PRAISE FOR THE NOVELS OF STEPHEN COONTS

LIBERTY

"Frighteningly realistic."

—*Maxim*

"Gripping . . . Coonts's naval background and his legal education bring considerable authority to the story, and the narrative is loaded with detailed information about terrorist networks, modern weaponry, and international intrigue . . . the action is slam-bang."

—*Publishers Weekly*

AMERICA

"The master of the techno-thriller spins a bone-chilling worst-case scenario involving international spies, military heroics, conniving politicians, devious agencies, a hijacked nuclear sub, lethal computer hackers, currency speculators, maniac moguls, and greedy mercenaries that rival Clancy for fiction-as-realism and Cussler for spirited action . . . [Coonts] never lets up with heart-racing jet/missile combat, suspenseful submarine maneuvers, and doomsday scenarios that feel only too real, providing real food for thought in his dramatization of the missile-shield debate."

—*Publishers Weekly* (starred review)

MORE...

"Fans of Coonts and his hero Grafton will love it. Great fun."

—*Library Journal*

"Coonts's action and the techno-talk are as gripping as ever."

—*Kirkus Reviews*

"Thrilling roller-coaster action. Give a hearty welcome back to Admiral Jake Grafton."

—*The Philadelphia Inquirer*

HONG KONG

"Move over, Clancy, readers know they can count on Coonts."

—*Midwest Book Review*

"The author gives us superior suspense with a great cast of made-up characters . . . But the best thing about this book is Coonts's scenario for turning China into a democracy."

—Liz Smith, *The New York Post*

"A high-octane blend of techno-wizardry [and] ultra-violence . . . [Coonts] skillfully captures the postmodern flavor of Hong Kong, where a cell phone is as apt as an AK-47 to be a revolutionary weapon."

—*USA Today*

"Entertaining . . . intriguing."

—Booklist

"Will be enjoyed by Coonts's many fans . . . Coonts has perfected the art of the high-tech adventure story."
—Library Journal

"Coonts does a remarkable job of capturing the mood of clashing cultures in Hong Kong."

—Publishers Weekly

"Filled with action, intrigue, and humanity."
—San Jose Mercury News

CUBA

"Enough Tomahawk missiles, stealth bombers, and staccato action to satisfy [Coonts's] most demanding fans."

—USA Today

"[A] gripping and intelligent thriller."
—Publishers Weekly (starred review)

"Perhaps the best of Stephen Coonts's six novels about modern warfare."

—Austin American-Statesman

"Coonts delivers some of his best gung-ho suspense writing yet."

—*Kirkus Reviews*

"Dramatic, diverting action . . . Coonts delivers."

—*Booklist*

FORTUNES OF WAR

"*Fortunes of War* is crammed with action, suspense, and characters with more than the usual one dimension found in these books."

—*USA Today*

"A stirring examination of courage, compassion, and profound nobility of military professionals under fire. Coonts's best yet."

—*Kirkus Reviews* (starred review)

"Full of action and suspense . . . a strong addition to the genre."

—*Publishers Weekly*

STEPHEN COONTS'

DEEP BLACK:

PAYBACK

**Written by Stephen Coonts
and Jim DeFelice**

St. Martin's Paperbacks

STEPHEN COONTS' DEEP BLACK: PAYBACK

Copyright © 2005 by Stephen Coonts.

ISBN: 0-312-93698-2
EAN: 9780312-93698-3

Printed in the United States of America

St. Martin's Paperbacks edition / October 2005

St. Martin's Paperbacks are published by St. Martin's Press, 175 Fifth Avenue, New York, NY 10010.

10 9 8 7 6 5 4 3 2 1

Authors' Note

The National Security Agency, Central Intelligence Agency, Space Agency, Federal Bureau of Investigation, National Security Council, and Marines are, of course, real. While based on an actual organization affiliated with the NSA and CIA, Desk Three and all of the people associated with it in this book are fiction. The technology depicted here either exists or is being developed.

Some liberties have been taken in describing actual places and procedures to facilitate the telling of the tale. Details of some security procedures and apparatus at real places have been omitted or recast as a matter of the public interest.

1

Charles Dean glanced toward the sky as he stepped away from the building, noting the direction and speed of the clouds as they moved. It was an old sniper's trick, a habit burned into his being long ago, so ancient he did it unconsciously. And yet if he had to use the information—if he were sighting a target at five hundred yards across a hill obscured by thick vegetation—his eyes and upper body would adjust to the light breeze as automatically and easily as his feet adjusted to the uneven sidewalk.

"How's it lookin', pardner?" boomed a voice in his head.

Dean pulled a satellite phone from his pocket, fussed with it for a few seconds, then held it to his ear. The phone was just a cover—like all Deep Black field ops, he communicated through a device implanted in his skull behind his ear. A tiny microphone sewn into his clothes picked up his voice; his belt held the rest of the unit, which transmitted through a satellite system.

"Same as yesterday afternoon," he told Kjartan "Tommy" Magnor-Karr. "Two guards outside. I just finished setting up the video bugs."

"Booster transmitter is set."

"Signals are strong," said a third voice. Though the other words were as loud as Karr's, the man who said them—Jeff Rockman—was sitting in an underground bunker some five thousand miles to the north.

The video bugs were miniature video cameras about the size and shape of a button. Their signals went to the booster Karr had planted. The booster uploaded the video stream to a satellite, which then relayed it to Rockman in the Deep Black nerve center known as the Art Room.

"We have sharp visuals all around," said Rockman. "You're good to go. Lia's plane is on schedule. Estimated time of arrival at Lima airport just over two hours."

"Rockman, you sound like you're an air traffic controller," said Karr.

"Is that supposed to be an insult or a compliment?"

Dean turned and began walking down the street as Karr bantered good-naturedly with Rockman, who was their mission "runner." During a mission, the runner maintained communications and coordinated operational support for the team in the field. The runner could access a wide array of intelligence, ranging from radio intercepts to satellite imagery, in real time.

He could also be a bit of a noodge.

"You guys ought to get hopping if you're going to make the airport in time," said Rockman.

"Plenty of time," said Karr.

As Rockman began lecturing the other agent about the notoriously heavy Lima traffic, Dean stopped at a small newsstand and bought a newspaper. The headlines shouted about a car bombing in the city the night before, the work of terrorists the government had claimed were stamped out months ago. Dean considered practicing his Spanish with the vendor, but the man's somber face warned him off.

Karr was waiting in the rented car around the corner.

"What do you say to a little breakfast, Charlie?"

"At the airport, sure."

"Airport food? Aw, come on."

"We don't want to be late."

"We won't be. I'm driving."

"We also want to get there in one piece."

"Always," said Karr, squealing the tires as he lurched into traffic.

2

The crisp, late May air of the northeastern Andes stung Stephan Babin's face as he looked out across the valley. Natives would think the brilliant sky a harbinger of a grand, dry day; they would welcome the beautiful chill as a sign of good fortune. But Babin was a foreigner here, a prisoner, though not bound by bars. The mountains would never seem hospitable, and as clear as the sky might be, it would never portend anything for him but bitterness and death.

He pushed himself forward on his crutches. To most of the world beyond this tiny patch of northern Peru, Stephan Babin was a dead man, killed in a plane crash three years before. There were many days when he thought of himself as a ghost, a spirit haunting the earth.

If he wasn't a ghost, Babin was certainly less than a physical man, his body a diminished wraith of what it had been before the crash. Most days he had so little feeling in his legs he might just as well not have them. What he could feel, hurt. His back alternately felt numb and screamed out in pain. Only his shoulders, strengthened by his need to use the crutches to walk or even balance consistently, were as they had been before the accident.

Babin was also as single-minded and bitter as any spirit haunting the earth. He existed only for revenge against the people who had crippled him—who'd betrayed him and left him for dead. His plan to extract it had taken shape slowly over the past eighteen months, but his hatred seemed to have existed forever. It was as deep as the nearby mountains were tall, as cold and vicious as the wind howling at their peaks.

"Señor Stephan, what are you doing without a coat?"

Babin turned and looked at Rosalina, the housekeeper General Atahualpa Túcume had installed here to watch after him.

"The general would not want you to catch a cold," said the old woman gently. "He would blame me—he worries about you constantly, like a father."

"General Túcume is not my father."

"Señor Stephan, he has been like a father to you. That you cannot deny."

No, that he could not deny, not at all. Túcume had saved his life and kept him alive. Babin had repaid him handsomely, and by any measure the debt would be completely requited within the next few weeks. Then, like a son, Babin would strike out on his own, fulfilling his own dream of revenge. The American CIA had shot down his plane; their countrymen would burn for it, burn in the most fearsome fire the world had ever known.

"Señor Stephan?"

"Rosalina, you are always right." Babin worked his crutches backward. "I'll come inside. The general is counting on me after all, is he not?"

3

Lia DeFrancesca handed her passport over to the customs officer, watching as he squinted and held it up to the light.

"Name?" he asked in English.

"Li Shanken."

"Business or pleasure?"

"Business."

He frowned. Before he could ask any more questions, Lia handed him a letter on fancy UN letterhead explaining in Spanish that she was an employee of Complete Computing on loan to the U.S.-based election consultant firm FairPlay International, which had been retained to assist the election commission overseeing Peru's presidential election this coming Sunday. The man read the letter twice, then shook his head.

"Is there a problem?"

"Go," he told her, mumbling something under his breath as he handed the documents back.

"Hello, Lia," said Rockman in her ear. "We can see you through the airport's security system. Your UN escort is waiting at the end of the hall. We think he's Julio Fernandez, the security liaison for the election committee, but we haven't gotten a good shot of him yet. Make sure to verify his identity with the retina scan."

Lia spotted a twenty-something man holding a sign with her name on it a few yards away.

"I'm Li Shanken," she told him in English, pointing to the sign. "From FairPlay."

He blinked twice, his wire-rimmed glasses nearly falling off his nose. Tall and thin, he towered over Lia, though he probably weighed less than she did.

"Yes," he said. "Oh."

"You were expecting a man?"

"Well, no." He pushed his glasses up on his nose.

"Not all computer experts are men," said Lia.

"No, I knew—I thought you would be an older woman, not one so beautiful."

"He covered that well," snickered Rockman.

"Where's your car?" asked Lia.

"I came by taxi," he said, starting for the door.

"Please get a retina scan to confirm his identity," said Rockman. "And listen, with the taxis, use the official ones at the kiosk. The independents can't always be trusted."

That was the thing with the Art Room. They were always looking over your shoulder, playing mother hen.

Of course, the one time she'd actually needed them to help her, they were nowhere to be found.

Not entirely true and definitely not fair, she thought as she followed Fernandez outside. But being raped tended to change your perspective on both truth and fairness.

The UN official waded out onto the pavement, ducking a succession of vehicles. He waved at an empty taxi, which ignored him, then practically stood in the middle of the road for another. It didn't stop because it already had a passenger.

"Let's try over here," said Lia, starting to the right.

"Lia, what happened to the retina scan?" asked Rockman. "Don't get into the cab with him until you're sure. One hundred percent *sure*."

As Fernandez walked to a car that had just pulled up, Lia feinted for it, then sprinted to the one stuck behind it.

"Oh, wait," she said, ducking away and going to a third car, which was back by the curb. Her maneuver would not only cross up any arrangement Fernandez had with an accomplice waiting to kidnap her, but it also allowed her to see how he reacted.

His confused look and shrug told her more than the retina scan ever could. She did the scan anyway, opening the case and seeing to her makeup as Fernandez slid in next to her.

"So what do you think?" Lia asked him, tilting the faux mirror toward him. "We should be at National Trust in what, two hours, give or take, depending on traffic?"

"You want to get right to work?"

"No sense dallying. We can drop off the luggage at the hotel on the way."

"Dean and Tommy are right behind you," said Rockman. "Next time, though, stick with the program, OK? Some of these taxi drivers are scam artists."

"Don't worry," sighed Lia, leaning back against the seat.

"Worry?" said Fernandez.

"What is there to worry about, except the traffic?" Lia said to him. "Do you mind if I practice my Spanish? It's rusty. Your English is so good."

His face brightened. "As I come from Spain, my Spanish here is too stiff," he said. "Between American Spanish and peninsular Spanish, there is a difference."

"Mine is basically from high school," said Lia, skipping the months of intense language training she'd taken in the Army. "*¡Hola, Julio!*"

"*¡Hola, Li!*" Fernandez laughed. "My first lesson in English was 'Hello' as well."

"All right, he checks out," said Rockman.

"*Gracias.*"

"*Muy bien,*" said Fernandez, thinking she was talking to him. "As you wish."

4

General Atahualpa Túcume paused for a moment as he turned the corner on the trail, catching sight of the valley and the soaring mountains beyond. Though he had been born here in the foothills of the Andes, each time he saw them he was filled with awe. Lush and warm here in the north because of the proximity to the equator, the mountains towered over green plateaus and lakes so pure they looked like the tears of the sun god, crying for his lost people. Trees seemed to explode from solid rock. Water tumbled down in clear streams that glowed with a light stolen from the sun, not merely reflected.

A thousand years before, one of the world's great civilizations had ruled these mountains and their valleys, the nearby jungle, and the exotic desert coast to the west. They built massive temples that rivaled those of Egypt, constructed elaborate forts and luxurious villas, studied the sun with the precision of the Greeks and Arabs, and talked to the gods who ruled the universe. A few of these men were gods themselves, passing among the living so that destiny could be fulfilled. Only the arrival of European diseases they could neither see nor fight brought them down.

Some saw their decline as the way of the universe, with its endless cycles, its rising and setting sun, its ever-changing moon. Others saw it as the result of grave sins that had to be expiated in the blood of the people, a stain on the

soul of the mountains themselves. A few thought it temporary, a mere night in the long day of existence, the passage
of a dark moment in an hour of great achievement.

General Atahualpa Túcume was one of the latter. A modern man, he had been educated in the finest schools of Spain
and the United States. But it was no accident that General
Atahualpa Túcume's first name was that of a great Inca ruler
or that his last recalled a regional capital during the Inca
reign. The general was the rarest of rare Peruvians—a modern man wholly of Inca blood, whose ancestors had not been
polluted by compromise with the Spanish conquerors.

Technically, the word "Inca" referred to the aristocratic
family of rulers who presided over the empire of the Four
Quarters, called Tahuantinsuyu in Quechua, the empire's official language. The empire included a large number of
tribes of different backgrounds; at its height in 1500, the
Great Inca governed a population of 10 million from his
capital at Cusco in the Andean mountains. His domain
stretched to modern Bolivia and down to what is now Chile,
from the Pacific to the headwaters of the Amazonian river.
Túcume's ancestor, according to carefully handed down traditions, had been a great ruler in the north at the time of the
Spaniards' arrival. Sometime after Pizarro beheaded the
Inca ruler Atahualpa in 1533, Túcume's direct ancestor fled
the approaching conquistadors and took shelter with an eastern tribe. There the family bided its time, telling stories of
past glories and dreaming of future ones.

Túcume had been raised on the stories. Long before he
attended Madrid and Miami University, he had memorized
the oral poem commemorating the legend of his namesake,
Atahualpa. The entire epic was a thing of beauty, but especially poignant were the lines of his beheading. Atahualpa
predicted that he would return to avenge his people as
Inkarri, the messiah of the earth. Túcume knew in his heart
that these words were not fiction but the strongest truth.

But as a thoroughly modern man, Túcume knew better
than to rely on stories or even religion for his power. Power
came from the ability to destroy, and he alone among the

Incas, among the Peruvians, possessed the modern equivalent of the sun god's arrow: a small nuclear warhead hidden not too far from here.

It might be said that obtaining it had been a matter of luck, rather than fate. Certainly the circumstances argued that. The bomb fell almost literally at the general's feet. But the tangled weave of events that had brought the warhead to him was so improbable that Túcume was convinced his ancestors had taken a hand. The Incas, and all natives of the land, would rise again, and Túcume, selected by luck or fate, was the man who would lead them.

He began walking again, turning another corner on the path. The man Túcume had come to meet was standing amid a knot of bodyguards about twenty meters away.

"Mr. President!" shouted Túcume, greeting Hernando Aznar as he drew close.

"Still only a candidate," said Aznar. "And a distant one at that. With a short week to go."

"A long week," said Túcume, who knew what it would include.

"You take a huge risk meeting me."

"Here? Never. This is not Lima, where spies are everywhere."

"A risk for me."

"Nonsense. Is it against the law for a candidate to speak to a general? No. Absolutely not."

"Your contributions—"

"Ah." Túcume waved his hand. "You are doing extremely well. Extremely well."

"The papers all say I won't finish above third."

This was why they had had to meet; Aznar had become defeatist and needed propping up.

"All of the journalists are on the government's payroll," Túcume assured him. "Who else would call the vice president a man of the people? Ramon Ortez, who owns an armor-plated Mercedes and whose wife shops three times a year in Madrid, a man of the people? Victor Imbecile—who votes for a communist anymore?"

As was his custom, Túcume mangled the candidate's name and his political affiliation: Victor Imberbe represented the Peruvian Centrists, and his moderate views were in no way left of center, let alone communist. In the past, this distortion had pleased Aznar, and he would jokingly add something of his own about one of the other candidates, Bartolo Lopez, who really *was* a communist. But today Aznar merely frowned.

"Our polls," he said. "We have barely twenty percent."

"And climbing," said Túcume quickly. "It's the direction that is important. Ortez has lost votes. They will go to you. Imberbe has barely forty percent. You are catching up."

"With this many candidates, the lead is insurmountable."

Not for the first time, Túcume wished that he could have run for the office himself. But the uniform had become a political liability in Peru, thanks to the criminal antics of some who had preceded him.

"You are going in the right direction," Túcume told his man firmly. "Continue to make your speeches. Do your work. We must all do our work."

The general glanced toward the knot of aides standing a respectful distance away. Among them were Aznar's speechwriter—a mumbling Jew from Argentina who had somehow been gifted with a golden pen—and the candidate's political adviser. Both were secretly on Túcume's payroll. He called them over, pretending not to know them very well.

"Geraldo, how are you?" he said to the speechwriter. "What are the high points of today's speech?"

"The poisoners of our country," said the man, his beaky nose pointed almost straight down. "We must band together to fight them and seize the future."

"There, you see?" exclaimed Túcume. "What stronger argument can you make? The Maoist rebels are trying to steal our country."

"People don't believe the rebels are a serious threat," said Aznar glumly. "The cities are especially smug, even after the latest attacks."

"They will see," said Túcume.

Aznar stared at him, puzzled.

Túcume grabbed the candidate's arms, bracing him as if he were in the borderlands again, encouraging his men to chase the Ecuadorian scum.

"Peru is counting on you. My people—our people—our ancestors, they are watching and helping you. Look around you; look at this—"

Túcume turned Aznar 360 degrees, shaking his shoulders as he went.

"This is our history and our destiny," Túcume said. "Peru will be a great nation again. The others will stand up and respect us. Brazil, Argentina, the Ecuadorian dogs. Even El Norte, the demons of America, in the end they will respect us. No longer will we be considered the poor rabble of the world. Peru!"

Túcume ended his speech by staring into Aznar's face. The man had Quechua blood in him; his features made it obvious. But the European was there, too, diluting the courage that was necessary for greatness.

"I will do my best," said the candidate.

"Your best will inspire the nation," said Túcume. "Go."

5

William Rubens pushed his chair back from the table as the waiter approached. As a general rule Rubens hated luncheons such as these, which he derisively termed chicken and pea affairs. The food was actually poached salmon and scalloped potatoes, but it could easily have been rubber as far as his taste buds were concerned. If that weren't bad enough, he faced the unwelcome prospect of sitting through three long speeches on the "state of the world" by people who knew less about international affairs than Jay Leno did.

Sensing his self-control slipping, Rubens rose and walked to the portable bar at the back of the room. He ordered a seltzer with a lime twist, then turned to survey the room silently.

"I'd say, 'A dollar for your thoughts, Bill,' but you'd probably feel insulted."

"Debra." Rubens turned and nodded at Debra Collins, the CIA deputy director of operations or DDO.

"Charming lunch."

Collins' tone would have sounded sincere to anyone who didn't know her as well as Rubens did. Her rise in the CIA had been fueled by a healthy disdain of many of the people she worked for, contempt she kept well hidden. Under oath, Rubens would have admitted that she was smarter than most of the people she worked with and in her own way quite brilliant, especially when it came to manipulating people.

He could speak from first-hand experience: they had been lovers for a brief time some years before. He still rued the mistake.

"Thank you for your personal attention on Peru," he said. "Your people were insightful."

"Of course," she said. "How is that business?"

"Proceeding."

"An interesting election."

"All elections are interesting."

"The president sees it as a cornerstone of his South American policy. I hope it proceeds fairly."

"Yes," said Rubens.

The CIA had made several officers available for background briefings prior to the current Deep Black mission to Peru. It was a gesture of cooperation facilitated by the DDO, no doubt intended to show that Collins had no hard feelings about the mission, which had been authorized directly by the president and national security adviser. The complicated and delicate mission was precisely the sort Desk Three was invented to handle, but Rubens knew Collins felt that her people should have conducted it. Undoubtedly she saw it as yet one more instance of Deep Black encroaching on her agency's domain. The CIA had made a strong play to "own" Desk Three when the high-tech covert group was first proposed, and Collins was nothing if not a sore loser.

"Vice President Ortez is still running second, I see," said Collins, sipping her drink—it would be a very weak vodka martini.

"Yes," said Rubens. "But the race is very close."

Much closer, in fact, than the polls showed—assuming the information Deep Black was working on was correct, Ortez was the one who was trying to steal the election.

"Imberbe would be a good president," said Collins. "Though I wouldn't call him pro-American. Don't you agree?"

"I really don't have an opinion," he told her.

"Oh, you always have an opinion, Bill. You're just very careful about sharing it."

Touché, thought Rubens. But he refused to be provoked. "I would say that the problems in Peru are so intractable that any leader would have a difficult time. Ortez has always been anti-American, and he's been much more vocal about it than the present president. As for Imberbe, he is a reasonably intelligent man. The fact that the company he owns had done much business with America is a plus, and his statements would certainly lead one to think he would be more in sync with us than most of the others. But who can see the future?"

"Not you."

"Not I."

There was applause. The first speaker was ambling toward the podium.

"If we can do anything more to help you, you'll let us know," said Collins.

She tapped his shoulder gently. For just a moment, the shadow of what he had once felt for her crossed over him. It quickly lifted, but it left him confused and off-balance, uncharacteristically paralyzed.

He forced himself to nod graciously. He reminded himself that she was a viper. He told himself that she must have some ulterior motive, that nothing Debra Collins did was accidental, that surely she had been watching for her chance to accost him all through the lunch. By the time Rubens returned to his table, he was back in control, his feelings—misguided, surely—safely locked in a place where they could neither interfere with his judgment nor surprise him with their ferocity again.

6

"The vault room dates from the late nineteenth century," said the Peruvian election official who met Lia and Fernandez at the bank. "It has survived several robbery attempts, including one by Yankee banditos. There are still scratches on the outside of the door from the dynamite when they tried to blow it up. The room here—" He swung around, gesturing at the high-ceilinged lobby. "*Mucho* damage. Very severe. But not the vault. The gold remained safe."

"Tell her who the bandits were," Fernandez prompted.

"Butch Cassidy and the Sundance Kid. It is rumor, only."

A false one, Lia knew—it had been mentioned during her briefing. The western outlaws had spent time in Bolivia and elsewhere in Latin America, but they'd never come to Peru.

Not to mention the fact that the safe had been built several years after they died. But it was a good story, and Lia saw no sense in interrupting the man as he fleshed it out with a legend about a local romance between Cassidy and the wife of the bank president. Feigning interest, Lia turned her real attention to the security setup, making sure it jibed with what she'd been told by the Art Room on the way over, as well as during her earlier briefing.

The vault was a large steel and concrete encased room, partly underground, sealed by an impressively massive steel door. The room had its own level a few steps down from the lobby. There were two restrooms to the left along a narrow hallway and two equipment closets jammed with gear to the right. Surveillance cameras, both video and infrared, monitored the lobby and vault entrance. There were also motion detectors, but the system had been turned off because guards were now in the bank around the clock.

Two stood just inside the main entrance. They were armed with MP5 submachine guns. Two more guards, also with submachine guns, stood along the rail above the vault floor. A final pair stood just outside the vault door. There were plainclothes guards at the foot of the steps from the lobby; they checked credentials of anyone entering the vault. A trio of Peruvian election officials assisted them and tried to look as important as possible.

A reporter had come to the bank to do a story on the procedures that had been adopted to ensure a fair election, as well as some of the security surrounding the voting machines and related equipment. Though not allowed into the vault itself, he was being given a lecture near the security checkpoint by a carefully coiffured Peruvian government official, who assured him the special voter cards stored here guaranteed an honest result.

"They must have done a dozen interviews here in the last week and a half," Fernandez told Lia. "The cards and the vault have become symbols of the fairness of the election."

The official had a model of one of the cards in his hand, holding it out for the man to see. About half as big as a credit card, it looked like a Bic cigarette lighter that had been flattened by a cement mixer. A tapered end housed eight small tonguelike connectors, the slivers of metal looking a bit like flat piano keys. The indentations in the connectors added to the complexity of counterfeiting them.

"This allows the vote to be recorded," the official said in a sonorous voice. "No impostors."

He explained that there would only be three cards per voting place and that they had to be entered each time to record a vote. The cards included a chip that produced a 128-byte "key" that "unlocked" communications between two different parts of the system, which as a layman's explanation of the security system was nearly as good as the considerably more technical brief Lia had received during the mission planning. Since the chips were custom designed and had been delivered only a week before, anyone interested in beating the encryption, let alone duplicating the cards, faced an almost insurmountable task.

Unless the cards had been hacked before they were supplied. In that case, rather than guaranteeing a fair vote, the cards could be used to steal the election rather easily. Which was the reason Lia was here.

Six days ago, an informant at the company that made the chips told the FBI that twelve cards had been engineered to guarantee that Ramon Ortez, the current vice president, would win. The informant had supplied a list of serial numbers for the chips used on the cards; the IDs were not written on the chips or the cards but could be obtained by querying them with a special reader.

The hack was extremely sophisticated—so much so that it had taken the NSA's experts nearly a day and a half to decide that it was conceptually possible and then design a way to test the cards, which were already in Peru.

Making sure Peru's elections were held had become a priority for the U.S. following several reversals for democracy in other South American countries over the past six months, including a coup in Brazil. But the fact that Ortez was known to be rabidly anti-U.S. complicated the situation, as did his intimate relation with the current government.

The U.S. couldn't announce that the cards had been hacked without being absolutely certain that they were. The hack had gone undetected by all of the earlier tests the monitors employed. Working undercover as a specialist brought in for a last-minute check, Lia would upload data from one of the cards so that the NSA specialists could determine whether it was indeed a clever hack or an even more clever hoax.

The question was, what happened next? If the cards had been tampered with, simply revealing the hack might backfire. The company that had made the cards was American, and Ortez would surely claim that the U.S. had set him up.

Public sentiment in the region was running heavily against the U.S., and it was very likely he'd be believed. Meanwhile, the UN election committee had indicated that if it detected fraud it would call for a delay in the election. That would also hand Ortez the presidency—the current president was very sick and had already indicated that, election or no, he would retire in a month. Ortez would assume the presidency and most likely cancel the election completely.

Desk Three had been tasked with verifying that the cards had been hacked. If that proved to be the case, the NSA's covert action team would then clandestinely replace the bad cards with good ones—assuming the U.S. president gave the final OK.

The cards were stored temporarily in the large vault before being shipped to the regional election centers just before voters went to the polls. They were packed three to a tamper-evident envelope and stacked in narrow, shoe box–size boxes inside. Even though the envelopes could be identified by numbered bar codes on the outside, the odds against picking all twelve cards out of the thousands and thousands of envelopes were greater than one in 15 million.

Fortunately, Deep Black had a way to beat the odds. The cards had been placed into the envelopes by a random sorting machine, ostensibly to further decrease the possibility of fraud, since no one on the production line would know where the cards were going. But like many supposedly random number generators, the sorting program was not *really* random. It used only two variables, and since the NSA analysts already knew one—it was a set permutation of the time the program was initiated—they could easily solve for the other. All they needed were the IDs of the cards in two envelopes; from that, they could map the entire collection. They would know where each card was without opening the envelopes. (Technically, they only needed the serial numbers from one card in one envelope to find the solution. But they would use two envelopes and test the full set to be sure.)

Lia's first priority today was to map the location of the cards in the envelopes. Then she would locate one of the suspect cards and swap it with the duplicate that had been fitted to the back of her belt buckle. The card would be taken out and tested; if it was hacked, the team would proceed to replace the rest of the cards. They had developed several different plans to do this and would choose the best depending on the specific circumstances at the time. Unlike many Deep Black missions, which involved weeks and even months of planning, the Peru operation had been mounted in only a few days. Its success—for Lia, there was no option other than success—depended to a large degree on the ability of the field ops to adapt to the situation.

One option would be for Lia to return the next day to swap out the rest of the cards. Her cover gave her carte blanche to randomly test the cards as well as the machines, so she was guaranteed all the access she needed; all she had to do was wait for her opportunity. She could also opt to swap all twelve cards if the opportunity presented itself inside, using the complete set of twelve cards hidden in the lining of the bag. Lia had suggested that option herself, arguing that it might prove simpler to simply replace all of the suspect cards on her first visit if she wasn't being watched too carefully.

The setup outside the vault argued that wasn't likely. Even though she'd already passed through a metal detector and an explosive sniffer at the door, Lia had to run a similar gamut at the base of the steps leading down to the vault room. The sniffer could detect common explosives such as HMX and RDX, the major components in plastic explosives, as well as old standbys like nitroglycerin and TNT. Lia's shoes, handbag, and briefcase were put through a separate X-ray machine and then hand-inspected, with each item in the bag and case closely examined.

She watched as the detective laid out the items in the briefcase, beginning with the laptop and its related equipment. He checked the pages of her two bound marble composition notebooks, which were blank. He turned on her phone, which wouldn't work because of the thick metal and concrete surrounding them. He even tested her pens. Finally satisfied, he handed the case back.

"And my pocketbook," said Lia.

The man began to explain that unnecessary personal items were kept outside the safe.

"I have female stuff in there," she said sharply, first in Spanish, then in English. The man's face turned red, and he quickly handed over the bag.

It worked every time.

Lia's "female stuff" amounted to two lipstick cases and a compact. She wasn't likely to need the compact, which was actually a retina scanner, but the lipstick might come in handy—one shade concealed a solvent to unstick the bottom of the voter card envelopes without visible trace and the other a glue to reseal them. But what she really wanted were the voter cards. They'd been fitted precisely so that their outlines merged with the zipper and rivet design on the bag's exterior and wouldn't show up on the X-ray machine. The bag's design was so elaborate that it had cost more to make than the cards it held.

Shouldering her bag, Lia walked to the vault with Fernandez and the bank president, who was bursting with pride about his vault and the honor of helping his country preserve its democracy. The massive safe door, with its locking arms and gear work, sat to the right, folded back on its hinges against the wall. It looked like it would take two or three people simply to open or shut, but as the bank president explained, it was so carefully balanced that even a child could move it.

Two UN observers—frail-looking black women from Uganda—sat on stiff-backed chairs inside the vault. According to the Art Room, they would stay the entire time until the vault was closed with the rest of the bank. One of the women held out a clipboard with a form on it, asking Lia to sign in. She did so as illegibly as possible.

"I need a card table or something," Lia told Fernandez. "I don't want to set up the laptop computer on the floor."

"Oh, right."

"A chair would be nice, too."

"Come with me," said the bank president. "I'll find something suitable."

Lia put down her bags and then ran her hands over her face, as if rubbing some of the fatigue from the flight away. "Charlie, are you here?" she whispered.

"At the check desk, waiting to open an account," said Dean. "How you doing?"

"Just setting up."

One of the local election officials came inside, introducing himself and going on in Spanish about how important the election was—and, Lia gathered, how important he was since he was connected with it.

"You will ensure a fair election by checking all the cards?" he asked.

"Just a few."

"Such a lovely tester," said the man. "I would wager the machines will all be at their best to please you."

Lia bit the inside of her cheek to keep from smacking the sexist slob.

Rubens looked at the large screen at the front of the Art Room, where a diagram of the bank's interior gave Lia's and Dean's locations inside the bank. To the right of this were four small panels showing video feeds from the surveillance cameras.

"The election official who asked Lia what she was doing—do we know who he is?"

"Schoolteacher from Tarapoto, north of the country."

"Does he have a link to Ortez?"

"No."

"You're positive?"

"Everybody in the bank has been checked pretty carefully, Mr. Rubens."

"Check him again," said Rubens, walking toward the screen. "Is Lia out of direct communication inside the vault?" Rubens asked.

"The vault walls and ceiling interfere," said Rockman. "It's like being deep inside a bunker. We can hear her through the directional booster Dean brought in, but we can't talk to her directly. We needed the bandwidth to transmit the data into her laptop."

Rubens folded his arms in front of his chest.

"Did you want me to pass something along?" Rockman asked Rubens.

"That won't be necessary," said Rubens. "Mr. Karr is outside the bank?"

"A block away. Charlie's pretense for being in the lobby is that he's opening a bank account. If Charlie is called, Karr will come inside and take his place."

"Are we ready to map the cards?"

"Everybody's standing by."

Rubens glanced toward the back of the Art Room, where the team's specialists were gathered at their own monitors. The actual work of mapping the cards and envelopes would be done in another part of the large complex, then transmitted back.

"I don't think Lia will have any problem," volunteered Rockman. "She's recovered from that business in Korea."

"That business in Korea, Mr. Rockman, is not the sort of thing that one recovers from."

Lia opened the briefcase and took out one of the notebooks. She began counting the plastic boxes holding the voter cards. Every so often she pulled a box out, ostensibly to count the envelopes that held the cards, but actually to record the serial numbers on the envelopes to make the cards easier to find later on. One of the Ugandan UN women stood annoyingly close behind her as she worked, so close Lia nearly bumped into her several times. The survey took nearly a half hour; Lia was just finishing when Fernandez returned with a small folding table.

"Sorry it took me so long," he said, setting up the small card table. "I ended up having to go down the street to get one. The bank president wanted to bring an eight hundred–kilo mahogany desk down here."

"Pick an envelope at random," she told him, booting the computer.

"Any one?"

"First one is up to you. The computer will generate the list from there. Something from the middle."

Fernandez walked to the wall of plastic boxes. One of the UN observers got up and stayed at his elbow as he tugged a box forward. He pulled it out about two-thirds of the way and tilted it forward just far enough so he could get the top envelope out. The eight or nine boxes on top of it nearly tumbled down on top of him.

It's going to be just luck that the envelope I need will be at the bottom of the pile, thought Lia as he brought the envelope over to be opened.

"Oh, your chair," said Fernandez. "I'll be right back."

Dean leaned over the check-writing counter as Lia continued to talk.

"Here we go," said Lia, ostensibly talking to someone inside the vault.

The relay system used low-power, discreet-burst transmitters. The units could not be detected by conventional radio scanners or most other devices generally used to intercept radio signals—an important consideration, given that Dean and Karr had found two detectors operating in the lobby area when they had checked out the bank the day before.

"Looking good," said Rockman. "We have the signal. You can pass the word on to Lia."

"Uh-huh."

"Señor Garcia?"

Dean looked up to find one of the bank officials standing over him.

"You wanted to open an account?" asked the man in Spanish.

"Yes, I do," said Dean.

"Stall for a second if you can, Charlie," said Rockman in his ear. "We have two more sets of numbers to go. The signal may degrade if you move and we'll have to start over."

"I would like to open an account," Dean told the bank officer, first in Spanish, then switching to English. "I, uh—my Spanish might not be that good, though. So if we could use English?"

"But of course," said the banker. He smiled apologetically. "It is possible that your Spanish is better than my English."

"*Mucho gracias.* But for money, and legal matters . . . I sometimes get nervous. If it is OK?"

"Of course," said the banker. "Come this way."

"Another few seconds, Charlie," said Rockman. "She's just plugging in the third card from the envelope."

"Is it going to take long?" Dean said.

"Just a few seconds," said Rockman. "Tommy's on his way in."

I wasn't talking to you, thought Dean.

"Twenty minutes," said the banker. "A few very easy things. You have a passport?"

Dean reached into his jacket, pretending to fumble as he fished it out of his pocket.

"We're good, Charlie. Go ahead."

Fernandez came back with the chair as Lia put the voter cards back in their box and returned them to the stack.

"We're ready for the next set of cards," she told him. "Where do you think envelope B-5983 is?"

"That one, specifically?" said Fernandez.

"That's what the computer says. It generates a random pattern so that we spread out through the system," said Lia. "We get fourteen envelopes with three cards apiece, selected for a statistical cross section of the production run."

The story was a bunch of bull, but it sounded good, and Fernandez nodded as if he understood what she was saying. While this selection didn't matter, Lia wanted to introduce the pretense so that the third selection—and the eleven after that, if she decided to try to swap them all out at once—seemed routine. He found the box with help from her list and gave her the envelope. She slit it open and took out one of the cards, twirling it in her hand before pushing it in. The screen generated what looked like an old-fashioned TV test pattern, which dissolved into a multicolored mosaic. A series of numbers and letters filled the bottom two lines; the ID began on the top line at the left, in case she needed to read it off.

"So this screen tells you the card works?" asked Fernandez.

"Not precisely. It only tells me it's not broken."

He hovered over her as she put the cards into the reader. Lia went as slowly as she could; she'd heard Dean being called away but hadn't heard anything from Karr yet, and the screen hadn't blinked, which would have indicated the numbers had been uplinked and confirmed.

When she was done with the third card in the envelope, Lia got up, stretching as she resealed the envelope with a tape and tag that identified when it had been tested. As she did, the laptop blinked.

"What was that?" asked Fernandez, pointing at the screen. "It went out for a second."

"I don't know." Lia reached over to the reader, pushing in the cord.

"Problem?" asked Fernandez.

"I'm not sure. This cord may have been loose. Let's run through that last envelope and make absolutely sure we're OK. I don't want to mess that up."

"Was that a stall, or did something really go wrong?" asked Karr, finally talking.

"I'm not sure what the problem is," Lia told Fernandez—though she was really talking to Karr. "Let's do it again."

"Okey dokey," said Karr.

Lia knew that the lighthearted, almost joking tone in his voice was just Tommy being Tommy, but it still got under her skin. She knew that if she told him to be serious, he'd give her one of his dumbfounded looks and say, *Yo, I am serious.*

Lia put the card into the reader slowly, fussing with the connector wire as if still not sure it was working properly. While she was running through the whole procedure again, Karr asked if she was going to take one card or get all twelve.

"Not sure," mumbled Lia. One of the UN people had taken up a spot at her elbow. And Fernandez was so close she might not even be able to get one. She had to get rid of him somehow.

"All right. They're dumping the envelope numbers down to you now. You can just hit the function keys and you'll see them," said Karr.

"Look at this," Lia said to Fernandez, pointing to the lower left-hand corner of her computer screen. "My battery's starting to wear down. This is just not my day. I'm down to sixty percent, and we've got a ways to go. I'm going to have to plug in."

She rose and got the power cord from the briefcase.

"There are no outlets in the safe," said Fernandez.

"Oh." Lia feigned surprise. "Can we bring in another extension cord?"

"I'll see."

As soon as he was gone, Lia pulled out her notebook and jotted down the numbers, just in case something was wrong with the machine. Then she rose to get the envelope she needed.

As she did, Lia nearly knocked one of the UN women over. Surprised that she was so close, Lia shivered involuntarily. The woman followed her over to the boxes, so close she could feel the woman's breath on her neck.

As Lia began to search for the envelope, her fingers began to tremble.

She wasn't scared—she shouldn't be scared—but . . .

But what?

"I'm sorry. I'm *really* sorry," she told the woman standing next to her in Spanish. "But could you like, just give me a few feet? Sometimes I get claustrophobic."

The woman blinked at her but didn't move back.

I'm not going to get all twelve cards, Lia thought to herself. I'll be lucky to get even one.

The woman stayed within six inches of her as Lia walked back to the laptop. Sitting down, she suddenly felt lightheaded and then doubly spooked—first, somehow unnerved by the woman's proximity, and second, unnerved that she had been unnerved. This sort of thing *never* happened to her.

Lia slit open the envelope, cutting through the tamper-evident tape. Her mind blanked. She couldn't remember which of the several numbers that flashed on her computer screen were the ones that told her the chip's serial number.

First step, find which of the three cards she needed. Second step, swap it. Third step, leave.

"Please give me a little space," she told the UN observer. "You're as close as my shadow."

If the woman moved, it was less than an inch.

One and out, Lia told herself. Just get the card and go.

The number was at the bottom of the screen, in the corner, right there.

Tommy was outside, and Dean was nearby. If she needed something, all she had to do was say so.

Lia pushed the card in. It wasn't the right one. She pulled it out, arranged it on top of the table next to the envelope. Would the next card be right?

No.

That made it easier, didn't it? Card three.

She turned to the UN monitor, standing over her shoulder. "Did you want to see how this works?" Lia asked her.

The woman didn't respond.

"Do you not speak Spanish?"

"I do," said the woman.

"Well, could you move back then?"

The woman took a baby step backward.

"Thank you," said Lia sarcastically.

Her heart revved as she slipped her left hand to her belt and unhooked the replacement. She pulled the envelope into her lap, starting to hunch over so she could pretend to drop the envelope to the ground. Lia felt a pain in her throat, a sharp, stabbing pain, and for a moment her whole body was paralyzed.

The envelope teetered on her lap. Just then, Fernandez came into the vault. She turned to glance at him and saw the monitor's head had turned as well. In an instant, Lia had the cards swapped and was tucking the suspect one under the belt clasp.

Her heart raced as she sealed the envelope with the new tape and sticker. Everything around her seemed tinged with a dull red light.

"You know what? I think we're done for today," she said, rising slowly. She handed Fernandez the envelope. "I'm starting to get some jet lag."

"Not a problem."

"Wait," said one of the UN observers as Lia started for the door.

A fresh wave of anxiety froze Lia in her place.

"You didn't sign out on our form," said the monitor. "You signed in. Now you have to sign out."

"Of course," said Lia, hoping no one else noticed her hand was shaking.

9

"The post office attack was a success," Keros told General Túcume. "Most successful. The government is being ridiculed."

"Excellent," Túcume told him.

"Four more car bombs will go off in Lima tonight. In Pisco—"

"I do not believe we need any more car bombs."

Keros looked stricken.

"The plan," said Keros. "As you outlined—"

"Yes, I know. But too many attacks will not help us. We have the effect we need. To go too far may damage us more than help."

So far, twelve people had been killed in the various car bomb attacks in Lima blamed on Sendero Nuevo, the New Path guerrillas; another dozen or so had died in similar incidents in other cities. Túcume regretted this, as necessary as it was. Even though the bombs had been exploded in areas that belonged to the descendants of the conquistadors, there was no way to guarantee that they alone were the victims. He had ruled out attacks in areas heavily populated by natives and especially in Cusco and similar cities, where Inca blood remained strong.

The takeover of the Lima post office—orchestrated by Keros with the help of a few sympathetic police officers and hand-picked men from Túcume's division who posed as the terrorists—seemed an apt climax of this phase of the campaign. It had gone perfectly, with no injuries among the hostages. A congressional member of Aznar's party had "negotiated" their release, as well as the surrender of the guerrillas; this was mentioned prominently in all of the stories.

The next phase of Túcume's plan to install Aznar would be even more dramatic. There was no need for more bombings.

"I will cancel the attacks, General," said Keros.

"You've done well. I have every confidence in you. When our time comes, you will be richly rewarded. Your ancestors would be proud."

Keros bowed his head rather quaintly and backed away a few steps before turning to leave the general's hotel suite. Túcume had a very modest office at the army building in the city. It was bugged, so he never did real work there, certainly nothing requiring secrecy. Instead, he commandeered hotel suites and even whole floors when he had business in the city.

Túcume turned his attention back to the weather report he had received before Keros came in. Heavy rains were anticipated tomorrow in the area where Túcume's military unit patrolled; beyond that the forecasts were unsettled. If heavy rains did come, some of the precarious mountain roads in the area would be washed out—including the road to the village where he had originally intended to "discover" the rebels' secret weapon.

He reached down for his briefcase and took out a topographical map of the region. There were not many roads in the area to begin with, and so his choices were limited. He looked again at his favored target on the Ecuador border. It was perfect; not only was it isolated enough that he could control access, but the proximity to Ecuador would naturally imply that their traditional enemy had been aiding the rebels. This would undoubtedly prove useful in the future.

But if the truck was to get stuck before it reached the village . . .

There were two other possibilities, located farther south.

There was a knock on the door. He made his decision—an unnamed hamlet northeast of Boria—then folded his map.

"Come," he said.

"General, your helicopter has been refueled," said Captain Chimor, his chief of staff.

"Very well." Túcume rose. "Captain, see if you can arrange a meeting with the American CIA officer at the embassy. Tell him I want to have lunch. Call him from the division phones."

"The general staff will know instantly."

"Yes, that is my intention. Mention Sendero Nuevo," Túcume added. "Say this with an offhand tone, something casual, as if it's spontaneous. But make sure it comes up. Tell him that it would be useful for him to have lunch. Tomorrow. At the club in Lima."

"Yes, General."

Túcume rose. "We are moving forward, Chimor. Always forward. I will be back by early morning."

10

Rubens felt his shoulders and arms sag with relief as Lia left the bank, her image caught on a video bug Karr had planted on a light post near the entrance earlier.

"She's going to the hotel," said Rockman. "We're looking good. They're getting into a taxi. Dean and Tommy are right behind her."

"Very well." He turned to Marie Telach, the Art Room supervisor. "I want to know the results of the tests on the cards as soon as possible. I'll be in my office."

When Rubens reached it upstairs, he found John Bibleria waiting to talk to him. "Johnny Bib" was a classic NSA staffer—a mathematical genius and certified eccentric. While Johnny Bib had cut his teeth at the agency working on cryptography, he now supervised the operations of a multi-disciplinary research and analysis team assigned to Deep Black. He was also in charge of H Group, a collection of computer specialists who were used for a variety of tasks in the Deep Black operations.

Rubens pulled out his chair and sat down behind his desk. Though the top was clear, he habitually covered it with a gray blanket, intended to keep anyone from inadvertently seeing highly classified information. Rubens wouldn't keep truly important data in his office, but by definition everything at the NSA, even the weekly bill for the vending machines, was classified.

"My team was not established for history work," said Johnny Bib, following him inside.

"I don't have time for riddles today, Johnny. What are you referring to?"

Johnny Bib looked deeply offended. He took a specially designed flash drive from his pocket; the memory device could only be read on certain NSA computers and would erase itself in forty-eight hours. "You needed a summary for your briefing? The political situation in Peru?"

"Oh yes. I'm sorry."

Rubens had asked Johnny Bib to have someone pull together the critical background so that he would have the facts ready if the president questioned him; he had not been present for the CIA briefing and did not want to rely on the skimpy handout the briefers had left behind.

"Petra did the work. I reviewed it. So did Segio. I was just pointing out that this sort of work is not our forte. This is not what we were assembled to do."

"I'm sure it's fine. How long will it take to determine whether the voter cards have been hacked?"

"Once the data is uploaded, eleven minutes and thirty-seven seconds," said Johnny Bib. He drew out the pronunciation of "thirty-seven"—it was a prime number, of almost mystical significance. "Segio will report to you directly, from the computer section. We have Gallo working on it."

Segio Nakami was the number two man on the research and analysis team. While he wasn't *quite* the genius Johnny Bib was—Rubens blamed this on an affinity for set theory—Segio was refreshingly uneccentric, even normal. Which might be the ultimate eccentricity at the NSA.

Gallo was Robert Gallo, a young man who had hacked his way into an FBI computer at the tender age of twenty. Fortunately for Gallo, he had done it as a member of Johnny Bib's staff, taking part in a "friendly" demonstration of security lapses. In the two years since, Gallo had handled a number of tasks; as far as the agency was concerned, his best was inserting a virus into the control code for North Korea's test missiles.

Gallo himself preferred the hack that allowed him—and only him—to obtain free root beers from one of the soda machines on the main level.

"I had some new thoughts on Fibonacci sequences," said Johnny, lingering. "A new set of rules regarding exponential division. I'd like to discuss it—"

"Unfortunately, I can't right now."

The mathematician looked as if he had been shot in the stomach.

"I'm due at the White House," said Rubens. "I have to read your report first, and deal with everything else."

Johnny nodded stoically.

"Have you spoken with DiGiacomo about it?"

Hope sprang into Johnny's face. "I hadn't thought of her."

"She may have new insights. She's fresh from Princeton," said Rubens.

"No need to hold that against her," said Johnny Bib, running out of the office.

Rubens quickly went through his important phone and e-mail messages, then turned his attention to the report on Peru and recent Peruvian history. The Shining Path revolutionaries—psychotic crazies spouting Marxist nonsense, in Rubens' most charitable opinion—had been battled into submission by a properly aggressive response in the 1990s. While there had been a few abuses, the military campaign against the so-called revolutionaries had been effective and relatively free of scandal, certainly when compared to similar campaigns in other Latin American countries.

The same could not be said for the administration of Alberto Fujimori, president at the time. Fujimori was ousted after videotapes showing aides soliciting and taking bribes on his behalf were aired on Peruvian TV. The president and the head of Peru's intelligence service, Vladimiro Montesinos, who'd acted as his bagman, both fled the country.

The current president was considered an honest man, though an inept politician. Ortez, one of Peru's two vice presidents, seemed poised to return to the more corrupt ways of the past. Worse—while the current president was, at best, mildly pro-U.S., Ortez was a rabid U.S. hater, nearly as vicious as Fidel Castro on "the North." Except for the fact that he backed the free-market system, Rubens thought, he and the aging Cuban dictator would be perfect bedfellows, scoundrels of the first order.

But that had yet to be proven, Rubens reminded himself, reading through the rest of the report.

The summary was brief and succinct. Nothing wrong with that, though more depth on who was who in the political parties would have been helpful. The leading candidate in most polls was Victor Imberbe, whose Peruvian Centrist Party was a coalition of several groups representing the middle of the Peruvian political spectrum. Ortez trailed by about five points; his numbers had been trending downward for some time. The number three candidate, Hernando Aznar, was said to be anywhere from five to twenty points behind the front-runner. His Futuro (Future) Party was two years old, but the report had nothing on its political philosophy, beyond the fact that it was considered slightly right of center.

Johnny Bib had a point about the research team being out of its depth. Desk Three's Achilles' heel was its lack of a historic perspective when dealing with world affairs. There was no organization better at collating current intelligence and using it, simply none. But when it came to supplying perspective on a world situation, Deep Black's superintelligent math prodigies might as well have been walking cold into a seminar on medieval art. They could supply plenty of facts but had trouble putting them into a wider, deeply nuanced historic context.

What Rubens needed—what Deep Black needed—was memory. Not the simple memory of archives, as Johnny Bib's team had provided, but an interpretive memory, the sort that could be provided by a human being who had lived through at least part of it.

Rubens got up from his desk, stalking back and forth. Collins' innocent remarks at lunch earlier—were they truly innocent? Was there something in the background his people should know?

If the mission were in Europe or Russia, he would feel much more confident. But he'd only been to South America himself a few times.

Was he missing something?

Rubens found himself standing in the middle of the room, arms folded, eyes gazing at his blank computer screen.

I am overly concerned with Collins, he told himself. But perhaps there is something there that I should know. At the very least, a fuller perspective on Peru would be useful after the election if the vice president does not win.

Rubens berated himself for not thinking of this sooner. The mission had come up suddenly, but still—he had failed to anticipate the situation.

Who could supply a perspective without an ax to grind?

Hernes Jackson came to mind.

Jackson had served as the American ambassador to Chile before retiring only last year. Rubens thought most career diplomats were soft intellectually and naive pragmatically, but Hernes was an exception. His ambassadorship capped a distinguished career that included several different posts in the State Department Intelligence Agency. Virtually unknown outside of the diplomatic corps, he didn't have the sort of smooth patter and distinguished looks it took to be a talking head and so had never made the jump to the media or consulting circuit—points in his favor as far as Rubens was concerned.

Rubens found Jackson's phone number himself and dialed it. He was pleasantly surprised when the ambassador picked up on the second ring.

"This is William Rubens, Mr. Ambassador. I would like an opportunity to pick your brain," he said, plunging in.

"Dr. Rubens. At the NSA?"

"Yes, sir."

"Of course. When?"

"As soon as would be convenient."

"I was on my way to the library, but I suppose I could put that off until tomorrow," said Jackson with the casual ease of someone who really was retired. "Sometime this afternoon?"

"Actually, I expect to be tied up for the rest of the day," said Rubens. He checked his watch. The report on the cards should be ready within the hour; he would head to the White House as soon as he had it.

They could meet after that. Jackson lived near Alexandria.

"Perhaps for dinner?" said Rubens. "Seven or so."

"Dinner? Well, I suppose it would be possible. Yes. Dinner would be good, Dr. Rubens."

"Few people call me doctor," said Rubens. He had two PhDs, a fact he had been somewhat egotistical about when he was younger and at a junior government rank. Now he found the doctorates mostly useful to remind some of the younger mathematicians he employed that he was not simply an empty suit. "I'd be more comfortable if you called me William or Bill. Give me directions and I'll pick you up at your house at seven."

11

Neither Karr nor Dean was at the café when Lia arrived for the rendezvous. She decided to have a glass of red wine, something she almost never did, especially when she was on an operation. She was about halfway through the glass when Dean showed up, pretending not to know her.

"You're an American, right?" he asked.

"Yes."

"Mind if I ask you for a few directions? My Spanish isn't too good." He took out a guidebook, thumbing through it.

Oh, Charlie, just sit down, Lia thought. No one's paying any attention.

"I'm a little lost," said Dean.

"You may sit if you wish."

Dean pulled out the chair and asked a question about how to get to the Museo de la Inquisición, which was located in Lima's historical district.

"Let me see your book." Lia slid the card from her sleeve into the book, then passed it back. "That's not a very good neighborhood at night," she told him.

"I can take care of myself." Dean began folding up the map. "Thank you very much, *señora*."

"That would be *señorita*. Though I am spoken for."

Dean smiled. "Where's Julio?"

"That's the best pickup line you can come up with?"

"What happened to him? I thought he was supposed to escort you all day."

"He's not my bodyguard." Lia frowned. "I told him I had a headache. An oldie but a goldie."

"I'll remember that. Thanks for the information."

"Wait," she said as he turned away. "Stay and have dinner."

"Can't."

"Charlie. I mean it. Stay and have dinner."

He shook his head. He had to send the data back to the Art Room as soon as possible.

"I got scared in there. Really scared."

"When?"

"In the vault. I can't—it was nothing, but I just, I almost freaked for a minute. It was weird. I was scared."

Lia felt the sensation again, her throat tightening.

"Do you think I'm losing it?" she asked.

"I don't think you're losing it."

I came close, she thought to herself. *I really did.*

Instead of saying that, she told him that she loved him.

He nodded.

Watching him go, Lia berated herself for mentioning her fear. She'd known he wouldn't understand. He never got scared of anything.

12

"How'd the food look?" asked Karr as Dean slid into the front seat of the car outside the café.

"I didn't notice."

"Jeez, Charlie. You have to work on your powers of observation. How are we supposed to gather intelligence, if you're not watching?"

Karr put the little Toyota in gear and began talking about how hungry he was. Dean didn't pay attention. He'd heard the complaint many times.

He'd never heard Lia say she was scared.

She didn't look scared, and she certainly didn't act it.

Not that there was anything wrong with fear. Fear was a natural reaction in any number of circumstances. Everybody got scared sometime. You handled it as best you could.

It was the admission, and the look in her eyes accompanying it, that worried him.

Immediately after the assault in Korea, Lia had insisted on going back into the field. She'd pulled off a difficult mission, and if it weren't for her, half of Europe would have been wiped out by a nuclear-seeded tsunami.

She hadn't once mentioned the word "fear" or talked about being scared after the assault. Angry, maybe, but not scared.

Dean had never been a person who thought talk did much good. If something bothered you, you attacked it—you stalked and you fought it; you dealt with it. That was what he'd done as a sniper. It was what he'd done as a Marine and as a small businessman and what he did now with Deep Black.

Lia was the same way. Harder, really.

If she was worried, maybe he should be, too, About her.

"You figure that guy is with the Peruvian intelligence service, or somebody else?" asked Karr.

Dean looked up to see who he was talking about: a man sitting in a van across from their hotel's main entrance. The truck had a florist's logo on the front and side.

"Probably a local," said Dean. "*If* he's an agent."

"You think somebody delivering flowers is going to take the trouble to find a parking spot, let alone sit there?" said Karr. "He'd double-park, run inside, get going. Not wait."

They circled around the block. The truck was still there when they came back.

"I doubt he's looking for us," said Dean. "But let's not fool around. We'll just go for roof number two. The Leon."

"OK with me," said Karr.

The uplink unit was in the trunk and could be set up just about anywhere with an unobstructed view of the heavens. The transmitter looked like a standard satellite dish and had a slot specially designed for the voter card. The transmission rate was relatively slow, and from setup to teardown the process would take about a half hour. Their hotel had been chosen partly because it had a roof terrace that was rarely used and would be perfect for the transmission. But just in case, they had scouted several other possible transmission spots the day before.

Dean took Karr's handheld computer and brought up the map and a position locator so he could give him directions to the Leon, a business-class hotel in the Miraflores district. The side entrances were not equipped with alarms, and though they were locked from the outside, this didn't present much of a problem; Dean slid a plastic card into the jamb side and tickled the door open in a matter of seconds. Ten minutes later they were on the roof, leaning against the small service shack above the elevator shaft.

Karr handled the transmitter, donning a set of headphones to help him find the proper angle for the satellite. Dean stood guard, using the PDA to monitor the feed from two different video bugs they had left in the stairwell to warn them if anyone was coming.

"Here we go," announced Karr finally. He tightened one of the screws on the dish's tripod, pushed the card into the slot, and stood back.

"Good," said Karr, practically singing. "So what do you think, Charlie? Can we get in the bank vault?"

"Looked pretty well guarded."

"Yeah. But that's what makes it an interesting challenge, don't you think? I mean, Butch Cassidy and the Sundance Kid couldn't get in. And we can."

"Maybe we can, and maybe we can't."

"Oh, we *can*."

"Easier to take them on the road, once they ship them to the rest of the distribution points Thursday," said Dean. "And I prefer easy."

"Too many. We'll never get it done in time."

"Then Lia has the easier shot, going in tomorrow or the next day," said Dean. But as he said that, he reconsidered.

"Ah, you're no fun." Karr sat down next to Dean. "You're worried about Lia?"

Dean shrugged. He was surprised Karr had picked up on that.

"She'll be OK," Karr told him. "She's tough."

"What did Clint Eastwood say? 'Sometimes tough ain't enough.'"

"I say we do the vault ourselves. Keep her inspection as a backup."

"Yeah, that's probably best."

"Let's check out the bar downstairs when this is done. I kinda want to know what Peruvian beer tastes like."

13

In his last lifetime, Stephan Babin had consummated many of his deals in a Moscow after-hours club, an establishment he partly owned. He liked to fantasize about the place now, picturing the flushed faces and bursting bosoms, the red lips of Lida the hostess, and the purple jowls of Boyce, his German partner. Babin imagined he could smell the sweat and perfume, the overbearing breath of the drunks, and the vague metallic scent that clung to the bodyguards. He pictured it all in his mind, heard the sounds again. He saw himself at his table, watching the others with his quiet smile. He saw himself taking the bottle of champagne—he had sealed his deals with champagne, a trademark—and carelessly filling his glass to the brim. He would raise it slowly to his lips, pause to toast the room, then sip—a tiny, infinitesimal sip, all he would have.

Then he saw himself standing and waving his hands. The room exploded in a fireball. He heard a delicious shriek, a shout of recognition as well as fear and pain: an acknowledgment that Stephan Babin held the power of life and death in his hands and had chosen death.

The dream faded as Babin poked the smoldering rubbish pile in front of him. Encouraged, the fire leapt upward, its red tongue leering at the dark shadow of the nearby hills, as if to frighten the ghosts from the Inca ruins that lay there. The old stones were not quite visible from here—the Indians had oriented them to catch the sun at its zenith—but they loomed in Babin's imagination, charred and broken, their destruction a foreshadowing or the retribution he planned.

He heard a truck approaching.

Babin leaned his weight on his right crutch and reached into the back of his belt for the Walther pistol hidden there. There were no random visitors up the nearby road. It connected the old Spanish house and its accompanying barn to the nearby highway, where traffic was strictly controlled because of the military installation to the north. The vehicle would belong to either General Túcume or an American spy coming to finish the job they had botched three years before.

Babin listened carefully, trying to decide from the sound which it was. He couldn't tell. The general used a variety of vehicles, and the Americans—who knew what they would steal?

As the vehicle rounded the sharp switchback and drove onto the small terrace before the old Spanish building and its accompanying barn, Babin's pulse quickened. It was a small Toyota pickup. He held the pistol to his side, shifting his weight slightly so he would be as stable as possible when he fired. Despite his profession as an arms dealer, he had never been a very good shot. The gun in his hand did not have much of a kick for a pistol, but his crutches would add to the uncertainty. He would have to wait until whoever was in the truck came very close to be sure of killing him.

How ironic, Babin thought, to be discovered so close to his chance for revenge.

The truck stopped thirty feet from him. Belatedly, Babin realized that the fire silhouetted him in the darkness. It was too late to move.

"Excuse me," called the driver, rolling down the window of the truck. "Could you direct me to *Señor* Babin?"

"Why?" said Babin. He held the pistol at his hip, not quite concealed but not obvious, either.

"A package from Kleis."

Babin raised his arm, making the gun obvious. "Leave it."

"I was told to—"

"Leave it. Put it out of your truck—*carefully.*"

The driver ducked down in his cab. Kleis had supplied the parts for the general's dummy warhead—and a few parts Babin needed for himself.

Kleis was a scoundrel of the worst sort. He could easily have sold him out.

As the driver opened the door, Babin steadied his arm to shoot. From this distance in the dim light, the shot would not necessarily be an easy one for an untrained man, even if he had full use of his body. The bullet would have to strike the target in the head—surely anyone who came gunning for Babin would wear a vest.

And it would have to be on the first shot fired.

The driver sat back upright in the cab and opened the door. A box clattered to the ground.

Babin kept his finger against the trigger but did not squeeze. The truck backed down ten yards, twenty, then turned and hurried away.

Slowly, Babin began crutching toward the package. His left leg had enough sensation and strength to act as a sturdy pivot even on his worst days. Today was one of the better ones, with his right aching but able to bear more than its usual portion of weight.

He stood over the box for at least a minute. Then he turned it over with his crutch.

It could be a bomb. But anyone who wanted to kill him would have taken the much surer route of hiring an assassin to kill him in person, wouldn't he? Especially if he knew they had failed once before.

Getting to the ground was not difficult—Babin simply pitched himself forward and rolled onto his shoulder. He crawled to the package, then pushed his legs around and under him so that he could sit. He turned the package over, then took his pocketknife out and scored a small cutout in the side. He worked slowly, stripping off layers of the cardboard a few at a time until only a thin piece remained. He made a light perforation, then poked into the box.

Shredded newspapers filled the interior. By now it was

so dark out that he had to crawl back to the fire to see into the box.

But the fire was smoldering, much of its fuel gone. Patiently, Babin pulled himself up by leaning on the rake, then grabbed the can of kerosene. Babin made sure the rake was steady—the last thing he wanted to do was pitch forward into the flames—then sprinkled the contents on the embers. Nothing happened for a moment or two, but then some spark caught and the liquid flared so high he dropped the can. It bounced in the dirt in front of his right leg. Instinct took over, and he swooped forward to try to grab the container before it caught fire. But he didn't have nearly enough control of his body to do that, and he landed on the ground in a pool of the dribbling kerosene.

Babin rolled to his stomach and dragged himself back to the box, pushing it with his face.

So close, he thought to himself. I was so close to my goal.

He heard a loud whoosh behind him and felt the warmth as the fire roared with its new fuel.

Not yet, he thought to himself. Not yet. Not yet.

Babin hunkered down in the dirt and pushed forward, continuing until he no longer felt the flames scorching his side. He twisted around, half-expecting to see his legs on fire, but they weren't. Provoked by the kerosene, the flames climbed ten or twelve feet high, consuming the last pieces of wood and rubbish in the pile.

He sat up, then pulled the package to his lap. Caution on the one hand, foolhardiness on the other—that had been the story of his life. It was a character flaw that had cost him his legs.

Babin tore open the package quickly. Wrapped at the center of the newspaper and a wedge of bubble wrap was a small timing circuit that could be used to trigger a bomb.

He had asked Kleis for it with the other items months ago. It had never been delivered, though he had to pay in advance. He assumed that the dealer had simply forgotten or perhaps kept the money as an extra payment. Now it seemed that he had had trouble obtaining it.

Babin's warhead had come from an antiaircraft missile modified for use against ballistic missiles. It was relatively small; it weighed just over two hundred kilos and fitted in a crate about the size of a small bathtub or office desk without the legs. The main trigger was essentially a proximity fuse wired with an altimeter circuit. "Proximity" was relative— the bomb was designed to explode above thirty-five thousand feet when a fast-moving object was within a half mile. The altimeter circuitry also acted as a fail-safe detonator, triggering the bomb if the primary fuse failed.

Babin had modified the fusing circuitry so that he could "trick" the fuse into exploding when triggered by an elementary detonator: a cell phone circuit, an astoundingly easy and versatile trigger he had first seen used by Chechnyans on roadside bombs more than a decade before. He'd wanted the timer as a backup but had resigned himself to doing without one.

He clutched the circuit board tightly in his hand as he crawled over to his crutches. As he rose, the fumes in the kerosene can ignited. It exploded with a low boom, the flames flowering like a red-yellow lily. But Babin no longer paid attention. He crutched quickly to the barn, opened the door with the key he kept around his neck, and went to work.

Unlike the nano-switches that actually did the work, the circuitry that Babin had modified to set them off was not particularly complicated; even if he had not been an engineer by training, Babin would have known how to wire the timer in simply by virtue of having built train layouts when he was a child. Still, there was a certain delicacy involved, not least of all because the weapon was packed in a large, shielded crate and maneuvering the sheathing was not easy. It took several hours, and by the time Babin was done, he was physically drained. He made his way out of the barn and slowly to the main house; he was so tired that he crawled up the steps rather than pulling himself on the banister.

He'd just closed the door when he heard the housekeeper's voice from the rear of the house.

"Señor Stephan, are you OK?"

Rosalina hurried to the foyer, a worried look on her face.

"I'm quite all right," he told her.

"I saw the fire," she said.

"I was in the barn."

"I thought, yes, but then when you did not come . . . In a little while, I would have gone over."

"I'm OK. Just checking on things," he told her.

The barn was not off-limits to her; not only did the general trust her completely, but Rosalina would not comprehend what was in there anyway. Still, she seemed to fear the building, and her weekly forays were quick visits to empty the trash can in the workshop. Maybe the spirits she sometimes talked to—like many Yahua Indians, Rosalina thought she could talk to the dead—had warned her away.

"Señor Stephan? For breakfast?"

"An egg would be fine."

She bowed her head but did not leave.

"Was there something else?"

"I was going to ask for tomorrow afternoon and the next day off. My daughter's son is to make Holy Confirmation. I can get a ride with a truck if I wait at the edge of the road."

"You must have the day off," he told her. The timing was perfect, though of course he didn't tell her this. "Both. This is the daughter who lives near the city?"

Rosalina nodded. The daughter's husband was a mestizo—a mixed-breed who worked at a small farm.

"The general—"

"Don't worry about the general," Babin told her. "He will never know. But if he were to find out, I would say I gave you the day off for your hard work. You deserve it. It's too little time. A week—you should have a week."

"You are very kind, Señor Stephan. Thank you. I will be here Friday."

"Take Friday, Saturday, Sunday, too—make a vacation of it."

"I could not do that. The cleaning would not be done."

"I don't think there is a house in Peru as clean as this one," he told her. She smiled, but Babin knew she would report to work Friday, bright and early.

By then he would be gone, as would the warheads, both the general's and his.

"Good night, Señor Stephan. Stay warm."

"Oh, I'm very warm, Rosalina. Very, very warm."

You wouldn't believe the inferno that burns inside me, he thought, making his way to his room.

14

"The FBI information was right," Segio told Rubens over the phone line connecting him to the Desk Three analysis center. "The cards are programmed to increase the votes of the candidate in the first position on the ballot—Ramon Ortez. They pull off the votes under a complicated formula to make it harder to detect a pattern, and they spread it out over the whole network, taking advantage of the fact that the machines are all connected as a security feature."

"Is removing one card enough to disrupt the effect?" Rubens asked.

"We're debating that. We don't think so. It looks like even one card would add votes. I would get them all."

"Good work, Segio. Please extend my gratitude to the staff." Rubens reached to the telephone console, switching into the Art Room.

"Telach."

"This is Rubens. The cards have been tampered with. I'm on my way to the White House. I expect we will have authorization from the president to proceed within a few hours."

"We'll be ready," she said.

Thirty minutes later, Rubens' helicopter set down on the lawn of the White House. The wash from the blades pushed at his suit as he walked toward the building, his pace so brisk that his leg muscles stiffened. An aide met him, telling him that President Marcke wanted to meet him in the national security adviser's office.

"I thought Mr. Hadash was still in China."

"He is, sir. But the President wanted to talk to you there. Mr. Hadash will be calling in as well."

They went up the stairs to Hadash's office, which was just around the corner from the president's. The national security adviser was working on a set of strategic agreements with the Chinese and trying to get them to increase their pressure on North Korea to disarm. He was supposed to visit Japan afterward; he wasn't expected back for another week and a half.

Rubens nodded to Hadash's secretary and went into the inner office. He had no sooner sat down in one of the chairs in front of the desk than the president walked in.

"How are you, Billy?"

"Very well, sir."

"I'm stealing George's office because we're shuffling delegations in and out of the Oval Office today. I have a group of third graders and their teacher waiting for me inside."

Marcke sat down behind Hadash's desk. "I'm not sure we'd want them listening in," said the president. Then he chuckled. "On the other hand, I suppose their advice might be as insightful as Congress's. And twice as useful."

Rubens smiled. Marcke's party controlled Congress, but in some ways that made it harder to deal with.

"The FBI information on Peru was correct, I gather?" said Marcke.

"Yes, sir. The voting cards are rigged to put a worm in the computers, delivering the election to Ortez."

The president glanced at his watch. "I expect George to check in any moment. The call will come here. You're ready to move ahead?"

"Yes, sir. We can replace all of the cards that we believe have been altered. There are only a dozen of them."

The telephone buzzed. Marcke snagged it with a practiced motion. "How are our Chinese friends, George?" he said.

Rubens couldn't hear the answer, but it may have been

off-color, because Marcke roared with laughter. "I have Billy here. I'm going to put you on the speakerphone." The president punched a button. "Hear us?"

"I hear you, Mr. President," said Hadash. His voice echoed slightly. "Bill?"

"I'm here, George."

"The Peruvian election cards were compromised, as we thought," the president said. "I want to revisit the question of where to go from here." He had snagged a paper clip from the desk in front of him, and he began straightening it as he talked.

"I still think we should swap out the crooked cards, as we discussed the other day," the national security adviser said. "Let the election proceed."

"Lincoln thinks we should let the UN handle it," the president said and looked at the speakerphone. Lincoln was James Lincoln, the secretary of state.

Rubens took a deep breath. He had a long list of objections to working with the UN on a matter like this, starting with the fact that it would put one of his covert ops in the spotlight. Nor would the hack of the voter cards be easy to explain: the hack could not be detected by normal diagnostic tools, which was how it had gotten this far in the first place. And the politicians at the UN would wring their hands and dither. . . .

"Even assuming that we wanted to trust that crowd," Hadash said, "UN meddling in Peru will only result in postponing the election. All indications are that the president will retire as he said he would—he's a damned sick man— and Ortez will take over. Lincoln knows that. Once Ortez is in, he's in and that's that. There will be no election."

The president had the paper clip completely straight. Now he began twisting it. "Thanks for your thoughts, George," he said abruptly, and his hand shot out to the telephone. The tinny hiss stopped. "What are your thoughts?" he said to Rubens, looking him in the eye.

"I think we can pull off a card switch and the election can go forward."

The president got out of his chair and came around the desk. He sat in a chair beside Rubens and leaned toward him. Marcke was still twisting the paper clip, which had taken on the shape of a pretzel.

"If the United States gets caught with its fingers in a ballot box in Peru, the shit is going to hit the fan," he said softly. "That would be the biggest American foreign policy disaster since Pearl Harbor. We're trying to encourage democratic regimes all over the globe, and we would instantly lose all credibility. My assessment is that Latin America would become too hot to hold us. The countries in South America owe so much money to the World Bank that they could bankrupt it if they renounced their debts. With the Chinese economy slowing, oil prices rising, the Middle East bubbling, and North Korea ranting about nukes, that would be one more disaster than we could handle."

"My team won't get caught," Rubens said.

"The prisons are full of people who thought that." The president concentrated on the wire as he manipulated it. "By God, they had better not. If they do, this government never heard of them." He eyed Rubens. "Understand?"

"Yes, sir."

Marcke lowered his gaze back to the wire. "My gut tells me that we should tell the president of Peru that we think the election computers are compromised and let the Peruvians figure it out. After all, it's their country."

He tossed the paper clip onto the desk and stood up. "The truth is that it doesn't make a hill of beans' difference who gets elected down there." He went to the window and stood looking out. He stretched and scratched his head.

Rubens sat silently.

"It's been a bad year for Latin American democracies," the president mused. "Not that they've had many good ones. Still, until the folks in Latin America learn to have honest elections and live with the results, the place is always going to be a breeding ground for tyrants."

When the silence that followed that remark had dragged on too long, Rubens said, "I believe it was Abe Lincoln who pointed out that it's difficult to drain the swamp when you're up to your ass in alligators. Lincoln or Confucius."

Marcke turned to look at Rubens, flashed a smile, and headed for the door. "Switch the cards," he said in passing, "and don't get caught."

15

Lia checked her room for bugs as soon as she got there. She found three, all of which appeared to belong to the Peruvian intelligence service. She left them where they were and made a phone call to her "mother"—actually an NSA operator briefed to play the role—and told her how beautiful the country was. Then Lia turned on the TV and flopped down on the bed. Finding her eyes starting to close, she called down to the desk to ask for a wakeup call in three hours. Lia put the phone down and within moments was sleeping. The next thing she knew, the phone was ringing to wake her.

A quick shower restored some of her energy. Dressing in a long, loose skirt and a flowing knit top, Lia went downstairs in full tourist mode.

She knew she'd be shadowed, but she didn't spot the two Peruvian agents who'd been assigned to track her until she got out of the taxi at Manos Morenas, a popular tourist spot. The restaurant pulsed with Peruvian music so loud the pavement under her feet shook, and by the time Lia reached the iron gate at the entrance, she was bouncing with the beat. She walked through the porch and went inside, sliding through a knot of guests as if she were meeting someone inside. After continuing toward the ladies' room, she spun around in the hall and doubled back ito the main dining room, looking to see whether her tails had come into the restaurant or were going to stay outside. They were both in the car, which made them easy to duck; she walked back and went right through the kitchen, striding purposefully out the door and then down the alley to the side street.

A few blocks later, Lia went into a small *penās* or bar; the nightly show of homegrown music wouldn't start until midnight, and the place was nearly empty. But it suited her purpose well—she planted a video bug at the front and then headed to the ladies' room, where she used her handheld computer to make sure she wasn't being followed.

Sure she was clear, she went out the back door. A block away, Lia found a taxi and asked the driver to take her to La Posada del Mirador, another bar popular with tourists, not far from the waterfront. Here she went up to the balcony, gazing out toward the sea. A band downstairs began playing *música criolla,* a catchy jazz tune that lifted her mood.

She ordered a bottle of water. When the waiter left, Lia took her handheld computer out and scanned for listening devices. Finding none nearby, she got up and went to the railing, posting a video bug there. She scanned again, then went back to her table. The balcony was about three-quarters full, and the buzz of the music was loud enough to mask her conversation if anyone tried to listen in with a parabolic mike.

"Are you with us, Lia?" asked Rockman as she got back to the table.

"Just waiting to dance."

"Dean and Karr are in a bar a block away from you. Give them a minute; they're ordering food."

Lia wished they were with her, Charlie especially. She knew that would be a security risk, but she still wished he were here, that she could put her hand on his.

"Are we go or no-go?" she asked.

"The cards were definitely hacked," replied Rockman. "We're in the process of figuring out where the envelopes are going. I'm expecting the data any second."

"Hey," said Karr, his voice very distant. "Lia, how's the beer over there?"

"I wouldn't know."

Rockman repeated what he had said for the benefit of Dean

and Karr. The cards in the vault were to be distributed the day after next, sent to different voting sites around the country.

"I say we go with the break-in plan tomorrow night then," said Karr. "Hit the safe. Get them all in one place without anybody looking over Lia's shoulder."

"That's what we're thinking," said Marie Telach, joining the conversation. "If you're all up for it."

The electronic guardians and physical barriers in the bank and vault were easy to defeat. While the area was patrolled at night, a window on the second floor of the building could not be seen by the guards outside and could be easily reached by climbing up on the roof of the neighboring building and crossing over. The video surveillance system had already been compromised; the Art Room could take it over at any point, supplying "reruns" showing all was well.

The safe itself had a mechanical lock. State-of-the-art in the late 1800s, it could be opened easily with the aid of a small unit the ops called a cracker that in effect listened to the tumblers as they turned. It might not be necessary to use it, however—the Art Room had researched old archives and discovered what they believed was the original combination, which they would try first.

A set of voter cards matching the "good" ones in the envelopes would be delivered by a special courier in the morning. They already had replacement envelopes and the tamper-evident seals; they would use them to prepare the envelopes beforehand and simply swap them once they were inside the vault.

The only real difficulty was the two guards who worked in the lobby at night. The plan was to knock them out by intercepting a tray that was delivered to them every night around 10:00 p.m. The tray always included two sealed bottles of water; they'd substitute a pair with a strong synthetic opium to make the guards fall asleep.

"What if they don't drink?" asked Lia.

"They will," said Karr. "They did last night and the night before. And if they don't, Charlie nails them with the blowpipe. Right, Charlie?"

The blowpipe was a small air gun that shot a tiny dart with a muscle relaxant and barbiturate cocktail; within ten seconds of being hit by the needlelike bullet, the victim fell asleep. The sharp needle could penetrate clothes, and the drug could be calibrated to put just about anyone to sleep. But there was a downside: the needles stung when they hit.

"I can get them," said Dean. "But they'll realize they were hit by something before they go down."

"We grab the needles on the way out. They'll think they were stung by bees," said Karr. "And if not, heck, the computer surveillance cams will show nothing happened. Nobody will believe them."

"What do you think, Lia?" asked Telach.

"I think the regional centers will be easier. The security arrangements look like they're nonexistent."

"Normally, I would agree with you," said Telach. "But according to the list we've decrypted on where the cards are going, we'd have to hit seven different regional centers. The security at the sites won't be very strong, certainly nothing compared to what's here in Lima. But the distance is considerable. One's near the border in Chile; another is in a small city in the Amazon region near Iquitos. That's a lot of traveling to do in only two days."

"I'll take three cities," said Lia. "Tommy and Charlie can split the others."

"Our strong preference would be to keep you together. But if you think this is too difficult—"

"Hey, come on. We can do this," said Karr. "Lia, this is like twenty times easier than the Georgian embassy last year, right? It's just breaking into a safe."

"Lia, what do you think?" asked Dean.

"It's all right with me. You and Tommy have the hard part."

16

The directions Ambassador Hernes Jackson gave Rubens led to a condominium complex a few miles south of Washington, D.C. This was not one of the ultrachic enclaves with gates at the entry road and Mercedes S's in the guest spots. The units were small one- and two-bedroom town houses jammed four by four into postage stamp lots.

Rubens wondered if he'd made a mistake. But the number on the unit was correct, and when he rang the bell Jackson pulled open the door.

"Mr. Ambassador," said Rubens, sticking out his hand.

"How are you, Dr. Rubens?" said Jackson. He was a short man, whose gray head barely came to Rubens' chest.

"Very well, sir. A little hungry, perhaps."

"Is it warm out?"

"Yes. My car's right here."

The outside door opened into the living room. A plaid couch at least twenty years old dominated the sparse furnishings.

"I neglected to ask about your wife," said Rubens. "If she'd care to join us."

"My wife, unfortunately, passed on a year ago."

"Oh, I'm sorry."

"Is it going to rain?"

"I think it will hold off."

Rubens took Jackson to a restaurant he knew a few miles

away. The food was dependable and, more important, he knew he could get a table in a private corner. The wine list was also excellent, but when his guest said he didn't drink wine, Rubens stuck with sparkling water.

"Does retirement suit you?"

"Not particularly," said Jackson. "You needn't beat around the bush, Dr. Rubens. I'm not much for chitchat, really."

Rubens felt instantly relieved—he wasn't much for chitchat himself.

"I'm interested in Peru."

"Peru? In all honesty it was never a focus of mine."

"It was in your purview."

"For a time," said Jackson. "Before I was ambassador."

Rubens nodded, waiting for him to continue.

"A beautiful country, with a rich history, good ore deposits, but in terms of its strategic or economic value, well, it pales beside Argentina and Brazil."

"What did you think of Vladimiro Montesinos?"

"The head of the intelligence service? A thief and swindler. You're aware of the Jordanian business?"

"Only vaguely."

Jackson reviewed the highlights. Among other things, the head of Peru's intelligence service, Vladimiro Montesinos, had arranged to buy shoulder-launched antiaircraft missiles from Jordan. The CIA had signed off on the deal—only to realize much later that the missiles had been sold to Colombian narco-guerrillas.

"Was there ever any talk that one of our people may have been involved?" Rubens asked.

"No one had an opportunity, I would think."

Rubens nodded.

"The undersecretary of state was quite livid when he found out what had happened. Rightly so. Everyone was. Is that what you're interested in?"

"I'm not sure," said Rubens honestly. "Did the CIA run an operation to recover the antiaircraft missiles?"

"I didn't hear of one," said Jackson. "I'm not entirely positive I would have."

Neither had Rubens, a strong argument that they hadn't—or rather, that they hadn't gotten the weapons back if they had.

"Peru is not like Bolivia or, God save us, Colombia," continued Jackson. "Their border wars with Ecuador in the 1990s piqued some interest, but otherwise they're part of a blur to most people. Outside as well as inside the Beltway, I'd suppose."

"There is a good deal of drug production there," said Rubens.

"Yes, absolutely. During my time, the estimates were as high as two hundred thousand people involved, mostly in the Amazonian regions and nearby. This was where the mess with Air Bridge came in."

"Regrettable," said Rubens. Air Bridge was a CIA program intended to cut down on the use of airplanes by drug smugglers in the region. Two civilians had died in a case of mistaken identity in 2001 when they were shot down by an Air Bridge aircraft. The program was subsequently suspended.

"The CIA does have a habit of tripping over itself in South and Central America," observed Jackson.

The waiter came over, and Jackson turned his attention to the menu. After they had ordered, the ambassador spoke about the Incas and their remarkable civilization. He had taken several trips to Inca ruins, including Machu Picchu, a royal estate in almost impossible to reach (but breathtaking) terrain. He described some of what he had seen, his details of the stone and chiseled figures as precise as if he were looking at a photo.

"You realize why the guerrillas, the Shining Path, ended in failure?" said the ambassador, abruptly shifting from the travelogue to politics.

"It was foreign to the people," said Rubens. "Maoism doesn't particularly fit in South America."

"Absolutely." Jackson smiled, and Rubens had the distinct impression that the ambassador had posed the question as a sort of test.

"It was also rather psychotic," said Rubens.

"Sanity has never been a requirement for running a country," Jackson remarked.

"No, I guess it hasn't."

Dinner arrived. The ambassador spoke of the sights in Peru and then Brazil and Argentina, peppering his descriptions with observations about the people. Rubens let him go on, waiting until they ordered coffee to return to serious matters.

"I find myself in need of someone who could deliver a good perspective on the region," said Rubens, using a formula that would let the ambassador bow out gracefully if he wasn't interested. "My people are often in need of background on different situations."

"I didn't realize there was a need for that at Fort Meade."

"There is, from time to time. Someone who could look at recent cables, briefings, findings, reports, put them all into perspective for us. Someone who was independent, who had a great deal of mature knowledge, that person might fit in very well."

"Someone who came with the proper clearances?"

"Those would be a start."

Depending on what he gave the ambassador access to, the security checks could be quite extensive and include invasive lie detector tests. But Rubens decided not to go into the details until he was sure that Jackson was willing.

"And if I say no?"

"Of course you can say no, Ambassador. This is entirely optional. It's rather routine. Probably boring for a man of your talents."

"I don't know that it would be that boring," said Jackson. "But I must ask, isn't this usually the sort of thing that a CIA analyst does? Or someone from the State Department? Surely they would give you a full rundown on the region if you ask."

"We have asked. And we have had briefings," said Rubens. "I have questions about whether I've received the entire story. That's why I emphasize independence."

Jackson put his thumb and forefinger to his closed lips, massaging them gently. His brow furled, and his eyes narrowed, as if he were reading something inside his skull.

"Oh. You're not sure what has been left out. And that's your problem."

"Very possibly, nothing has been left out."

"Oh, something is always left out," said Jackson.

"That would be my fear."

The spider's nest of lines at the sides of Jackson's face grew deeper. When Rubens had picked him up, he thought Jackson appeared at least five years younger than the age in his bio, which was seventy-two. Now he looked ten years older than that.

He's going to turn me down, Rubens thought. He's worried about offending someone he used to know. Or maybe he just doesn't want the trouble.

"When do you want me to begin?" asked Jackson.

"Tomorrow morning would be good," said Rubens.

After he dropped the ambassador off at his house, Rubens checked in with the Art Room. Telach had gone home for some rest; her relief, Chris Farlekas, filled him in on the situation in Peru. They had hacked their way into the computers where the list for the voting machine distribution was kept, decrypted the list, and determined that the cards would be shipped to too many places to make intercepting them convenient. Therefore, they were going to have to break into the bank the next night.

"We have a good plan," said Farlekas. "Tommy Karr's chomping at the bit."

"Mr. Karr would be eager to tap-dance into Hades. What does Mr. Dean think?"

"Charlie says fine. Lia agrees."

"Very well. Move forward with the plan. I will be in first thing in the morning."

Rubens snapped off the phone.

The CIA people had analyzed past elections and predicted that the cards would be sent en masse to a single city or at most two, most likely in the south where Ortez was weak.

Wrong.

Surely not a deliberate mistake, thought Rubens, just a simple mistake. And yet he couldn't quite convince himself.

17

The day began for Calvina Agnese like most days of her life for the past five years: walking in the dark for an hour and a half from her apartment on the outskirts of Lima to a restaurant in the city's tourist area. Calvina's steady pace was somewhat faster on Wednesdays than other days, for two things happened on Wednesday that she looked forward to: her boss Señor DeCura always arrived at 6:00 a.m. for coffee in the kitchen, and she was paid.

The latter was far more important to her than the first, for her meager wages supported not only Calvina but also her mother and father, along with her sisters and brothers. But she liked also to listen to Señor DeCura, who would spend an hour describing the wonders he had seen in his life, in America especially.

Señor DeCura had gone to the United States during the 1980s. His first job had been as a busboy at a diner in a city called Goshen. He lived in a trailer with three other workers from the restaurant. Señor DeCura said the trailer was considered a hovel in America and claimed not to like it very much, but when he described his days there it sounded to Calvina like a palace. So did every place he spoke of—the restaurant where he worked as a short-order cook, the one where he began as sous chef, and finally the grand establishment where he commanded the kitchen. By the time he was thirty-five, Señor DeCura had saved enough money to return home and open his restaurant in an old mansion. He had not only earned a great deal of money, but he had learned what the Yankee tourists liked and were willing to pay for.

Señor DeCura had opened the doors to his restaurant five years ago. Since that time, he had become a hero and inspiration for others. Many of his young workers left for the U.S., most after gaining advice (and a few dollars) from him.

Calvina wanted to join them. If she were a boy—or if her money were not so important to her family with her father out of work—she would have left by now.

As she neared the block where the restaurant sat, Calvina sensed that something was wrong. Two of the employees she worked with were sitting on the sidewalk in front of the building, heads in their hands. She quickened her pace until she was almost running.

"Carlos, Jenna? What is going on?" she shouted when still several meters away.

Jenna moaned and Carlos shook his head. The iron gates in front of the restaurant door had not been opened. A new chain wound through the bars, clasping it closed.

"What happened? Where is Señor DeCura?" Calvina demanded.

"Dead," said Jenna. And she began to sob.

"Who?"

"He killed himself, God save his soul," said Carlos. "He had debts."

"Debts? Señor DeCura was a rich man. His restaurant—"

"All gamblers have debts," said Carlos. "And this restaurant has not been his own for more than two years."

"But will we be paid today?" said Calvina. Tears streamed down her face. "Is there money to pay us?"

The others stared at her, unable to speak.

18

Hernes Jackson had visited Crypto City several times during his years with the State Department, and so he was prepared for some of the security gauntlet he had to run when he reported for work at seven o'clock the morning following his dinner with Rubens. He began at Operations Building 1, which looked very much like a modernist-style corporate headquarters building, its black-mirror glass adding style to the cold cube of its form. The fact that the building sat on a high berm and could only be approached after passing two different security checks might have tipped off the uninitiated that it was something else entirely. If it didn't, then the gamut inside would, since all visitors had to pass through a set of special gates that not only checked for bombs and weapons but sniffed out electronic devices as well.

On the other side of the gates, Jackson was met by not one but two "men in black"—members of the paramilitary security detail assigned to protect the NSA's secrets. The men were representative of the breed—unsmiling and huge. Behind them lurked a man of medium height and slouchy build, whose walruslike blond mustache seemed at first glance a stage prop. He wore a turtleneck beneath a blue blazer; about fifty, he looked like an Ivy League professor enjoying the benefits of tenure as his career wound down.

"Ambassador Jackson, hello," said the man. "I'm Kevin Montblanc. I work for Mr. Rubens. I'll be your escort today.

That badge you're wearing doesn't allow you to go where we're going without a friend, so think of me as your best friend."

Montblanc and the escorts led Jackson down a corridor to another security station.

"I hope you haven't picked up a weapon in the last thirty seconds," said Montblanc good-naturedly. "Otherwise we'll all have to be strip-searched."

"Do you have a pacemaker or similar device?" asked one of the guards.

"No."

"Do you have an iPod or a PDA or anything like that, sir?"

"I'm not entirely sure what that is," said Jackson.

The man smiled and began waving his hand around Jackson's body. It took Jackson a moment to realize that the guard had some sort of detector in his hand.

"An iPod is the modern equivalent of a Sony Walkman," said Montblanc. "A PDA is a small handheld computer. They have memory, so they're forbidden to be brought in and out. A lot of the younger people have iPods for music. You can have one kept here if you wish, however. It's easily arranged."

"I'm not sure I want one."

Jackson looked down at the man who was using the miniature searching device. Most people who wielded metal detector wands passed them swiftly and sloppily around someone's body, especially if he had already been searched. This man moved slowly and carefully, pausing and occasionally doubling back. He didn't touch Jackson, but when he finished there was not an inch of his body that the detector could have missed.

"This search is just part of the protocol. Even Mr. Rubens goes through it," said Montblanc, holding out his arms.

Down the hall they boarded an elevator. There was no control panel or floor indicator.

"Close doors, please," said Montblanc, and the doors gently shut. The elevator started with the gentlest tug imaginable.

Jackson realized they were descending, but he had no way of knowing how far. The doors opened on an empty hallway; they walked down it to a second elevator.

"Mr. Rubens would like your immediate impression on some reports he has. As it happens, it all falls under your old clearance," said Montblanc as the car began to descend. "You understand the drill, don't you, Mr. Ambassador?"

"I understand."

"He hopes to speak to you about it within an hour. Unfortunately, he's wearing two hats this week and next. He's filling in for the admiral—our director."

"I understand."

"There will be an extensive process involving your clearance. We have to go through it. It's a little more involved than when you were at the State Department."

"I see."

"There will be lie detector tests. It's rather routine."

"Oh?"

"Have you ever been under a psychiatrist's care?" said Montblanc.

"No," said Jackson, surprised as much by the nonchalant tone as the question itself. "Why do you ask?"

"We tend to be nosy about that sort of thing. A psychologist?"

"No."

"Marriage counselor?"

"Not at all."

"Get along with your wife?" said Montblanc lightly, trying to keep the conversation easy. "That's good."

"My wife unfortunately passed on."

"Grief counselor?"

"I'm not a nutcase, if that's what you're getting at."

Montblanc chortled, his cartoonish mustache rocking back and forth. "Oh, don't get offended. We have plenty of nutcases working here. It's practically a job requirement in some areas."

The elevator stopped. Jackson attempted to keep his dislike of Montblanc in check as they passed through yet one more security hurdle, this one confined to a retina scan and ID check. Montblanc brought him down the hall to a small conference room.

"Our facilities are a little primitive here," Montblanc told him. "We're not really set up for visiting scholars, not in this department. Down the line, we may be able to do better."

Jackson did not mind the temporary office, but he was beginning to sour on the entire idea of working with the NSA. Extra money would be welcome, certainly, and he welcomed a chance to do something useful, but the atmosphere here seemed very strange, as if he'd stepped into a science fiction movie.

"I'm to review cables? Briefings?" he asked Montblanc, gesturing at the empty table.

"Someone will bring you the file in a moment. Even though, as I said, it may not be highly classified, as a general rule—well, let me put it to you this way: *I* shouldn't even see it. Our friends here won't see it. Only you. It's our protocol, you know. The way of life. We wouldn't share a lunch menu."

Jackson nodded.

"If you need to use the restroom or get some exercise, one of our friends will escort you. Are you OK?"

"Yes."

"Good, then I'll leave you to your work."

A few minutes later, a man in his thirties wearing a business suit but without a tie appeared at the door. Without introducing himself, he walked over to the table and put down a blue envelope. Jackson rose and started to introduce himself, but the man acted as if he weren't even there, turning and walking away without speaking.

To Jackson's surprise, the envelope contained only one item, a CIA briefing paper that was prepared as part of a presentation. It was a background report on the country, discussing the political situation and the upcoming elections, which were due to be held this coming Sunday. It was stamped TOP SECRET, but a decently diligent college undergraduate would have been able to find the same points with a few hours of work. Its conclusions were rather rudimentary: democracy in Peru was precarious; the indigenous peoples— aka Indians, natives, or *campesinos*, as they were sometimes called—were poor and underrepresented; the military would remain neutral.

"You seem perplexed, Ambassador. I hope you're well."

Jackson looked up at Rubens, who for a big man managed to tread very lightly and had entered the room without him hearing.

"I am well, Dr. Rubens. Thank you. I've been reading the briefing."

"And?"

"It's a rather thin summary. You're concerned about the elections, obviously."

"Yes, we are."

Jackson flipped back to the beginning of the document. It had been printed from a computer slide presentation, which probably accounted for its shallowness. In Jackson's opinion, no one over the age of thirteen should be allowed to use a program such as PowerPoint.

"Jorge Evans was one of the people who prepared this?" asked Jackson, pointing to one of the authors' names. "He's not an analyst."

"I believe you are correct. The Office of African and Latin American Analysis acted as the lead preparing the brief, but there was input from the Operations side."

"Yes. He was involved in paramilitary operations in some way, and not simply in South America."

"I understood his expertise was there."

"I daresay he knows a great deal. I would expect that he's rather senior at this point, however."

"Indeed."

The CIA could be seen as several large companies operating under the same umbrella. Usually, intelligence reports and backgrounders would be prepared by the analysts, who worked for the CIA's Directorate of Intelligence. Covert action and actual spying—called humint or human intelligence, never spying—would be handled by an entirely different side of the operation, the Directorate of Operations. In simple terms, the Intelligence people would take information developed from a number of sources, including the Directorate of Operations, and prepare a briefing. Jackson gathered that while the main report had been prepared by the analysts, the Directorate of Operations had been asked to participate. There could be several reasons for this, though he guessed that the most likely one was unstated: the NSA wanted a heads-up if there was an ongoing mission there.

"Did Evans mention any ongoing projects?" asked Jackson. "Assuming I'm at liberty to know about them?"

"No, he did not bring any to our attention," said Rubens. "That report is in fact a reliable summary of the briefing."

"And he is still in Operations?"

"Yes. I'm not sure what his exact position is," added Rubens. "I myself was not at the briefing."

If there had been an ongoing operation, Evans' presence might make sense, since he would brief it. But a "nothing's up" would come from someone lower on the totem pole.

There were exceptions, certainly. Jackson wasn't sure how deeply to read into this.

"The reason this strikes me as interesting," he told Rubens, "is that Evans was involved in Iron Heart. The focus there was Brazil, not Peru, however. Iron Heart—a very interesting program."

"I'm not familiar with it," said Rubens.

"Yes. Well, that was during the last days of the Clinton administration." Jackson was only partly successful in masking his disgust for the former president. "Be that as it may, the project was not without merit."

Rubens listened impassively. It was difficult to tell what he was actually thinking; Jackson realized that Rubens' face was such a complete mask that it was possible he already knew everything he was saying but wasn't letting on.

On the other hand, Rubens seemed to be the sort of person who didn't play those kinds of games.

"Brazil was trying to obtain nuclear weapons from a Russian arms dealer, and came very close to pulling it off," said Jackson. "Iron Heart managed to upset the sale at the last moment. It was partly because of that, incidentally, that Brazil turned to trying to create a weapon on its own. But that's another matter."

"It didn't involve Peru."

"The Brazilians were dealing with an intermediary in Ecuador. The intermediary had made some sales to a rebel group there—these are the sorts of people who get involved in these kinds of situations. You have to hold your nose somewhat. There were several meetings in Colombia, and then Ecuador. Aside from the fact that the countries share a common border, I don't see a connection."

"So what happened?"

"Iron Heart succeeded. I don't know the particulars. Brazil was not my assignment then. Frankly, I'm not sure how many people from State were informed. Clinton, you know."

Rubens folded his arms and stared at the desk for a moment before speaking. "I wonder, Ambassador, if you would be willing to go through some more invasive security procedures. I realize that they can be very annoying. They include a psychological evaluation as well a lie detector test."

"I must look very unbalanced," said Jackson. "You're the second person today who has been asking about my mental health."

"No, I have no question that you're very sane. But the procedures can seem . . . invasive. The psychological evaluations seem for some reason more objectionable to people than the lie detectors and the background checks. They're not abused, rumors to the contrary."

"I'm sure."

"The reason I'm asking—I would like to give you real access to the situation we're involved in here. Obviously, your old clearance—it's not *irrelevant,* you understand, but we do have our own requirements. Some may seem quite preposterous to outsiders. I realize the process can be a burden."

"Well, if it's important—"

"We only do important things. Especially in this bunker."

Jackson's last months at the State Department had not been pleasant; he was essentially put out to pasture, his advice ignored. He was looked at as just an old man with outdated notions. Now he was being told exactly the opposite—that his age imbued him with "mature wisdom."

He felt it somewhat ironic. But he also was flattered and even touched.

"There is one thing," said Jackson. "I have an outside commitment that I couldn't, that I wouldn't want to break."

"What is it?"

"Tuesdays. I'm a volunteer for the local Meals on Wheels and they rely on me."

"I'm sure we can accommodate that," said Rubens, turning and leaving the room.

After he left Jackson, Rubens went upstairs to a secure reading room in the Desk Three analysis section so he could access information about Iron Heart. The project papers and summaries had been digitized and were available on the NSA network, though they could only be accessed by people with very high clearance or a specific need to know.

Rubens began reading the documents, scrolling past the security warnings and the presidential finding that had authorized the covert action. The file was extremely brief, summarizing things that had happened. There were no after-action reports or assessments.

As the ambassador had said, Iron Heart had been a success—a spectacular one, in fact. Were it not for Iron Heart, Brazil would have become the first South American country to possess nuclear weapons. And given its volatile politics and recent conflict with Argentina, it might very well have used them by now.

A Russian arms dealer with ties to the *mafiya* had "obtained" two nuclear warheads from a Russian air force storage facility in 1998. The warheads had been intended for

SA-10 "Grumble" missiles that were to supplement A-135, the antiballistic missile system ringing Moscow. (The SA-10s, originally designed for use against aircraft, ordinarily carried conventional explosive warheads.) Mounted on trucks, the SA-10s were soon replaced by better-suited missiles known as Gorgons, but not before a dozen or more nuclear warheads had been prepared. The arms dealer, unnamed in the summaries but clearly a high-ranking Russian official, had diverted the pair while they were on their way to a facility to have their plutonium recycled.

The warheads were not designed to destroy ground targets, but modifying them to do so was not a difficult task. The man who obtained the bombs did not like Muslims—the war with Chechnya was at its height—but otherwise was perfectly willing to sell the bombs to any interested party. At least two countries were interested; neither was named in the report. At this point, another Russian arms dealer became involved, bidding on behalf of Brazil, which had already been approached. The arms dealer was connected with the CIA in some manner, but his identity was a closely guarded secret; even his code name had been blacked out from the report.

The dealer won the bid, and preparations were made to ship the warheads. At this point the Russian authorities learned of the transaction somehow. Rubens had to read between the skimpy lines of the report, but it seemed clear that the CIA had not tipped them off; he guessed that the second weapons dealer had been under some sort of surveillance by one of the internal security forces, which tripped over the transaction. In any event, American and Russian intelligence joined forces and moved against the man selling the warheads. One of the weapons was seized in Russia. The other, however, made it to Guinea in Africa, where it was placed on an aircraft to be flown to South America—not to Brazil but to an isolated airstrip in southeastern Ecuador where the exchange was supposed to be made. The "Brazilians" on the ground there were actually CIA paramilitaries. They completed the transaction, and the aircraft then took off. At that point, the airplane experienced mechanical difficulties and crashed in the nearby mountains.

Convenient, thought Rubens as he got up from the computer. Stiff, he bent over and did a simple yoga stretch, loosening the muscles in his back.

The report did not name the CIA people who had been connected with the operation. But after his stretching, Rubens sat back at his computer and checked Jorge Evans' CIA personnel file. He was a member of the operations directorate at the time, with a pay grade that suggested he would supervise the assignment. More interestingly, he was now with the Office of Military Affairs as a staff officer. His exact assignment was listed as "training consultant," which could cover any multitude of sins.

On paper at least, this was at best a lateral move, though it could easily be a cover for something else, including an extended working vacation for an officer who had seen quite a lot of heavy action or a parking spot for someone on his way to DDO. Still, it begged the question: why did Collins send him to represent her at the meeting?

Rubens stretched again. Probably Evans was just one of her fair-haired boys, given a flexible job so he could do her bidding. His real purpose wasn't to brief the NSA team—he hadn't said anything of any value. He'd been sent to try to figure out what Deep Black was *really* up to. He was an expert in paramilitary operations; Collins probably figured he could tease out the hidden agenda.

Except, of course, that there wasn't a hidden agenda. But Collins, being Collins, would suspect that there was.

The alarm on Rubens' watch buzzed. He was due upstairs for a budget meeting.

Rubens picked up the phone and punched in Montblanc's extension. He got his voice mail. "Kevin, this is Rubens. Work Ambassador Jackson through the intake process, would you please? Make it as expeditious as possible. I want him examining everything by the morning. I realize that's not enough time, but please do your best. Remember that he

was an ambassador. Have Porter do the lie detector. And
have Johnny Bib find him a good office—no, no, let's keep
him down near the Art Room. Best not to spring Dr. Bibleria
on him until he's been here a few days."

19

Lia woke to the incessant ringing of the phone. For a moment, she didn't know where she was—Peru, France, Morocco? Her assignments blurred together, her life a kaleidoscope of danger in exotic places.

Korea, always Korea—the memory of pain permeated her confusion. A cold and barren fear rose in the room. Lia was paralyzed, unable to move.

"No," she said aloud. "No."

She reached over and picked up the phone. It was her wakeup call: 9:30 a.m. She was meeting Fernandez for breakfast downstairs in fifteen minutes.

She got up with a lurch, shoving herself from the bed and to the floor. She took a cold shower to push the lingering memories away and got dressed.

Fernandez was waiting in the dining room on the second-floor balcony when she arrived. Tables lined the railing, giving breakfasters a view of the wide lobby; on the other side, they could look out the window and see the city, already wide awake.

"Coffee?" asked a waiter, pulling the seat out for her.

"Yes," said Lia.

"Sleep well?" asked Fernandez.

"OK."

"Voter cards again?"

"I thought I would rearrange my schedule, if you don't

mind," Lia told him. "Let's do the voting machines today. The ones for Lima."

"The cards will begin shipping to regional centers Friday."

"I think I can do the rest of the tests tomorrow. If not, I have to make tests in the field anyway," she told him. "Besides, that safe feels a little claustrophobic."

"Yes, of course. Whatever you want. You're in charge," said Fernandez.

Her coffee arrived. Lia drank it quickly, then signaled for more. She was not much of a coffee drinker and ordinarily would not have liked the harsh taste of the local brew, but this morning she needed the caffeine.

The voting machines that would be used in the Lima area were stored in two warehouses on the outskirts of the city. Lia would test six at each spot. Fernandez took her first to the warehouse northeast of the city in the direction of the Huara Valley and the nearby Andes. Though the building was only a few miles out of town, the traffic in the city was so bad it took nearly two hours to get there.

Security at the warehouse was strong but not as obsessive as it was at the bank. Two dozen armed guards were scattered around the outside of the building; an armored car and a gray fire truck with a water cannon sat near the entrance as well. Water cannons were often used for crowd control in Peru and were a common sight at political rallies, though Lia wondered if the powers-that-be were expecting some sort of mass demonstration *against* voting that would necessitate its use. A metal detector was used at the door; a gray-haired Kenyan monitor nearby shook Lia's hand, then went back to a card game with some of the local election officials and guards.

The machines were stacked in large black cases about half as big as a small desk. They were secured by numerical tumbler locks, but the combinations had not been changed since the boxes were packed at the factory, and so they were secured by the same combination: 1-1-1.

Fernandez complained that the election commission had not authorized him to have the combinations changed.

"So change them yourself," suggested Lia as she arranged the machines on a pair of tables at the front for testing.

The locks were of a simple type and could be reset with a master reset tool.

"I couldn't do that without approval. I don't have the authority."

"Do you have the reset key?"

"Yes, but that's not the point."

Lia didn't bother to argue. Some people were destined to be flunkies their entire lives.

The voting machines looked like flat-screen TVs mounted on oversize shoeboxes. Essentially simple computers optimized to record and transmit votes, the machines' electronic guts were hidden behind the screens, which voters simply touched to indicate their choices; the base units were there solely for ballast. Considerable engineering skill had been put to use designing units that could withstand heavy use. As with many technological achievements, success would be measured by the absence of problems; if the machine was essentially invisible to its users, it would be judged a great success.

Lia connected her laptop to the first unit with a special cable, inserted a diagnostic card into the slot where the voter card would ordinarily be placed, and put a control card in the remaining slot, just as the poll supervisor would do on the day of the election. The machine responded with a series of beeps, and an automated diagnostic procedure began. A report of the process was stored on the voting machine as well as Lia's laptop, one of several precautions against tampering.

It took nearly as long to hook the laptop to the machine as it did to run the diagnostic. Lia entered the serial numbers of the machines she tested in her marble notebook, then added a confirmation number from the diagnostic screen when the test was completed. Within an hour and a half, she had tested six machines.

"Good timing," said Fernandez. "We have to leave for lunch."

Lia thought about begging out of the luncheon, even though the Art Room had asked her to get a feel for what the commission members were thinking. But she decided not to; there would be plenty of time for a nap in the afternoon. Realizing that she had failed to check in since arriving at the warehouse, she reached to the back of her belt and activated the communications system as she packed up.

Rockman had apparently been waiting for some time back in the Art Room and greeted her with a sarcastic, "Hello, lost soul."

"Ha, ha," muttered Lia.

"Lunch with the commission still on?"

"So where's lunch, Julio?" she said loudly, indirectly answering the runner.

"Nice place downtown. You'll like it. Very chic."

They were about two blocks from the restaurant when a traffic snarl of epic proportions stranded them amid a rising chorus of honking horns. Fernandez, spotting a parking area nearby, suggested they get out of the car and walk. A block later, they discovered the problem: a group of protestors had closed down the avenue in front of the restaurant where the UN election committee was having lunch. The police had lined up across the roadway, standing stoically but unemotionally as the protestors chanted *"¡Claro!"*, a Spanish word that might be translated as "clear" or "transparent." In the context of this election campaign it had become a slogan for "fair and open."

It wasn't clear to Lia why they would be demonstrating in front of the people who had come to Peru to ensure that those demands were met, but in her experience protestors rarely exhibited any kind of logic. Less than a hundred men and women were walking back and forth across and near the roadway. They ranged from a baby in the arms of a well-dressed man of twenty to a pair of gray-haired grandmothers.

"You see the slogans?" asked Fernandez, pointing to the signs. "They're the same ones Victor Imberbe of the Peruvian Centrists uses as part of his campaign."

"So these people are with him?"

"They're his supporters. They're afraid the government is going to steal the election, and they want us to do our job."

"Fair enough," said Lia. And though just a moment ago she'd looked on them with condescension at best, she decided that the protestors did have a point. And more than that, for the first time since coming to Peru she felt what was at stake in her mission. *Felt,* not intellectualized, how basic the right of democracy truly was and what was at stake for the people around her.

"Does the campaign pay these people to protest?" Lia asked.

"I doubt it. Imberbe doesn't have the money. They're organized, but they're volunteers. They might be part of a church group; they have a lot of grassroots support there." He pointed to the left. "We can go this way. Come on."

As Lia began to follow, a black shadow loomed in the corner of her eye. She whirled around and saw two men dressed in black emerge from the building behind where she had been standing. One raised his arm, pointing something toward the crowd. He had something in his hand.

A gun.

"Get down! Get down!" yelled Lia, though in her heart she knew it was too late.

20

General Túcume had little use for the psychological games many of his fellow generals played with the North Americans, such as keeping them waiting for an appointment to demonstrate their power. So he showed up for lunch at the yacht club in Lima's most exclusive oceanside district precisely on time.

This meant that he had to wait fifteen minutes for the CIA officer to show up. But it was time well spent. Túcume settled details with Captain Chimor on what must be done here in Lima over the next few days.

Túcume also received word from Keros that the action near the restaurant had begun. This time the police would not emerge as heroes, but that was not a problem for their allies on the force, who needed room above to advance.

"General, a pleasure to see you again," said Greene, not bothering to apologize for his tardiness when he finally arrived. But perhaps he had taken the time to check Túcume's file: he mentioned Miami University and the basketball team there as soon he sat. Túcume had gone to Miami but had about as much interest in basketball as he did in dressmaking. Still, he knew enough to hold up his end of the conversation for the few minutes until lunch came.

"I'm not often in Lima," Túcume told Greene as they ate, turning the conversation toward its aim. "There is a great deal going on in the countryside with the rebels. Of course, with Ecuador active as well—"

"You're worried about Ecuador?"

"A traditional enemy. As is Brazil. Consider, if Brazil were to develop its nuclear weapon."

"The government renounced the program," said Greene. "And it's been discontinued."

You argue too much to be a good spy, Túcume thought. But this was typical of Yankees.

"I think you'll find that our neighbors will admit to only a portion of the sins that they actually commit," the general told the CIA officer.

They continued in that vein for a while longer, Túcume taking care to underline the external dangers his nation faced, Greene doing more to knock them down than listen. As their plates were cleared, the general turned to the real reason for the conversation.

"We face internal threats as well," he told Greene. "Serious ones."

"The New Path?"

"Sendero Nuevo." The words practically spit from Túcume's mouth. "Communists of the old school. Why would they resurrect ideas that have failed utterly?"

"I guess there are only so many ideas to go around," said Greene.

"It's fascism at the core. Fascism is not the future. Democracy is."

"The military hasn't always believed that," said Greene.

"You'll find the new generals do."

"The government and the president's party work very closely together," said Greene. "The military seems to be aligned with him."

For once the American was not far off the mark, Túcume thought. The general staff surely wanted Ortez to win.

"There's no doubt that many of us would prefer the vice president to be elected. I myself intend to vote for him," lied Túcume. "But I can take orders from any president. And I can back most of the men running for office. Aznar for one. The candidate of the New Peru or Future, whatever he calls his party these days."

"What about Imberbe?"

Túcume made a face. "I will take orders from him if I must. That is the law. But secretly, he is a communist."

"You're not serious."

"Perhaps I exaggerate." Túcume shrugged. "I don't want to talk about the election. I can't. We have sworn neutrality, every officer in the military. Not a word."

He reached for his coffee, which had just been poured.

"You were speaking of the rebels," said Greene.

"Yes. They're becoming more reckless. The post office in the city was their latest outrage."

"The police seem to have acted very quickly."

"A miracle." Túcume put down his coffee cup. "I'm afraid that these latest rounds of attacks are only an omen of what is to come. We have intelligence from my region of various threats being prepared. Lima itself will be targeted. The specifics have been vague."

"The post office?"

"No, a much larger target. The rumors I hear are for a very big action. I believe they will aim to shut down the city, or worse."

Greene was finally listening.

"Some of my colleagues don't agree with me that we face a serious threat," Túcume told the American. "My warnings are discounted."

"Why?"

"My background—my heritage is entirely native. That is a serious handicap in Peru. Worse than being black in your country. And ironic, since we are the majority."

"You're a war hero."

"To some. To other members of the general staff, I'm a vain and ambitious native who found himself in the right place at the right time and made the most of it." Túcume laughed. "I am probably some of that. I am ambitious—I would not mind being head of the military someday. It would be a great honor, and yes, I believe I would do a good job. I don't think there's anything wrong with ambition, do you?"

"It depends."

"Some of my colleagues are jealous because I have proven myself in battle. I make no apologies for that."

"I don't think you should."

Túcume pulled his sleeve back to look at his watch. The American took the hint.

"Let me ask you, General," said Greene, folding his napkin. "Who do you think will win the election next week?"

"I'm not good at predictions," said the general. "But I would assume the vice president. I would think he holds all the cards."

"His poll numbers are slipping."

"Are they?" Túcume feigned a moment of concern, then made a show of dismissing it. "I wouldn't believe those things. In your country, people are used to dealing with surveys. But here in Peru? No."

"Did you have something specific you wanted to bring to my attention?" asked Greene.

"Keeping allies and friends informed of volatile situations seems a good practice," Túcume said. "Sharing views with senior partners—this can be mutually beneficial."

Túcume knew that the CIA officer would think he was just one more general trying to cozy up to the Yankee gringos in hopes of it paying off down the line. But in a few days, after the predictions he had made came true, Greene would think of the meeting differently. He would see the general as a person to be cultivated—and feared.

Babin had warned Túcume that the warhead was bound to be recognized. This was necessary—Túcume wanted there to be no doubt that it should be taken seriously immediately before the election, and if the government had any doubt, the CIA would disabuse them. At the same time, Greene would remember this meeting and consider Túcume a friend, or at least someone he could deal with.

"I hope your information is pessimistic," said Greene as he got up. "I would hate to see violence in Lima."

"I would hate that as well," said Túcume. "And I will do my best to prevent it."

21

"Don't get involved, Lia! Get out of there!" yelled Rockman, pounding on the console of his workstation as the scene on his monitor blurred. The images whirled. They were fed from a video cam hidden in a button on Lia's jacket, and Rockman knew from experience that she had attacked one of the gunmen from the side, taking him with a karate-style kick.

"Run away!" Rockman repeated. The image blanked, and for a moment he thought he'd lost the feed. Then he realized that she had fallen to the ground, face-first.

"Lia!"

Telach leaned over the front of his station, staring at him but saying nothing.

"Did you see them?" asked Lia.

"Are you talking to me?" asked Rockman.

"No, the Invisible Man. Did you see them?"

Rockman put his finger on a button under the screen, isolating her voice from the background sounds erupting around her.

"I didn't see them, but we can review the images later. Are you OK?"

"Where did the others go?"

"Are you OK?"

She replied with an expletive so fierce he knew she had to be fine. He looked up and nodded at Telach.

"Tell her to get out of there," said Telach. "Now."

"Lia, get out of there."

Another expletive.

The street was chaos around her. Police ran left and right. Some people were lying on the ground; others were crouched on their haunches and pointing, apparently in the direction the gunmen had fled.

"Lia," said Telach, keying her microphone into the circuit. "Remember your job. Leave the area."

The op still didn't respond. Once Lia DeFrancesca decided she was going to do something, not even a nuclear bomb could stop her.

Literally, as she had proven beneath the English Channel.

22

Lia lurched to the right, ducking a fleeing protestor as she tried following one of the men who'd fired the submachine gun in the crowd. She saw him stop at the doorway of the building and threw herself down as he began firing again. When she looked up, a woman roughly her age lay on the sidewalk nearby, blood spilling slowly from her mouth.

"Ambulance! Get an ambulance!" yelled Lia, deciding to help the woman rather than chase a gunman she could no longer see. The woman convulsed, bending at the midsection. There was a large blot of blood on her shirt. Lia leaned over the body and saw that the woman's eyes were glossy. Then Lia realized the victim had stopped breathing.

Lia jumped up, determined to help someone else. But Fernandez grabbed her.

"We have to get out of here. The police are going crazy."

"The police?" said Lia. "Why?"

"Come on."

The police were clearing the area, but they weren't going crazy. True, they were yelling and emphatically herding people away, but the reactions were normal.

"Let's go," insisted Fernandez.

"We have to help the people."

"Let's go before the police shoot us, too."

"The police didn't do this."

Lia looked left and right quickly. Only when she was sure

there were no other victims on the ground, she let Fernandez tug her away, passing through the area where the police line had been earlier. They turned the corner and went half a block, where they found a television crew already interviewing a hysterical man covered with blood.

"Stay here with the TV people," Fernandez told her. "The car's just up the block. I'll get it and pick you up."

"Go ahead," said Lia.

She took a step toward the man who was being interviewed. The Spanish was a little quick, but Lia easily understood the gist—the man was accusing the police of firing on the crowd.

"No. It wasn't the police," Lia said. "Two men came out of the building. They weren't police. At least they weren't dressed like policemen."

The man who was being interviewed spoke louder and more quickly. The reporter didn't seem to hear her.

"No—that's not what happened," said Lia.

"We'll get to you in a second, honey," said the cameraman, waving at her to pipe down.

"Lia, get out of there," said Rockman in her ear. "Get out of there, now."

The witness who was being interviewed said that a number of policemen had fired. Some had singled out their victims very carefully before taking aim.

"That's just not true," said Lia.

Something exploded in the street behind the cameraman. She started to duck, but a hand caught hold of her and threw her back. As she spun, another set of hands grabbed her and threw her into the backseat of a car.

"Go!" yelled a familiar voice.

It was Charlie Dean.

"What are you doing?" Lia demanded from the floor of the car as it squealed into reverse.

"Saving you," said Dean, next to her on the seat.

Overcome by rage, Lia pulled herself up and swung her fist hard into Dean's chest.

"What are you doing, Charlie? What are you doing?"

He grabbed her arm. She pushed against his grip, then forced a release with a sharp snap of her forearm.

"You hit me again, I may hit back," he warned.

"Charlie Dean!"

"Hey, you lovebirds, let's calm down back there," said Karr. "It's a little hard navigating as it is."

"I'll strangle you, Tommy," Lia sputtered. "Just stop. *Just stop.*"

"The car?"

"I swear—"

"Let's just calm down," said Dean. "Let's all just calm down." He leaned forward to talk to Karr, who was wearing his usual *What? Me worry?* grin. "Take a right and go down that boulevard. There ought to be a place where we can have a drink."

"I don't need no stinkin' drink," said Lia.

"Well, I do," said Dean. "I think you broke one of my ribs."

23

Rubens hesitated for a moment before picking up the phone.

"Yes, Debra, what can I do for the CIA today?"

"It's what the CIA can do for you, Bill."

Rubens was thankful he did not have a videoconferencing phone; Debra Collins' smirk would have turned his stomach.

"We were contacted in Peru this afternoon," she told him. "Less than an hour ago. An army general from one of the northern provinces predicted that the rebels would make a large strike against the capital. I know it's an area of interest, so I thought I would pass it along."

An hour ago? Rubens wondered why the information had traveled so quickly—and if Collins had an ulterior motive.

Well, of course she did. The question was what it was.

"That's very kind," he told her. "Which general, if I may ask?"

"Túcume. Does it ring a bell?"

"I'm afraid not."

"He commands several divisions in the north and northeast, primarily the Amazonian area and near the Ecuadorian border. He saw action in the wars against Ecuador in 1995 and 1998. He was a colonel in 1998, and proved himself so irrepressible he had to be promoted. He doesn't quite get along with the general staff because of his background. Which may be a factor here: the natives really hate the rebels, and that may be coloring his views. In any event, he seemed quite serious, and we have no reason to doubt that he at least believes his information is correct."

"Túcume?" The general's name was not immediately familiar to Rubens, though in itself that meant nothing.

"I'll save you the trouble of looking him up," continued Collins. "He claims to be descended from relatives of Tupac Amaru, who was the last ruler under the Spanish and executed in 1572. His people supposedly escaped and went to live with natives in the northeastern jungles. Whether the claims about his ancestry are authentic or misguided, it's impossible to tell at this point."

"And he was warning about which rebels?"

"Sendero Nuevo. The New Path. Successors to the Shining Path. Same philosophy, different faces."

"Did he have any comment on the riots in Lima?"

"Riots?"

Now Rubens wished he *did* have a video hookup.

"There were some protests and gunfire," said Rubens, who'd just gotten the report from the Art Room. "The army is being called in. I'm surprised you hadn't heard."

"Unfortunately, I've been very busy, and Peru is not among my priorities."

I wonder about that, thought Rubens.

"If there's anything else we can do," Collins added, "please call."

"I'll do that."

24

Dean rubbed his rib as they drove, wondering if Lia actually had broken one.

"That's the restaurant, up there," he told Karr. He slid back in the seat and turned to Lia. "You want to talk about it?"

"There's nothing to talk about."

"I don't see a parking space," said Karr, pulling up near the restaurant. "I think I'll stay with the car while you guys cool down."

Dean thought that was a good idea.

Lia got out of the car on the other side. Karr grabbed Dean as he started to follow.

"This is why I call her Princess," he said. "Packs a heck of a punch, huh?"

Dean followed Lia into the restaurant, where she found a table in the back and pulled out her handheld computer, scanning for bugs.

"You two shouldn't have come, Charlie," she told him when he sat down. "I didn't need to be rescued."

Dean pointed at the PDA.

"Yes, it's clean," she said.

"What about the window?"

She got up, sighing like a teenager who'd just been told to go clean up her room. She slipped a small device nicknamed a shaker onto the corner of the glass near the curtain. The NSA-designed device disrupted vibrations, making it impossible to use them to pick up conversations inside. While Lia was slipping it on, a waitress came over and Dean ordered two beers.

"I'm not drinking," said Lia, pulling out her chair.

"I'll have them both. Tell me what happened."

"It was some sort of setup," Lia told him. "They're blaming it on the police."

"You should have gotten out of there," said Dean.

"Would you have done that?"

"Depending on the circumstances."

"The circumstances? The circumstances are, two men came out of a building, shot some innocent protestors, then took off. Ten minutes later, a guy who wasn't even there blames the police."

"Do you know he wasn't there?"

"I didn't recognize him."

"For all you knew, it was an operation aimed at kidnapping you."

"It wasn't."

"But you didn't know that at the time."

"I wouldn't be talking if I were you, Charlie Dean. You and laughing boy tried to break up a purse snatching in England a few months back."

"That was different."

"Why? Because it was you, not me?"

The waitress came over with the beers. True to her word, Lia pushed hers to his side of the table.

"You seemed shaken yesterday," said Dean.

Lia's face flushed. "That was nothing."

"I was just—"

"I'm fine."

"OK."

"We're here to make sure the election is fair, right?" said Lia. "They can steal it using the media just as easily as they can using the machines."

Probably easier, thought Dean.

"You shouldn't have thrown me in the car like that," she told him. "It looked like a kidnapping."

"The Art Room wanted you out of there."

"The Art Room is in charge now?"

"The Art Room is in charge of the mission while it's running," said Dean.

She snarled. "Is that what you really believe, Charlie Dean? *You?*"

"I thought you were in trouble," he told her.

"Well, I wasn't."

"You were."

Her eyes flashed with anger.

"You *were* scared in the vault," he said.

"Well, I wasn't scared here."

They stared at each other. Dean realized he might be as angry as she was.

"Let's get you back to the UN people," he said, reaching for some money to pay the bill. "You'll have to make up something plausible."

Lia caught his hand as he got up. He stopped, gazing down at her beautiful face, luminescent with the reflected light.

"The cops were framed," she said.

"I believe you."

"That doesn't bother you?"

"I'll pass the information on," said Dean.

He was tongue-tied. He wanted to say—he couldn't even tell himself exactly what it was. He loved her. He was worried about her. He wanted her to be OK.

Instead, he ended up lecturing her. "We have to stay focused on what's important."

"What's important?"

"You."

"Well, thanks for that," she snapped, walking out.

25

"Do you miss your wife?"

"I don't believe that would have much relevance to my work, do you?" said Jackson.

"Please answer the question."

"Of course."

Jackson watched the technician flip the pages of the yellow pad on his clipboard. The interviews were supposed to uncover "vulnerabilities" that would make a person a security risk, but to Jackson they were an odd mix of prurience—"Have you ever practiced deviant sex?"—and shallow pop psychology. This was the third go-around for the questions about his wife. He'd already explained that they had led somewhat separate lives when she was alive but that yes, he hated the fact that she was gone.

"Can we get back to your son?" asked Montblanc. He'd sat in on this session, hardly saying anything, but it occurred to Jackson that Montblanc had formulated most of the questions that weren't routine. He clearly was in charge; everyone else silently deferred to him.

"Yes, my son," said Jackson. "He died five months ago. He had been in a coma for eighteen months before that."

"Actually, yes, I was more interested in the doctor bills," said Montblanc. "If you—"

"The doctors are actually a small portion of the total. Most of what is still owed is to the hospital. It's a bit over two hundred thousand," said Jackson.

"Do you mind if I ask a personal question?"

Jackson laughed. The sensor band slid on his forehead.

"Don't touch that, please," said the technician, rising to adjust it before Jackson could.

"All of your questions are personal," said Jackson. "Ask whatever you want."

"Why did you take on your son's debts?"

"I thought it only right. He didn't have insurance. Someone has to pay. If not me, every patient who's treated there."

"It's put you in financial straits."

"Not really. I don't need to live ostentatiously." Jackson saw that the technician was frowning. "I'm not taking the job for the money. I'm doing it to be useful. I'd like to think that I'm still of some use to someone, especially my country."

And that, thought Jackson, was as candid as anyone could ask him to be.

26

After she found the doors to the restaurant where she worked gated and chained, Calvina Agnese spent the morning walking through the city, trying at other restaurants to see if they might have a similar job. She was still stunned by what had happened and all that she had heard. Calvina was not a naive girl, but it seemed impossible that her beloved boss had been a bankrupt and gambler.

And a thief. For he had killed himself without paying her the week's salary he owed. It was the same as taking money from her pocket.

Early in the afternoon, discouraged and tired, she went home. Her mother took the news better than Calvina had feared: she only cried, not shouting or demanding to know what role Calvina had played in her employer's demise.

Losing the job meant immediate difficulty for the family. Calvina promised her mother that she would find a new one soon. Her mother tried vainly to stanch her tears and finally succeeded in smiling for her, but Calvina could tell that she was not optimistic. Calvina's fourteen-year-old brother had been laid off from a job with one of the markets a year before and, though he had tried to find another, had not yet managed to do so. Her mother made a few soles a week doing piecework for a clothing manufacturer; Calvina volunteered that she would ask for work there herself. While this was unlikely, her mother nodded enthusiastically and said it was a very good idea.

To take her mind off what had happened, Calvina filled a bucket and began washing the kitchen floor, her hands circling in the steady rhythm she would have used at the restaurant. The floor there was stone and here it was linoleum, but the familiar motion felt reassuring, and she moved on to their bathroom and then the hallway and bedrooms.

With each room, some of the comfort melted away. Her thoughts returned to Señor DeCura. She thought of the priest who would say his mass—if this was even allowed. Was it allowed? Could a man who took his own life be buried in the church?

Calvina's thoughts grew darker still. She filled her bucket again and began washing the hall outside their apartment, hoping the sense of relief would return. Eventually she realized it would not, but the task had assumed an importance of its own, and she continued to work her way down the hall past the other apartments here, carrying her bucket back and forth several times for fresh water.

She was near the stairway when her cousin Rosa arrived home. Two years older than Calvina, Rosa worked as a cleaner at a small office building on the other side of the city. Ordinarily, she came home well after dark, and Calvina looked up with surprise when she heard Rosa's familiar steps on the stairs.

"You're home?" said Rosa.

"My boss, Señor DeCura—" She began crying, unable to continue.

Rosa knelt next to her on the wet floor and wrapped her arm around her. After a while, Calvina told her cousin what had happened, punctuating the story with soft moans that she would never be able to find a job again. Rosa comforted her, assuring her that something would be found.

"Finding that job was so difficult," Calvina complained. "So impossible."

"You should come to the United States with me."

"When? When are you planning this?"

"Within a few days." And Rosa explained that she had been let go more than three weeks before. She had kept it a secret from her family, making plans instead to go north.

"Where can you get the money for the trip?" asked Calvina.

"There are ways to make money," said Rosa.

Calvina froze. Her face must have turned white, for instantly her cousin reassured her that no sin was involved.

"I'm sure you could do it as well," added Rosa.

"What would I do?"

"You carry things. They pay for your flight and give you documents."

"It must be dangerous."

"Not so."

"What would you do in the North?" asked Calvina, already considering the offer.

"There are many things to do. Clean rich people's homes, care for their children—the pay is ten times for a week what you make in a month in Lima."

"Could I stay a year?"

"A year? The rest of your life."

"I would work very hard." Calvina felt a rush of hope. She could become a person such as Señor DeCura.

Except that she would not fall victim to temptation as he had.

"How?" she asked her cousin.

Rosa put her finger to her lips. "I will explain later. Don't tell them. The old women will worry. But we will take a trip first, arrange everything, then leave. I will help you, Calvina."

"Thank you," she said.

27

After getting into the car, Fernandez had been shunted in a different direction by soldiers who arrived to quell the disturbance. Sure that he had lost Lia forever, he spent the two hours they were separated alternately roaming the streets and calling everyone he could think of to help look for her. By the time Lia finally caught up to him at the election commission's temporary Lima offices, he was on the verge of having a nervous breakdown. He greeted her as if she had survived an earthquake, blaming himself for abandoning her.

The Peruvian army had moved in and shut down the center of the city. Order had been quickly restored—it had never really been threatened—but the police found themselves besieged on all sides. The media accepted the allegations that the police had fired into the crowd and another demonstration had spontaneously erupted a few blocks away from the first.

The UN delegation had decided to push up a scheduled tour of Cusco, the major city to the south. They had boarded a hastily chartered aircraft and left Lima, hoping to keep themselves from becoming the focus of any more attention. That left the local staff to try to deal with the press. Even Fernandez's voice mail was overwhelmed with requests for comments.

"You should tell them it's definitely a setup," Lia said. "The police weren't involved."

"The gunmen were able to get very close."

"So were we."

After a few minutes of arguing, Lia realized that having him say nothing was better than the alternative. She watched TV accounts of the disturbances for an hour or so. Several thousand people blocked off Javier Prado Avenue, a main thoroughfare in the Lince section of the capital, but there was no violence. In the other parts of town the crowds were much smaller and just as peaceful. Traffic was hopelessly snarled, but that was a normal state of affairs in Lima.

By early evening even the most breathless television commentator was saying that the city had returned to normal. The incident's effect on the election was already being measured; it was generally agreed that the disturbance would harm the vice president, who was seen as the government's candidate and therefore connected to the police. Victor Imberbe of the Peruvian Centrists had already given a press conference denouncing the violence, though he was careful not to directly criticize the police force.

He had a round, almost cherry-red face, with slicked-back blond hair. He had the smooth patter of a host on an infomercial. Lia started shaking her head as she watched him talking to an interviewer.

"Don't do that," said one of the UN people.

"Don't do what?"

"We have to be neutral."

"I can't shake my head?"

"Here, we are among friends, but elsewhere, you never know who may see you. We have to be neutral."

"Three people died. Five were wounded," said Lia. "We have to be neutral."

"The election—"

"Fine." She got up.

"What's wrong?" asked Fernandez, coming over.

"I think I'm going to call it a day," she told him. "I'm going back to my hotel."

"I don't think that's a good idea."

"I do. My work is done for the day."

"What I meant was, you should stay here where we have some protection."

The UN had hired security guards to protect the election workers; the men were from Spain and Portugal, to help ensure that they could be trusted.

"I'll be fine."

"Maybe we could have dinner first?"

"Another time."

28

Dean felt his "pre-go" adrenaline build as he and Karr placed fresh video bugs around the bank. Some people were stricken with all manner of jitters; Dean had known a sniper in Vietnam who always threw up before leaving camp. Dean didn't get nervous before an assignment, but he did feel his pulse quicken and stomach tighten. There was nothing to do about it but wait for the mission to begin.

While the batteries in the small video units were state-of-the-art, they could provide power for only a few hours and had to be replaced for the night's mission. The Art Room had analyzed their earlier coverage plan and come up with a few tweaks, improving what the geeks called the redundancy of the system—if one or two bugs failed, they'd still have a complete virtual surveillance net over the area. Dean moved along planting his share of the bugs, nonchalantly pressing them against different surfaces. The fit wasn't always perfect, and in some cases the sticky material on the back had to be reinforced with a small blob of additional stickum. Doing this wasn't exactly hard—but doing it without attracting attention took finesse and patience. Dean felt his adrenaline working against him, pushing him to rush the task. He kept reminding himself to move more slowly and not press.

Karr passed him as he worked a bug onto the back of a road sign. The other op smiled but didn't make eye contact. To provide possible diversions in case things got complicated inside the bank, Karr was planting small explosive panels along the block. About the size and thickness of a check-book calculator, the devices were essentially flat firecrackers that could be ignited by radio signal. Their sound was much worse than their bite, and they were meant only to temporarily confuse the police unit that would normally be stationed outside, or anyone arriving to assist them.

Dean finished planting his last bugs and went to meet Karr at a café a few blocks away. By the time he got there Karr had used his very elementary Spanish to order himself a hot chocolate, which was advertised here as French Cocoa.

"Why do you think this is French Cocoa?" asked Karr as Dean slid into the booth. "Do Peruvians think the French make great chocolate?"

"Maybe they realize it's not as good as Swiss," said Dean.

Karr laughed. "I'm kind of tired. What do you say about going back to the hotel and taking a nap?"

"I have to talk to Rubens," Dean told him.

"Why?"

"I want to make sure he knows that was a setup at the demonstration."

"Telach told him by now."

"I want to tell him myself. I told Lia I would."

"I'd leave that part out. Or make it a group thing—tell him we're all concerned."

Karr's protectiveness was touching, and Dean remembered it two hours later, back in the hotel, when Rubens called him back. He was in a helicopter—even the Deep Black communications system couldn't completely erase the turbines and blades in the background.

"Mr. Dean, you wanted to speak with me?"

"The incident in front of the restaurant where the UN monitors were gathering seems to have been a setup. Lia saw two men who were not policemen come out of a building and fire into the crowd. A short while later, there was a television interview with a victim who lied."

Rubens listened impassively, not even muttering a "yes." Dean couldn't tell if he was interested, uninterested, or even still on the line. Maybe it was just the nature of the communications system they were using, but Dean felt like he was talking to a machine. He expected *some* sort of reaction.

Was this just Rubens being Rubens? Or was it a subtle way of telling a field op that his job was to simply follow orders and not analyze what was going on around him?

"I don't know who was behind the riot," added Dean. "Lia wasn't sure, either. Someone trying to make the police look bad."

"Very well. Anything else?" asked Rubens.

"That's it."

"Please do your best."

The line went clear.

29

Since Dean and Karr were going into the bank, Lia handled the task of doping the guards' dinner by herself. Dean and Karr had already scoped out the arrangement: a waiter at a restaurant across the street took the plates and some bottled water and carried them over to the bank at eleven. The tray was prepared at the waiters' station between the kitchen and the dining area in a hall that connected to another hall with the restrooms.

Two bottles with a heavy dose of a barbiturate ordinarily used to sedate patients for operations had been prepared; Lia carried them under her long skirt, strapped to her calves.

Her first task after getting a table in the restaurant was to plant a video bug near the waiters' station; since it was out of view from the dining room the Art Room would have to tell her when to make the switch. But when she went to plant the bug, she found the corridor filled with waiters; they were gabbing about a soccer game, milling around making it impossible to simply sneak over and put the bug in one of the light fixtures as she'd planned. And she couldn't just mount it on the baseboard, either; the shelf of the waiters' station blocked the view.

One of the waiters noticed Lia as she eyed the corridor, looking for a solution. He asked if he could help her, and she said that she was looking for a job.

She could tell instantly from his expression that was the

wrong thing to say. Not only was she too well dressed to be a service worker, but she was female—all of the servers here were men.

Lia froze for half a second before plunging into a more believable story—she was a chef in training who hoped to gain experience overseas. As the words rushed out of her mouth she began to feel more comfortable. The waiter's face brightened and he insisted she come with him to the kitchen and meet the chef. Lia followed him around the divider into a small area of controlled chaos, where four rather large men threw pans and pots around, jabbering in a kind of kitchen patois about the food they were preparing.

Lia spotted a shelf that had a view of the window over the waiters' station; she moved next to it, scratched her hair, and in a smooth, well-practiced motion, planted the video bug.

"Good. We have a full view," said Rockman.

But now she was trapped by her own cover story. The chef had interned at a number of restaurants in Europe and the U.S. and apparently saw an opportunity to pay back the kindness of others—and not coincidentally gain some free labor and an attractive protégé. With great enthusiasm, he began telling Lia his philosophy of food preparation as well as his methods, giving a running commentary on what he was doing that would have put many a TV chef to shame.

He had just started to hold forth on the importance of fresh herbs when one of his assistants plucked some chicken out of a pile, spooned up some rice, and set out two plates for the waiter to finish and take over.

"Have to go," Lia told her would-be benefactor. "Ladies' room."

It was an effective if overused excuse, and she escaped back into the hallway just in time to see the waiter who had introduced her earlier take the tray from the station and start toward the back door.

Lia followed, waiting until he was at the threshold to call to him.

"There you are," she said. "I wanted to thank you. You're very kind."

The man looked at her with the puzzled expression he'd had earlier. Once again Lia felt herself freeze, her brain refusing to move ahead smoothly.

She got over it by touching the man's shoulder, feigning something more than casual interest as she thanked him again. The look of desire in his eyes as he glanced down revolted her, even as she realized it meant that she would succeed. She reached up to kiss him—and as she did, knocked the tray to the floor. The contents went flying, the plastic water bottles rolling down the hall.

"I'm sorry; I'm sorry," she said, grabbing them.

Exasperated, the waiter left the bottles where they had fallen and went into the nearby kitchen for replacements. Lia switched the bottles, holding the replacements out to the waiter when he returned.

"I'm sorry," she told the waiter.

He forced a smile and this time kept his leers to himself as he walked out the back.

30

Dean heard Rockman grumbling in the background as he climbed in through the second-story window of the bank.

"They're just taking forever with that food," said Rockman, referring to the guards outside the bank, who had to check the tray and bring it inside to the other guards. "The last two nights they went right in. Now they have to taste it? What gives?"

Dean smiled to himself. The runner—and the rest of the Art Room—tended to get testy when events didn't precisely match their preconceived script.

Karr waved at him from the inside doorway, pointing to an infrared beam of light running across the threshold. The light was easily visible with their glasses; they'd decided to let the system alone, since it could be easily avoided.

Dean turned back to the window, lowering it carefully so that he didn't jostle the device Karr had used to defeat the alarm. Then he placed a satellite transmitter on the sill, making sure it was oriented toward the clear sky. The transmitter— it had been designed to look like a small personal satellite FM radio receiver—would pick up signals from the booster they would place downstairs, allowing the Art Room to communicate directly with them if they were both in the vault. In the event they had to leave it behind for some reason, the Art Room could send a signal to fry its circuitry, and they'd pick it up the next day.

"Transmitter's good here," Rockman told him.

"Good," said Dean. He checked the replacement envelopes in his backpack before cinching it back up, then moved across the room.

"Finally," said Rockman. "They're bringing the food inside."

Karr was waiting for Dean by the stairwell, once again pointing out the beam of ordinarily invisible light. Once Dean acknowledged it, the other op tapped his watch. They had agreed before going in that if the guards weren't sleeping by 11:40, they would use the blowpipe. They had ten minutes to go.

Dean took the weapon from his belt and loaded it. About the size of a .22-caliber air gun, the blowpipe had a highly accurate scope integrated into the housing; the weapon had no kick and could be held at just about any angle without harming its accuracy.

"Guard One is drinking," said Rockman, watching them through the bank's own video system. As soon as the other guard had left, Rockman had begun feeding the command post a tape they had made from the feeds the two previous nights. "Saying something. Guard Two thinks it's amusing. He's opening his bottle. Should be out any second."

Dean followed Karr down the staircase, moving as quietly as he could, each step, each breath, deliberate.

"Guard Two is getting up!" hissed Rockman. "He didn't drink yet. Don't let him see you."

No kidding, thought Dean, pushing back against the wall and raising the blowpipe so it was ready.

"Going back," hissed Rockman. "All right—taking a slug, another slug. Sitting down. Any second now. Bingo. You're clear! You're clear!"

"You ever think of doing baseball play-by-play?" Karr asked as he raced across the lobby.

31

Lia sat in a car three blocks away, listening to the conversation at the bank. She wanted to run over and try cracking the safe herself. It would be a useless gesture—they were already doing everything that could be done—but it would be better than sitting here helplessly.

Was this what it had been like for the people in the Art Room the day she'd been raped?

A loud tap on the car window jolted her to the present. Lia glanced up as a flashlight glared against the window. A shadow loomed behind the light, a voice.

"Out of the car, miss."

Lia glanced to the other window and saw that she was surrounded by soldiers.

32

"Isn't working," said Karr, pushing on the handle again. "Next set of numbers."

Rockman started reading the numbers. The cracker worked by listening as the wheels of the safe's tumbler fell into place. It also guessed on the approximate positions of the numbers in the combination sequence by measuring the sound, but it was only a guess, and with eight wheels there were still many different possibilities.

Karr messed up halfway through and had to start again. The combination failed to open the safe.

"I'm thinking a whole big box of nitro," said Karr. "Just blow it right out."

"That won't work, either," said Dean. "Been tried."

"Sequence number three," said Rockman, starting to feed him the numbers.

Karr dialed in the combination, but the safe still didn't budge.

"I felt something that time, on the sixth turn. Let me try again, reversing steps five and six."

"Tommy, we really want to do this according to statistical probabilities," said Rockman. "We're starting to cut things tight."

"Stay with me."

Karr tried the combination with his variation, but it didn't work. Dean tapped his watch next to him. "We're down to four minutes," said Dean.

"Next sequence," Karr told Rockman.

Rockman began reading the numbers. This time, Karr swore he felt something tingling at his fingertips—and finally the safe unlocked.

"Let's go, Sundance," he told Dean, stepping back to open the vault.

33

Lia silently berated herself before rolling down the window. This wasn't the result of some random twist of fate; she'd gotten sloppy, not paid enough attention to her surroundings.

The flashlight banged again. Lia reached to the manual crank at the side of the door, pulling down the window.

"¿Sí?" she said.

"What are you doing?" demanded a soldier. He shone the light into her face.

"I was thinking," she said.

"Thinking?"

Apparently this was the most preposterous answer the man could imagine, because he demanded she get out of the car.

"Lia, tell him you're with the UN," said Telach over the communications system. "Let's not fool around. He has no right to detain you—there is no curfew."

"I had a fight with my husband," Lia told the soldier. "I— I can't stand him anymore. He's a cheating slime."

"Where's your wedding band?"

"I threw it into the sea where it belongs." Lia practically spit the words. She grabbed at the door, missing once, then getting the latch, and stepped from the car. "He's a lying slime," she said. "I caught him with his secretary. I'm sure there have been others. Men—they are all slime. Are you married? Do you cheat on your wife?"

One of the Art Room translators tried to correct her

pronunciation, but she was on her own now, completely on her own. Anger welled up inside her—that part wasn't an act. She seemed to have an endless supply of it. Her whole body grew warm as she complained and cursed her supposed philanderer of a husband.

"I hate him. If it weren't for my children I would kill myself," said Lia. She slammed her hand on the roof of the car, seemingly out of control. At the same time, she scanned the area, counting the soldiers, gauging exactly how convincing she had to be. She had a small Glock at her belt and another near her ankle.

Four other men, in the roadway. They all had M16s.

She could shoot her way out if she had to, but it wouldn't be easy and it would complicate things immensely.

The soldier who had banged on her window didn't know exactly what to do. "Calm down, miss," he said, then corrected himself. "Ma'am."

"Miss, yes—alone. Men are pigs—lying, cheating pigs. They take what you have and then where are you?"

Lia held her hands out, trembling.

Another soldier came over—an officer. "Why are you not with your children?" he said. "Go home to them. All men are not like your husband. He's a dog, but you must make the best of it—for your children."

"My mother came to watch them." Lia looked at him. Something in his face told her he was skeptical, that he didn't believe her. It reminded her of the Korean officer, the man who had raped her.

Then, she had met the look with scorn.

She didn't have that in her anymore.

"I can't face them," she cried, grabbing the officer's arms. And she really did begin to cry.

The officer pushed her back against the car. The gesture began harshly, but then weakened, and as he held her there Lia could see that there was compassion in his face.

"Go home," he told her gently. "That is where you belong. There are patrols throughout the city tonight. You will only end up finding trouble. Your children need you."

Lia nodded. Silently, she got into the car and started it.

"Academy Award performance," said Rockman as she drove away. "You're smokin' tonight."

For some reason, she felt insulted, as if she'd been accused of lying.

34

Dean laid out the replacement envelopes on the floor as Karr located the bins containing them. The vault room was very dark; while they could see with their night-vision glasses, the numbers on the envelopes were printed in red and Dean had to resort to his small LED flashlight to make out the numbers.

"We're running behind," said Dean as he gave Karr the first envelope and took the original, stuffing it into the rucksack. "I'll locate the boxes and pull them out. You get the envelopes."

"Don't let them fall," said Karr. "We'll be here all night shuffling them back into the right containers."

Dean started to work his way across the stacked rows. He still had two more to find when Telach hissed a warning in their ears:

"Charlie, Tommy: the supervisor is coming up the street to the bank ahead of schedule. Pack up and get out of there now."

35

By the time General Túcume arrived at the house under the Inca ruins, it was nearly midnight. He had stopped earlier at his divisional headquarters and was very tired from the long day. But the sight of Stephan Babin standing before the house filled Túcume with energy. The crippled Russian arms dealer looked like an Inca wraith emerging from the Spaniards' mansion—the ghost of Tupac Amaru, just after he slaughtered the inhabitants in revenge.

"You return, General," said Babin, crutching his way toward him. "Later than I expected, but good evening nonetheless."

"And to you. Everything is ready?"

"Yes. The mock warhead is in the barn. Be careful who sees it. It may not fool a well-trained eye—or a sophisticated radiation meter. Three meters. Remember. And your devices must not be given up; anyone recalibrating them is very likely to realize they have been tampered with."

"I intend to be most cautious."

When Túcume had discovered the warhead along with Babin in the wreckage of the plane three years before, he had sensed it would allow him to fulfill his dream of taking his rightful place at the head of a restored Inca Empire. But within a few hours he realized something else—the bomb was as much of a liability as it was an asset. There was no possibility of using it as a weapon; his enemies lived too close to his own people, and in any event Túcume knew that no leader who destroyed his own country would be followed. The weapon could be used as a bargaining chip only, and even then the circumstances had to be just right.

Once the warhead was revealed, any number of things would happen. Questions would be asked about where it came from. The general staff would assert their authority to take control of it. The Americans, who according to Babin did not know it existed, would realize their mistake and try to recover it. So Túcume had to construct exactly the right scenario for its "discovery"—one where he would not be responsible for its past.

The plot he had arrived at, with Babin's help, solved many problems. The weapon would be "discovered" in the rebels' possession in a remote area. Its discovery right before the election would help Túcume's candidate win. After the election, Aznar would appoint him to head the military—a natural appointment, given his record against Ecuador and the guerrillas—and any other complications could be smoothed out.

However, the plan put the warhead at risk. First because the area where it would be "discovered" had to be a dangerous area, and in order for the operation to appear authentic he could not send troops to guard the bomb ahead of time. And second, because there was bound to be at least some jealousy among the Spaniards who controlled the general staff, who would eventually order the warhead delivered to them.

It was Babin who had supplied the answer. He had crafted a dummy warhead, which to Túcume at least looked precisely like the real one. That would be the one discovered and transported. The genuine bomb would stay hidden in the barn where it had always been; at some point in the future when it was safe—and necessary—the warhead would be brought out from hiding.

"How is your election going?" asked Babin.

"We will win," said Túcume. "Events are moving. The people will see the way they must vote."

"You're an optimist, General. Democracy is rule by the mob, the lowest of the low. I'd never trust them."

"One uses what one can," said Túcume. "Just as the Spanish made use of disease, I make use of democracy. A wise man finds weapons at his feet."

"Is that one of your Inca proverbs?"

"It could be, couldn't it?"

Túcume smiled at the Russian. Túcume did trust the people, the natives, his people—he trusted them because he trusted their spirit. He'd told Babin this before, but the Russian did not understand.

"I'm going to take a nap now, Stephan. The truck for the warhead will be here in a few hours. Good night to you."

Túcume turned and walked toward the main house, aware that Babin's eyes would follow him until he disappeared into the blackness.

36

Dean grabbed Karr's arm as he reached for another of the plastic boxes. "Now, Tommy. They're coming in."

"I still have two more."

"No. We'll get them at the regional centers," said Dean. *"Come on."*

They grabbed their backpacks and hurried out of the vault room, but before they could close and reset the lock on the vault to the number where it had started, there were shouts at the far end of the lobby.

"Domir!" shouted one of the men who'd just come in. He followed this with a string of Spanish curses violent enough to boil paint off the walls. "Sleeping at your post? What in the name of the saints has gotten into you, you worthless scum?"

Dean crouched behind the security equipment at the base of the steps down to the vault. He could hear the guards being roused. One jumped to his feet and began babbling an apology.

"Silence!" said his supervisor. "Wake him up!"

"One of the guard supervisors brought an army officer in to show him the security arrangements," Telach explained. "We switched the video signal back—it's real time. There's a lavatory down the hall. If you wait there, we'll tell you when the supervisor has gone. We'll interrupt the security feed again and you can get them with the blowpipe. No one will believe anything they say if they're caught sleeping a second time."

More likely, thought Dean, the guards would be replaced.

Karr had taken out the MP5 submachine gun he'd packed as a personal weapon. The weapon had a silencer on it, but silence was a relative concept for a submachine gun.

The second guard groaned, then protested that it was not time to get up. This was too much for the supervisor, who told them that they were both fired and must leave on the spot. The other guard began pleading for his job, saying that he had just dozed off for a moment. Even though the tape would have backed him up, the supervisor wanted no part of any excuses. Pleading that he needed the job, the man began to cry. But his boss wouldn't give in. He herded the two guards toward the door.

Karr tugged Dean's shirt and gestured toward the ladies' room. Dean followed, easing in as Karr held the door open.

"The visitor is still there," said Telach. "He's looking for something—going toward the vault level."

"Good thing we went in the ladies' room," whispered Karr.

Sure enough, Dean heard footsteps coming down the hall. They waited in the dark, heard the man go into the lavatory next door.

"Let's go," whispered Karr, starting to pull open the door. "We can get in behind the tellers' boxes if we can't make it all the way to the stairs."

But as he pulled open the door Telach warned them the supervisor was coming back.

The supervisor yelled to the other man, asking where he was. The man explained gruffly that he would be right out. The supervisor walked to the lavatory door and told the man that he was very sorry, but he had to arrange for some substitutes.

"How long do you think it will take him to find new guards?" Karr whispered as the toilet flushed.

Dean shrugged.

"You think it's worth waiting? Or should we just take this guy down and get out now?" asked Karr.

"Better to wait on the chance that we can sneak out," said Dean. "We take him out now, they'll realize we were here anyway."

"Wait," suggested Rockman.

The officer was at the sink in the next room, washing up. Suddenly he began to curse.

"No paper," Dean whispered to Karr. "He'll come here next. Get into the stalls."

"Let's just bop him and be done with it."

"We've come this far. We'll tough it out another few seconds. Into the stalls."

Karr slipped into the one on the right; Dean took the left. A second later, the door flew open.

37

Lima might not be under a curfew, but the streets were all but deserted. Lia drove about ten blocks before parking again, this time in a lot that wasn't visible from the street.

"Tommy and Dean are having a little trouble in the bank," Rockman told her.

"They need a diversion?"

"At the moment, we think they're going to play through on their own. But maybe."

Wary now, Lia decided that she would plant video bugs near the street to make sure she wasn't snuck up on again. She got out of the car and began walking toward the Dumpster near the driveway. As she came close, something moved to the right. In one quick motion, she dove, rolled to the ground, and retrieved the pistol at her ankle, bringing it to bear on the old bearded man who'd stirred from the small blanket of newspapers he'd spread as a resting place for the night.

"*Vamos,*" Lia told him harshly. "Go! Get away."

The man got up, then began to run.

"Lia, what's going on? Are you OK?" asked Rockman.

"I'm OK," she told him. "I'm always OK."

38

Dean held his breath as the Peruvian fumbled in the darkness for the light switch. Instead of finding the light, he happened on the paper towel dispenser; he pulled out some paper and made his way back to the nearby door.

Dean slipped out of his stall, holding his breath as he tried to hear the man's footsteps.

"He's back up in the lobby," said Rockman.

Dean opened the door and slipped out. He had the blowpipe in his hand and his rucksack slung over his other shoulder. Karr went to the safe, spinning the dial to clear the combination.

"Are you there, Rockman?" asked Dean, stopping near the steps.

"We're here, Charlie," said Telach. "The lobby's clear. The replacements are on their way from the police station. You have about three minutes to get out. We're controlling the video. Go!"

Fifteen minutes later, Dean and Karr were outside the back of the building, moving slowly along an alley toward the rendezvous spot with Lia. They had to duck an army patrol before crossing the street, but once past that, reached the avenue where they were to meet without seeing anyone. Lia, approaching in the car, blinked her lights twice and pulled over. Dean and Karr both shoved into the back and she took off.

"I feel like a chauffeur," she said.

"Not a bad career move," said Karr.

"We couldn't get them all in," Dean told her. "There were two left when the guards came in."

"I'll get them tomorrow," said Lia.

"We can always get them once they're shipped Friday," said Dean.

"It's no big deal."

39

On his second day as a "permanent consultant" to the NSA, Hernes Jackson found that his biometric identity had been programmed into the agency's security system. Not only could the computer confirm who he was by checking his retinas; it could also use face recognition and body-shape software to make sure it wasn't being fooled.

He was allowed to make his way to OPS 2/B Level Black (the official name of the subbasement where the Art Room was) without an escort, but that didn't mean he was proceeding unwatched; the walls were embedded with sensors, and video cameras along the hallway ceiling swung around as he passed.

A woman met him at the door of the second elevator.

"I'm Marie Telach. I'm the Art Room supervisor," she told him. "You're Ambassador Jackson."

"Yes. You could call me Hernes."

"Thank you. I'm Marie. I'm going to take you to our library room. I'm afraid it's not the most comfortable working environment, but it's only temporary."

Jackson followed her down the hall to a small, windowless room. There was nothing on the whitewashed Sheetrock walls or the tile floor. Two computers sat on a simple table in front of a secretary's sideless swivel chair. One looked little different from the small Dell unit Jackson owned, with a seventeen-inch flat screen as its display. The other had a larger keyboard and a screen that measured thirty inches. There was a phone at the edge of the desk, but nothing else.

"This computer can access SpyNet, and all of the secure databases and systems you'll have access to," said Telach, pointing at the larger screen and keyboard. "There's also a segregated version of most of the DoD archives as well as our own, and—"

"Excuse me," said Jackson. "What do you mean by segregated?"

"I mean that we have our own copies, so that our access can't be monitored and there are no unguarded back doors into our system. DoD, the Department of Defense, and SpyNet—you know what that is?"

"Sure. It's our government intelligence web network. I used it at the State Department."

"Good. The Dell computer connects to the Internet through a dedicated line. It uses a series of anonymous servers so it can't be traced. The data you can send out is very limited, and it's also monitored for security reasons. You can't buy anything," she added lightly, "so no shopping at Amazon.com on your lunch hour."

"I get a lunch hour?"

"Mr. Rubens runs a very tight ship, but it's not that tight. We have our own lounge down the hall. It's small, but you're probably better off eating there today. It'll save you some of the hassles of going back upstairs. You place an order and it will be delivered."

Jackson nodded. Montblanc had told him that there were very nice cafeterias—more like small commercial cafés or restaurants—upstairs, but he had no idea where they were. This would be fine.

"Someone from our analysis section is coming down to show you how to use the systems," Telach added. "I assume you don't know how."

"I can use the Internet and e-mail."

"Good. This is a little different, but once you get the hang of it, it's fairly simple."

"What exactly am I looking for?"

Telach gave him an odd smile. "Mr. Rubens didn't tell me."

Jackson already knew his way around SpyNet, an internal "intranet" service used by American intelligence agencies to access and share information. It was very similar to a commercial intranet, the internal Web-like systems used by many companies to allow different departments to share data easily.

The other databases he had access to were simply mind-boggling. He could, for example, look through the government's entire archives on World War II—the military as well as diplomatic records not only had been digitized but also were indexed and could be searched in a variety of ways. Jackson, who'd always been interested in history, felt a bit like a schoolkid introduced to the library for the first time.

The only question was what he was supposed to do with all this information. Rubens didn't seem to know, either—or if he did, he wasn't telling.

For want of a better idea, Jackson decided to start where he had left off the day before, looking at Iron Heart. The report was skimpy, but that was all right—the more things that were left out, the more places there were to look next.

40

Drinking her coffee in the hotel's balcony restaurant while waiting for Fernandez to meet her, Lia watched through the window as the rest of Lima woke. The city reminded her of Los Angeles, mixing tall buildings and highways against the backdrop of the sea nearby. The contrasts were much sharper here, the colors riotous; the wall on the building across the way jammed a violent pink against the brightest yellow she'd ever seen. But the same wild mix of dreams, wealth, and desperation that made Los Angeles such a vibrant place filled Lima's streets. From where she sat, Lia could see seven or eight cranes rising in the distance, towering over new buildings. On the street below, men and women recently arrived from the highlands to the east walked swiftly past, bundled in clothes that could have been woven four hundred years before.

Why were these people struggling for democracy, Lia wondered. Why were their governments so chronically corrupt? Was history to blame? Had the Spanish planted some irredeemable seed here that prevented men from doing the right thing?

"Lost in thought?" said Fernandez, startling her as he arrived.

"Good morning," said Lia coldly.

"Yesterday's storm has blown over, at least for the moment," said Fernandez. "The president is holding a news conference this morning to ask for a full investigation and to pledge free elections. We think that will help. There's a march to the main police station scheduled for this afternoon. I guess that will tell us how this is going to go."

"The police were set up," Lia told him.

"Latin America is different than your country and mine," said Fernandez. He nodded as the waiter came with his coffee. "They don't have the same traditions here."

Lia didn't feel like arguing.

"We'll visit warehouse number two to test the voting machines after breakfast," she told him. "Then we'll go back to the vault and finish the checks on the voter cards."

"Oh."

"Problem?" asked Lia, pretending to be surprised.

"We decided to rearrange the shipment schedule because of the, uh, problems yesterday. The cards are being shipped out right now."

"Peachy."

"Excuse me?"

Fernandez didn't understand the expression, and Lia didn't bother translating it.

"It's not a problem," she told him. "I'll finish the machines here and then go to the regional centers. I'll need a list of the sites and where the envelopes are going so I can use the same test pattern."

"I don't know if we have that," said Fernandez. "Let me check."

He took out a cell phone and called over to the commission's headquarters. Lia knew that they did have a list—the Art Room had already obtained it. She wondered what it would mean if he told her it didn't exist—would the logical conclusion be that he was somehow involved in a scam?

"We can get it," he told her, glancing up from the phone. Then he went back to talking with his co-worker in rapid Spanish, complaining about all of the bureaucratic problems they had to deal with.

"Arranging transportation may be a problem," said Fernandez when he hung up. "Depending on where you're going.

Near the coast isn't a problem, but once you're up into the mountains, it can get rather tortuous."

"I thought there were helicopters available."

"There are, and we will try to get one for you. But between the weather and altitude, they sometimes can't physically make it there and back, not safely."

"Well, hopefully we can figure it out," said Lia. "Should we order? I'd like to get going."

41

Rubens' day began with a National Security Council sub-committee meeting at the White House. Given the president's interest in the Peruvian election scheduled for the weekend, Rubens expected that a good portion of the meeting would be devoted to it.

He also expected that he would run into Debra Collins there. Which he did.

"You look tired, Bill," said Collins as they walked down the hall toward the conference room in the basement complex. "Thank you for the information about the riot. I always appreciate a heads-up."

"Yes." Rubens glanced down the hall. No one was coming down behind them. Except for her aide, they were alone. Rubens touched her sleeve to stop her. "Why was Jorge Evans part of the briefing team on Peru?"

"Jorge?"

"I find it odd that he's not a member of your staff but was representing you."

Collins made a face as if she didn't understand—which, to Rubens, meant exactly the opposite. She nodded to her aide, indicating he could go on without her.

"First of all," she told Rubens when they were alone, "Jorge was there on behalf of the Latin American Division, not me personally. And second of all, he was the person we could spare who knows the area."

"There are no present operations in Peru we're going to trip over?"

"You know me better than that. I'm not going to jeopardize your people or our interests by playing some turf war garbage game."

"Oh, that's rich."

"Bill, don't talk to me like this." She leaned forward slightly. "Get beyond the personal."

"This isn't personal. Why are you so interested in Peru?"

"Me? You're interested in Peru."

Her voice was too loud. Rubens thought this was a tactic to get him to be quiet.

"Why are you interested in Peru?" he repeated, lowering his voice further.

"The president is interested in Peru—in fair elections. Otherwise I don't give a shit."

"Four-letter words don't impress me, Debra."

"Good."

She started across the hall, but he grabbed her arm. Her eyes flashed; he let go.

"Why did Evans brief us on Peru? Did he volunteer?"

"This is what happens when I give you a heads-up about a contact that approached the agency? You go paranoid on me?"

"If my people are in danger—"

Collins didn't let him finish. "I'm neither a fool nor a traitor." She spun and strode angrily into the conference room.

About ten minutes of the meeting was devoted to Peru, and most of the time was taken up by the undersecretary of state for Latin America, who reviewed the election situation. The undersecretary mentioned the disturbance the day before and put it into political perspective: Vice President Ramon Ortez's numbers in the overnight tracking polls had plummeted. Victor Imberbe of the Peruvian Centrists now had a ten-point lead. Hernando Aznar had picked up a few points as well, though he was still in third place.

Collins chimed in with the warning that had been delivered by what she called a "high-ranking potential source."

She said his information was still being evaluated; technically, it would be up to the CIA's analysis side to put it into perspective, though obviously events would show how trustworthy he was.

Rubens watched her as she spoke. Maybe she was right—maybe she didn't have an ax to grind and he was just being paranoid. Evans might have just been available, or even been sent over as part of a gradual plan to make sure he knew all the players as he climbed further up the echelon.

Chaired by one of Hadash's deputies in his absence, the session moved along expeditiously, and in less than thirty minutes Rubens was packing up his things to go. He thought he might actually get ahead of his daily schedule until a member of the chief of staff's office met him outside.

"President wants to talk to you upstairs," said the staffer, a twenty-two-year-old fresh out of Yale. "And you, too, Ms. Collins."

Rubens gritted his teeth. Neither of them said anything as they made their way upstairs. The aide led them to the Oval Office, asking them to wait in the hallway. Rubens held his arms together at his chest, folded there as if they were an armored suit. Collins stood with her back to him, feigning interest in some document her aide had given her downstairs. For perhaps the millionth time, Rubens berated himself for ever having any sort of interest in her, romantic or otherwise. Truly it had been a moment of lunacy, utter lunacy.

When they were shown in, Marcke was in the middle of a phone call, apparently with a governor whose support he was courting for a highway initiative. He motioned at them to sit down, then continued cajoling the governor, who apparently was refusing to sign off on a change in allocation formulas. It was obvious the president wasn't getting anywhere; he finally signed off by telling the governor that they would have to agree to disagree.

"Is Peru going to explode?" Marcke asked as soon as the call ended.

Collins answered before Rubens could even open his mouth.

"I don't think so, Mr. President."

Rubens was tempted to ask whether she had taken over the analysis side of the agency as well as operations but knew better than to snipe in front of the president.

"Billy?"

"The Peruvians can be unpredictable," he told the president. "But whatever happens, our mission will succeed."

"I don't have a doubt about that."

Marcke got up and went over to the corner of his office, where he kept a golf club. He lined up a putt and took a shot at a target cup before speaking again.

"George is doing very well in China. He sends his regards," said the president. "It seems as if they will agree to cut relations with North Korea if the North doesn't disband their nuclear weapon program and allow full inspections. I don't know if we should give George too much credit, though. It may go to his head."

The president smiled, then turned his attention back to the golf ball. He took another shot.

"George mentioned something else during our conversation. He's thinking seriously of retiring."

Rubens suddenly realized why Marcke had called him upstairs: he was being considered as a replacement for his mentor.

As was Collins.

"I just wanted to make sure that you both knew about this," Marcke told them. "I promised I wouldn't try and talk him out of it. It won't be official for a while. Hopefully, no rumors start until after he's come back."

That was intended to be a warning, Rubens realized.

Obviously aimed at Collins.

"You tried to talk him out of it?" she asked.

"No, he made me promise I wouldn't," said the president. "But if either of you want to take a shot at it, be my guest."

42

THE EVENTS OF YESTERDAY WILL NOT GO UNPUNISHED. ALL OF LIMA SHALL WITNESS THE FEROCITY OF OUR WRATH.

THE POLICE STATE WILL BE ABOLISHED BY FORCE. FOREIGN INVADERS AND COLLABORATORS WILL BE PUNISHED. HEED OUR WARNING: YOU HAVE TWELVE HOURS TO LEAVE THE CITY, OR DIE FOR YOUR SINS.

General Túcume couldn't help but grin as he finished reading the copy of the unsigned communiqué from Sendero Nuevo. The general staff had ordered it distributed two hours after it had been received by e-mail at the Lima headquarters. The threat was considered so important that commanding officers were to acknowledge in writing that they had received it.

"A bit over-the-top," said Babin, standing on his crutches next to him.

"Very much in their style," said Túcume, hitting the keys on the laptop to save the message in an encrypted file.

"You would know," said Babin, crutching across the room.

Túcume reflected on the Russian's tone. Had he become more bitter since they had met?

Certainly. And it was understandable. Babin had been happy to be alive that first afternoon. He had no idea what had happened to his body. It was only later, over much time, that the full reality sank in. Túcume could not blame him.

Túcume intended to reward all of his people lavishly in the best Inca tradition, and Babin would be no exception. Perhaps a doctor could be found to cure his legs and back or at least ease his pain. The general made a solemn promise to himself to help his friend.

"You'd better take care to plan your ambush for the cameras," said Babin. "You may not get the right light for the TV cameras."

"There won't be any television cameras."

"I can't believe you'd miss the opportunity."

Actually, there would be something much better—a BBC stringer had asked to join the general on a patrol in the Amazonian jungle weeks before. They were to meet in a few hours.

The announcement of the discovery of the weapon was critical to Túcume's plan; keeping it a secret from the public would accomplish nothing. He had gone to great lengths to make sure the news could be broadcast and would seem spontaneous at the same time. He'd settled on the British reporter over several Peruvians because the unprejudiced words of praise from a foreigner would surely be worth more. Members of Peru's media were commonly thought to be bribed by officers looking to advance, and Túcume did not want his discovery tarnished by such suspicions.

Babin watched the general's SUV as it made its way down the mountain trail, staring after it until all that was left was a thick cloud of yellowish-brown dust. He admired Túcume; in many ways the Indian was like a countryman. The general had the ambition of a Slav and the ability to plan that made Russian chess masters so unbeatable. The plot he had woven to win the election for his candidate—and to cement his own hold over the country—was worthy of Peter the Great. Túcume did not possess the ruthlessness of a criminal like Stalin, who had massacred people on a grand scale; this was a flaw in a great leader, Babin thought, but not an unforgivable one. More problematic was Túcume's loyalty to people he trusted. Not that Babin had not benefited: a truly ruthless leader would have executed him long ago. Túcume gained very little by keeping him alive, and yet Babin knew very well that he would not even entertain the thought of killing him.

He also knew that Túcume was unlikely to help him get revenge against the people who had crippled him. Like most Latin Americans, Túcume had a love-hate attitude toward the Yankees. He might criticize the U.S. and take advantage of its foibles, but in the end he would not do anything to seriously enrage it. He was wise enough to understand that doing so would only endanger his vision for the future. Túcume lived for the time when the native peoples were once more the lords of the Andes.

Unlike Babin, who only lived for revenge.

Babin pushed back on his crutches, heading toward the barn where the real bomb was still stored. The truck he had sent for would be here within the hour. He had to make sure everything was ready before it arrived.

43

They spent the day following Lia from a distance as she inspected the second set of voting machines and then went over to the UN to meet with the board of observers. Lia's meeting took place near an Internet café, and Karr told Dean he was tempted to send his girlfriend an e-mail.

"So go ahead," said Dean.

"The problem with working for the NSA, Charlie, is that I know how easy it is to trace things."

"You can't figure a way around it?"

"Somebody's always watching. No matter how good you are."

"How's your girlfriend?" asked Dean.

Karr's face flushed. He'd met Deidre Clancy during their last mission in Europe several months before. She was the daughter of the American ambassador to Great Britain and one of the most beautiful women Dean had ever seen.

After Lia, of course.

"She laughs at all my jokes. There's something in that," said Karr.

"There's a *lot* in that," said Dean.

"You ever been married, Charlie?"

Dean smiled—not at the memory of his own marriage but at the fact that Karr was thinking about it.

"Didn't work out," Dean told him. "Doesn't mean it wouldn't work out for you. Probably would be pretty good."

"What happened?"

"Long story."

"We got time."

Karr was right, but Dean didn't feel like talking about his marriage. He glanced across the street at the restaurant where the UN people were meeting with Lia.

It wasn't a thing to talk about—wasn't important at all, just a passing mistake. Fortunately, it was one without many consequences—they hadn't had kids, and no money to squabble over. Just something best forgotten.

"So?" prodded Karr.

Dean changed the subject, provoked by another billboard proclaiming Vice President Imberbe as THE HERO OF THE PEOPLE.

"You think of yourself as a hero, Tommy?"

Karr laughed. "I think of myself as a mathematician."

Dean stared at him. It was hard to know with Karr how sincere he was being. "A mathematician?"

"That's what I went to school for. I'm just a big geek." Karr laughed. "I'm not old enough to be a hero. Heroes are the guys in the reviewing stands at the end of the parade."

"Yeah," said Dean.

Karr gave him a look. "Ah, you're not old enough to have served in Vietnam. I know your war record's phony."

Coming from Karr, the joke somehow felt like a great compliment, and Dean laughed along with him.

44

Rubens' car had just turned off the highway when the phone that connected him directly to the Art Room began to ring. He pulled the phone from his pocket and flipped it open, carefully placing his thumb at the side where it could be read by the unit's biometric security device.

"Rubens. What is it, Ms. Telach?"

"The Peruvian rebels have issued an ultimatum threatening Lima. Their military is on full alert."

"I'll be down as soon as I arrive," he told her.

By the time Rubens made it to the Art Room forty minutes later, the analysts had prepared a fresh report on Peru's military, showing where its various units were deployed. Satellite photos revealed that two battalion-sized groups of soldiers and materiel had been dispatched to the central Andes where the rebels had been active in the past. A much larger force had gone to the south. Logically, this did not make much sense, and the analysts concluded that the military might be thinking of using the alert as a pretext to settle a local score.

Rubens noted that no reinforcements had been sent to the Amazon and northeastern areas of the country—the ones with the heaviest activity. The forces there were widely spread out. They were also under the command of the general who had warned the CIA earlier that the rebels were planning something.

Either the general staff wanted him to fail or didn't care if he succeeded. The briefing showed that his force was undermanned to begin with—he wasn't trusted, probably because of the prejudice against natives.

The UN election committee was alarmed about the developments and had sent several messages back to the UN Security Council, in effect asking for direction. So far they had not received an answer.

Rubens put in a call to the White House and got through to the chief of staff; he gave him a quick update. He also called the secretary of state and the U.S. ambassador to the UN, neither of whom was available to take his call.

Ordinarily, Rubens would have called Hadash first. But he didn't want to talk to the national security adviser from the Art Room. Rubens wanted to speak someplace where he felt free to ask why Hadash hadn't told him he was quitting.

As he started to leave, though, it occurred to Rubens that delaying was exactly the wrong thing to do. For one thing, he would be letting a personal consideration interfere with his job—a gross violation of his responsibility. And second, he didn't particularly *want* to talk to Hadash about his resignation. He didn't know what to say.

Rubens pushed the buttons and sent the call through. Most likely, he thought, Hadash would be sleeping and he would have to leave a message with an aide. But the national security adviser's voice came right on the line.

"George Hadash."

"George, this is Bill Rubens. The rebels in Peru have issued a threat against Lima. The military has mobilized. They've sent a sizable unit to the south, though their intentions there are not clear. The city itself is quiet."

"Yes, I know. The CIA briefed me a few minutes ago."

"Very good," said Rubens. It *was* the CIA's job, after all—but he felt as if they were interfering somehow. "Our mission is proceeding."

"You haven't accomplished it yet?"

The question stung Rubens, as if he had failed somehow.

"We're moving at a prudent pace," he said stiffly.

"I see," said Hadash, his voice unusually cold.

Rubens wondered if he had misread his friendship with Hadash all along. Perhaps the fact that it had started as a teacher–student relationship had always colored it; maybe Hadash still thought of him as an eager but untempered young post-grad.

So be it. There was nothing he could do to change it now.

"I will keep you informed," he told Hadash.

"Thank you."

When he looked up, Telach was standing a few feet away, waiting to speak to him and pretending not to have overheard his conversation.

"Where are we with the mission?" he asked, eager to move on.

45

Hernes Jackson spent most of the day finding indirect ways to get information about Iron Heart. While the report didn't mention them, Jackson guessed that there would be NSA intercepts related to the operation. His new clearance allowed him to search through files using time and location as search terms, and with a little help from an NSA librarian he managed to network considerable information about the weapons dealer who had acted as the go-between and arranged the "sale" to Brazil. Jackson's interest in history as much as his State Department background helped him play detective; he felt as if he were reconstructing a time and place a hundred years before by bringing together information from dozens of sources, just as a good historian would do.

While the CIA's report had made Iron Heart seem like it was a sting operation from the start, it wasn't—the Brazilians were already involved when the CIA's plant entered the picture. Aside from the fact that he was Russian, he wasn't identified anywhere. This was not unusual. The agency went to great lengths to protect its foreign "assets," and the identity of a particularly valuable one was generally so restricted that only two or three people knew who he was.

The "asset" in this case was very important and had been before Iron Heart. By cross-referencing some of the CIA people involved and looking at unrelated reports, Jackson concluded that the agent had been set up in business or at least helped by the CIA around the time of the conflict in Bosnia, possibly as part of a program to stop underground weapons sales to the government there.

Jackson was so involved in his work that by the time he broke for lunch it was after three. The small lounge room was empty, but he discovered that he could order something at a computer terminal at the side of the room. The result was like something out of the *Star Trek* science fiction series—within a few minutes a metal window near the terminal hissed and opened; his sandwich was packed on a tray inside.

After lunch, Jackson turned his attention to obtaining information about the military units that had backed up the finale of Iron Heart. Again, he had to work obliquely, reading between the lines and patching things together based on inferences and educated guesses. He was at a bit of a disadvantage in dealing with the Department of Defense records (accessed over a special hard-wired link to a military Web-like network called SIRNET, for "Secret Internet Protocol Router Network"), not because he was unfamiliar with the database system but because he didn't understand half the abbreviations. And he wasn't sure exactly what sort of protocols covered different situations. Was it normal, for example, that a U-2 spy plane had undertaken ten sorties over the crash area? And if so, why did they begin six hours after the bomb had been found?

Jackson knew several military people he could call for background, but he wasn't sure whether he was allowed to or not. Not wanting to bother Telach or Rubens too much, he did some more searches and discovered that the "package" that was deployed followed almost exactly the pattern that would be followed in the case of a "broken arrow" incident— the loss of a nuclear weapon by a U.S. asset.

Interesting, considering that the operation had begun *after* the warhead had been recovered at the airstrip by the CIA's paramilitary team.

"You're still here?" asked Marie Telach, entering the room unannounced.

"Still digging," said Jackson, looking up.

"It's past nine. You ought to go home."

"I didn't realize it was so late."

"Anything interesting?"

"I don't know," said Jackson. "I haven't really figured it out yet."

"Well, go home and get some rest. We may need you to be fresh tomorrow."

"Thank you," he said, turning around to sign out of the system.

46

Calvina and Rosa had arranged to meet at the bus station at 10:00 p.m. Wednesday. The journey was complicated—they had to travel to Nevas, a small city far in the north of Peru northwest of Santa Cruz on the Rio Marañón. That journey alone would take two days. Once there, they would meet a person who would give them some type of exam and tell them what to do next.

Calvina's cousin had been very vague about what the job called for; she claimed not to know the specifics. Calvina guessed that something illegal was involved. Most likely she and her cousin were to carry drugs to the United States. Calvina decided that if it was all right with Rosa, it was all right with her.

The thing that puzzled Calvina was why it would be against the law. There was no commandment against taking drugs, and none of the sins that she had been taught involved them. Drinking too much, yes—but even that wasn't a mortal sin, as the priests would readily attest. So why would taking drugs be wrong?

She put the thought out of her mind as the bus she was supposed to take was called. Where was Rosa? There was only one bus per week to Santa Cruz, where they would take other transportation to Nevas; if they missed it, they would have to wait seven days.

Worse, if Calvina missed it, she would have no place to go.

She had already left her mother a note explaining that she wouldn't be back. To return home now . . .

If she didn't leave now, she would never be able to get away. Ever.

"Calvina!"

The voice that called her was not her cousin's, but Calvina turned anxiously, expecting to see Rosa. Instead, she saw Rosa's friend Maria, who lived two buildings down.

"Your cousin gave me this to give to you," said Maria, pressing an envelope into her hands. "She's sorry."

"Sorry for what?"

Maria shook her head. Instead of explaining, she turned and began walking away.

"Maria! Wait!"

The announcement that her bus was leaving in another minute stopped Calvina from following. She opened the envelope. There was money, a bus ticket, and a note.

I'm sorry. Go for both of us. The Blessed Virgin be with you.

Calvina stared at the words, reading them over and over.

"Señorita?"

She looked up. A bus company employee who had helped her earlier was standing nearby.

"You said you were going on that bus," he told her. "Did you get your ticket?"

Not knowing what to do, she held up the one Rosa had supplied.

"Come. I will take your bag. Not very heavy, is it? But we had better run. The driver does not like to wait, and tonight he is running behind."

47

Lia studied the map on the PDA as Chris Farlekas explained the situation. Telach had gone over much of the information the night before, but Farlekas tended to be anal-retentive when it came to mission prep—not necessarily a bad thing. Lia sipped her coffee, holding the sat phone as if she were using it to talk. The restaurant was empty except for an American couple in their early fifties several tables away.

"One of the cards is going to La Oroya. That's a few hours away from Lima, up the mountains," said the Art Room supervisor. "The setup there is very straightforward. They're using a building that was a cafeteria for one of the mining operations two miles outside of the city; the voting machines were trucked there last week. Tommy and Dean will get there ahead of you. They'll scout the situation, but we think that it'll be the easy one.

"The second is going to a city just on the edge of the Amazon area in northeast Peru, called Nevas. As you can see on the map, it's very far from the coast, and very isolated. There aren't many roads in that area. The most reliable transportation is by air or boat. The UN will probably give you a helicopter; they hadn't made a final decision yet."

"Is this the jungle?" asked Dean. He and Karr were sitting on a park bench across the street.

"The edge really. The wilderness, the thick Amazonian jungle, is further east. This is definitely jungle. The area around

Nevas is pretty primitive, and there are narco-traffickers all through that region. A lot of cocaine."

"And we get to walk?" asked Karr.

"We'll have a light aircraft standing by for you and Dean. You'll be covered as businessmen looking for botanicals that may be of medicinal use."

"New age nuts?" Karr laughed good-naturedly.

"There's big money in botanicals," said Farlekas. He didn't sound like he was joking.

"How serious is the threat from the terrorists?" asked Dean. "There have been news reports about it."

"Very good question. Opinions vary. You won't be in Lima, which is their alleged target. We think it's much more likely that the rebels will strike in the north if they strike anywhere. So we'll have paramilitary teams in Ecuador standing by in case things get rough when you go to Nevas," said the Art Room supervisor. The units could not be located in Peru, since that would have raised obvious questions with the Peruvians about what they were up to. "Their base is roughly three hundred miles from Nevas by air, which is just inside their range. At top speed, they'd be there within an hour and a half. Depending on the situation, we may have them in the air when you're going in.

"But just for reference, most of the rebel activity has taken place to the *east* of the area you're going to—fifty, a hundred miles away. And I have to tell you, the military has made no obvious move to deal with any threat over the past twenty-four hours; it may just be a false report.

"Let me show you the building up there," Farlekas continued. "It's a school with a clinic, some health offices, things like that. It's one of the major, what would you call it? Civic services places in the city. They don't have a video system there we can break into, so you're going to have to plant flies. According to the instructions and the communications we've seen, the cards are kept in an upstairs room at the side, here."

An X appeared on Lia's map.

"I have to caution you, though, this is not confirmed,"

added Farlekas. "You may have to scout it before going in. We'll keep working on it. Just for your reference, the voting machines up there are in a separate warehouse close to the river. Like I say, the security is very light; they've authorized funds for a total of a dozen people and sent only metal detectors up there.

"Lia, if you get to La Oroya this afternoon and then reach Nevas Friday, that will give us twenty-four to thirty-six hours of leeway," said Farlekas. "That's the schedule we'd like you to keep. One complication here is that sometimes the electricity goes off. They don't have backup generators at either place, so that may be a pain."

"I'm sure we'll survive," said Lia. "Are you going to be on all day?"

"Just until noon. Then Marie and the rest of the A team come on."

"You're the A team as far as I'm concerned."

"Hey, thanks. Us Greeks have to stick together, right?"

Lia smiled. "We'll keep you updated. Enjoy your breakfast."

"Yeah, enjoy your breakfast," said Karr. "Have some for me."

Two hours later, Lia got into a battered Land Rover with Fernandez and set off for La Oroya as part of a convoy of election officials and equipment. There were crates of leaflets explaining how to vote, tables and chairs that were to be used by poll watchers, and enough odds and ends to fill four trucks. Another four trucks of soldiers had been detailed to escort them. Fernandez complained about this, saying that the rebels were forever making threats that no one took seriously. He seemed to think the soldiers were intended to somehow intimidate them.

After a few miles his complaints became too much and Lia told him that he seemed much more sympathetic to the rebels than to the government.

"I thought we were supposed to be neutral," she said.

"Yes, to the extent possible. But I don't trust the government," he said. "The riot was a pretense for a clampdown and intimidation. I've seen it before."

"Maybe," said Lia. "Or maybe it was instigated by the rebels to make the government look bad."

"That's not their style. I don't pretend that they're angels," added Fernandez, "I'm only saying that no one takes them seriously. If they did, this road would be clogged with people running away from Lima. You see it's practically empty. There's no traffic here. They're buffoons. Lightweights. The military is much more of a serious threat."

"They're not talking about murdering people."

"I didn't say I liked Sendero Nuevo," insisted Fernandez.

He concentrated on the road for a while—pouting, Lia thought, because he didn't like being shown his prejudices.

"Coming from Spain, I have a different perspective, perhaps," said Fernandez finally. "I distrust the government because I've seen how corrupt it can be. The colonial government here was often unfair to the people. I understand that legacy."

And maybe, thought Lia, you feel a little guilty about it.

"Peru liberated itself almost two hundred years ago," Lia told him. "The government is on its own."

"And as corrupt as its oppressors."

Fernandez seemed to surprise himself with the remark. He said nothing for the rest of the trip.

48

General Túcume leaned back in the Jeep to hear the BBC reporter's question. The man's Spanish was very good, but it was Castilian and had a heavy English accent besides. The words were hard to catch in the open truck.

"There is quite a lot of poverty here," said the reporter, Charles Ross. "The government can't do more to help?"

"A question, I'm afraid, beyond my scope," said Túcume.

"But you come from this area. These are your people, the Indians."

"True," said Túcume. He liked Ross; he was not as condescending as many journalists he'd met and not stupid, either. The man recognized that Túcume was a man of the people and felt a strong bond to them. Ross' questions were actually good ones, though answering with candor was inconvenient for Túcume, who knew that the general staff would be sure to study what he said.

Then again, in a short while it wouldn't matter what the general staff thought, would it?

"Native people want only fairness," said the general, deciding to answer honestly. "You have to remember that since the days of the Spanish—the early days of the Spanish—the people you call Indians have been treated very badly. Even those who were leaders of the people, they were hounded and persecuted, made to give up their beliefs and convert to

Catholicism. Even then, it wasn't enough. Many were killed or reduced to peasants."

"History is more complicated than that," said Ross.

"More complicated than what you've read in books, yes. I would agree. Some Incas were allowed to remain on as leaders under the Spanish, as long as they kowtowed to their real masters. My people remained true, and they suffered greatly for it. For many generations they lived in hiding, in the jungles, far from the Spanish and the cities. That was a blessing in disguise, for it kept them pure."

"Pure genetically?"

"In thought," said the general. "In the way they lived. To be an Inca—to be a ruler—is not an easy thing."

"If you feel that way, why don't you run for political office?"

"Politics." Túcume waved his hand dismissively. But then he grew serious, once more speaking with as much candor as possible. "I could get many votes. Here. In the country among native peoples, I believe I would have a landslide. You saw them in the village."

"They worship you."

"That's too strong a word. And don't be mistaken: they flocked around the Jeep because they know we give out presents and bring money, and they would act the same way to anyone, to even you, Señor Ross. But you noticed the respect from the little boys? Their fathers have spoken of me to them. That is something that one cannot buy with a few sols or dollars. Respect for my ancestors. That is a serious honor."

"So why don't you run for office?"

"You didn't let me finish. I could do well here. But in the cities, never. I would be isolated in Parliament." He shook his head. "I would not have my position if it were not for the war with Ecuador in 1995 and again in 1998. If others had done well, I would not be here."

"I've heard that."

"It's true. It's also part of the reason that my command is so far from Lima."

As he spoke, gunfire began echoing through the canyon. Túcume cursed to himself—the encounter was supposed to be over when they arrived; he did not wish Ross to think it had been prearranged. But there was nothing to be done about that now.

Túcume grabbed his driver's arm as the gunshots continued.

"To the side," he said. He turned around to his aide who had the communications gear, but the man's blank face answered his question: there had been no warning.

As the truck skidded to a stop, Túcume jumped out. He pulled his pistol from its holster, then helped Ross from the back, pulling him down and pushing him against the side of the truck for cover, as if he were the reporter's bodyguard.

"General, what is going on?" asked Ross.

"I'm not sure. The peaks around us make the radios almost impossible to use at times. At the moment we're out of communication. Don't worry; we will bring this under control."

The soldiers in the vehicle behind them had fanned out along the narrow shoulder of the road. One of them began firing.

This was definitely not part of Túcume's plan. Seething with anger, he turned to the communications man, who had been with him for many years.

"Stay with Señor Ross," Túcume said. "Guard him with your life."

The aide hesitated before nodding. Belatedly, Túcume realized that he had pointed the pistol in the man's face and he had probably thought he was threatening him. Without apologizing, Túcume turned to the reporter and handed him the pistol.

"Be careful and stay here."

Ross looked at him doubtfully but took the weapon. Túcume rose and trotted up the road in the direction of the soldier who had started to fire. By the time Túcume reached the man, three other soldiers had joined him.

"What are you shooting at?" the general demanded.

The man didn't hear him, squeezing off another three-round burst. Túcume put up his hand, warning the others not to fire.

"What are you shooting at?" Túcume asked again.

The man began to explain that he had seen something moving through the high grass off the side of the road.

Túcume saw nothing.

"You've chased him off," he told the soldier. "I need a gun. Give me yours."

The man handed over his rifle, then dug into his combat vest for a fresh magazine. The general took it, then began up the road. The soldiers—they were all privates—followed.

The road dipped to the right, turning around sheer rock, which formed a wall on that side of the road. A sparse field sat on the other side; its width varied from ten or fifteen yards to just a couple of feet as it followed the road around the curve. Beyond the field was a cliff.

Túcume darted across the road to the scraggly grass, then began moving ahead toward the curve. As he reached the apex of the turn, gunfire began again; it was too far away to be aimed in his direction, though the surrounding geography made it difficult to get a precise sense of where it was coming from. He signaled to the men to move with him, then trotted around the turn, pausing a moment before heading to the next, a sharp cutback that would have made the road look like an inverted 5 from the air. As he gained the straightaway, he heard the echo of voices ahead. Túcume dropped to his knee, steadying his rifle. He wasn't a general now; his quick-beating heart had made him a young soldier again, a bold lieutenant eager to prove himself.

Two men appeared on the road, coming up from a shallow dip. They had bandanas tied around their heads, the blue scarves guerrillas here sometimes used to identify themselves to one another in battle.

Túcume sighted up his rifle but did not fire. Were they real guerrillas? Or part of the sham force that was supposed to stage the attack farther up the valley?

One of the men stopped, spotting him.

"Surrender!" he yelled.

The man squared the AK-47 to fire.

Túcume squeezed his trigger. Three bullets leapt from his M16. Two hit their target, striking the guerrilla in the face. The soldiers behind Túcume began to fire, and the man's companion was cut down in a hail of bullets.

"Stop," yelled Túcume as the man went down. "Conserve your bullets! Discipline! Discipline!"

The soldiers ran forward to the downed bodies. Túcume huffed to keep up.

"There will be more!" he warned, and within seconds they heard voices and fresh gunfire. "Our people will be fighting with them," said Túcume. "Be careful that we do not shoot our comrades. Take positions in the field. Spread out."

Túcume knelt down next to the man he had shot, taking the guerrilla's AK-47 and the spare magazines from his bandolier. Túcume preferred the M16, but the Russian-made assault gun was a serviceable second choice.

Three men with bandanas ran around the bend. Túcume rose and yelled at them to surrender. One of the men began to throw down his rifle, but it was too late; one of the soldiers with Túcume began to fire. In a few seconds all three men were lying in the dust of the road.

And then something roared around the curve, dust and bullets spattering. It was a pickup truck filled with guerrillas. Túcume, still on his feet, emptied the M16, pouring bullets into the windshield. Then he threw himself down.

The vehicle skidded across the road. A grenade exploded; men screamed and the air filled with the smell of dirt and metal turning into incandescent flames. The general picked up the AK-47 but could not find a target in the cloud of smoke and dust around him. The rocks cracked and shuddered, as if they were coming apart. Finally the cloud in front of him cleared and Túcume saw a guerrilla running toward him, gun held as if it were a sword, a wild look in his eyes. Túcume fired two bursts, catching the man in the chest. The man continued toward him. Túcume fired again, then threw himself to the right as the man ran on as if propelled by some supernatural power. Finally his legs folded beneath him and he collapsed.

The truck had overturned at the side of the road, spewing its passengers into the field. Black smoke curled from the engine compartment, and little fingers of flame poked out from the side of the hood. Túcume started to shout a warning, but as the first word came out of his mouth a fireball surged from the underside and flashed across the road. The percussion was so strong that it knocked the general off his feet.

Before he could get up, he saw a guerrilla taking aim at him at the edge of the road. Túcume tried to turn around and bring his own weapon to bear, but he felt as if he were moving in heavy oil, his body held back by some strange form of gravity. Before he could pull the rifle up, the guerrilla pushed down his shoulder, pumping the weapon's trigger.

But no bullets came out; the guerrilla's weapon had either jammed or gone empty. Túcume fired his own weapon, missing with his first shot but not his second. The guerrilla grabbed at his stomach, then slid down to the ground.

The clatter of gunfire began to recede. Túcume, breathing heavily, got up. One of his soldiers lay on the pavement a few feet away. At first, the general thought the man was lying in wait for more trucks, but then Túcume saw the red creases across the side of his head and turned away.

"General, we have suppressed the rebels," said one of the privates running up behind him. The words sounded almost comical to Túcume, the report so official and antiseptic, far at odds with the chaos around them.

"Jimenez is dead," he told the private.

The man squinted. Túcume realized the young man was in a state of shock; this was his first experience in combat.

"You did well, son," the general told him. He gripped the young man's shoulder, but the stony expression did not change.

"More!" yelled another of Túcume's men. "Coming down the road."

"Back here," shouted Túcume. "Behind the truck!"

As the others ran to take cover, Túcume realized that this new group would not be guerrillas but his own soldiers, the men who had ambushed this group or been ambushed by them on the road ahead. Rather than taking cover, he ran toward the roadway, raising his rifle in his right hand and holding out his left. Two young khaki-clad soldiers appeared, Ml6s at their waists.

"I am General Túcume!" he yelled as the men squared off to fire. "We have killed the enemy."

One of the men pressed his trigger. Bullets flew to the left of the general.

"I am your commander! Put down your gun! Put down your gun!"

Men flooded around the corner. More gunshots were fired and there were screams.

"I am General Túcume and I command you to stop firing!"

The air burned again, and the smell of blood mixed with the scent of pulverized stone.

"I am General Túcume and I command you to stop firing!"

And then there was silence. Túcume stood at the edge of the road, unharmed. The soldiers began running toward him, shouting, tears streaming down their faces, apologizing.

My ancestors have protected me, Túcume thought to himself. Yes. I knew they would.

Yes.

"Your comrades are down the road," he told the men. "Approach them carefully. We do not want any accidents."

By the time the Jeep caught up with him, Túcume had reached the two trucks the rebels had ambushed. Three of his men had been killed by a grenade, and two peasants who'd been nearby had been caught in the gunfire.

The two trucks were supporting the sweep into a rebel village about a mile ahead and had been surprised by fleeing guerrillas. In Túcume's opinion, this showed that the lieutenant in charge of the element was derelict, but the man had paid with his life for his lack of preparation and awareness. The soldiers had done a reasonably good job rallying. The peaks had prevented them from communicating with the units farther north, just as Túcume had been.

The BBC reporter tried to give Túcume his pistol back, but the general told him to keep it. "It's possible you may need it yet," Túcume said. "It will be dark soon. I'm not sure what we'll find ahead."

The privates who had accompanied Túcume earlier got into the SUV and led the way. The adrenaline from the fight swirled in his veins. Images from years ago floated up from his memory—he felt as he had in Ecuador, the sting of battle pushing him on.

It was too easy to become the bull, prodded in the ring to the point of madness. He had to stay within himself. Túcume glanced at the AK-47 he still held, reminding himself that he was a general now, not a lieutenant; his ancestors might indeed be protecting him, but he must still move with the caution and prudence befitting a leader.

The guerrillas were devils, arrogant devils, believing that they had the people's interests at heart. What did they know of his people? Only what they had learned in school, from vapid professors drunk on the sham power of words. Communism—what was that but a mad European theory, another disease to poison his people?

When the election was over he would eradicate the guerrillas. Vidal's operation against the Senderistas would be his model. He would go beyond General Vidal; when Túcume was finished, no Maoist would remain anywhere in the Andes or the surrounding land.

"That was a brave thing you did," said Ross from the back.

"What was that?" said Túcume, still distracted.

"Leading the soldiers."

Túcume shrugged. "Just a soldier's reaction."

"Not all generals would do that."

"True generals would. In any event, I did not think about it."

The driver hit the brakes. Túcume turned around and saw two of his men standing in the road, hands out to stop them.

One of his trucks was parked in the road ahead. A knot of men were gathered at the rear.

"General!" shouted a sergeant near the truck as he got out of his Jeep. The men around him snapped to attention as a unit. Túcume recognized the man—he had served with him against Ecuador in 1995, when he had been a rail of a boy, barely sixteen. He'd proved himself under fire and now led others as thin and raw as he had been.

Major Sican, in charge of the unit, came up and greeted him. Túcume had chosen Sican, a dull but honest man, to command the mission because he was related to one of the generals in Lima; his account to the general staff would be believed without question.

The major's eyes widened as he saw Túcume's uniform.

"We ran into some guerrillas trying to escape," Túcume told him. "Otherwise we would have been here sooner."

"There's blood, sir. Are you hurt?"

Túcume hadn't noticed the blood caked on his pants legs. "This is our enemy's blood. What is the situation?"

The major looked to his left. Ross had come up behind him and had his notebook out.

"Don't worry. He's all right," Túcume told the major. But then he turned to Ross and told him to put the notebook away. "It may make some of my people nervous," he added in English. "The young men especially. Many are illiterate, and they associate writing with problems."

Ross nodded and put the notebook away.

"There is a bunker a hundred meters beyond the village," said Major Sican. "It is an incredible find."

"How incredible?" asked the general.

"There is a large bomb there, with curious figures. It is a large bomb, in a crate. There was a truck nearby. We suspect it was to have been loaded and we interrupted them. The villagers say there has been no one here in some time, so we think it was a hiding place."

"Show me this," said Túcume.

They started up the road. After a few paces, Túcume turned to Ross and told him that he should wait near the truck.

"You promised me full access," said the reporter.

Finally, it was as the general had rehearsed.

"I think on this—"

"You told me you never went back on your promises."

"This area is still dangerous," said Túcume.

"As dangerous as being ambushed? I doubt it. Come on, General. You gave me your word."

"Come then. Stay next to my sergeant there. He is a veteran and has a good head."

Túcume turned and gestured to the major to show the way.

49

To Lia, La Oroya looked like an old European village dropped into the mountains, decorated with a few modern signs and lights, then populated with Indians who'd been given a ragtag assortment of clothes from a Goodwill drop-off bin.

The UN convoy drove around the outskirts, up a narrow road made of paving stones, then around a square and back down toward the countryside. Fernandez had to veer sharply twice to miss llamas in the roadway; the large animals didn't seem to notice, standing placidly and munching on the bare vegetation at the side of the road.

A string of old buildings sat behind a long rusted chain-link fence on the way out of town, part of a mining operation abandoned some years before. The air smelled of copper, smog from the nearby processing plants clinging to the peaks. Just past the fence, the caravan of trucks and cars turned off the highway onto a hard-packed mountain road that twisted around a cliff and then entered a wide valley. A quarter of a mile later, they came to the warehouse where the area's voting machines were stored.

A single guard in a policeman's uniform stood at the entrance. He greeted the convoy with unabashed glee, no doubt happy to finally see someone after standing for hours or maybe days alone at his post. The workers jumped down and began unloading the trucks.

Lia had planned to get something to eat and come back once the machines and cards were settled, but she decided to go inside now and make the switch; the chaos of the group's arrival would make it easier, and she saw no reason to wait. She took her pack and the briefcase with the laptop and walked inside, Fernandez in tow.

After the careful security of Lima, the laissez-faire was shocking—even if it did suit Lia's purposes. There was no one at the door and no one inside. The interior consisted of a large front room and a smaller back room, divided by a thick plaster wall with windowlike openings and an arched doorway. The front had been the eating area for workers in the nearby mine complex. Except for the voting machines stacked against the wall and the box of voter cards atop one of them, it was completely empty; there was no furniture, not even a single chair. A string of work lights hung from the ceiling, their 100-watt bulbs barely enough to throw a few dim rays into the corners. The windows at the side were so caked with dirt that they might as well have been boarded over.

"Can we get more lights?" Lia asked Fernandez. "And maybe a table?"

"I'll get something," he told her.

The back room had been a kitchen. The lights did not extend this far, and shadows hung over most of the room. Lia took a small LED penlight from her pocket and shone it around the room. It had been stripped of its appliances and sinks; the pipes along the back wall were capped. There were two windows on either side, covered with large pieces of plywood.

Back in the main room, Lia examined one of the windows. They were secured by metal pins that were locked into the casing at the side. She pushed at it, trying to see how difficult it would be to open. The metal fell off and clanged to the floor.

"Whoops," she said, turning and looking at the two men who were carrying tables in. Neither man paid her any attention.

"Rockman?" whispered Lia.

"I'm here," said the runner. "Tommy and Dean are watching the warehouse from the hillside. Dean says we can get in real easy tonight."

Lia resisted the impulse to tell Rockman that she didn't see *him* standing anywhere nearby. She picked up her briefcase and pack and took them near the wall of the kitchen. Then she dragged one of the tables over, opening its legs and flipping it over.

"What's the envelope number?" she asked Rockman, opening the laptop.

"You're going to make the switch right now?"

"What's the number?" she said again.

He gave her the number. Lia found the envelope. But before she could swap it with the replacement in the lining of the briefcase, a parade of workers entered with boxes. Two local government officials also came in, looking around. She nodded at them; they stared stone-faced but didn't ask any questions.

Lia positioned her backpack so that it hid what she was doing. She turned on the computer, pressing the buttons that controlled the sound to flip it to the highest setting. A loud *ba-leep* filled the room.

The men were stacking the tables near the door, not paying any attention to her. One of the officials began berating the men for not being gentle enough with the tables.

"They are not sacks of flour," complained the man in Spanish. "Be careful. This is the future of the country in your hands."

Lia slid her hand into the case, opening the panel in the lining. She looked across at the workers, who were now being instructed by a UN supervisor who wanted the machines stored closer to the back of the room. The men looked at him with dazed expressions—he wasn't explaining why, just telling them it had to be so.

Do it now, she told herself, and she pulled the envelope up into her hand, slipped it down behind the laptop, and reached toward the box.

As she did, Fernandez walked in through the door. She dropped the envelope on the top of the pile, leaving it there as he approached.

50

"Marie, you better look at this," Rockman told Telach, pointing to the monitor with the feed from the Peruvian television station.

As Telach came over, he jacked the volume so she could hear. A woman in fatigues—not an army uniform but undoubtedly chosen to suggest one—was interviewing a middle-aged man whose Spanish had a decidedly British accent. He was a reporter from the BBC, and he said that he had been with the army unit that made the incredible find in the guerrilla village after heavy fighting a few hours before.

"What incredible find?" asked Telach.

"Wait," said Rockman.

The screen flashed to a still photo of a crated cylinder in what looked like a room dug into the hillside.

"That's a missile warhead," Rockman told Telach. "Russian. We briefed on those eight months ago when we were looking at the Russian ABM system. They're calling it a bomb, but that's a nuke. I remember the assembly at the rear."

"Are you sure?"

"I just punched the image over to the weapons people, so we'll get something definitive, but yeah. I'm sure of it."

"In Peru?"

"This is a pre-broadcast feed. They're just uploading it. It'll go over the air in a second. I haven't had time to pin down the location, but it's up in the north, west of Iquitos. This is a BBC affiliate. The reporter's an English guy."

Telach leaned over and hit a preset that took the feed back to the image thirty seconds before, freezing it so she could look at the bomb.

"It's a warhead, but it doesn't go on a Gorgon," she said, referring to the Russian ABM system. "There would be a set of blisters on the right there."

"I swear I've seen it," said Rockman.

"I'll alert Mr. Rubens. How's Lia?"

"She decided to go ahead and make the switch herself," said Rockman, sitting back upright at his station. "Hang on. She's almost done."

Rubens grabbed the dedicated phone to the Art Room as soon as it began to ring.

"Rubens."

"Mr. Rubens, there's a report in Peru that the military has found a nuclear weapon in the northern jungles, apparently belonging to the rebels," said Marie Telach.

Rubens prided himself on remaining calm under any circumstance, but even he had to take a moment before he could respond.

"Get me the details," he told Telach. "I'm putting in a call to the White House right now."

51

"What are you doing?" Fernandez asked Lia. He had found another set of work lamps similar to those strung along the ceiling.

"I figured I could get going, get done, and get out of here," she said. She reached down and took the authentic envelope from under the replacement, slitting it open with her fingernail.

"Don't you want something to sit on?" he asked.

"That would be nice," said Lia.

"There are some chairs in the trucks. Do you have enough power in your battery?"

Lia remembered the excuse she had given him at the bank.

"For one or two tests, I can get away with it," she told him. "But if not, I think I can reach the overhead cords. That's OK, right?"

"Sure." He glanced to her right, looking at the box of cards. Then he went to get the chair.

Once he was gone, Lia finished switching the envelopes. After the original was sealed inside the briefcase, she took another envelope from the middle of the pile and slit it open to "test" the cards. The diagnostics were just starting when Fernandez returned.

Besides the chair, he had a bottle of water and two green leaves in his fingers.

"Chew these. They're coca leaves. The natives around here use them for energy. They carry them in little bags. I got a couple from one of the workers."

Dubious, Lia took one of the leaves and nibbled at the corner.

Fernandez laughed. "It won't make you a drug addict; don't worry."

"Maybe I'll try it later," she said, taking a sip of water.

52

Dean picked up the binoculars and scanned the road back toward La Oroya. A large four-door pickup was heading down the road in their direction; the rear bed was empty and it was likely that the truck was heading toward one of the mining operations farther south.

"The army?" asked Karr, settling down behind him.

"Nah. Just a truck."

"They go to all that trouble in the city, and here anybody could walk in and take the cards, take the machines, take everything," said Karr.

"Maybe the people are too honest to steal the election," said Dean.

Dean rubbed his hands together. The thin air was crisp; it was at least ten degrees cooler than it had been in the city.

"Lia's done. Switch is made," said Rockman over the communications system. "No trouble. She's coming out."

"Man, she has all the fun," said Karr.

"I told her you guys could handle it," said Rockman.

"Tommy's only kidding," said Dean.

He rose, turning his glasses in the direction of the building. He could see Lia walking out with Fernandez. The UN escort put his hand on her shoulder and Dean felt a pang of jealousy.

"Hey, that pickup's going up the road," said Karr. "Going over to the UN people."

Dean raised his glasses, watching. The lone policeman at the site spotted the truck and walked over to meet it.

Dean pulled up the A2 assault gun he'd slung over his shoulder. Specially designed for Desk Three, the A2 fired caseless bullets with almost no kick and with extreme accuracy, a sniper's dream. But the gun was meant for relatively short ranges; six hundred yards was nothing for a Remington, but it was at the tail end of the A2's reach.

Dean zeroed in on the policeman who was walking over. They'd looked him over thoroughly earlier; he was armed with an ancient revolver and had been drinking most of the morning.

One shot, he'd be dead. Lia would be on her own.

He'd put a string of bullets across the windshield of the truck. That would give Lia enough time to find cover.

"There's a truck," he heard Karr telling Rockman in the background. "We're not sure what's going on. Tell Lia to watch it. Charlie's got 'em."

Did he?

Absolutely.

The door to the cab opened. Dean felt his heart leap. But the man who got out didn't have a weapon; he walked to the back of the truck and relieved himself while the other man spoke to the cop.

Karr started hee-hawing.

Dean kept his weapon aimed at the truck. The Land Rover with Lia made a U-turn and drove away. Dean waited until they were back on the highway to put his weapon down.

"Lia's done. They're going back to the village to get some dinner," said Rockman.

"About time," said Karr. "I want a beer."

"No time for that. See if you can get over to the airfield."

"I thought we weren't leaving until tomorrow morning," said Karr.

"There's been a change in plans. We'll give you a full brief when you get to the airfield."

"What about backing up Lia?" said Dean.

"She can take care of herself."

"Wait a second—"

"She's fine, Charlie," said Telach, breaking in. "Please just make your way to the airfield as soon as possible."

53

Stephan Babin laughed when he heard the news report. Túcume had added a delicious twist to his plan: not only had the army discovered that the terrorists possessed a nuclear weapon, but documents indicated that they had been in contact with the campaign director for Victor Imberbe—Victor Imbecile, as the general called him.

All across the country, people would be scampering through their garbage to find the government's printed guides to the election. Vice President Ramon Ortez was unacceptable because he couldn't protect Lima and had told the police to fire into a crowd of protestors. Imberbe was a terrorist.

Who could they turn to? Túcume's chosen puppet, Hernando Aznar, of the Party of the Future.

Túcume had told Babin that Aznar would do much better than the polls showed, because he had strong support among the natives, who were rarely polled. Yesterday he had been within eight points of Imberbe officially; by the general's rough estimate, this meant he was actually within four of the leader. By tomorrow morning, even the polls would show Aznar ahead.

Babin's own plan was proceeding as well. The real warhead—*his* warhead—was aboard a ship that had left a few hours ago from Chimbote on the coast. Babin would meet the ship in Mexico. Then he would take the warhead on its final journey.

His satellite phone rang. Worried that the man who was to pick him up in the morning had been delayed, Babin answered quickly—and found himself talking to the general, not the soldier he had bribed to take him to the coast.

"Stephan, have you been listening to the news?" asked Túcume.

"Of course. Congratulations."

"I owe you a great deal, my friend. After the election, you will have a villa, and a driver, and perhaps a girl or two to keep you company."

"I'm touched," said Babin.

"A driver is on his way. He'll take you to the helicopter— we have a suite for you in Lima. No more exile. And I've arranged for new doctors. We are grateful people, Stephan."

Babin didn't know what to say.

"There were rebels in the area, and they struck just at the right time," continued Túcume. "My ancestors protected me—I have never felt so optimistic. And you are the cause."

"Perhaps I should stay here until after the election," said Babin. "I don't want the Americans putting two and two together."

"Don't worry about them," said the general. "You'll be safe with me in Lima."

Babin had not foreseen this. Refusing the ride, that wasn't an option; he couldn't afford to do anything that would make the general suspicious. Shooting the driver or hiding—once Túcume realized something was wrong, Babin would have a difficult time escaping.

If he went to Lima, could he escape from there? Could he get to Ecuador and then Mexico, where the cargo container would land?

There was some leeway, but . . .

"Stephan, are you there?"

Babin heard a vehicle approaching. "I'm here, General."

"My aide will take care of you. He should be there any minute."

"I hear him."

"Excellent. I'll see you when I get to Lima."

"Godspeed," said Babin. "Godspeed."

54

Rubens swiveled in his desk chair, listening as Jackson detailed what he had discovered over the course of the last two days. When he had asked to speak to Rubens, the weapon had not been discovered. Now the images from Peru seemed a graphic verification of Jackson's work, though he apparently had not been told about them yet. Rubens listened to the ambassador, trying not to interrupt or prejudice him; he wanted as much raw information as possible before saying anything that might influence the researcher's opinion or presentation of the facts.

"The arms dealer worked in Russia and the Middle East, traveling back and forth," Jackson told him. "He must have been planted or cultivated around the time of Bosnia, because there are no references to him earlier than that. There are two different possibilities for the program that he was part of, but wherever he started, he quickly became more important. There's a reference to someone working with the CIA in Moscow in 1999. They used the code word Sholk or 'silk' in Russian, which is from 'шёлк.'" Jackson spelled the Cyrillic letters out. "I'm not very good with Cyrillic letters."

"That's quite all right."

"You see, the Cyrillic is important, because they use that for an operative in Syria the next year," explained Jackson. "And it's in several intercepts a few months before Iron Heart begins—the Russians may have been on to him by then."

"You don't think that's a coincidence?"

"Unlikely, given the way they were assigning identities at the time. But possible. Notice the parallels—again in Afghanistan after the American action there, and then in Moscow."

Jackson had unearthed a number of communications and vouchers for money, tracing through four different projects. While only the CIA officer who had "run" Sholk would know for sure, Sholk was most likely the asset who had gotten involved when Brazil tried to buy nuclear warheads from the renegade Russian in Iron Heart.

NSA intercepts of e-mails showed that a Russian arms dealer had supplied weapons to Middle Eastern terrorists after several meetings in Beirut. Sholk was in Beirut the same time as at least two of the sales.

He was clearly the same person. Which meant that the CIA had had a man who gave weapons to terrorists on its payroll.

And then they'd brought him into Iron Heart. He helped make the deal—and mysteriously died in a plane crash when it was done.

A very convenient plane crash. Though Jackson didn't say it, Rubens thought it very possible that by then Sholk had become a liability. Destroying his plane with a shoulder-launched missile or a bomb would have been child's play.

But Sholk's background wasn't the most interesting thing Jackson had discovered.

"There were three warheads discussed in one of the original communications from Brazil. 'Three bags of bread' were the words they used." The ambassador passed a yellow sheet of paper across the conference table to Rubens—the original decrypted translation of a communication sent to Russia that the NSA had intercepted, the message that had probably gotten Iron Heart started in the first place.

"And then there's this photo," said Jackson, laying the paper onto Rubens' desk. "This was of the shipping point, the evening right before the raid."

The paper was a print of a satellite photo taken by a KH-11A spy satellite. The warheads were small rectangular boxes in the lower right-hand corner of the photo, identified by a photo interpreter at the time as the payload of SA-10 "Grumble" missiles. Roughly five feet long and about three feet across, they looked like ordinary crates; the interpreter relied on information about packaging and other data to classify them.

"This is why the search in Peru was so extensive after the plane went down," said Jackson. "They had the warhead on the ground already. They got to the plane and for some reason worried that there was another one. They followed the exact same procedure they would if an American plane had gone down with a bomb. But they never mention it in the report."

"Because they didn't find anything," said Rubens.

"Probably. They might have seen something as simple as a flight plan suggesting another stop, or some document, or even an extra set of tiedowns and decided to investigate. They didn't find Sholk, either." Jackson pointed to one of the printouts. "You can see the report of the helicopter crew that took the bodies out—there are only two bodies, and they're identified as the pilot and first officer of the airplane that crashed."

"Perhaps his body was so incinerated they never found it."

"Maybe. But there's a long ground search near the plane and nothing is recorded as being found. They don't mention that his corpse was identified. There's no call for records that I can see."

"The CIA officer in charge of the mission would have known him by sight."

"Notice that he never specifically mentions in the report that the unnamed asset—Sholk—died."

Rubens got up from his seat and began pacing around the room. How much of this did Collins know? Rubens wondered.

Probably everything.

"I don't want to mislead you," continued Jackson. "There are many references to two warheads in the material. Both of those were accounted for."

"Three hours ago, a Peruvian army unit made a raid on a guerrilla hideout on the border of the Amazonian area of the country," Rubens told Jackson. "Not terribly far from Ecuador. They found something they believe is a nuclear bomb. They also found a truck and maps for Lima, along with some other documents."

"This bomb?"

"Obviously that's the question we'll have to try to answer. I have some people on the way there to make sure it is a nuclear warhead. It seems rather . . . interesting."

"Yes," said Jackson.

"I'd like to know the identity of the arms dealer, Sholk," said Rubens. "Can you figure it out?"

"Maybe. But it won't be easy," said Jackson. "Wouldn't it be much easier to ask the CIA?"

Rubens leaned against his bookcase without answering.

"You don't think they'll tell you," said Jackson. "And you don't trust them to tell you the truth."

Rubens pressed his lips together. "There is that."

"If he's dead . . ."

"Ordinarily that would make no difference. In this case, we could follow the procedure to get his name. We will follow that procedure. But I'd like you to undertake it as well."

Jackson nodded. In truth, the CIA did not appear to warrant any trust in this case.

"I'll look into it right away," he told Rubens. "May I make a suggestion?"

"Please."

"I wouldn't let that weapon stay in anyone's hands. It's too tempting."

"I quite agree."

As soon as Jackson had gone, Rubens picked up the phone to call Hadash. It was an ingrained reflex—he had always shared important intelligence, even hunches, with the national security adviser. If Jackson's theory was correct—if this was a warhead involved in Iron Heart—the implications were immense.

But in the few brief seconds it took for the call to go through and the national security adviser to come on the line, Rubens reconsidered. It wasn't that he doubted the evidence Jackson had just shown him; on the contrary. But he was unsure now of Hadash's standing in the government—and his attitude toward him. Maybe he couldn't depend on his former teacher for advice. Maybe telling Hadash was the worst thing to do.

"Bill? What's the latest on Peru?" asked Hadash when he came on the line.

"I have people en route to verify the find," he told Hadash. "I understand the president and the secretary of state have been talking with the Peruvian government. They seem to have very little information. Otherwise, nothing has changed in the last hour since our conference call with the secretary of defense. I did see a note just a short while ago that the aircraft carrier *Reagan* and her escorts have been ordered to sail for Lima. They're three days away."

Hadash grunted.

"I'm drawing up a plan to take custody of the weapon, drawing on resources we have in the area for the existing mission," continued Rubens. "It can be put into motion as soon as the president gives the word."

"The president has not made that decision yet. It's not a foregone conclusion that he will."

"I understand."

"We need to know definitively whether that is a warhead or not," said Hadash. "We need precise data on it, an absolute location, information about the unit that found it—"

"We'll have all the information within hours."

Should he tell Hadash about the connection with Iron Heart? It was best to wait. Dean and Karr would be there soon; at that point, he'd know for sure.

"Did you read the draft of the president's statement?" said Hadash.

"Yes."

Marcke was due to go on national television at 9:00 p.m. eastern time, announcing the discovery and saying that he had asked Peru to turn the weapon over to the International Atomic Energy Agency for dismantling. He was also going to reiterate what had been American policy since John F. Kennedy confronted Khrushchev during the Cuban Missile Crisis: no nuclear weapons would be allowed in the Western Hemisphere.

What else he would say depended in large part on what the Peruvians said to him.

"Was there something else, Bill?" asked Hadash.

"Why didn't you tell me you were thinking of resigning?" blurted Rubens.

Hadash didn't answer. It had come out unbidden, but now that it had, Rubens told his old friend what he truly felt.

"I think, considering how long we've known each other, you might have mentioned it," he told Hadash.

"I really can't discuss it at the moment," said Hadash. "I'm sure you understand."

No, I don't, thought Rubens. But instead of saying that, he simply hung up.

55

Dean and Karr were supposed to meet the airplane in a small field about five miles north of the city, but when they got there the field was empty. It bore only the vaguest resemblance to an airstrip, and if it hadn't been for the GPS coordinates, Dean would have continued on. He turned the car off the road and immediately sank into the soft turf. Dubious, he shut off the engine and got out. Karr had already leapt from his seat and was wading into knee-deep grass.

"The field is mud," said Dean. "How's a plane going to land here?"

"Maybe he's just going to slow down so we can jump aboard," said Karr.

Dean went to the trunk and got their bags. He opened them and started rearranging things, making sure the most important items—like extra bullets—were in a single bag, just in case they had to leave extra weight behind. It reminded Dean of his early days on patrol. Many Marines had realized that luxuries like clean underwear weren't worth displacing necessities like ammunition. He made those same choices now, unsure of what they were facing.

The A2 rifle was packed in a small box of its own. Both men carried two pistols, one under each arm in shoulder holster. Besides being easier to conceal under a bulky jacket, the shoulder holsters made it easier to retrieve the gun, especially when you were sitting in a car. Dean checked his pistols—both Glocks, solid and dependable 9mm handguns—then filled his pockets with as many extra magazines as he could stuff in.

"It's only wet by the road, Charlie," yelled Tommy. "There's a macadam strip under this dust. Check it out."

As Dean started toward him, an airplane turned hard around the nearby mountain. It came down so fast it looked almost out of control, more plummeting rock than glider. A small, high-winged plane with a boom tail, one engine at the nose and another at the rear of the cockpit behind the boom, the plane made almost no noise as it landed, bumping along the short field for only a hundred yards before slowing and starting to turn.

The aircraft's basic shape reminded Dean of spotter airplanes he had seen long ago in Vietnam—Air Force close-air-support planes built by Cessna and officially known as 0-2As. This plane was painted green, the shade so dark it looked almost black. It rode across the field on tricycle landing gear with thick shock absorbers and tall wheels that were mounted four across at the axle.

Dean and Karr ran for their gear while the airplane turned and taxied back toward the end of the runway where it had landed. By the time they caught up to it the front prop had feathered to a halt. The hatch at the side of the cockpit popped open and a short bearded man wearing a baseball cap and a monstrous frown emerged from the craft.

"Fashone!" yelled Karr. "You? What are you doing here?"

"Suck it, Karr," replied the pilot. He jumped down, kicked at the surface of the field, and shook his head. "This is an improved airstrip, huh? Rockman wouldn't know dirt from concrete if he ate it."

"Hey, that's no way to say hello," shouted Karr. "Long time no see." He gave Fashona a shoulder chuck that nearly sent the lightly built pilot tumbling to the ground. "What's happenin', my friend?"

"Usual BS," grumbled Fashona. He went to the belly of the short fuselage and opened the hatch on a cargo bay.

"Hey, Ray," said Dean. "How are you?"

"I'm all right, Charlie. How about yourself?"

"Pretty good. Lia told me how you saved her in Korea."

Fashona's face turned red. "I didn't save her, man. I just got a plane to where she was. That's all I did. How is she?"

"Holding up."

"Yeah, she's tough. That's good. Give me your bags. They have to be tied down in the back."

"What kind of airplane is this, Fashone?" said Karr.

"Knock off the Fashone crap."

"It's pretty quiet," said Dean. He'd met Fashona on his very first mission in, as one NSA briefer had put it, the good part of Siberia. Fashona was a contract pilot for the NSA who could handle everything from helicopters to airliners. He tended to be moody, and Karr always seemed to rub him the wrong way, even though the two men had worked together for a long time.

"The plane is pretty quiet," Fashona told Dean. "These engines were specially built. But I have to tell you, they would not be my first choice. They're more temperamental than my first girlfriend. They got borderline personality disorder. For real."

Dean gave Fashona his bag. The pilot stood five-four or five-five and had to lift the bag up against his shoulder to slide it into the bay because the special gear on the aircraft lifted it so high off the ground.

"Spooks built this plane ten years ago," said Fashona. "Typical CIA project—you can land the thing in mud just about with these wheels, no one can hear you coming until you're two feet away, and there's no stinking heat in the cockpit."

"So, really, Fashone. What are you doing here?" said Karr.

"Knock off the Fashone crap. It's Fashona. Uh. *Uh.*"

"What are you doing here, Ray?"

"I'm on vacation. You brought fuel?"

"We have gasoline in the car," said Karr.

"Oh, that'll work great in a turboprop." Fashona slapped down the cargo hatch. "Rockman said you might have fuel. Of course, he also claimed this was a decent airstrip."

"Didn't tell us about it," said Karr.

"Just as well. Probably be too heavy to take off. You put on a few pounds, Tommy."

"Get out. You think?"

"You oughta work out like Dean."

Karr laughed. "I will when I'm his age."

"Your parachutes are inside." Fashona pulled open the cockpit door. "You better get it on before we take off. Fat boy in back, Karr. Sit in the middle of the plane. We have to worry about weight distribution."

"It's that razor wit that sets you apart, Fashone. That's why we love you."

"Wait," said Dean as Fashona started to climb into the plane. "We're jumping?"

"Hey, we'll have chutes," said Karr.

"Rockman didn't tell you?"

"No. He's supposed to brief us once we're airborne. They're still pulling information together."

"Ah. You've jumped before, Charlie, right?" said Karr.

"Yeah." Dean had jumped before, several times—and liked it about as much as putting his finger in a light socket. The last time he had parachuted had been into a desert—and even with all that sand to land on, he'd nearly busted both legs.

"You're worried because it will be a night jump?" asked Fashona.

"No." That was an honest answer—Dean hated jumping in daytime, too.

"Hey, if you're worried, Charlie, we can always do a tandem," said Karr. "I'll just strap you onto my belly and away we go. No sweat."

"Thanks," said Dean. "I'll manage somehow."

56

La Oroya was about 112 miles east of Lima, but the real distance was measured vertically: the city sat in the mountains at 12,385 feet. The thin air took some getting used to. Lia felt light-headed, and her lungs seemed to scrape against her ribs for more air. Maybe she should have taken the *coca* leaves, she thought.

A group of small boys gathered around their SUV when Lia and Fernandez stopped for dinner. The kids clamored for money, blocking their way with outstretched hands and plaintive faces. When Fernandez told them there would be none, they responded by cursing him.

"Tourists have polluted their minds," he said after he and Lia had pushed their way through and gone inside the restaurant. "They think they're entitled to handouts."

"Is this a big tourist town?"

"No, but tourists come through. It's like a disease, the mentality. It's really twisted. You saw."

Lia tried a soup that included quinoa, a grain grown in the Andes. The vegetable base had a pumpkinlike flavor, and the grain filled her up. When they got outside, it had turned cold, and Lia pulled her jacket tight around her as they drove to the Hotel Meiggs, a small building about a quarter of a mile from the center of town. La Oroya did not have the array of first-class international hotels Lima featured; Hotel Meiggs was considered one of the town's fancier establishments.

The hotel had been named for Henry Meiggs, the American industrialist who had brought railroads to the Andes in the nineteenth century.

Lia thought the building and most of its dirt had probably greeted Meiggs when he surveyed the area. Her room was a dingy affair with a bed piled high with blankets—necessary, because she could see her breath in the frigid air.

Fernandez suggested that they share a drink in the café across the street. The café had American beer as well as some local concoctions. Lia ordered a Budweiser; Fernandez had an *aguardiente,* an herbal rum that smelled like an oregano liqueur.

A TV was on in the corner of the room. The regular programming had been preempted by reports on the discovery of an "apparent nuclear weapon" in the possession of the rebels far to the north. The skimpy footage of the find was played several times before the screen switched back to a pair of talking heads who speculated on exactly what the country's president would say in his speech that evening at nine o'clock.

The Art Room had already filled Lia in, but Fernandez was hearing this for the first time. He stared at the screen in disbelief.

"It must be a hoax," he said. "The rebels would never be able to get a bomb. Never."

"They have photos," said Lia. "Didn't you just see? And they're working with one of the candidates."

Fernandez stared at the TV, finally absorbed in something other than himself.

"They backed Imberbe? Impossible," he said. "I can't believe he would work with them. Never."

"Will that have an impact on the election?"

Fernandez shrugged. A new set of talking heads came on, noting the gravity of the situation. A spokesman for Imberbe was interviewed saying that the candidate denounced the rebel movement; he was immediately followed by a statement by a longtime political correspondent who said Imberbe could not be believed.

Lia sipped her beer slowly as she watched the program. The show was entertaining in a bizarre way, as guest after guest speculated endlessly on something they knew almost nothing about. The medium is the same the world over, Lia decided.

Fernandez ordered another drink and then a third. Unprompted, he began telling Lia his life story, which amounted to an epic struggle against academic demons as he went to five different schools before earning a master's degree in international law. Fernandez seemed to feel that he had struggled mightily in his years as a student, which made him appreciate the realities of poverty and hardship even though his family regularly sent him checks from Madrid.

Lia nodded every so often, one eye on the TV. Finally, bored and tired, she got up to go. Fernandez accompanied her shakily back to the hotel; as they walked up the stairs to their rooms she wasn't sure whether he would get sick or make a pass at her when they reached their floor.

He did neither, which was something of a relief as she eased into her room.

The door had no lock. Lia pushed the bureau in front of it; the bureau was too light to keep anyone from entering, but it would at least slow them down. Though it seemed ludicrous, she took out her PDA and scanned the room for bugs. When she saw it was clean, she checked in with the Art Room.

"Same old, same old on your end," said Rockman, telling her nothing was new. Dean and Karr were on their way to check out the warhead; she was to proceed as planned.

Kicking off her shoes, Lia climbed under the covers still fully dressed. She'd no sooner shut her eyes than she heard a scratching sound. Jerking up in bed, Lia pulled out the pistol she had left under the covers next to her. Her first thought was that Fernandez was scraping at the door in some sort of drunken plea, but she quickly realized that the sound was coming from above her.

Lia took her gun and got out of bed. She reached into her pocket and took out her small penlight, shining it around the ceiling. There were several patches where the plaster had fallen out, exposing the lath.

As she shone her light upward, the sound turned into a scampering drumbeat, then stopped. Lia climbed up onto the bed and shone the light into one of the lath-filled holes. The light made shadows through the blackness, but it was impossible to see beyond them.

She flicked off the light for a moment. The scratching resumed. When she flicked it back on, a pair of red beads glowed down at her from above.

The ceiling space was filled with rats.

"Oh, just peachy," Lia said to herself, shivering involuntarily as she climbed back beneath the covers.

57

When he was a corporal, Charlie Dean had learned to parachute on the advice of a top sergeant, who said the skill
would help him advance. The sergeant, a short, ugly man
with a large heart and a very soft voice, was the smartest
noncom Dean had ever had, and so he followed the advice
even though he knew he would hate every minute of it. For a
man who had served as a sniper in the waning days of the
Vietnam War and witnessed the evacuation of Saigon, the
training could not be honestly described as difficult duty. But
Dean would have gladly swapped his weeks there for a year
anywhere else, including Vietnam.

His three night training jumps—all successful, all utterly
routine, all scary as all get-out—came back to him as he
waited for Fashona's signal to go. The aircraft had a specially rigged door on the right side that allowed it to slide out
of the way, making egress easier for parachutists. Wind kicked
through the cockpit like a hurricane, and Fashona groused
about how hard it was to keep the plane on its circular course
over the patio-sized field they had targeted for the drop.
All three men had donned oxygen masks because of the
thin air.

The area they were jumping into sat in the foothills between the Andes and the thickest parts of the tropical forest.
Not as wet as the jungle to the east, nor as high as the peaks

to the west, it mixed qualities of both—wide rivers divided green valleys; dusty plateaus were shaded by craggy rocks. Their targeted landing zone was a grassy field a mile and a half from a river; bounded on one side by a sharp drop and on the other by a dozen or so trees, they had about two and a half acres of clear landing zone.

It might just as well have been a square foot as far as Dean was concerned, looking out at the darkness.

"Five seconds," said Fashona.

Karr stood next to a large equipment pack that contained most of their gear as well as an inflatable boat. Rather than using a static line to open the parachute, an altimeter trigger would open the chute at nine thousand feet above sea level, which was fifteen hundred feet above the ground, if, of course, the altimeter setting they had chosen was somewhere close to the true barometric pressure. The nylon canopy was designed so that the gear would fall in as straight a line as possible; Fashona had to fly the plane along a very precise line and the gear had to be ejected at the right moment for it to hit the landing zone.

Dean couldn't recall the name of the top sergeant who had told him to learn to jump—Jones or Jacobs—but heard his voice in his head as if he were right behind him.

Well-rounded Marine is a good Marine. The way of the future, kid. Educate yourself.

What did jumping out of an airplane have to do with *education,* anyway?

"Now," said Fashona.

Karr pushed the pack out. Dean leaned forward, hands still gripping the sides of the doorway.

"Geronimo!" yelled Karr, pulling Dean from the plane with him.

Caught off-balance, Dean's left arm was grabbed and twisted by the wind. He focused on bringing it back, pushing his body into a flying wedge. The specially programmed goggles they were using worked with global positioning satellites as well as an altimeter reading to present visual cues as the parachutist fell. While the goggles weighed almost seven pounds, the weight was worth it—a green arrow appeared before him, telling him he was perfectly on course.

Good thing, thought Dean. At least if I splat I'll do it in the right place.

58

Robert Gallo got up from his workstation in the Desk Three subbasement and began walking around the NSA computer lab. His eyes had started to water and blur from staring at the LCD computer screens. He'd run out of eyedrops earlier and struggled not to rub them—he knew from experience that would only make them worse. He had another bottle of the drops in the lounge, but that was a staircase and a security checkpoint away. Better to tough it out for a bit, if possible.

But not to itch! Gallo lay down in the middle of the floor and shut his eyes. The tears had just stopped streaming out when he heard someone come into the room.

"Ah," said Johnny Bib above him. "There you are."

"Hey," said Gallo. "Did Angie find the source of the guerrillas' communiqué?"

"No," said Johnny Bib.

"They must not have used a landline to transmit the message. Otherwise Shark Siphon would have found it already, right?"

"Maybe yes, maybe no," said Johnny.

Shark Siphon was an automated program that snagged communications on the Internet. It had taken all of the communications from Peru over the past twenty-four hours, examining them as possible sources of the communiqué by applying a variety of decrypting techniques. Unlike the smart viruses and worms that Gallo specialized in, it was a brute-force tool, made possible only by the agency's massive computer capacity.

"Another possibility is Peru's cell phone network," said Johnny Bib.

Gallo sat up, eyes still closed. "We could hit the wireless companies' databases, look for some transmission that would be long enough to send the message. I bet we could narrow it down to maybe a hundred phones or so. Even a thousand— we could check the names on the list against Peruvian intelligence files."

"Yes," said Johnny Bib in the singsongy way he used when someone had shared a good idea with him. "Ye-es. Very good thinking."

"Want me to get in?"

"Ye-es. Ye-es."

"On it." Gallo opened his eyes gingerly. They felt a little better; once he launched the attack on the cell phone network, he'd run up and put the drops in.

"Are you having a vision?" asked Johnny Bib as he got up.

"Huh?"

"You were on the floor."

"Oh." Gallo laughed sheepishly. "My eyes just got teary with the screen."

"Too bad," said his supervisor, leaving the lab.

59

The green arrow in Dean's goggles began to blink, indicating that he had three seconds before pulling the rip cord. He reached his hand to the ring, waiting. As the arrowhead changed to a plus sign and a tone sounded in his helmet's headset, Dean pulled.

It was a good, solid tug, exactly as he had been taught as a Marine Corps "guest" at the Army's Fort Benning airborne training center nearly three decades before. The parachute jerked him against his restraints—a very welcome jerk, given the alternative—and he reached for the control toggles. The green arrow was solid again and stayed there the whole way down, showing he was right on course.

Even so, his anxiety and adrenaline continued to build. Dean did everything right, braking the chute on cue and even managing to flex his legs as he hit the ground. But he tumbled over like a sack of potatoes and found he was hyperventilating so badly he had to rest a moment before getting up.

"Hey, Charlie, right on target," yelled Karr, landing a few yards away. "Our gear and the boat are back about a quarter mile. Just missed landing in one of those funny-looking trees."

Dean's legs were so unsteady he thought he was going to collapse as he undid his harness.

"Hey, you OK?" said Karr, giving him a hand.

"I've been better."

"Aw, come on. Don't tell me it wasn't fun."

"Barrels," said Dean. "I wish I could do it every damn day."

The river was a half mile from where they landed. The large pack of equipment contained a small raft that inflated in a few seconds once Dean twisted the plastic lock on the air canister. As Dean loaded the backpacks into the raft, Karr assembled a small electric outboard motor. It looked like it had come from an oversize kids' Erector set. The sturdiest part was the battery, which was about the size of a dictionary. But it proved not only quiet but relatively powerful, propelling them upriver against the current at about seven knots.

The village where the warhead had been found lay three and a half miles upriver, perched on the side of a cliff about two hundred feet above the water. Dean and Karr planned to stop at a bend about a half mile south of the village, hide their boat, and then sneak through the jungle. They had to get close enough to the warhead to get good pictures of it, take readings with a radiation meter Fashona had given them, and if at all possible plant a tracking device on the bomb or its transport.

Dean sat in the front of the boat, working as lookout as they made their way upriver. He tried warding off the memories of Vietnam, but they marshaled among the shadows along the riverbanks. He'd worked in terrain somewhat similar to this when he got the North Vietnamese sniper they called Fu Manchu. That had been in the highlands, too; drier on the whole, but there'd been a stream there as well.

As much as he tried to focus on the present dangers, the past ones clawed their way into his consciousness.

Fu Manchu had been hitting a South Vietnamese army outpost southeast of the demilitarized zone. The South Vietnamese were supposed to be interdicting the stream of North Vietnamese supplies, weapons, and men south, but what they were mostly doing was hunkering in an abandoned American bunker and trying to stay alive.

The ones who hadn't deserted, that is.

A Marine unit was sent to stiffen their resolve. After they set up a post on the military crest of the hill near their ally's bunker, the North Vietnamese sniper began taking shots at them as well. Dean and another Marine sniper called Turk ended up going after the man, volunteering one muggy afternoon and ending up on a cat-and-mouse chase that stretched nearly five days.

It was difficult to say who was the cat and who was the mouse. Turk was a gunnery sergeant, a veteran of two tours as a sniper in Vietnam, and as wily a hunter as Dean had ever met. Dean had only been in country a month and, though he'd seen quite a bit of action, was a novice at the trade.

Fu Manchu—Turk gave him the name for no particular reason—slipped through the jungles on both sides of a five-meter-wide stream so smoothly and silently that for much of the time they weren't sure whether he was one person or three. They eventually discovered that he had several hides, where he prepositioned weapons and ammunition.

Something splashed in the water ahead. Dean jumped back to the present, raising not a sniper's gun but the A2.

"Something?" whispered Karr.

Dean stared at the riverbank through his lightweight night goggles. A medium-sized cat hunkered down a few dozen yards away, eyes fixed on the strange craft as it sailed past them.

"Jaguar," Dean said.

"I thought jaguars were extinct."

"Then it's a ghost," said Dean.

Karr's chuckle cracked the stillness.

They made landfall and stowed the boat under some foliage. A collection of small satellite-launched audio bugs had been dropped on the village, allowing the Art Room to scout the general layout of the troops there. Their runner, Sandy Chafetz, wanted Karr and Dean to launch a small unmanned aerial vehicle, or UAV, nicknamed a crow, so they'd have real-time visuals of the village. (It was called a crow because it was about the size of a large bird and looked like one, at least from afar and at night.)

"Not worth it with this foliage," said Karr. "We won't be able to see much, and it'll be tough to recover. I think we just slide in and out. Plenty of gaps."

"Your call," said Chafetz.

"Thanks, sweets," said Karr.

As they pulled on their rucksacks, Dean thought of the strange pack Turk had used in 'Nam. Taken from a North Vietnamese sapper, it was a big, sturdy bag with handy pockets and pouches. Turk had found a rigger or someone who could sew and added a few more of his own. At the time the Army was using very basic packs, and everyone who saw it was envious.

Fu Manchu had sent one of his bullets through the side of the pack. It was the sniper's other bullet that had taken Turk, drilling through his temple.

Dean's thought when he heard the second shot was that their quarry had failed—a second shot meant you had missed the first time.

And more important in this case, the second shot showed Dean where Fu Manchu was. He put his bullet there.

It took him several hours to get to the sniper's body. Fu Manchu had crumpled into a pile of bones. He was so skinny he looked as if his flesh were made of paper.

He was a kid, younger even than Dean, who'd gotten into the Marine Corps the year before at sixteen, fudging on his age.

"Sentry, fifty yards," said Karr, pointing to the left. He took point, moving through the trees toward the low-slung huts ahead. For a big man—and Karr was *very* big—he moved extremely quietly. He would have been a good sniper.

The village consisted of six small huts scattered around a clearing near the water. The woods on the south side were so thick that even with infrared night glasses, Dean and Karr had trouble seeing more than a few feet ahead. That helped them more than hindered them; the soldiers in the village had no night-vision gear at all.

Several vehicles were parked at the edge of the clearing and on the rough trail of a road, which snaked off to the west. Two men walked back and forth in the center of the compound.

Dean and Karr observed the area carefully, comparing what the Art Room had told them with what they saw, making sure they knew where everyone was. Knots of soldiers were strung out along the roadway and shoreline, but they were all far enough away that they could be ignored. Several soldiers were sleeping in the huts; they, too, wouldn't be a problem—as long as they remained sleeping.

The target was a large military truck parked behind an SUV on the dirt road that ran in front of the huts. Dean counted seven soldiers, each about thirty feet from the truck, strung out in a loose circle around it. When they were sure they knew where everyone was, Dean and Karr backtracked ten yards into the jungle, circling to the east, where the brush and the alignment of the guards left a narrow lane they could use to get close to the truck without being seen. The night was almost pitch-black, but they couldn't entirely count on the darkness to hide them; at least one of the guards had a flashlight on his belt, and Dean suspected flares would be kept nearby.

When they were five yards from the road and about a dozen from the truck, Karr pulled off his pack, dropped it to the ground, and handed Dean his rifle. Then he removed a small device about the size of a TV remote control. This was a radiation detector "tuned" to find specific isotopes of plutonium—the common warhead material for Russian missiles—and a uranium by-product that often accompanied the material.

Just in case there was any shielding, Karr carried a device that would look for extremely dense material by sending X-rays through it. Nicknamed "the interrogator," it was about the size and shape of two fat coffee thermoses put back-to-back together. The interrogator had two modes, one for simply detecting large mass elements and the other for estimating their size. The X-rays were extremely powerful; the beam could burn flesh and cause radiation damage if you stood too close.

"Give me a whistle if anybody's coming," said Karr, and before Dean could say anything he began gliding toward the vehicle.

Just like Dean had done with Turk on the third day they were out.

"You got more guts than noodles," the old-timer had told him. "Before we go anywhere we fully reconnoiter the situation, figure our in and our out, get our signals straight—then we go."

The old-timer was right; acting impulsively was a good way to get killed.

Old-timer?

Turk was, in a sense, but he'd probably been in his early thirties at most. Maybe less. Certainly younger than Dean was now.

Unlike Rockman, Chafetz said almost nothing while the ops were in the middle of a mission. Karr transmitted the readings back through a link in the com system; she acknowledged with a simple "got it" as each one came through.

Dean saw something moving near the back of the truck. He raised his gun, then realized it was Karr, already on his way back.

"Fake. It's a fake," whispered the op. "The readings are all wrong."

"I didn't hear the Art Room say that."

"They will. It's a phony."

"You sure?"

"I had a mission just like this in Russia six months before you joined us, babysitter," said Karr, resurrecting the very first nickname he had given Dean. "Cruise missiles. Pretty much the same gig, though. Come on. Let's blow."

60

Rubens picked up the phone to call the White House as soon as he heard from Telach.

Peru's president had pledged a few hours before to cooperate with "the U.S. and the entire world" in securing the weapon, so Rubens' plan to retrieve the warhead would probably not have gone forward. But the readings Karr and Dean had obtained ended all possibility.

Still, the information that the warhead was phony would be welcome at the White House, enhancing Rubens' reputation there.

Not that he needed to do that. Not that it was or should be or could be a consideration now.

If this "weapon" had been involved in Iron Heart, Rubens realized, the fact that it had been fake explained why the CIA had missed it in the jungle. Indeed, it was possible that the agency had known all along that it was a phony and not been worried about it.

No. If they had, they wouldn't have launched the massive search.

Perhaps it *was* genuine at one point and material was removed. If so, it could still be hidden somewhere in the jungle.

More likely sold on the black market. But such a sale would have been discovered, Rubens thought, by any of the half-dozen standing missions assigned specifically to watch for them, including the NSA's.

He'd have them quickly reviewed for gaps.

Rubens took a deep breath as the phone was picked up on the other end.

"Bill Rubens for the president."

"Go ahead," said Marcke, coming on the line immediately.

"The warhead does not contain plutonium or uranium," said Rubens. "We have high confidence on this. It's a fake."

"You're sure?"

"Yes, sir, I'm sure. One of my people crawled under the truck with the bomb in it. We have X-rays of the weapon; it does not contain nuclear material."

"Very good. Very, very good." Rubens could practically feel the relief in the president's voice.

"There was one other thing, Mr. President," said Rubens. "The warhead bears a very close resemblance to warheads Brazil tried to obtain several years before. The CIA had an operation to stop it. One of the warheads was seized in Russia. Another was snatched on the ground. However, there was a possibility at the time of a third warhead."

"A third warhead?"

"Yes, sir."

"Are you saying that the CIA missed one, Billy? This one?"

"I'm not really in a position to say. The operation was a CIA operation. I would think that it's possible that this dummy warhead was somehow involved. I should note that it's possible that this may have been a legitimate warhead at one point, but the material, the bomb kernel, was removed. Honestly—candidly—I simply don't know."

I suspect a great deal, Rubens thought to himself. I suspect that the CIA messed up in a very big way and then *covered up* that possibility. They also covered up the fact that they had bankrolled an arms dealer responsible, indirectly, for the deaths of dozens of civilians around the world, including several Americans. And then assassinated him.

But it was best to hold his criticism of the CIA, until the immediate crisis in Peru passed. Especially under the circumstances.

"We're talking about Iron Heart?" asked Marcke.

"Yes," said Rubens, surprised that the president knew of the operation.

"Ms. Collins informed me that there were questions about it earlier this evening," Marcke said.

Rubens balled his fingers into a fist. She'd gone to the president ahead of him with the information to make herself look good. She had outmaneuvered him at every turn.

"Please keep me updated if anything else develops," said the president. "We'll have a conference call update tomorrow at six. I guess that's today at six now, actually."

"Yes, sir."

"Ted will let you know if there's anything else."

Ted was Ted Cohen, who'd replaced Art Blanders as chief of staff when Blanders became secretary of defense the year before.

"Yes, thank you, sir."

The line snapped clear.

61

Fifteen hundred cell phone calls had been made from the region where the guerrillas operated in the twelve hours before their communiqué was released, much more than Robert Gallo would have thought. A first pass through showed that the calls were made almost exclusively by phones registered to businesses in the area, with the remainder apparently ecotourists. Gallo tried coordinating call times with the length of the data set in the communiqué but couldn't get a match. Or rather, he could match just about anything by adding or subtracting different encryptions and compression schemes.

Up against a brick wall, Gallo took a break. When the team was working on a project like this, a page was set up in a network file as a kind of journal to allow the members to post different results, hints, and frustrations. It was very much like a Web log or "blog," randomly organized, with large sections of references to data files rather than Web addresses. The idea was to make it a common, open notebook to share information and provoke new ideas and directions—though in practice it often degenerated into a log of rants and complaints: this didn't work; this was dumb; can you believe how easy (or hard) it was to get this?

Gallo added some comments about his efforts and then began paging through what others had written. Certain members of the team could be counted on for off-the-wall notes, and Johnny Bib often put in mathematical dissertations of little apparent relevance. But today the blog was extremely businesslike and to the point, the notes terse.

Not a good sign, Gallo thought.

Intercepts of electronic signals was the NSA's raison d'être. There were several minor gathering programs active in Peru, and between them, regional listening posts, and a dedicated satellite network focusing on the Southern Hemisphere, there were plenty of electronic signals to sift through. As Gallo cursored through some of the lists, a single entry jumped out, simply because it was surrounded by white space.

RUSSIAN MILITARY SATS?

"Sats" meant satellites, and the question was a suggestion by one of the analysts that someone check and see if any Russian observation satellites passed over the region and might have gotten optical data. But the suggestion reminded Gallo that he had been looking only at wireless cells rather than satellite communications networks—a much more likely source, and yet one he hadn't even thought about.

But maybe Johnny Bib had given it to someone else. Rather than calling around or instant messaging to find out, Gallo typed the term into the search engine slot on the page. The search engine came up empty as it scanned the blog. Then, a few seconds later, it spit out a list of results from SpyNet and two NSA-only databases tracking intercepts. (The two-part search was a default "simple" search procedure, designed to save time when the analysts were helping on a mission.) The entries included a few lines summarizing the reference. The first one stuck out immediately: the Russian embassy in Peru had been queried a week before about the continuing unauthorized use of a Russian military communications network.

Gallo had to get help from one of the librarians, but within twenty minutes he knew everything that mattered about the Russian system, and a half hour after that he was looking at intercepted cables saying that the Russian embassy had been working with two military specialists trying to track the satellite phones down.

They were roughly forty miles from the village where the bomb had been found.

Johnny Bib greeted the news of this with his highest praise: *"Ha!"*

Shouted twice, at the top of his lungs.

"The Chinese record all of the Russian transmissions," Johnny told Gallo. "Break into their system and get a copy. Go."

"Not a problem," said Gallo. "But, like, the Russians were complaining that they couldn't figure out the encryptions that were being used on the messages."

"Fortunately, we're not the Russians."

62

Dean and Karr traveled downriver to a village where an international drilling company had set up a base camp. There they "borrowed" a larger boat, a rigid-hulled inflatable with a conventional engine. The engine propelled the little boat at a healthy clip. Dean sat in the bow, keeping an eye out for logs and shallow drafts. About two miles after setting out, they came to an area of rapids; the boat tipped slightly as they wormed through, but they made it past intact.

"That was a pretty wild ride," yelled Karr. "There's more about two miles ahead. Keep bird-dogging for me."

Dean leaned forward against the gunwale, staring into the darkness. He spotted a thick log ahead, lurking like an alligator in the shadows. Karr made it around it, but as he steered back toward the channel, the river dropped through a jagged set of rock outcroppings.

"Left," shouted Dean as the shadows metamorphosed into rocks. "Left!"

The next thing he knew he was flying over the gunwale as the boat pitched wildly beneath him. He managed to get his right hand hooked into the rope that ran along the top of the side of the hull; he hung about two-thirds out of the boat, water furling over him as the boat charged through the obstacle course, dragged along by the current despite Karr's efforts to stop it. As he struggled to get his feet back in, the boat struck something and Dean found himself underwater. Waves twisted around him and the current grabbed him again, pulling him downstream into a pool of calmer water.

Karr bobbed to the surface nearby, cursing a red streak to heaven.

"I just lost it. I just lost it," Karr complained. "You OK, Charlie?"

"Yeah, I'm OK."

"I can't believe I lost it."

They struggled to shore. Dean lay on his stomach, coughing the water from his lungs.

"Stay here. I'm going to try and get our gear," said Karr.

"Tommy, wait—"

"No, it's all right. My mistake; I'll fix it."

Dean turned himself around and sat, still trying to gather his senses. He reached into his pockets and began inventorying what he had, but his mind seemed to be working in a different dimension and he handled the objects two or three times before their identities registered. He found his small flashlight and turned it on just as Karr lumbered up the shoreline to his left.

"Boat's tangled in some branches downstream, in one piece. Motor snapped off," said Karr. He dropped a pack at Dean's feet. "Stinking A2s are gone. They're supposed to be waterproof. I'd really like to see if that's true. But I can't find them."

Dean, still in something of a daze, reached to make sure his pistols were strapped in his holsters.

"Your communications system working?" Karr asked.

Dean reached to the back of his belt and felt for the switch. It had turned off in the tumult.

"Charlie?" asked Rockman.

"I'm here."

"You guys OK?"

"We just went for a swim," said Karr, joining in. "We were getting bored."

Dean's legs had been battered by the rocks, and they ached

as if he'd just run two marathons back-to-back. But otherwise he seemed intact.

"You all right?" Dean asked Karr.

"Yeah. I keep telling you: I'm still numb from all those painkillers they gave me in France. I figure I won't feel anything for another year yet. You feel like walking?"

"No," said Dean, opening the pack. "But it beats standing here."

"Or swimming."

Dean traded his sodden boots for a pair of dry walking shoes. After two miles through the rough terrain his ankles began to ache so badly he took some aspirin from the small first-aid kit in the pack.

Following directions from the Art Room, they headed toward a nearby village used by an ecotourist company as a jumping-off point for tours through the local jungle. They arrived about an hour before dawn and waited on a bench near the water for something to open. Small, modern wood buildings dotted the main area of the settlement, muscling out huts that seemed to have been left standing for atmosphere. There were signs in English as well as Spanish advertising everything from "native" handcrafts to AAA batteries and shaving gear. Karr joked that the handcrafts probably came from China; since they included coffee mugs and T-shirts, he might not have been far off.

Dean sat on a bench, resting his legs while Karr went to explore. Barely five minutes later, Karr returned with a ceramic mug filled with coffee.

"No Styrofoam," said Karr, handing the cup to him gingerly. "Watch this stuff—it'll burn holes in your throat going down."

The smell alone was enough to wake the dead. Dean took a small sip and felt his sinuses loosening up.

"We can catch a ride in a half hour over to Iquitos," said Karr. "Have the Art Room arrange a room for us there. We can use a generic cover as adventurers."

"That'll fool them," said Dean sarcastically.

"No one there we have to fool," said Karr. "And we won't be there long anyway."

"I'd like to get some sleep," admitted Dean. "About twenty-four hours' worth."

"Yeah."

Dean could tell from Karr's answer that sleep was unlikely anytime soon. There were alternatives stronger than the coffee—the Deep Black ops had specially formulated "go" pills, supposedly high-tech stimulants that were non-addictive and had no adverse side effects. Dean didn't trust them; he'd heard the same sort of bull in Vietnam and later in the first Gulf War. Anything artificial always came back to bite you somehow. At least the coffee was predictable.

"There's a place we can wash up a bit," Karr told him. "They even have these vending machines with little shaving kits in them. When we're done we have to head over to what they call the south dock. It's about a quarter mile from here."

"Where are we meeting Lia?" asked Dean.

"In Nevas," said Karr. "She should be there this afternoon. We'll have to get an airplane or at least a boat—it's pretty far from Iquitos."

"She shouldn't do the switch without backup."

"I'm not saying she should, Charlie. Let's go get a shave, all right? My chin gets cranky if I don't shave off the peach fuzz every forty-eight hours or so."

63

Considering that her bed was under a rats' nest, Lia slept comparatively well, waking only when Fernandez knocked on her door. She dressed quickly—all she needed were her shoes—and got an update from Farlekas in the Art Room, which told her that the nuke was a phony and that the Peruvians did not yet seem to realize that.

"What's this mean for me?" she asked.

"That you continue as assigned. Fly up to Nevas and do the swap."

"Fine. What about Charlie?"

"Dean and Tommy are on their way to Iquitos," said the Art Room supervisor. "They may meet you there."

"May?"

"Things are still up in the air right now, Lia. I'll let you know what's going on the second I know. I promise."

Fernandez was waiting downstairs in the small breakfast room. There were two other tables of guests, and they were listening intently as a radio at the side of the room proclaimed the latest on the plot by the "notorious and desperate enemies of the Peruvian people" to destroy the country's capital. The hero of the moment was a general named Atahualpa Túcume, who had fought valiantly against the Ecuadorian bandits and was now engaged in a battle to the end against the guerrillas. A small snippet was presented from an interview with the general. He declared that "luck and the grace of our ancestors" had allowed the army to foil the terrible plot to destroy the nation and Lima.

A commentator followed, giving some biographical information about Túcume. "He is not well known in the coastal areas of our country, but should be," said the man. "He believes he is descended from the Inca aristocracy. . . ."

Fernandez hunched over the table, his face pale and his eyes bloodshot from all the alcohol he had consumed the evening before. Clearly, he had had his last taste of *aguardiente* for a while.

"Can you deal with the helicopter?" Lia asked him.

"I'll survive. Let's get going."

64

Rubens' helicopter was about five minutes from the White House when Johnny Bib buzzed him on the secure line. One of the computer experts—Johnny Bib hated the term "hacker"—had broken into Chinese intercepts of a Russian satellite phone system and obtained several conversations that had taken place not far from where the warhead had been found. The transmissions used an encryption popular among some members of the Russian *mafiya*. The NSA had the "keys" to decrypt it and the conversations were being translated now. They were extremely brief and unenlightening: in one case, a ride was apparently solicited; in another, a question was asked about how much it would cost to buy a truck. The analysts were divided on whether these might not be code for something else. But the implication of the dated Russian encryption and the use of the phone network were much more important at the moment than anything in the conversations: it suggested that the CIA agent involved in Iron Heart was still alive.

"Or that someone found his satellite phone," said Rubens.

"Well, yes," said Johnny Bib. "That, too."

Johnny's voice dropped, and Rubens realized he hadn't thought of the obvious possibility.

"You have an exact location?"

"Yes. It's within a military reservation in an unpopulated area."

"Inform Ms. Telach." He glanced at his watch. "Tell her that I would like Tommy and Mr. Dean to check it out. Tell her to prepare a mission, but to wait for my word to launch it."

Fifteen minutes later, Rubens entered the cabinet room at the White House to find Collins giving a full briefing on Iron Heart. She was flanked by her boss, CIA Director Louis Zackart, and Jorge Evans—the CIA officer who had supervised Iron Heart. Secretary of Defense Art Blanders, who'd never been a big fan of the CIA, looked furious. Secretary of State James Lincoln, nominally a Collins ally, had his arms crossed and was shaking his head. In fact, only President Marcke seemed nonplussed by the disclosure that the CIA might have lost track of one of the warheads in the operation.

Collins glanced at Rubens as he came in. He was surprised that the look seemed not only benign but almost one of relief, as if he were an ally she'd been waiting for.

"Our best information then, and now, is that there was no third warhead," said Collins. "But it should have been mentioned in the report."

"That's an understatement," said Blanders.

Collins nodded. Her strategy was rather transparent: since this had all happened before her time, she could easily distance herself from it while claiming to give full disclosure.

"A search of the wreckage was conducted," she said. "A wide range of assets were used. Just as a precaution."

"Was this all mentioned to the president at the time?" Blanders demanded.

"I don't personally have that information," said Collins. "It was a different administration."

That response didn't sit well with Blanders, whose opinion of the previous administration was as low as his opinion of the CIA. He began telling Collins how idiotic—"I'm putting it politely," he said—it was to transport a real nuclear weapon to South America to begin with.

Collins could have chosen to tell Blanders that the operation had been approved at the highest levels of the government—it had been authorized by a presidential finding and in the due course of things would have been subject to several reviews. She might also have mentioned that elements of the military had been involved in the operation and that the *targeted* weapon was never far from a sizable strike force. She could even have said—and here Rubens would actually have agreed with her—that having the operation end up in South America was no worse, and possibly a whole lot better, than having it take place in the Middle East or some other country where the local governments might be less than cooperative if things went sour. But instead she answered mildly, "I don't disagree."

Rubens glanced at Evans. Clearly, he was going to end up taking the brunt of whatever fallout ensued, the designated patsy for decisions made several pay grades above him. He seemed rather stoic today; then again, the paramilitary types tended to be like that. They'd seen their share of blood in the field, and little fazed them, at least outwardly.

"What the report should or should not have included is an issue for a different time," said the president. He turned to Rubens. "And I'm in office now, not my colorful predecessor. We need to know now what it is we're dealing with. Billy, you have an update for us?"

"As we all know, the warhead that has been discovered in the Amazonian area is not real." He pulled his chair out and sat. "Or rather to be precise, it does not contain what the experts refer to as a radioactive pit—a bomb kernel, if you will. There's no nuclear material. But the fact that it's very similar to the warhead that was involved in Iron Heart does raise some possibilities."

"We're not sure it was the same as the ones in Iron Heart," said Collins. "The data that your people brought back is less than definitive."

They could have brought the warhead back here and dumped it in your lap and you'd still find some way to criticize them, thought Rubens.

"Everything I've seen, not just the Deep Black pictures but the images on Peruvian television, leaves absolutely no doubt," said Blanders. "More than a dozen analysts have looked at it at the Pentagon. And these Deep Black people—the agents who were there—are experts in Russian nuclear arms. They've dealt with this sort of thing before. They're not going to mess this up."

"One of the people is an expert," said Rubens mildly, referring to Karr. "He disarmed the weapon in southern Siberia last year. Not the same type of warhead, though there are many similarities."

"There are two possibilities," continued Rubens. "One, the warhead that has been discovered was a dummy from the very start. The CIA asset—I believe you refer to him by the name Sholk or Silk; am I right, Mr. Evans?"

"Sholk," he said with a stony glare.

"Perhaps he intended to use it somehow, or used it when he made the original deal. When you shot down his plane in Ecuador, it was still inside. The rebels recovered it, maybe then, more likely in the recent past."

Rubens glanced at Evans, unsure whether he would argue that the CIA had not shot down the plane. He didn't.

"What's the other possibility?" asked Lincoln.

"The other possibility is that the warhead *is* real, or rather *was,* but that the bomb material was removed at some point after the crash. The guerrillas could have the material or they could have sold it. Or perhaps someone else sold them this bomb, either as a dummy or even as a legitimate weapon, since they might not know how to test it properly. We've found no financial transactions or communications backing that theory, but it remains viable."

"Let me straighten Mr. Rubens out on a minor point," said Collins. "Two points. One, the crash occurred in Peruvian territory. I realize that the report is imprecise, but it was just over the border in the contested area. And two, the CIA did not shoot down the aircraft."

"Are you sure, Debra?" said Rubens.

She turned to Evans. He in turn glanced at the director, then began to speak. "There was a misunderstanding at the airstrip. The pilots refused an order to get out of their airplane.

As they took off, gunshots were heard. A shoulder-launched missile was fired."

"A misunderstanding?" said Rubens. "That's hard to believe."

"That's what happened," said Evans.

Rubens met his gaze and realized that Evans had decided he could tough this point out.

Blanders, who was having trouble controlling his temper, asked with the help of several expletives why *that* wasn't mentioned in the report.

"It wasn't relevant," said Evans. "The plane crashed. That's noted."

"Not *relevant* that you shot it down?"

The two men stared at each other. Rubens looked over at Collins, who sat stone-faced, gazing dead ahead at the wall opposite her. Most of the people looking at her would think she'd been blindsided, but Rubens suspected—knew—she hadn't. She would have read the report and, just as he did, realize how convenient the crash had been. Not only that, but she would have known Sholk's entire background—she would have known that the CIA was responsible for setting him up in business.

"OK, enough of this crap," the president said. "I'm not going to waste my day sitting here listening to a rehash of a fucked-up CIA operation that occurred under the previous administration. I want a complete investigation done of this mess and I want to see the report. Mr. Zackart, see to it."

"Yes, sir," said the CIA director.

"Let's move on. But before we do, one question: What happened to this guy, Sholk? Was he killed in the crash?"

"He was incinerated in the crash," said Collins.

"Oh?" said Rubens. "We've discovered that a Russian satellite phone has been used in the area where the warhead was found over the past several months. The encryption code is several years old, one the Russian mafia likes."

"If he had survived the crash, I would've seen him," Evans insisted. "I was there myself. He died in the crash or the fire that burned up the plane."

Rubens asked Evans, "How long did it take for you to reach the wreckage?"

"Not long."

"Hours?"

"In that country it can take a day to go two miles," Evans explained. "It's all jungle straight up and down. I don't remember how long it took. Not all day. Less than that. A few hours, maybe."

"Was the body in the wreckage?"

"The wreckage was ashes. The plane had fuel in it and burned fiercely. By the time we got there the fire was almost out. The bodies had been consumed."

"No corpus delicti," the president said. "Enough. We've got a hell of a mess right now that needs all our attention. We've got a fake bomb in Peru that the Peruvians think is real. They're sitting on it. There may be a real bomb, and we need to find it if it's there. Our entrée to Peru is to help them dispose of the one they have and search to ensure there aren't any more. I spoke to the president of Peru on the telephone just before I came here. He promised full cooperation."

They discussed the arrangements. A Delta Force team and a team from the State Department were en route. The entire Southern Command, headquartered at Fort Sam Houston in Texas, had been placed on alert. An emergency response unit trained to deal with disasters was heading to Lima so that it could respond immediately in a catastrophe. Two platoons of Marines and some aircraft had been dispatched to provide additional security at the embassy. Reconnaissance assets, planes and satellites, had been dedicated to the search. And finally, the USS *Ronald Reagan* and her task group were on the way to the waters off Peru, just in case the folks in Peru didn't feel like cooperating in the search. "Sometimes a little intimidation prevents serious problems," the secretary of defense said.

"The Peruvians will cooperate—are cooperating," the secretary of state said.

"I don't want to talk contingencies," the president said. "The people at the Pentagon can handle that." He turned to the chairman of the Joint Chiefs. "I understand you want Jack Spielmorph to head the search force?"

"Yes, sir." Spielmorph was a two-star general.

"Fine."

Collins weighed in. "One thing that needs to be determined is whether or not the Peruvian army manufactured this fake warhead. The generals are very much suspects."

"So is our mysterious Mr. Sholk," someone interjected. "Why do a fake warhead? Why not a coup?"

"Maybe the new generation is more subtle," Collins replied. "The army found the weapon and got the political credit."

"And the election is this coming Sunday," the president said sourly. He glanced at Rubens, who suspected the president was wishing he had told the Peruvian president about the rigged vote-counting computers.

"Thank you, gentlemen and ladies, for sharing breakfast with me." The president rose and left the room.

65

The helicopter stuttered to the left as it took off. Lia's stomach floated in the wrong place for a moment, waiting for the rest of her body to catch up. She closed her eyes to regain her equilibrium; by the time she reopened them the helicopter was over a long valley, the mines and smelters behind them. The mountains stretched in all directions. The air had a dark purple hue; the ground mixed green and brown like a mottled blanket. It seemed to Lia the terrain rushed by while they stood still.

The drone of the helicopter's engines shut her off from the others, putting her in a little cocoon where she could rest for a while. She had one more card to swap. Hopefully that would be done quickly and she could go home and rest, retreat to a beach or someplace quiet where rats didn't run in the ceiling while you were trying not to freeze to death under blankets stiffer than cardboard and not half as warm.

The helicopter wove its way north following a series of long, deep valleys, generally staying a few hundred feet below the nearest peaks. It seemed impossible that anyone could live in these mountains, and yet the slopes were dotted with houses, new and old, as well as massive stone ruins. Some had come for gold and silver: large strip mines were scattered around as well, along with old-fashioned tunnels. But the terraces along the mountainsides, the cultivated fields a thousand feet high, showed that more than the hunt for treasure had kept them here.

After about a half hour's flying time, Lia grew tired.

"I'm going to take a nap," she told the others—and Rockman. She reached to her belt and clicked off the com system. Within a few moments, she felt her mind starting to drift and she was sleeping.

In her dream, she saw Charlie shaking his head at her.

Why?

She was back in the vault, looking at her hand trembling before her. But this time she stopped it, staring crossly at it.

I will not be afraid.

Charlie materialized again, once more shaking his head.

Why? she asked him.

Before he could answer, there was a soft pop, followed by a louder bang. Lia felt herself lurch upward. Caught between sleep and consciousness, she thought she saw the nose of the helicopter skitter upward and then back down. The tail slid to the left, then back; in an instant the helicopter was yawing back and forth as well as up and down, flying in a large, un-guided corkscrew through the sky.

Fernandez grabbed Lia's arm and shouted something. As he did, the chopper pitched hard to the right, and Lia's mind seemed to lift up away from her body, soaring into the azure sky.

66

Not only did fresh orders meet Dean and Karr in Iquitos, but Fashona did as well, this time at the helm of a large single-engine amphibious plane. Fashona was in an appreciably better mood than he had been the night before, giving Dean a thumbs-up and even half-smiling at Karr as the two men boarded the plane.

"New airplane, huh?" Dean asked.

"Very pretty beast," said Fashona. "Cessna Caravan. Straight-at-you, what you see is what you get. With water wings."

"Water wings," echoed Karr in the back.

"I hope you haven't let him eat those jungle leaves," Fashona told Dean. "I'd hate to see him high."

"Probably slow him down," said Dean. "Like taking Ritalin if you're hyperactive."

Fashona throttled up. The aircraft felt more like a graceful sailboat than a speedboat, gliding along the river so smoothly that Dean didn't even realize they were airborne until they started to bank. They flew south for about five miles, then began heading to the west. Their target was a pair of buildings near a military outpost above the Rio Orona.

As the crow flew, it was only about forty miles southeast of where they had been the night before, though by ground the journey would have been close to a hundred over unimproved roads and rickety mountain trails. Once at the installation, they would use a boat and then their feet to hike another ten miles before reaching their destination in the shadow of half-forgotten Inca ruins.

The Art Room wanted to know who, if anyone, was there. Specifically, they were looking for an old Russian satellite phone somehow linked to the warhead they had checked out the night before.

It sounded like a wild-goose chase to Dean. He wouldn't have minded so much, except for two things: one, Lia was working without backup, and two, he was so tremendously tired now that he couldn't keep his eyes open. He gazed out the side of the aircraft at the green jungle, teetering on the edge of slumber. His mind wandered back and forth, confusing the thick foliage with Vietnam. They were worlds apart, and he was even further from the kid he'd been thirty-some years before. But they jammed close now in his head, his consciousness giving way to the dreamscape of memory.

Turk was the one who'd deserved the medal for taking out the Vietnamese sniper. Without Turk, Dean would have been another notch on the wooden stock of Fu Manchu's ancient Russian weapon. Dean followed Turk out of the bunker area and through the hills, learning more in their first day together than he had during the entire year he'd been a Marine.

But Turk wasn't around to get the medal. So it fell to Dean, who'd been the one to take the shot.

One shot, one kill, one shiny medal, one star in the firmament.

One certificate signifying you are the man.

Paper.

Was that why he was so cynical?

He wasn't cynical. On the contrary. He valued honor and duty. He believed in them and lived them, did his best to— not for medals, not for anything of that, but because he felt sick, literally queasy, when he realized he'd let down someone who was counting on him.

Like Lia in Korea. Even though it wasn't his fault— wasn't even his mission. He'd been thousands of miles away at the time, but he still felt as if he should have been there for her.

Maybe it was medals he didn't care for. He didn't hold them against men who felt they were important. On the contrary—if he knew the man, especially if he knew the man, he took the medal as a sign that he'd been through hell and lost something important, trading it for something that couldn't be explained. That experience set a person apart.

Didn't make him better, just different.

Offered proof that he had been tested and come through.

That wasn't cynicism.

Maybe it was just his own medals he didn't care about, the way smart kids in school were about grades. Dean had been an OK student, but even his B's came with considerable effort. One of his best friends, Mikey, yeah, good ol' Mikey, he always got A's, but just shrugged.

"Ain't nothing."

Mikey became an officer in the Army and died in a dumb accident in Panama two years before the invasion.

They didn't give medals for that.

The shot that had killed Fu Manchu hadn't been an accident. Skill, a good idea, a lot of patience, training, experience—Turk's mostly—those made the shot, not luck.

There *was* luck involved, though. Dean had turned left at the edge of the stream a half hour earlier, when he wasn't sure which way to go. Turn right, and things would have been different.

Not to mention the luck involved in not being in Fu Manchu's sights.

"Beautiful country, huh?" said Fashona.

"From a distance, everything's beautiful," said Dean, his mind rising back to full consciousness.

"You never saw my first wife. You all right?"

"Just tired."

"You want to sleep, go ahead."

"It's not that easy in a plane."

Fashona glanced behind him. "Karr's snorin' up a storm back there."

"Yeah." Dean was surprised to see Karr sleeping, his head thrown back and his mouth wide open. "He's a piece of work."

"Yeah, he's a real asshole."

Dean hadn't meant it the way Fashona took it.

"I guess we all are sometimes," he told the pilot.

The side of Fashona's face turned bright red. "You aren't, Charlie. And I hope I'm not."

"You're not, Ray. You're just a damn good pilot."

Fashona didn't answer—or rather, if he did, Charlie Dean didn't hear what he said; he surrendered to fatigue, slumbering against the side of the plane.

67

"There's a problem with Lia's helicopter," said Rockman. "She's not moving forward."

"Are they landing?" asked Telach.

"I'm not sure. Her com system's off."

Telach glanced up at the map screen displayed at the front of the Art Room. Agents' positions were tracked in two different ways. One was by a simple locator that worked with the communications satellites. It was similar to the global positioning technology embedded in many cell phones and 911 systems. Because it involved radio signals, however, it could be detected. Since field ops had the option of turning off communications for safety (and, Telach knew, to get the Art Room off their back), there was also a backup system using implanted radioactive isotopes. The system had technical limitations, but it was working now and showed Lia's position about eighty miles north of La Oroya.

"She's definitely not moving," said Rockman. "Can't tell if they're in a hover or what. Maybe they landed. Map shows a village nearby."

Telach leaned over to look at his screen. The locator showed they were about a half mile south of a settlement on the side of a mountain. The latest satellite image showed rough terrain, and it was an unlikely place to land.

One of the occupational hazards of working in the Art Room was something Telach called Mother Hen Disease—a tendency to worry that something had gone wrong simply because information had stopped flowing back. The field ops—Lia especially—were constantly complaining about it.

"What are the flying conditions?" Telach asked Rockman.

"Clear skies. Unlimited visibility."

"How long has she been at this position?"

"Two minutes."

"Call her on the sat phone. If she doesn't answer, see which one of the U-2s is closest to her, and get it over the area."

68

The security procedures seemed almost routine to Hernes Jackson now, and he donned a benign smile for the security people as he passed through their checks. Down in the Desk Three bunker, he found that he remembered the sign-in procedure for the computer networks without having to resort to the prompts or call the librarian for assistance.

A message popped up on the screen with a new assignment for Rubens: did any of the Peruvian guerrillas seem interesting in any way?

Amused by the broad, open-ended query, Jackson began paging through the accumulated files on the terrorists, including video clips from the discovery of the bomb and the attempted post office takeover several days before.

Nothing jumped out at him beyond the obvious: the guerrillas were more organized than the Peruvian intelligence service believed. The car bombings alone showed a great deal of coordination across a wide geographic distance.

Far more interesting, Jackson thought, was the fact that the warhead was a fake. Had it started that way? Had its weapons kernel been removed?

Taking a weapons core from a nuclear bomb was not technically difficult—if you were a nuclear weapons expert. Did the guerrillas have access to those kinds of people? A number were college-educated, but their majors were in subjects like literature. Someone could have been hired, perhaps.

Jackson spent about an hour learning how to use a watch list as a cross-reference before giving up. There were plenty of potential experts, most of them Russian, but no direct link to Peru or Ecuador that he could find.

But working with the lists gave Jackson another idea: how to determine who Sholk was. Jackson found the list immediately after Iron Heart and began comparing it with other watch lists, including several intercepted ones from foreign governments (allies as well as enemies). By fishing through the lists and several passenger manifests from the Middle East, he found four candidates. Only one was unaccounted for at present (two were in jail; another had committed suicide), and he happened to be Russian: Stephan Babin.

Babin was mentioned in a Department of Defense Intelligence Agency report from the early 1990s as a Russian military officer who might be worth cultivating. He was apparently serving as a liaison in Bosnia at the time. The NSA had Russian military files, but Jackson couldn't figure out how to access the special database. He called the librarian for help, but the man had gone out for a late lunch.

Was it lunchtime already?

Discovering Sholk's identity felt like a personal triumph, but Jackson didn't stop there. If there was a weapons expert with the rebels, it might very well be Babin.

Jackson paged through information on the encounter during which the bomb had been found by the Peruvian army. There was no list of the guerrillas taken. Nor did Babin's name show up in any of the lists of known or suspected guerrillas compiled by SIN, Peru's intelligence service.

If names were out, what about photos?

He'd need to find a picture of Babin in the Russian data; he wasn't sure whether one would exist or not. In the meantime, he brought up photos of the guerrillas, thinking he might be able to narrow down possibilities on the basis of age.

But there were almost no photos of the people connected with New Path. The best he could find were photos of a few of the dead bodies. Jackson tried a wider search and got names and photos from the post office takeover by the guerrillas a few days before in Lima, along with some additional incidents.

Still waiting for the librarian to return, Jackson opened the system's facial features tool—it used several hundred specific points to match faces—and began playing with it, capturing faces and applying searches to familiarize himself with the program. The tool was extremely easy to use. He moused a box around a face, "capturing" it, then simply clicked one of the search buttons on the toolbar and waited while the computer checked the face against a database. Of course, behind the scenes, the program went through a billion gyrations, computing and checking, but to Jackson the process seemed no more difficult than using the primitive drawing program one of his neighbor's little girls had shown him at Christmas.

The first search came back with what the computer called "no definites." However, it did give him about ten possible matches, none of which actually looked close when he opened the window under the dialogue box on the screen. He tried again, selecting the same face. This time the computer beeped immediately and gave him an error message: he was repeating the search against the same database. He opened the list of searches and saw that the computer had helpfully highlighted several databases that he might be interested in, based on the terms of the first search. Jackson carefully looked through the list, but it didn't include Russian military files. It did have Peru's, however, and he checked those off along with the computer's other suggestions. The computer returned with no match.

He moved the cursor to another person and repeated the search. This time he got a hit—the suspected guerrilla was an army lieutenant who, according to the small bio that popped on the screen, was still on active duty.

And in the same division that had discovered the nuclear warhead.

69

Lia felt the body on top of her, pushing and grunting, the devil incarnate. She struggled with all her might, resisting and fighting, cursing the others holding her down. She knew she would lose the battle, but it was the struggle that was important. To resist meant salvation, survival—she would be wounded, but in a greater sense still whole, the most important part of her preserved.

And then suddenly she was free, the rapist gone, light streaming in around her.

Voices murmured in her head. The Art Room?

"Hello?" said Lia. "Hello?"

She wasn't in Korea. She was in the helicopter, the ruins of the helicopter—they had crashed in the Andes.

She was pitched at an angle, her head and right arm resting on something soft.

Fernandez.

The aircraft had augered in on its starboard side, crushing the cabin downward. She couldn't see Fernandez's face, but his left arm next to her chest was drenched in blood. Lia looked toward the front of the helicopter. Bits of metal and wire hung like vines in front of her. Beyond them, instead of the pilot and the rest of the cockpit, she saw rocks and dirt, some scrubby brush. The sky.

Lia slipped down a little farther when she undid her seat belt. The door of the helicopter was above her left arm. It was intact. She pulled back the latch and pushed against the panel, but the door snapped back down, pushed back by gravity.

Squirreling around in the seat, she stood on Fernandez and pushed her way up and out of the aircraft. They had crashed against a mountainside. Rocks loomed above her. Moving as gingerly as possible, she got out, crawling head-first down and around the crushed fuselage onto the slope, then through the dirt to a level spot a few feet from the bits and pieces of the helicopter that lay scattered along the ground.

It was always the easy assignments, she thought, that ended up being trouble.

Lia took a breath, then pushed along the ground a few yards more, going across the slope. Finally she clambered to her feet, pulling herself up on the side of a big rock.

"Just peachy," Lia said out loud.

She reached to the communications switch. "Are you there?"

"Lia, are you OK?" said Rockman instantly.

"I'm in one piece."

"I called you on the sat phone twice. Why didn't you answer?"

Lia realized she had left her bag in the helo and started back to get it.

"Lia, what's your situation?" asked Marie Telach.

"Tangled and confused. The helicopter crashed. Everyone else is dead."

"Was it shot down? Or something mechanical?"

"I'm not sure. I was dozing, then I heard a bang."

"An explosion?"

"I'm not sure."

She looked into the fuselage. The bag with her clothes and the sat phone peeked out from under a large piece of metal that was anchored by part of the helicopter engine; there was no way she was getting it. But the briefcase with her laptop—and the envelope with the replacement voter cards—had wedged itself near Fernandez's body. She might be able to snake in and grab it.

"Lia, please," insisted Telach.

"I'm OK, Marie. The helicopter crashed."

"Was it shot down? Or was it a mechanical problem?"

"It happened all of a sudden. I heard a boom, but it might have been the engine. I don't know. I'm going to retrieve the briefcase and voter cards. Hang on. I'll get the PDA and take a picture for you."

"Don't do anything foolish."

"By whose definition?"

Lia ignored Rockman's suggestion to put a video bug on her clothes so he could see what was going on. She climbed into the helicopter head-first, leaning as gingerly as possible on Fernandez. She hadn't actually made sure that he was dead, and though it seemed obvious enough, she put her hand onto his neck to feel for a pulse.

A bone or vertebra had sheered through the skin. She moved her thumb farther up, stubbornly refusing to accept the obvious. His head had been wedged against a metal spar that had flown through the cockpit during the impact. Thankfully she couldn't see much of it from where she was, she thought, settling her fingers where she supposed his jugular would be.

Nothing.

What if he had gotten in first? Then she would have been sitting on this side of the helo. Dumb luck had saved her.

"Lia, what are you doing?" asked Rockman.

"I'm getting my laptop bag," she grunted, pushing herself to the left and wedging into the space in front of the seats. She had to push her left hand forward and down, snaking past part of the seat cushion to get the bag. It came easily—for about six inches. Then it caught against something and she dropped it.

Cursing, Lia pushed herself closer so she could get a better grip. She yanked, scraping her hand against the metal, but whatever was holding the bag down gave way.

"All right," she said, backing out. "Got it. I'll take some pictures of the wreck so you can figure out whether it was shot down or not. Stand by."

Lia thought she heard someone in the Art Room mumble something.

"I can't hear you," she said, pulling herself out of the helicopter. As she got to her knees on top of the twisted fuselage, she realized the Art Room hadn't been talking to her—six or seven men were standing a few yards from the wreckage.

"Buenos dias," she told them.

They didn't answer.

"Lia?" said Rockman.

"I have company." Lia eased herself down from the helicopter. She knelt, propping the briefcase so that she could remove the small Glock pistol strapped near her ankle without it being seen. She palmed the gun, holding it against her side; she'd use it only as a last resort.

"My helicopter crashed," she said in English.

"Helicóptero," started a translator in the Art Room, feeding her the sentence and then a few lines about wanting to call the authorities for assistance.

Lia repeated the words, twice, but got no response.

"Try it in Quechua," said Rockman, and another translator gave her a few phrases in the native Indian language. But that didn't work, either.

Several more men appeared, apparently coming from a trail that ran to the right. They didn't seem hostile, but they also weren't overtly friendly. They seemed puzzled by her appearance, almost as if they weren't sure what a helicopter was. But their clothing was modern, if somewhat worn and mismatched, and certainly helicopters must fly overhead here all the time.

"Are they guerrillas?" asked Rockman.

"How can I tell?" Lia asked.

"Ask them."

Lia kept her sneer to herself. That was just the sort of thing the Art Room would suggest—a naive question that could get you blown up no matter what the answer was.

"I have to get help," Lia said in Spanish. When they didn't respond, she repeated it, this time more emphatically.

"*¡Socorro!*" she said, pointing to the helicopter, though she knew Fernandez was dead. "Help!"

Even that didn't break the spell. There were now a dozen men standing four or five yards from her, staring but saying nothing.

"This is just too weird," she muttered, starting toward the trail. As she did, two of the men stepped aside. Two more men appeared from behind the bend. They had AK-47s in their hands. The men raised their weapons and she stopped.

"Well, at least we know where we stand," she said. "Two bozos with AK-47s," she added for Rockman in a quick stage whisper. Then in Spanish she told the newcomers that there had been a helicopter crash and help was needed.

One of the men with a rifle shouted something quickly in Spanish to the men who were standing near the helicopter. But they were as uncommunicative with him as they had been with her.

"What's this about?" Lia asked the Art Room. "Can you hear?"

"They're trying to decide who you are, and what to do with you. They're confused about the helicopter—they thought it was military, but it's not. They said something about waiting for a commander. Offer them a reward—tell them you can pay them if they'll help you."

Lia folded her arms in front of her chest. The briefcase was in one hand, the gun hidden in the other.

"What you're going to do," she told the men in English, "is call the local police."

"Lia, why are you using English?"

"Don't try and bluff them," said Telach, breaking in.

One of the men with the guns told Lia in Spanish to shut up.

"Why?"

As long as the men stayed relatively close together, she thought, she could take them—shoot them quickly in the heads, then dive for their guns.

Maybe not even dive for their guns. As long as she was

closer to the weapons than anyone else, she could ward off the others long enough to retrieve one.

She'd have to make *very* good shots.

Lia edged a little closer. The two men began talking to each other, trying to decide what to do. The one who had barked at her before said that she should put up her hands.

Just as she was about to drop her briefcase and shoot, a burst of gunfire echoed nearby. The two men with the AK-47s jerked around in the direction of the trail. Lia went to one knee and fired twice, dropping the first man with a shot to the temple and catching the second square in the back of the head.

She dove at the rifles as they fell, sliding into them. She fished around for the gun, spinning back, her head dizzy.

The men by the helicopter seemed like deer caught in headlights, staring at her with shocked expressions.

Lia went quickly to the other rifle, grabbing it and then retreating back toward the wreck. She made the mistake of glancing to her right; the sharp drop-off increased her wooziness and she threw herself down against the battered metal of the fallen chopper.

"What's going on?" Lia whispered to the Art Room.

"We're not sure," said Telach. "Put out a video bug."

Lia slipped her hand in the bag.

"I only have two, and one audio fly," she said. She stuck one video bug on the helicopter tail and the other near the front of the fuselage, giving as full a view of the area as possible. She left the fly with the bug, then ducked down the side of the hill, crouching with the guns.

Two soldiers appeared, rifles ready. One covered the men near the helicopter while the other bent to the two men Lia had killed.

"Two people in uniforms. They look like Peruvian army," Rockman said. "May be a legitimate military unit."

"*May be* isn't good enough."

The soldiers were joined by an officer, who walked to the small group of men and demanded to know who had shot the two dead men. He used curses when he referred to them, calling the dead men traitors and saying the shooter would be rewarded.

The men said nothing. The officer identified himself as a lieutenant with the army, but this failed to impress them as well.

"All right, we're checking him," said Rockman.

"I killed the guerrillas," Lia yelled in English. "Who are you?"

The officer craned his head to see who was talking to him. "Hello?" he said in English.

"Yeah, hello."

"I am Lieutenant Gomez. I'm here to save you from the guerrillas."

"Yeah, well you're a little late." Lia climbed up and walked toward the wreckage. She kept the rifles pointed toward the ground and walked straight to the briefcase she had dropped.

"Lia!" hissed Rockman. "We haven't verified that he's legitimate."

"He would have shot me by now if he wasn't," Lia muttered, grabbing the briefcase.

70

The ruins reminded Dean of the miniature villages the candy maker in his old hometown set out in windows at Christmastime to lure shoppers into the store. The ancient Inca estate was set at the side of a mountain on a narrow plateau that overlooked the valley. It glowed green in the light, its carefully fitted stones covered with moss and grass. Two large buildings perched over the cliffs; they lacked roofs but otherwise were perfectly intact, seemingly untouched by the five or six hundred years that had passed since the complex was last used. Below them were narrow terraces, once used for growing crops, which looked like steps from above.

To the north and east, the ruins of other buildings sprawled along a series of steps in the rock outcroppings. Farther north were long rectangles of stone, now just rubble; these were the remains of very large buildings that would have been used as temples or palaces.

"You're looking at the private estate of an Inca king," said Karr, leaning forward between the seats of the airplane. "There's a group of rocks, a trio there. See it? They would have made sacrifices to the gods there."

"Human?" asked Fashona.

"I think humans they just tossed down in ravines."

"Seriously?" asked Fashona.

"Oh yeah. You ever been to Machu Picchu?" said Karr.

"No."

"Way bigger than this. Blow you away."

"You were there?" asked Fashona.

"Nah. Travelogue."

Karr's description came from one of the videos they'd been given as part of the mission briefing. Dean stared at the complex through the windscreen of the airplane, looking not at the ruins but at the hills around them. Unlike the much larger and more famous ruins Karr had mentioned, these were not open to the public; they were part of a military reservation and off-limits to the general public. A radar site a mile and a half to the north was used as a listening post to spy on the Ecuadorians across the border.

"The Incas ruled from Ecuador all the way south through Chile," continued Karr. "Their capital was in Cusco, pretty far south of here, but they governed this area. Had some interesting beliefs."

"Like?" asked Fashona.

"They threw little kids into the gorges so that there would be no disease."

"For real?"

"Oh yeah. That was an honor."

"Some honor."

"Yeah. But their justice was pretty hard. If you slept with the wrong woman, she was buried alive and you were hanged. If you were already married, your family was slaughtered as well."

"This is as close as I can get without being picked up on their radar," said Fashona, banking the Cessna to the southeast. "We're below their horizon, but we can't push it too far. You guys are going to have a pretty good hike ahead of you."

"So what else is new?" said Karr. "You have a good sleep, Charlie?"

"Too short."

"Tell me about it."

They landed near a small village a few miles downriver of the ruins. While not large, the village was used as a transportation nexus by the military installation as well as some commercial mining concerns to the south, and there was a small marina of speedboats. There was even another float-plane at the docks where they tied up. Fashona was returning east to refuel and get more supplies; he told Dean and Karr that he would be back in twenty-four hours, or sooner if they needed him.

"What do you figure a good price on a boat is here?" Karr asked as they walked toward a small shack advertising rentals.

"Don't haggle," Dean said. "Let's just get going."

"You have to haggle, Charlie. Otherwise they don't re-spect ya."

Karr began negotiating with the help of an Art Room translator. Dean turned around and scanned the dock area, feigning interest in the boats but really looking over the few locals who were sitting nearby.

A tall, lanky man with blotchy brown skin approached him and asked in Spanish if he was looking to rent an air-plane. When Dean shook his head, the man asked again, this time in English.

"We just got here," Dean told him.

"What are you doing?"

"We're going downriver to fish," Dean said. The man looked at him suspiciously until Dean added, "And look for a little gold."

"Many people look for gold." The floatplane pilot nod-ded. Treasure hunting was a time-honored pursuit. "I know some good spots."

"I'll bet."

"You want me to show you?"

"We're really all right, thanks."

"Maybe you'll need another airplane."

Dean thought reserving the man's plane might not be a bad idea—there was always the possibility that Fashona would get tied up somewhere. But doing that might lead to more questions, and so he just shook his head.

"Two hundred dollars a day, plus fuel. A very good deal," said the man.

"That's a terrible deal," said Karr, looming behind him.

"No, a very good deal."

"Well, we don't need a plane. Maybe tomorrow. Come on, Charlie."

"One-fifty," said the pilot.

"Sorry," said Dean. "Maybe in the future."

"We could probably work him down to a hundred," said Karr, leading Dean to the speedboat. "Cheaper than Fashona, I'll bet."

71

Lieutenant Gomez told Lia that he had been pursuing the guerrillas through the rugged territory for weeks. The people who had gathered initially were from the local village and probably had a great deal of information about the guerrillas, he added.

"But these people never tell," he complained bitterly. "As if it is a matter of honor for them. They are Indians, ignorant natives. What can you do?"

The lieutenant was convinced that the guerrillas had shot down Lia's helicopter with a rocket grenade. The Art Room experts tentatively agreed when Lia surreptitiously fed them some pictures using the camera attachment on the PDA.

The UN had not announced the flight beforehand, and it seemed unlikely that the helicopter had been specifically targeted by the rebels—though given everything else that they had said and done over the past few weeks, it couldn't entirely be ruled out. The lieutenant said that he thought the guerrillas believed the helicopter was ferrying chemical company workers, who had occasionally been threatened in the past.

Impressed by her connection with the UN election commission, the lieutenant told her that there was a small settlement about a mile down the slope. If she went with one of his men, she would find food there and a telephone, as well as a small contingent of his men. They would consult his company commander and see what could be done about arranging transportation and alerting the UN. Lia thanked him and started to go.

"Stop. The rifles. You must leave them."

"Why?"

"They were the guerrillas'. We have a system," said the lieutenant.

"He gets a kickback for each gun he turns in," Rockman explained.

"I want to hold on to this weapon," said Lia. She held it up; two of the soldiers near the lieutenant interpreted this as a threatening gesture and snapped up their own guns. Frowning, she handed the AK-47 over.

The soldier detailed to escort her was a good-looking twenty-year-old who had a gold filling in a front tooth. Speaking in Spanish, he told her a story about how he used to kill chickens on his grandmother's farm by wringing their necks. Lia couldn't decide whether he was trying to repulse her or impress her; both seemed equally plausible from his expression.

The trail from the cliff led to a hard-packed road barely wide enough for a motorcycle, let alone a truck. After about a quarter of a mile they crossed a much wider asphalt road cut into the mountainside. On the other side of the road they found another trail, this one strewn with rocks. It zigzagged through a series of cuts before leveling off in a brush-filled plain. Then it meandered through the vegetation for twenty yards or so before funneling down another series of cuts. Stairs had been carved into the stones in a few places, their treads worn at the center by the shuffling feet of centuries of travelers. Lia felt as if she might come across a Spanish conquistador at every turn.

"What do the people in the village here do?" she asked the soldier, as much to stop his narrative of dying chickens as to satisfy her curiosity.

"Nothing," he told her. "They are just country people. Backward. Old Indians lost in a daze."

Lia would have laughed at the idea of a chicken killer calling other people backward, but at that moment a hail of bullets rained down from above. She dove to the ground, sliding on the briefcase for a few feet as if it were a sled. A shower of lead, dirt, and rock splinters pelted the narrow pass behind her. She managed to half-crawl, half-slide out of the gunfire. But when she raised her head to get her bearings, a fresh fusillade of bullets pelted the dirt above her.

"Lia!" said Rockman in her ear. "What's going on?"

"Gunfire. Automatic weapons." She glanced to her right, looking for her escort—or better, his gun. But he was nowhere to be seen.

As the gunfire relented, Lia looked around the stone cut where she had taken shelter. The angle of the path made it difficult to see above—a good thing actually, as it kept her out of the line of fire. The ledge opposite her was bare.

"How far am I from the village?" she asked Rockman.

"Another half mile by air. I'm looking at a satellite photo of the area from a few days ago. The trail zigs down to the north, then flattens out. We have a U-2 en route to your area; he's no more than five minutes away."

Lia took out her pistol and began backing down the trail in the direction of the village, dragging her briefcase behind her. She got about twenty feet when a fresh spray of gunfire percolated the mountainside, the rocks magnifying the guns' pop and making it difficult to determine exactly where they were. Lia froze and turned slowly, making sure the way she was going was still clear.

It wasn't. Shadows appeared near the bend, and she heard footsteps clattering nearby. She was surrounded.

"If you are a soldier," shouted a voice in Spanish, "surrender and join us or you will be killed."

"I'm not a soldier," she yelled in Spanish.

She leaned forward, peering back toward the cut she had just come down. She could see the noses of two AK-47s, their owners hidden behind the rocks.

"Surrender, miss," said a voice somewhere above her. "You are a prisoner of Sendero Nuevo, the New Path for Peru. We will treat you with kindness if you come peacefully, and show no mercy if you resist."

72

Dean and Karr took the small runabout downriver about a mile before turning back. There was little traffic nearby. Karr's PDA had survived the dunking, and they used it to help guide them to a spot a half mile below the Inca ruins that the Art Room had identified as a good place to hide the boat.

Fashona had left them with some new gear, including new radiation detection gear, an MP5 submachine gun, and night-vision goggles. He'd also brought replacement boots for Dean. They were a bit on the stiff side, but Dean changed into them when he got out of the boat, figuring they would be better than sneakers when climbing the rough terrain.

"You're not to engage any forces," Telach told them after they tied the boat up. "Especially Peruvian. Avoid contact."

"What if they're hostile?" said Karr.

"Avoid contact," she snapped. "Avoid contact. You got it?"

"You're no fun."

"Charlie?"

"Yeah, we understand, Marie. If we find this guy, though—"

"Simply report what you find. We'll handle the next step."

"Gonna send the Delta boys to finish the job," said Karr.

The hike to the buildings would be about ten miles long. Along the way, they would climb about five thousand feet, a little more than a mile. An unmanned aircraft known as a Global Hawk had been launched on a mission from the U.S. to supply overhead reconnaissance, which would make things easier than they might have been. There were a number of road patrols and checkpoints, and the eye in the sky would tell them which were occupied and which weren't. They'd also be able to use the trails without having to worry about being surprised by a patrol, even though they were walking in broad daylight.

Fifteen minutes into the hike, Karr suggested they snack while they walked. Before Dean could offer an opinion, the other op was halfway through his third sandwich.

"That food's supposed to last us until tomorrow," said Dean.

"Can't work on an empty stomach. Something will turn up. Worst case, we chow down on some of those MREs Fashona gave us. Good enough for the troops, good enough for us. Right?"

"I guess."

"You prefer C rations?"

"MREs will do." MREs—"Meals Ready to Eat"—were the modern equivalent of C rations, the World War II era canned food issued to troops in the field.

A few minutes later, Sandy Chafetz checked in with them from the Art Room, telling them she was taking over from Rockman as their runner.

"I'm sitting in for a bit," she told Dean. "I'm looking at you right now on the infrared feed from the Global Hawk. Going back to optical. You have a nice, easy walk around the perimeter of those Aztec ruins to the outpost. There are two soldiers down the road, but we think you can get around them easily."

"Incas," said Dean, correcting her. "The Aztecs were further north. How's Lia doing?"

"Lia's all right," said Chafetz.

There was a defensiveness to her voice, the tone a kid might use if he was being questioned about breaking curfew.

"What happened to her?" said Dean.

"Charlie—"

"What happened to her?"

"She's OK."

"Let me talk to Telach."

"It's under control, Charlie."

"If it were, Rockman would be talking to me."

Telach broke in. "What's wrong, Charlie?"

"Where's Lia?"

"Her helicopter crashed about eighty miles north of La Oroya. She was rescued by some soldiers there, but now they've been ambushed by local guerrillas."

"Where is she now?"

"We have it under control."

"I want the whole story," insisted Dean, stopping.

"That is the whole story, Charlie. We have a team standing by to assist."

"Standing by where? Is this the team in Ecuador?"

"Charlie, I really don't have time to explain this to you. Please let us handle it."

He slapped the communications unit off in a fit of anger.

"Charlie?" said Karr.

Dean pointed at his ear. Karr turned off his communications set.

"Lia's in trouble," Dean told him.

"Where is she?"

"North of La Oroya. She has no backup."

"We have the paras in Ecuador," said Karr. "And there's all sorts of Delta people arriving in Lima."

"Ecuador's a couple of hundred miles away, more. They're situated for a mission near Iquitos. She's down near La Oroya. One of us should be there backing her up."

Karr ambled over toward him. "You're not going to leave, are you?"

"I am going to leave."

"How are you going to get there?"

"I'll rent that airplane."

"You don't even know where you're going."

"Telach said the helicopter crashed eighty miles north of

La Oroya. It'll be in the same valley we took north with Fashona. I'll look for it."

"Come on, Charlie. Let the Art Room take care of it."

"This is just a sneak and peak. You can handle it by yourself."

"That's not the point."

"I have to go, Tommy."

Karr stared at him for a long moment before frowning and shaking his head. "I really don't think you should do this."

"Come with me."

"Aw, come on; I can't do that."

"We let her get raped in Korea, Tommy. We should have been there."

Karr frowned but didn't answer. As Dean started to step around him, Karr grabbed his shoulder. It was a strong, tight grip, and Dean worried that he would have to fight Karr to get by.

"I don't think you should go," said Karr. "But if you have to, all right. Just remember the Art Room is going to know right away."

Dean nodded.

"Take the boat. Hire the geezer with the plane," said Karr. "I'll catch up when I can."

73

The guerrillas took Lia over the face of a cliff about fifty yards from the trail, then almost straight down a chimney in the rocks where metal ladders had been anchored into the stone. She'd managed to conceal her pistol but had to give up the briefcase with her laptop and the replacement voter cards; it dangled precariously from the shoulder of one of the guerrillas as they descended to a ledge along the rocks. Every so often Rockman would say something he thought was encouraging; Lia would grunt in response. There were eight guerrillas, all armed with AK-47s.

She'd be able to get away eventually. It was just a matter of patience.

Unfortunately, patience was not one of her virtues.

Roughly three hours after her capture, they reached a hamlet about a half mile from the valley the helicopter had been flying along when it crashed. One of the guerrillas whistled loudly, apparently alerting a sentry, who responded with a similarly shrill call. The procession stopped for a moment to allow the group's commander to pass to the front. He led the way off the trail through a small copse of trees and underbrush. Lia tried to memorize the surroundings, realizing that the footpath ahead must be booby-trapped. She saw ax cuts low on the trunks of the trees—obviously guides, but they'd be difficult to spot in the dark.

The group emerged at the end of a semicircle of eight

small paste-gray houses built of some sort of masonry material or maybe even mud. They fronted an overgrown cobblestone street. There were ruins on the other side of the road, all overgrown by vegetation. Lia could tell from the lack of trees in the distance that the path extended down the mountainside.

The guerrillas led her to one of the houses with a large satellite dish in the side yard.

"You watch TV?" she said aloud, giving the Art Room a readily identifiable landmark. "Satellite TV?"

"Television can be useful," said the guerrilla leader, who'd stopped at the threshold of the house.

"You get pointers from reruns of *Mao Knows Best*?" snapped Lia.

"You have a good sense of humor for a UN employee," said the man.

"And you speak English pretty well for a Peruvian Indian."

"I studied at Cambridge. And I am not a member of the native tribes. Please, come inside."

The interior was dark and dank. A small table filled almost half of the front room; six chairs were crowded around it, and another half dozen were pushed against the walls. There were two doorways to other rooms at the right. Blankets hung across them instead of doors.

"Did you shoot down the helicopter?" Lia asked.

"That was an accident," said the man. "The army was conducting operations against us, and we believed your aircraft was a military one. Only after the weapon was fired was the mistake recognized. We were on our way to help."

"I'll bet."

"The army patrol that found you killed my men before they could rescue you. Our intentions were peaceful."

"Rescue or kidnap?"

"You aren't a prisoner. Our war is against the army. Not the people."

"So I can leave?"

"You would not do well on your own here. We will arrange for transportation."

"Maybe I ought to take my chances." Lia glanced at the door. Two men were blocking her way.

"Let him play the magnanimous warlord," said Rockman in her ear.

"We're not against the United Nations," said the guerrilla leader.

"What about the U.S.?"

"Why'd you tell him you were American?" asked Rockman. "Lay back, Lia. Lay back."

Shut up, Rockman, she thought to herself. He knows I'm American.

"The U.S. exploits the entire world," said the guerrilla. "I have nothing but disdain toward your leadership. The metals here are ripped from the ground for who? Yankees. But since you work for the United Nations, we will give you the benefit of the doubt."

"Thanks."

The guerrilla smiled. "Empty your pockets."

"I pulled them inside out for your man on the trail."

"Please do it for me."

Lia took out her PDA and placed it on the table, along with some change. The guerrilla picked up the handheld computer.

"It's a handheld computer. If you know what that is."

"I told you I went to Cambridge." He turned it over. "Is it a Palm?"

"Try and get a name," said Rockman. "We're searching the Peruvian intelligence databases."

"It's not a Palm. It's a cheap knockoff," she said. "I can't afford the real thing."

"It doesn't seem to be working," he said when it failed to boot up after he pushed the power switch.

"It broke in the crash." Actually, the unit would not activate without reading her thumbprint on the back. "Two hundred bucks up in smoke."

He slid it back to her. "So what do you have in your bag?"

"A laptop." Lia took it out. "When did you go to Cambridge?"

"Why?" asked the guerrilla. "Did you go there, too?"

"No. I'm afraid my family wasn't rich enough to send me to Cambridge." She just barely stopped herself from adding *or any college,* remembering her cover story—she was supposed to be a computer expert.

The rebel turned on the laptop. The computer beeped and booted into a safe mode designed for exactly this sort of situation. It would operate exactly as a normal machine running Microsoft Windows XP; any serious attempt to access the hidden programs and data would erase them.

"What's your name?" Lia asked. "Or should I just call you El Comandante?"

"What's yours?"

"Li Shanken. I work for a company that supplies diagnostics for the voting machines."

"You are one of the army of hundreds here to make sure the election is fair. According to the television, yes?"

"It will be fair."

"You're very naive, Li. The international corporations have already decided who will win the election. Will it be Imberbe, or Ortez, the Stone Age vice president? The dark horse Aznar? He is coming up from behind. That is an attractive story line, the underdog who comes from nowhere. Peruvians love such fairy tales. I predict he will be the winner. What does it matter? The corporations will still run things, with your country's help."

"He still hasn't told you his name," said Rockman.

"So when can I go?" said Lia.

"We will take you to the village when the time comes."

"When is that? Five minutes from now?"

"You have a sharp sense of humor."

"I try, *Comandante.*"

"You may call me Paolo. I am not a commander. Those sorts of titles are not of use among us."

"How did you get to Cambridge? You don't look English."

"I'm not. I was born in Chala, Peru. This is my country."

"Bingo," said Rockman. "All right. We can get it."

"Where's Chala?" asked Lia.

"On the coast, south of Lima. A pleasant place to grow up. But if you recognize the struggle of the peasants, you cannot live with yourself there. Or anywhere."

"And you're on the peasants' side?"

"Yes."

"Is that why you were going to destroy Lima?"

"I wasn't going to destroy Lima," said the guerrilla.

"Your movement was. With a nuclear bomb."

"No. Those reports are false. The government is trying to spread false rumors to discourage people from joining us. They're lies. Terrible lies."

"He's a lot more important than he claims," said Rockman. "One of the three or four leaders."

"Prove that they're lies," said Lia, trying to shut Rockman out.

"There are many ways. We would not turn such a weapon against our own people."

"You use bombs all the time."

"Not such as this." The guerrilla shook his head.

"That's the best you can do?"

He slammed the table with his fist. "It's a plot by the government. You'll see."

"Give me evidence to bring back to the people," said Lia, sensing an opening. "I'll spread the word for you. Give me proof."

Still angry, the guerrilla leader slapped the laptop closed and stuffed it into her briefcase. He took it with him as he walked to the front door. Lia started to follow, but the guards kept her inside.

"I thought I was free to go," she said sarcastically.

74

Dean untied the boat and jammed his hand against the throttle, pulling away from shore so quickly the hull seemed to soar above the water.

He left the communications system off; there was nothing the Art Room was going to tell him that he wanted to hear at the moment.

Eventually, he'd have to talk to them. But it would be better to wait until he was almost there.

Karr's advice not to go gnawed at him gently, but Lia's need overwhelmed it. As Karr had put it, the "sneak and peak" was easy enough for one person to handle on his own. Lia needed help.

Dean found the pilot sitting on the dock where he had left him, sipping a beer.

"You sober enough to fly?"

"Not a problem," said the pilot. "Where?"

"There was a helicopter crash in the mountains about eighty miles north of La Oroya. I want to go there."

The pilot's expression immediately changed.

"I'll pay five hundred dollars cash when we land," Dean told him.

"And fuel?"

"And fuel."

"Let me see the money."

Dean put his hand into his pocket and pulled out a wad of

bills. "And don't get any ideas," he added, leaning forward not only to intimidate the man physically but also to show the shoulder holsters under his jacket.

"I am not a thief," said the pilot. "I need sols for the petrol."

"I got them." Dean pulled out one of the maps he had folded into his pocket. "It's somewhere around here, in one of these valleys."

"Somewhere?"

"You think a crash is going to be hard to find?"

"From the air in a jungle, it may very well be, yes." The pilot took the map. "Where were they flying from?"

"La Oroya."

The man nodded. "This valley. But I have to tell you, it may be difficult to find a place to land where you're talking of going. Those are the mountains."

"We'll worry about that when we find it."

75

"I have great difficulty believing you told him to go, Mr. Karr."

"Seemed like a good idea at the time," Karr told Rubens. He was zigzagging around the edge of the Inca ruins, walking through an area probably used as a cemetery five hundred years before. If there were any ghosts—and if any civilization was going to have ghosts, it would be the Incas—Karr hoped they would be friendly.

"This was completely unnecessary," continued Rubens. "We are quite capable of dealing with the situation here. Your assignment is more important."

"Yeah, well, I really didn't need him. This is routine, you know?"

Rubens clicked off the line. A few yards later, Karr caught sight of the sentry post on the road thirty yards away. Two Peruvian privates were standing near the road, guns dangling from their hands. He watched them for a moment, gauging their boredom. As soon as one of the men walked off to the left, Karr scrambled down the embankment of stones, trotting down a short hill and continuing on for a few hundred paces. The thin air made even the short run a strain, and he finally had to stop and take a rest.

"You shouldn't have lied for him, Tommy," said Chafetz.

"Who's lying?" Karr got to his feet. "You don't really think I need help here, do you?"

"That's not the point. We have other assets, and the mission set is determined—"

"Keep an eye on the road for me, all right?"

"You're clear."

A half hour later, Karr came to the edge of the small compound where the satellite phone calls had been made from. There were two large buildings, both made of stone and dating to the colonial period. One was a large barn, the other a three-story house. The infrared sensors on the Global Hawk, which was orbiting above him at sixty thousand feet, had not seen anyone outside. Karr took his binoculars from his rucksack and scanned both buildings before going closer.

"Tracks from a heavy truck," he said, looking at the dirt in front of the barn. "Can't tell how old they are. When was the last time it rained?"

"Tuesday night," said Chafetz. "Can you get a close-up?"

"Anything for you, darlin'." Karr took out his handheld computer and slid a camera attachment on the end. Then he walked over and took three pictures. "Biggest tourist attraction in Peru."

The large side-by-side doors at the front of the barn were secured with a chain that ran through the handles and was held in place by a combination lock. The steel shop door next to them had a padlock. Either could be easily picked, but if he went in that way he had to leave the locks off and it would be obvious someone was inside. Looking for a less conspicuous way to get in, Karr walked around the side of the building away from the house. The windows were relatively new aluminum replacements for whatever had originally been there. He scanned one for burglar alarms; when he found none he tried to open it but found it locked. The same was true on the other.

Karr took out his night-vision glasses and held them up to the glass to peer inside. The interior of the barn had been stripped of stalls or whatever dividers it had once had. It had a poured concrete floor and steel beams across the ceiling. Thick electric conduit and industrial-style outlets ran along part of the wall and crisscrossed the ceiling. There were tools and a workbench on the far side.

"I think I'll break the window and go in," he told Chafetz. "This side can't be seen from the house, or the road up front."

"Go for it."

Karr broke the window with his elbow, then reached inside and undid the lock. The window was a surprisingly tight fit, but he got in smoothly, pulled it shut behind him, and crouched near the thick wall, surveying the wide space.

A metal door covered an opening in the floor at the northwest corner, and a few pieces of wood were stacked near the large doors; otherwise the barn was empty.

"Got a trapdoor in the corner here."

"Interesting."

"Could be a bunker or something. How deep can the Global Hawk see?"

"It has infrared and optical, no radar," said Chafetz. "Radar" would have been a ground penetrating device specially designed to look for bunkers and other underground facilities. "The Air Force has a U-2 with radar en route to Peru. We'll check with its mission tasking and see if we can have it fly overhead."

"OK," said Karr, examining the locked door. He pulled at it gently; when it didn't budge, he decided to save it for later. He walked through the rest of the building.

"Brought a truck inside," said Karr, kneeling near the tire tracks. "Probably the one that made the tracks."

A large truck had backed in through the double doors; dirt and grit were caked in little mounds from the treads. He saw black skid marks just beyond them.

"Check these out," he told Chafetz, taking out his PDA with its camera. "Maybe they're from a forklift."

"Why don't you run the interrogator on the area near the door?" she suggested. "That will give us an image. The U-2 is at least an hour away."

"Good idea."

"Are you going to try it?"

"Hold your horses," said Karr. "I'm getting some images of the work area for you first. You're getting as bad as Rockman."

"I'm sorry, Tommy."

"Rubens is breathing down your neck, right?"

"That's not it."

"Oh yeah, right."

The work area had the makings of a decent metal shop, with a multi-tester and an old, large oscilloscope. Karr walked around the large room, occasionally dropping to his hands and knees to look more closely at the floor or wall. The floor was rather clean; it looked like it was regularly swept.

Not that he was a real expert on barns.

Satisfied that there were no hidden rooms anywhere or trick panels in the concrete, Karr went back to his rucksack for the radiation detector and the interrogator. He started with the detector in the work area; it was clean. Then he made a series of slow passes across the floor, holding the detector below his waist. When he was done, he went back and turned on the other machine. As LEDs at the side began blinking, he reached into the ruck and took out the wire to connect it with his communications gear. He slipped it into the socket at the side of his belt, then attached an ear set directly to the device; a tone would sound if the machine's rays encountered anything thick enough to be interesting.

The techies who had first checked him out on the machine about a year before had warned him that it was really an oversexed X-ray machine; standing in front of it for any length of time was extremely hazardous for his short- as well as long-term health. They had also told him that there was a distant but theoretical possibility that the radiation in the device could trip a fail-safe circuit in a cleverly constructed bomb, causing the weapon to explode. He tried not to think about that possibility as he slowly worked the beam over the walls and floor.

It didn't help that he had recognized a mistake in the formula they showed him about the amount of radiation exposure from a ten-second blast by the machine. If they had made a mistake of the same magnitude on the probability of setting off a nuke, he might soon be a permanent part of the Peruvian hillside.

"Here we go," he told Chafetz. "If you hear a boom, you'll know I found something."

Karr laughed, but he felt sweat running down the side of his neck. He worked his way slowly around the concrete floor, once more reserving the area around the steel door for last. Finally, he went over to the door and pointed the interrogator downward.

No beep.

"It's a tunnel," said Chafetz. "Goes in the direction of the house."

"All right. I'll check that next."

Karr switched the interrogator off and started to whistle. He walked back to the rucksack, bending to put his gear back.

As he did, the lights in the barn switched on.

76

"It's about time you checked in, Mr. Dean."

"Hello, Mr. Rubens."

"Why did you leave Mr. Karr?"

Dean cupped his hand over the sat phone, pretending to use it as he spoke to the Art Room.

"I'm going to help Lia."

"That's really unnecessary, Charlie. We've put the paramilitary unit that was stationed in Ecuador into the air already."

"If they're flying helicopters, they'll have to stop and refuel at least once. I can get there first."

"Your mission was to check the site of satellite telephone transmissions with Mr. Magnor-Karr."

"He can handle that on his own."

"That is not your decision to make, Mr. Dean. You cannot be privy to all information such judgments require."

"I know enough to say the judgment was wrong."

Dean glanced at his watch. They were about five minutes from the valley the pilot said was the most likely spot for the crash.

"It would be helpful if you could tell me where she is," Dean continued. "Sooner or later I'm going to find her, but it would probably be better sooner."

"Do not think this means I approve."

There was a slight but audible pop on the line.

"Charlie?"

"Hello, Marie."

"Lia is in a small settlement fifty miles to the northeast of where you're flying. There's a large pond four miles south of it that we think your airplane could use to land; Fashona says it'll be tight but doable."

"OK."

"The paramilitary team has just landed to refuel. They're about a half hour of flying time away, but our preference would be to conduct the mission after nightfall, which is seven hours from now. Lia doesn't seem to be in any immediate danger. We're in contact with her—well, you know Lia; she says she's fine."

"I'll bet."

"The rebels realize she's here for the UN. They've told her they may release her. We're not taking them at their word, but they have been fairly benign toward her."

Dean scoffed.

"I'm not saying I trust them," noted Telach. "We have infrared imagery of the area where she is from a U-2 overhead. In addition, she's given us a good idea of the layout there. She believes that the area immediately outside of the settlement is either mined or booby-trapped in some way. It would be very useful if you could scout that for the rescue team. We'd like you to start by looking at two landing sites nearby."

"OK."

Dean told the pilot to change his course for the northeast, then unfolded the map. With prompts from the Art Room, he showed the pilot the mountainside where the helicopter had crashed and the lake where he wanted to land.

"I'd like to look at the area first," Dean told the pilot. "I'd prefer not to attract much attention when I do so, though."

"Let me ask you: Did the person you were talking to on your phone there say this was an accident? Or did someone shoot down the helicopter? Because there are guerrillas all through this valley."

"He wasn't sure."

"It would be better not to get too close."

"I agree."

They flew about a half mile from the site, just close enough to make out part of the wreckage twisted against the hillside. Sunlight glinted off the glass, helping mark the location. The guerrilla camp was not very far away, no more than two miles, but the rugged terrain and thick vegetation made it invisible from the air, even when Dean looked directly at it.

"I can't land on that lake," said the pilot as they passed over it. "The sides of the mountain there are too steep, and with the trees I would be taking too big a risk."

Fashona had said it was doable, but Dean wasn't in a position to argue.

"Where else can you land?"

"There's a stretch of that highway that's long enough. It's only a half mile away."

"You'll ruin your floats."

"There are wheels at the bottom of them. But we get only one pass. And it would be a good idea to have your gun ready."

77

Karr swung around as the light in the barn came on, but there was no one at the doors.

He pulled off the glasses, leaping back to his rucksack and grabbing his submachine gun.

"Lights are on here," he told Chafetz in the Art Room. "Must be some sort of timing circuit."

"In a barn, Tommy?"

"Good point. Anybody outside?"

"Negative."

Karr pulled his bag with him to the trapdoor. He was thinking about using it as a hiding place when he realized there was light coming through the cracks from below.

"OK, now I think I know what's going on," he told Chafetz. "This is a tunnel to the house. Somebody must be coming."

"Then get out of there."

"And miss all the excitement?"

Karr pulled his pack on his back so he wouldn't have to worry about retrieving it if he had to retreat. Then he stepped behind the hinge to the door, so he could surprise whoever was coming out. A minute later, the door creaked, and the metal swung upward slowly. Karr waited a second, then pitched his arms back, wielding the submachine gun like a club.

He stopped it just short of the small gray-haired skull that popped into the opening.

"Whoa!" said Karr, reaching down and grabbing the diminutive woman from the stairwell. He threw her aside, then scrambled over the opening.

The tunnel, its sides lined with closely fitted stones, was empty. Karr ran down about halfway and stopped. He took a video bug from his pocket and slapped it onto the tunnel ceiling, barely six inches above his head. Then he trotted back up the steps. The woman lay in a heap on the floor, still dazed.

"Jeez, I'm sorry, ma'am," he said, raising her head and trying to revive her. "*Scusa.* Like, really, I'm sorry. You all right? Ma'am?"

The woman opened her eyes, then jerked back in fright.

"Oh man, I'm really sorry. It's OK," he said. He slung the gun over his shoulder and pulled her up. "Chafetz, get those translators online here. Help me out. This poor old lady looks like she saw a ghost."

78

"You should have stopped him," Rubens told Telach as they stood under the large screen at the front of the Art Room.

"I don't have a magic wand," snapped Telach. "Frankly, he'll be of considerable help scouting the camp."

"I don't wish to argue that point, Ms. Telach. It's the principle of who is running the mission."

"Which is more important? Principle or results?"

Rubens took a step back. "Well put. But we must be mindful of both."

"Mr. Rubens, Marie—you want to listen in to Tommy Karr," interrupted Sandy Chafetz. "He found a housekeeper at the site where the Russian phone was used. She's telling him about large crates she saw, and mechanical equipment."

"Switch it on," said Rubens.

A brittle voice filled the room, its words a mixture of Spanish and another tongue Rubens wasn't familiar with. Rubens heard her describe large crates that had once been stacked at the side of the barn. One of the Art Room translators repeated what the woman had said in English. He was interrupted by Tommy Karr, asking for another piece of "whatever this great stuff is I'm eating."

"She works for a general," Chafetz said.

"Túcume?" asked Rubens. The area here was under his command.

"Tommy hasn't had a chance to ask her specifically, but it has to be. She thinks he works for him."

"So what happened to these crates?" Karr asked in English. The translator gave him the words in Spanish, and Karr repeated them.

"Perhaps Señor Stephan took them with him. He left a note saying the general sent a car for him Thursday night."

"Señor Stephan?" asked Karr.

"*Sí.*"

"Did he have a last name?"

The woman began explaining that he didn't use one.

"Tell Mr. Karr a last name isn't crucial," Rubens told Chafetz, guessing this *had* to be Stephan Babin—Sholk— regardless of what name he might or might not be using. "But a physical description would be most useful."

79

Lia stood near the door of the house, straining to hear what was going on outside. The guerrilla leader was saying something to two men about the military patrols in the area. As she leaned close to the door to hear, the floor squeaked slightly and one of the guards turned around. He angrily shooed her back toward the center of the room.

"I just wanted to know if I could get some food," she told him. "I'm hungry."

The man replied in Spanish that she would do as she was told or she would have a diet of lead. Lia went back and sat at the table.

"Could you make anything out?" she whispered to Rockman.

"They were talking about the military unit by the crash site. Your friend the commander is sending more men to reinforce the people tracking the soldiers. The guards don't seem to understand why the army doesn't surrender and join the revolution," said Rockman. "They killed most of the small unit that rescued you near the helicopter because they wouldn't give up. The commander used a lot of Maoist rant. Called each other 'comrade' and all that crap. I thought I was in a time warp."

"They say anything about me?"

"Not that we could pick up. They don't seem to think you're important."

"Story of my life."

"We'll take you tonight. Ought to be pretty easy. Charlie's headed in your direction."

"Charlie?"

"He's going to scout for the paramilitary team. He'll be on the ground any minute now. We're going to set up the paramilitary team so they can come in quickly if there's a problem, but like I said, we'll wait until nightfall, when things will be easier to pull off."

"I thought he was way up north with Tommy?"

"Charlie heard what happened and was worried about you, so he decided to help out," said Rockman. "Tommy said he didn't need him."

"I don't need him, either."

I should never have told him I was scared, she thought. The panic in the bank vault was a freak thing. She didn't need to be rescued or looked after.

Especially by Charlie Dean. She could take care of herself.

"Lia? You sound like you're mad at him."

"I'm all right."

She could get out of here herself, whenever she wanted. She still had her pistol. It would not be difficult to shoot the two guards at the door, grab one of their rifles, and then run into the woods nearby.

The gunshots would alert the others. And she didn't have the voter cards, which were still hidden in the briefcase.

As she pondered a way of retrieving them, a man she hadn't seen before came into the hut carrying a basket. He set the basket at the edge of the table and pushed it toward her. Then he quickly retreated, as if he might catch germs from being in the same room with her.

"Wait!" said Lia in Spanish.

The man froze.

"What is this?"

"Food." The man was large, nearly as big as Tommy Karr, but he seemed puzzled, as if he didn't quite understand her simple question.

"I want to speak to Paolo," Lia told him. "The commander. You understand?"

He nodded hesitantly.

"Go ahead; you can go," Lia said.

The basket contained two small loaves of bread. Though she was hungry, Lia didn't trust the guerrillas enough to eat it. Five minutes later, the guerrilla leader appeared in the doorway.

"There's a problem?" he asked.

"My computer. I would like to work."

"We can't spare the electricity. We have to generate our own."

"It has a battery."

"I'm sorry." He started to leave.

"You're stealing my laptop?"

The accusation of theft apparently stung, for the guerrilla turned around swiftly. "The revolution must make use of the resources it needs."

"To do what? Blow up Lima?"

"That bomb is not ours," he said. "This is a plot by the army to discredit us. The general of that unit—he is a notorious reactionary. He's the one you should denounce."

"Ask him how he knows it's not a guerrilla weapon," said Rubens, coming on the line from the Art Room.

"You told me you weren't very important," said Lia. "How would you know whether the bomb was real or not?"

"We don't have nuclear weapons."

"Tell him it came from Russia," said Rubens. "See what he says."

"The bomb is Russian, isn't it?" said Lia. "The UN people think so."

"Russia gave up the revolution long ago."

"There are still communists there. And people who would sell anything."

"Where would we get the money for it?"

"Ask him for some definite proof," said Rubens. "Tell him you'll tell the world—that the guerrillas are being libeled and you want to help."

Come here and tell him that yourself, thought Lia. "The world thinks you're murderers."

"I can't do anything about that. This is another government plot."

"What about the post office takeover in Lima the other day?" asked Rubens.

"You tried to take over a post office in Lima—"

"I did? No. And no member of our movement did. That was a government plot as well."

"Why do you say that? Are post offices off-limits?"

The rebel leader didn't respond.

"The post office takeover would have to be approved by the rebels' governing council," said Rubens. "And he's on it."

"You think of yourself as Robin Hood, don't you?" said Lia. "Take from the rich, give to the poor."

"That's not a bad philosophy," said the guerrilla.

"So you did rob the post office?"

"First of all, the post office was not robbed. It was taken over. It was a political action. So you can't accuse whoever did it of being thieves. Second of all, the men there surrendered. That on its face shows they were not members of the New Path. We would never surrender. We don't have to steal," added the guerrilla. "We have better ways of getting money."

"Like selling drugs?"

"That was our fathers' mistake." The rebel leader turned on his heel.

"I'd like my briefcase back at least. You can have the laptop," said Lia. "My mother gave me it when I left for college. Or does the revolution need that, too?"

The guerrilla left the hut without answering.

"Very good, Lia," said Rubens.

"He could be lying," she told him.

"Yes, certainly. His name is Paul Servico. He did go to Cambridge, incidentally, but dropped out three years ago. He came back to Peru and organized the New Path. His father was a member of the Shining Path, as was his uncle. Both were executed by the government."

Lia leaned back in the chair. "What do you want me to do?"

"Stay safe, at the moment. Mr. Dean is nearby. The assault

team is prepared to retrieve you as soon as it's dark, sooner if necessary. Please, do not put yourself in any greater danger," he added. "I mean that sincerely."

She knew that he did, but she'd always thought it curious that his tone became even colder and more formal when he said it. Rubens was not a "touchy-feely" kind of guy. This was reassuring in an odd way; his emotional distance somehow made him seem more reliable.

"I'm fine, Mr. Rubens," she told him. "Or I wouldn't be here in the first place. Right?"

"Very well."

The guerrilla who had brought her food reappeared at the door, carrying her briefcase. Lia got up from the chair to take it; the man held it out to her tentatively.

"I'm not going to bite," she told him, but as soon as she took hold of the strap, he fled.

The laptop wasn't in the case, but the card reader and her notebooks were. Lia opened the case and ran her hand down the lining; it hadn't been ripped open and the cards were still inside.

She adjusted the strap and tucked it under her arm like an oversize purse. Then she went to the doorway, hoping to overhear Servico talking to her guards. But he was gone; only the sentries remained, and when she bent her head close to the opening to see beyond them, one of the men turned and asked what she was doing.

"Nature calls," she said in English, sarcastic at first, then more diplomatically in Spanish. The guard frowned but beckoned for her to follow. Lia felt a twinge of fear as she passed the second guard—it would have been easy for him to hit her with the butt end of his gun. But the moment passed.

They went all the way across the compound to the last hut in the semicircle. The man put his hand up and ordered her to stop. He leaned inside and yelled, checking to see if there was anyone else inside.

The house had been converted into a shower and latrine. The toilets consisted of a row of plywood boxes over a pit in the ground; fortunately, she really didn't have to use them.

Lia looked around the room. The showers—there were two, with no curtains, on the right—had some sort of running water, because one of the faucets was dripping. There were windows at the side of the room and another pair at the rear; they held screens but no glass. The screens hung on hinges at the top and were secured by simple hooks at the bottom.

"I'd like to take a shower," Lia announced in Spanish, stepping out of the latrine building. "Can you get me a towel?"

Her minder seemed perplexed by the request.

"A shower, to wash," she told him. "I need a towel."

"I understand what you said," replied the guard.

"So?"

"What are you doing, Lia?" asked Rockman.

"You would need permission from Comrade Paolo."

"For a towel?"

"Yes."

"So let's ask him."

"No."

"Is he in here?" asked Lia, starting toward the next cottage.

The guard ran in front of her and blocked her way with his rifle.

"Well, if you don't want me to ask him, you do it," she said. "Can I take a shower or not?"

The man frowned and gestured that she should go back to her cottage.

"Are you going to ask?" she insisted.

"Maybe."

"That's not good enough."

"Lia, don't push it," warned Rockman.

"All right," said the guard. "But you go back first. I will ask." He gestured with his rifle. "Back with me, and then I will ask."

80

Paul "Paolo" Servico was a member of the New Path's ruling committee, by some accounts the number three man in the organization. He was also wanted in England in connection with raising money for terrorist groups.

He was worth capturing for several reasons, but kidnapping foreigners was expressly forbidden by U.S. law without prior authorization from the president. While he *could* say that Servico was merely taken in the course of an operation to free one of his agents, Rubens greatly preferred playing it straight and vetting the decision beforehand. So he called Hadash, who was on a plane en route to Japan from China.

"Will taking him compromise your operative, or your original mission?" asked Hadash when Rubens finished briefing him.

"I don't believe so."

"Hold on."

As he waited on hold, Rubens couldn't help thinking of Hadash's decision to resign. It had utterly blindsided him. Surely it must be something personal; he'd have heard political whisperings. Nor was there any noticeable animosity between Marcke and Hadash.

But if it was personal, surely Hadash would have mentioned it. So perhaps it was a scandal that Rubens was somehow blind to. In that case, Hadash's reluctance would make a great deal of sense.

George Hadash involved in a scandal? *Impossible.*

How ironic, Rubens thought, to have the machinery of one of the greatest intelligence agencies in the world at his fingertips and to be powerless to use it in this instance.

"Bill, the president would like to speak to you," said Hadash. "I'm talking with him on another line. I'm going to connect us all."

"Of course," said Rubens.

"Billy, what are you proposing to do with Servico?" asked Marcke as soon the connection came through.

"Debrief him. Then turn him over to Peru or even to London. It is still remotely possible that he has information about the warhead."

"Billy, your person comes first," said Marcke. "But if you can get him without jeopardizing the operative or your mission, do it."

"Yes, sir."

"Find a safe place to confine him. But I don't want this ending up on *60 Minutes.* Determine whether he has anything useful or not; then we'll arrange to turn him over to London. Or Peru, depending on the situation."

"Yes, sir."

"Was there anything else?" Hadash asked Rubens.

"Not at the moment."

"We'll talk to you during the conference call," said Hadash, and the line snapped clear.

81

Dean closed his eyes as the floatplane pitched toward the blacktop, its wings fluttering up and down. The aircraft seemed to be having second thoughts—its nose pitched up as the ground came closer. The trees were so close on either side that when Dean opened his eyes for a last-second peek all he saw was green.

The motor roared. Sure that the pilot had pulled off at the last possible second, Dean braced himself. Finally he opened his eyes and realized they were stopping.

"This space ahead is more open," said the pilot. "I need it to take off. I don't like feeling hemmed in when I leave a place. Landing is one thing, but to take off—a bird needs an open sky."

Dean was not about to argue with him. He reached into his pocket and took out the agreed-to five hundred-dollar bills—and then added five more, along with some sols.

"This will cover whatever other expenses you have," he said, holding the money out. His other hand gripped one of his pistols. "And buy silence."

"Silence is a very necessary quality in my profession," said the pilot, taking the bills as the plane halted, straining against its brakes.

Dean grabbed his gear and jumped out, running to the nearby field. The aircraft began to move instantly, and by the time he reached the field it was roaring up the road. The airplane pulled up easily, banking off to the east.

Dean trotted parallel to the road a few hundred feet, then zigged farther into the field, angling toward a high spot he could use to survey the area. The relatively flat parcel had been used until recently as a farm field; he passed an old iron plow overgrown in the weeds.

"How we doing, Charlie?" asked Rockman as Dean stopped to get his bearings.

"I'm fine. Yourself?"

"Bit of a cold. I'm going to take you from here. Sandy's staying with Tommy."

"How's Lia?"

"Still in the compound, but she's setting up something to slip away."

"Tell her to hold on."

"I've only said that five hundred times. The first landing site we need you to look at is two miles due north of where you are. Parallel the road for a mile; then we'll tell you where to turn. We have a U-2 overhead, but we want you to double-check the jungle perimeter. Lia thinks there are mines near the village. The trees that show the safe path are marked with a notch. See if there's anything like that near the landing site."

"All right. I know the drill."

Dean checked his weapons, bent to retie his shoes, then started walking double time in the direction of the guerrilla compound.

82

Between Jackson's information about Sholk and Tommy's Indian housekeeper, Rubens now had no doubt that the arms dealer had survived the crash. The link to General Túcume was irrefutable. And the old woman's story confirmed Rubens' suspicion that there was another bomb.

Ambassador Jackson's surprise identification of one of the post office hostage takers as an army soldier was not just another intriguing connection with Túcume. While Rubens realized that it was not definitively proven that the man was working on the general's behalf—as Mr. Dean so recently illustrated, an underling could easily act on his own—it suggested that at least some of the guerrilla operations in the capital and elsewhere might have been staged by the general. Until now, all of the military was believed to favor Vice President Ortez. Túcume in his meeting with the CIA station chief some days before had come as close as he was allowed by military policies to endorsing Ortez.

But the guerrilla attacks had had hurt the current government and Ortez. While this might have been the result of miscalculations at first, surely someone running a clandestine campaign to bolster Ortez would have stopped them when he saw that the results were the opposite of what he wanted.

The "discovery" of documents linking the guerrillas with Imberbe at the same time the bomb was found—a matter of considerable importance in Peru—told Rubens that Túcume was not trying to help Imberbe, either. So what was Túcume's agenda?

A coup?

Túcume did not have enough soldiers under his control to pull one off; his units were spread thin over a vast area hundreds of miles from the capital, where forces loyal to the general staff were stationed. Even the Peruvians on the general staff who hated Túcume were having trouble scaring up any evidence of that—though the latest intercepts from the country indicated they were spreading rumors and probably laying the groundwork for such accusations.

Whatever Túcume was up to—assuming he was the mastermind and not being used by someone else—the U.S. needed to find where he might have the bomb hidden. Aside from obvious places like the military bases under his command and the village where his relatives lived, the list was rather short. Johnny Bib's people were trying to expand it, so that it could be turned over to the Peru Task Force as it searched for the bomb, but when Rubens met him in one of the Art Room conference centers for an update, Johnny's demeanor made it clear there had been little progress before he even began to speak.

"The problem is, we don't really know all that much about Túcume," said Ambassador Jackson, who along with Segio Nakami had accompanied Johnny Bib to the session. "The CIA dossier is far too brief. His military records are extensive. His finances, for example: clearly he must have access to more money than it would appear."

"Yes," said Rubens. "Have we looked at the finances of his relatives?"

"We have the bank accounts," said Segio. "They have money from mining interests. We haven't finished tracing all of the various family members and company holdings. But the flow to him—that's what we're missing."

"Drug money?" asked Rubens.

"Supposedly very honest, incredibly honest," said Jackson. "I'm relying on the CIA assessment, but his statements and military career would seem to back it up. And his name never appears in the various files on the narco trade in the north."

"The assessment is skimpy," said Rubens. "There's not even mention of a girlfriend in the backgrounder."

"According to the State Department backgrounder, the man is a military saint, brave, honest, and celibate. In a world as big as ours, there must be at least one, and apparently he's it," Jackson said sourly.

Rubens rubbed his forehead, trying to think of some shortcut to make their work, if not easier, at least more expedient. Much of the agency's available manpower was being used to examine different intercepts and electronic data relating to army movements and the government. Desk Three had showered several of Túcume's camps as well as suspected guerrilla strongholds with satellite-launched listening devices to help gather intelligence. Even with computers doing a large part of the work, however, collating and interpreting the information took considerable time and energy. It was a brute-force solution to the problem, a necessary approach certainly, but it couldn't be expected to yield immediate results.

And they needed immediate results.

"The candidate who has benefited most from recent events," said Jackson, "has been Aznar. He's been something of a lightweight in the past. Perhaps there's a connection between him and Túcume."

"We haven't seen one," said Johnny Bib.

"Obviously they'd have to hide it," Jackson murmured.

"There must be a connection," Rubens insisted. "There are many ways to help a campaign. Companies provide in-kind services—telephone banks for example. You have to look beyond financial records."

"Silver," said Johnny Bib.

"What about silver?"

"The Incas had silver." Johnny Bib jumped up and ran to the door. "I'll update you," he said, disappearing.

"Odd duck," said Jackson.

"More than odd," said Rubens.

Segio simply smiled.

"What do we have new on Babin?" Rubens asked.

"There are no photos of him," said Jackson. "We have a description based on Mr. Karr's interview with the house-keeper. Someone who uses crutches or a cane, although he can walk some on his own. Rough idea of his height, hair color, weight. It can be passed on to Peruvian intelligence."

"Yes," said Rubens, though doing so would beg the question of why the Americans were looking for Babin.

"We're looking at intercepts related to the radar station near the farm where he was," added Segio. "There is a faint possibility that there might be something there, such as money transfers in the region, that sort of thing. Nothing has come up yet. If they used messengers, if he handled things himself, it will be difficult to find any of that."

"Let's find out everything we can," said Rubens. "I'm sure there are other things we don't know."

"What is the CIA doing to find their prodigal son?" said Jackson.

"They're looking," said Rubens, refusing to be more specific.

The agency would leave no stone unturned. What they did with Babin once they found him—well, that was hardly a matter for speculation, was it?

If Rubens' people grabbed Babin, what tales might the Russian tell? The CIA, and by extension Collins, would be embarrassed, possibly worse. A leak to the right Senate staffer and Collins' candidacy for national security adviser would be torpedoed, no matter how cleverly she tried to distance herself from the initial operation.

Rubens winced internally. He liked to think of himself as someone who did not play political games, certainly not with the president and national security. Sholk—Babin—had to be found, but not because doing so would benefit Rubens. If there was a real nuke, Babin would know. And he would probably know where it was.

"Do you think the agency was operating under presidential

orders to shoot down Babin's plane?" Jackson asked as he and Segio got up to go.

"I have to say, Ambassador, you would be in a better position than me to make that judgment. You were closer to that administration than I."

"Well, I wouldn't say I was close. Different parties, among other things." Jackson smiled, or was it a grimace? "I'd say it's a good possibility that the agency had marching orders. Of course, they will have to take the rap now."

"No way to avoid it," Rubens agreed.

Jackson zeroed in. "You don't particularly like the agency, do you, Dr. Rubens?"

"We've had our differences," Rubens admitted, then felt compelled to add, "We are carrying heavy burdens, and we're only human."

"You're sure there's another bomb?"

"Highly likely."

"Will we find it?"

Peru was being crisscrossed by a growing armada of U-2s, Global Hawks, and other reconnaissance aircraft, searching for hiding places and trucks similar in size to those that would have left the tracks Karr had found. Army personnel, CIA officers, a number of experts from the State Department and other agencies were working with the Peruvians to watch their ports, airports, and borders. NSA teams were sorting through mounds of signal intelligence, looking for different links with the bomb. Thousands of people were working on this.

But the task was immense. Peru was about the size of California, Oregon, Washington, Nevada, and Utah put together. It was covered with thick tropical forests and inhospitable mountains. The warhead was smaller than an office desk.

"You'll have to excuse me, gentlemen; I have a phone call that I must make."

General Spielmorph, the officer appointed to head the task force dealing with the weapon in Peru, moderated the secure conference call with the president and others directly involved with the American response. The general briefly summarized the situation in his native Oklahoma drawl, starting with Karr's discovery, which had been shared with the task force commander minutes after it had been made. The general informed his listeners that the search grids, already concentrated in the north, were being shifted to focus around the houses. Ground-penetrating radar would be used to map possible underground bunkers and hiding places. He was sending a Delta team to inspect the house and barn a second time—unnecessary in Ruben's opinion, though he didn't say a word.

"We don't want this to look too much like an American operation," the secretary of state said. "It's better for Peru to be perceived as dealing with this very forcefully—it's not only a model for similar crises, God forbid, but it removes some political problems."

"It's a matter of efficiency," the general replied. "The Peruvians are very, shall we say, deliberate."

"Are they dragging their feet?" the president asked.

"No. This is all happening very quickly. They're used to a slower pace than we are, generally speaking. From their perspective, they may think they're rushing right along. Major General Maduro, the chief of staff, has been cooperative. Prickly, but cooperative. They don't want us talking directly to Túcume, although we are. They have the equivalent of a reinforced battalion physically protecting the warhead. That's actually the largest concentration of troops in the region. The guerrillas can't get it, at least. I'm certain of that."

"Is there a second warhead?" George Hadash asked from Japan. He sounded tired.

"Mr. Rubens?"

"We haven't turned up any hard evidence," Rubens said. "If handled properly, a warhead doesn't leave radiation behind. In fact, to detect nuclear material, one has to be very close, generally within nine meters, in some cases less. That said, we can state positively that whatever else was done in that barn, the pit of a weapon was not disassembled there."

"Or was never there in the first place," Collins said.

"That is correct. We simply don't know. These things don't tie themselves into very neat knots."

"I'd like as much of the search as possible completed before the Peruvian public learns that the known weapon lacks nuclear material," the president interjected. "After that comes out, political pressure will build quickly for us to leave the country. Build . . . it'll go up like a rocket."

"The international team of inspectors will probably get around to examining that weapon on Saturday," the general said. "I can't guarantee our search will be complete by then."

"I appreciate your frankness, General. Still, do everything humanly possible."

"Yes, sir."

Rubens' computer beeped, signaling an alert on his secure messaging system. He tapped the keys to bring the note onto the screen.

TUCUME FAMILY OWNS INTEREST IN MINERALE INTERNATIONALE, WHICH HAS WORKER ON AZNAR PAYROLL. WE HAVE FOUND DONATIONS TO AZNAR THAT APPEAR TO HAVE BEEN WASHED THROUGH THIRD PARTIES. PERHAPS HALF AZNAR'S FUNDS IN QUESTION. GALLO CHECKING FOR MORE.

—BIB

So the link between Túcume and the candidate was silver, and Johnny Bib found it. Gallo had probably hacked into the company records and begun comparing what they found to what they knew of Aznar's finances.

Rubens informed the conferees of the message and filled them in on the silver mining company. "Any contributions from a soldier or his family to a political candidate would be contrary to Peruvian law," Rubens explained. "This could be part of a sophisticated plot to get Aznar elected, or part of a plot to discredit him."

"That's obvious," Collins said. "It would be nice to know which possibility is the correct one."

Blanders ignored Collins. "Getting Aznar elected might

be one reason that a fake bomb would surface at this time," he said.

"Be nice if we had some evidence for that," someone retorted.

"What if Túcume has a real bomb?" Hadash asked.

"Having a weapon and using it are two completely different things," the president said. "Which may be the reason we are looking at a fake bomb on the world news. Billy, how good is the Túcume–Aznar connection?"

"We're getting it nailed down."

"How much money are we talking about?"

"I don't know yet. Perhaps half Aznar's campaign money."

"That's enough to buy most of the politicians I grew up with," the president said thoughtfully. "Of course, sometimes the bastards didn't stay bought—that was always the risk. Do we have any evidence that the candidate knows Túcume is giving him money?"

"No, sir."

"OK. And the Peruvians are having an election on Sunday. Well, I know a thing or two about politics. State, have the ambassador in Lima find Aznar and inform him of the connection."

"It'd be better to keep this at arm's length," said the secretary of state. He had spent a career in politics, too. "This way we can deny it if blows up in our face."

"All right," said the president. "Billy, can one of your people deliver the message convincingly?"

Someday, Rubens thought, he was going to have to tell the president that he hated to be called Billy.

"I have someone who might be credible," said Rubens. "Hernes Jackson, the former ambassador to Chile."

"Fine. Leak it to the Peruvian press after Aznar is informed. Don't get caught doing it."

"Yes, sir."

The conference ended on that note. Two minutes later Rubens' line buzzed with another call. Expecting Hadash, he picked it up. It was Collins.

"You're just full of surprises today," she said.

"How so?"

"You parceled out that info on the Túcume connection as if you were Santa Claus handing out presents. You were lucky it wasn't a videoconference; they would have seen you gloating. How long have you known?"

"I reported the information within sixty seconds of the time I received it."

"I'll bet. Stop playing games."

Rubens couldn't think of a thing to say.

"All you do is play games," she continued. "You want Hadash's job and you're trashing the agency to get it. You're manipulating information. You are playing with lives and careers here."

He hung up without answering.

83

Roughly an hour passed before the guard returned to Lia's cottage. He carried a small towel and soap.

"This is the best I can do," he told her. "The water is not very warm."

"It'll be fine," said Lia. "No bag?"

The guard didn't understand what she meant.

"To put the towel and soap in? Oh, never mind," she said, stuffing the towel and soap into the briefcase. "I'll use this."

She walked with the guard to the shower building. He went inside, pointing out the faucets and soap, as if these weren't obvious.

"Yes, very good," she told him finally. She reached down and untied her ankle-high hiking boots. He didn't take the hint.

"Excuse me. You're not going to watch me take a shower," she told him.

"I have to take your shoes."

"My shoes?"

"You won't need them in here."

Lia rolled her eyes, but this had no effect on him.

"Take them. You want my bra, too?"

The guard turned red, embarrassed, but he still took her shoes. He also left the door wide open. Lia went to it and closed it just enough to block the view of the shower and window. She stepped back and threw her socks where they could be seen.

"I'm going for it," she told Rockman.

"We'd prefer you wait until dark."

"That's four hours from now. I can get out right now." Lia saw no reason to stay in the compound until nightfall. For one thing, it was very possible that the rest of the rebels would return, beefing up the defenses.

And for another—she didn't need to be rescued like a damsel in distress. She could take care of herself.

"All right," said Rockman, his tone still slightly disapproving. "Charlie's about four hundred yards away, coming toward the front of the compound. They're down to six people total in the hamlet and nearby, counting your friend Paolo. You have just that one guard in front of the building. Two others on the perimeter—we don't have exact locations on them because of the foliage. They were at the north side three minutes ago."

Lia slipped the envelope with the voter cards out of the briefcase and tucked it into her waistband below her shirt and sweater. She slipped back, turned on the water, and yelped.

"C-old," she said, stepping back and watching the door. "Oh. Whoa."

She stepped over to the window and pushed it open.

"Here we go," she whispered to Rockman, and she pulled herself up and out. The screen smacked against the frame as she slipped to the ground. It sounded almost like an explosion to her, but she was committed now—with two quick steps she was in the brush behind the building.

As she started to slip into the larger trees, something moved twenty or thirty yards away. Lia froze as a pair of guards ambled through the jungle, guns raised toward the sky. They walked a few paces and stopped, chattering about some sort of food they'd recently eaten.

Lia backtracked to the hut, heart pounding. She slipped along the wall to the front, dropping to a knee to peer around the corner. The guard was still at his post, eyes cast down on the ground.

Lia had her pistol in her hand and could take him down

easily. But the gunshot would bring the others, and she decided to wait until he went inside to check on her. At that point, she could cross the open area to the jungle opposite the settlement.

The young guerrilla was extremely patient. Lia crouched for five, then ten minutes. She was starting to doubt her strategy when finally he went to the door, knocking and then asking if it was OK to come inside.

Lia took off from a sprinter's position, keeping herself as low to the ground as possible in case anyone else came out of the buildings. As she dove into the foliage on the other side of the path, she heard the guard yelling the alarm from the window she had used to escape from. She crawled forward, rolled in the dirt, then jumped to her feet.

As she did, something caught her from behind and threw her to the ground.

A hand clamped over her mouth.

"Sshh," hissed a familiar voice. "You're making way too much noise."

It was Charlie Dean.

84

General Túcume squinted at the video monitor, trying to decide which of the reporters in the audience outside were actually spies, for either other countries or his own government. He had already given a briefing to the general staff and Peru's president on the discovery of the weapon; it was clear from their questions that they were in favor of allowing a thorough examination by "neutral observers" as soon as possible. Túcume had feigned indifference.

The fake bomb was currently at a small base southwest of Puerto América under heavy—and well-trusted—guard. He had proposed moving it by water to a regional base near Santa Cruz, which would still be under his jurisdiction. The president seemed willing to go along with this, but some members of the general staff wanted it airlifted to the airbase at Iquitos, where it would fall under the air force's jurisdiction. Túcume had turned this aside by pointing out that the field was part of an international airport and inconveniently close to Brazil, which surely would be interested in acquiring such a powerful weapon.

Túcume wanted to delay giving over custody of the bomb for another twenty-four hours. That would guarantee that it wouldn't be discovered to be a fake until voting was under way.

When the weapon was found out to be phony, his reputation would suffer slightly. There would be some carping—he envisioned headlines declaring he was "General Duped." So his real goal at the press conference today was to lay out his future defense, cautioning everyone that "real tests" would have to be made.

"They're getting restless," said Chimor, his aide.

"The powerless often are."

Túcume went to the mirror and inspected his uniform, making sure his ribbons were in place. His ancestors would have done the same with their garments made of *cumi*, the fine weave reserved for rulers. A ruler was supposed to look the role.

"Let us talk to the press," he said, striding toward the hall.

Babin arrived at the hotel in time to see Túcume's press conference on TV in the suite room. It was a revelation. In person, the man was rather short and, while hardly a stuttering fool, not given to poetic turns of phrase. But here he commanded the stage. He looked regal, and the reporters scribbled frantically to take down his words about the importance of Peru and its future. There was no question in the Russian's mind that the stories Túcume had told of his ancestors were true.

Túcume fended off questions about the discovery. He said that he had personally shot several Maoist scum just a half hour before the bomb was discovered. He was shocked by the discovery of the warhead and claimed not to have believed his weapons expert when he told him what it was. He still had doubts, he added, because "one does not want to believe a countryman can be so evil."

As the camera panned the crowded room, Babin thought he recognized one of the low-life CIA slimes who had been involved in the operation to double-cross him. Was it Jones? Was it really him? Babin's anger flared, but he couldn't be sure.

The one face that had been burned into his memory was that of Jorge Evans. Evans he would never forget. He knew much about Evans—enough to ensure that his wrath would be fully requited.

The CIA would undoubtedly aim its weapons at Túcume next. They'd be watching the press conference; whether Babin was right about the man or not, someone would be here. Someone would be plotting to get the general's warhead and to kill the general in the process.

Babin would have an easier time if the Americans succeeded; the general was the only person who knew enough to stop him. But as he watched Túcume and listened to him talk about his heritage, Babin felt his emotions aroused. He liked the general and wanted him to succeed.

Babin could not afford to feel sentimental. He steeled himself, and by the time Túcume found him waiting with some of his aides, Babin would have shot the general himself if he thought it would bring him closer to his goal.

"Good, you managed to make the trip quickly," said Túcume as he came in. "I have some things to discuss. Technical concerns."

Babin nodded. The general dismissed the others.

"Would the warhead pass an inspection by the International Atomic Energy Agency?" asked Túcume.

"No, I've told you that several times. They check for a specific isotope. They have to be very close to the device, but they come prepared and they know what to look for. And then of course they will dismantle it."

"What about the real warhead? Would they damage the warhead if they examined it?"

Babin's heart jumped.

"The bomb would not be damaged, but letting anyone close to it is the last thing you should do." Babin reached to his right leg, which hung off the couch at an odd angle. "Whoever is sent to inspect will include American agents."

"CIA?"

"Of course. I recognized a man at your press conference. He stood at the back and didn't say anything."

"I'll get a tape. You can point them out."

"Yes. I will. But it's not going to end there."

Babin's lower back began to spasm—this sometimes happened when he sat in one place for a long time. He tried to relax, pushing a slow breath through his teeth. Túcume waited patiently.

"The CIA will have people trying to recover the bomb," Babin said finally. "It's just a question of when. They'll use—I would suspect that they would use the cover of an international inspection team. Then they will strike."

"They can have that weapon. The president has already volunteered to turn it over to the Atomic Energy people."

"It's the other one I'm talking about, General. Don't even think of showing it to them." Babin reached for his crutches. "Do you mind if I move around a little? My back is in knots."

Túcume gave him a hand, supporting him while he found his balance. For just that moment, Babin felt sorry for the general and wished the circumstances were different. But their courses were set.

"After the election, any difficulties will be swept away," said Túcume. "You'll see. The Americans will not dare to move against me then—it will be like declaring war on the country."

Babin crutched his way around the room slowly, bending his neck to stretch his muscles, as this sometimes helped relieve the pain farther down.

"You're sure your opponents will allow a fair result?" said Babin. He had to force the words through his teeth; even the muscles in his mouth were knotting.

"The army will guarantee it," said Túcume. "And with UN observers, the process will be fair."

Had he not been in so much pain, Babin might have laughed at the irony of someone who was trying to steal the election calling it fair. He maneuvered himself so his back was against the wall, then pushed his head to flex the muscles. The pain relented ever so slightly, then surged up his spine, cramping his shoulders.

He would endure. Only a few more days. Then it would be gone forever.

85

Dean kept his hand clamped over Lia's mouth as two guerrillas ran up the path in front of the houses and turned toward the back, going in the direction they thought she had taken. They shouted back and forth. Someone on the other side of the buildings apparently thought he saw something and began firing.

"You all right?" asked Dean, letting her go.

"I'm fine."

"Where are your shoes?"

"I left them in the shower."

"Get on my back," he told her. "I'll carry you."

"No."

"You are the most stubborn human being in the world."

"My feet are fine," insisted Lia.

"Then come on, for cryin' out loud. Before they figure out which way you went."

86

"They're out of the camp," Telach told Rubens as soon as he entered the Art Room. "Lia saw a chance and she took it. She's with Charlie. We've launched the helicopters."

Rubens nodded.

"You still want Servico, the *comandante*?"

"Yes," said Rubens—and then immediately he second-guessed himself, realizing that he hadn't entirely considered the situation before speaking.

He'd told the president that he could get Servico, and now Rubens didn't want to disappoint him. His prestige would be dented, or at a minimum he would be losing a chance to enhance it.

It was ego. And it was more than that—it was chits to become national security adviser.

Was that going to color every decision he made now?

That is not who I am, Rubens told himself. I am above those sorts of political games. I have no need for them.

Would he be above petty politics if he were national security adviser?

The pressure would be worse.

"Just one second, Ms. Telach, as I reconsider this," he said. "Can Servico be retrieved without further endangering our people?"

"We planned it that way." Her cheeks, never plump, had

pulled tight and hollow. Her upper body was stiff with tension. "The helicopters are nineteen minutes away."

Would it be safer for all concerned to concentrate on simply picking up Dean and Lia?

Absolutely.

Was the risk worth it?

Yes, because snatching Servico might give them more information about any possible rebel connection to the bomb—or more likely, rule it out. And he might be of use in dealing with Peru.

"Lia's safety is paramount," said Rubens.

"I understand that," said Telach.

He didn't have to be pure—no one could entirely divorce himself from all possible influences. But he did have to make a decision.

"I want Lia safe," he told Telach. "Beyond that, if there is an opportunity to snatch Servico, who is wanted by the British government as well as Peru, then do so."

"Yes, sir." Her shoulders relaxed slightly, and she looked less like an enraged scarecrow.

"Where is Mr. Karr?"

"Making his way back to the river. I have Fashona on his way there."

"Have him move into position to make the switch with the voter card at Nevas. If possible, Lia can meet him. Or, if necessary, he can proceed alone."

"Yes, Mr. Rubens."

87

Dean led Lia to a spot about three hundred yards from the camp where a pair of fallen tree trunks gave them cover and a vantage point to watch for guards.

"We're at the trunks I told you about," he told Rockman.

"Good. Helicopters are sixteen minutes away," said Rockman. "One group is going to take out Servico. The other will meet you at LZ One."

"You're taking Servico?" said Lia.

"Yes. He's wanted by the British as well as the Peruvians, and we want to talk to him about the bomb."

"All right. Tell the landing team we'll locate him for them," said Lia, sliding off the tree.

"Hey, hold on," said Dean, grabbing her. "We just got out of there."

"*We?*"

"Lia, Charlie? Just relax a second," said Telach. "There are two helicopters of paramilitaries on their way. You'll hear them shortly."

"So will the guerrillas," said Lia. "Servico will get away."

Dean recognized the defiant look in her eye, the look he called *Lia DeFrancesca takes on the world.*

"There's only six of them. They're mostly kids. They're not very well trained," Lia said. "Do you really think we need to wait for help?"

"All right, let's do it," said Dean, taking the lead.

• • •

By the time Lia caught up to Dean, he was crouched a few yards from the point where she'd come into the jungle. Two men were talking in front of the shower hut. One was Servico; the other was the man who'd been guarding her.

"On the left," said Lia.

Servico started walking in the direction of the huts. The other man went down the road to the right, probably to join the hunt.

"Rockman, where are all the guerrillas?" she asked.

"They sent one to the road, probably to go to the others four miles away where they're searching for the military stragglers. We have two on the north side, one just walking to the south. One in the village near the cottages."

"That leaves one more."

"Has to be still inside Cabin Two. Is that our guy?"

"Servico's the one walking toward the cabin," said Lia.

"OK, got it. Helicopters are now ten minutes off."

"Wait till they're five," Dean said. "We'll take him before they hear the rotors."

"Charlie, it'd be much easier for you guys if you just waited—"

"Servico isn't going to surrender," Lia told the runner. "He made a real point of that before. If you want him alive, we have to grab him before he knows he's in trouble."

"Charlie? Lia? Are you sure about this?" said Telach.

"We're sure," said Lia.

"Charlie?"

"Yeah, we can do it."

"Eight minutes," said Rockman.

Lia looked at Dean. He scanned the village slowly, as if he were a robotic surveillance camera, taking it all in, analyzing every inch.

"I didn't need to be rescued," she whispered, checking her pistol to make sure it was ready, even though she'd done that just a few minutes before.

"Didn't say you did."

Right, she thought to herself.

Dean glanced at his watch, then held up a finger: one minute.

"Right or left?" Lia asked.

"I'll take the right."

"Call him out in Spanish," she suggested.

"Yeah, good."

"Rockman, where are the guerrillas?"

"Two to the north are about eight hundred yards away, searching at the edge of a ravine. Your target is in the cabin, with another man. The one on the road is out of the picture. We're missing one to the east, at least fifty yards from you, most likely more. Woods are too thick."

"Let's go," said Dean.

Lia ran on the left side of the door. Dean took the right. Pistol ready, he cupped his left hand over his mouth and called to the guerrilla leader in Spanish.

"Comrade Paolo," he said. "*¡Vamos!* Come on! Hurry!"

Someone answered with a grumble. Dean saw the door open; as a man stepped out he leapt onto his back, smashing his neck and then the back of his head with his pistol. The figure collapsed and Dean fell with him, rolling in the ground as the guerrilla's AK-47 clattered behind him.

The rebel clawed at the ground, trying to pull himself away. Dean caught him and gave him another smash, this one so hard it felt like he had knocked the man's skull off. Yet the guerrilla still struggled, and it wasn't until Dean hit him on the other side of the head that the man finally collapsed.

Dean grabbed the guerrilla's shoulder, planning to haul him up over his back into the nearby jungle. As he did, he caught a glimpse of the man's face and realized it wasn't Servico.

Lia leapt through the doorway as Dean took the guerrilla who had come out. There was a desk and a chair to the left, a rifle hanging on a hook in the corner.

And a man just starting for it.

Servico.

"Don't move!" she told him. "I'll shoot you."

"Shoot me then," he said, and he twisted around to seize the gun and fire.

Lia fired two shots through his right knee. Servico managed to get his hand onto the gun stock but fell, crippled by the pain of the bullets that smashed his patella and the adjacent bones.

She ran to him quickly, grabbing him by the shirt and pulling him across the floor. She started to lift him up to carry him over her back, but he struggled ferociously, grabbing her hair. A kick to his wounded knee drained the fight from him; another quick blow to his neck paralyzed him.

"Let's go, let's go," Dean yelled from the doorway. He had the other guerrilla's AK-47 in his hands.

Lia took hold of Servico's shirt and pulled him to the doorway, rolling him over to check for a hidden weapon. As she looked around for something to truss him with, she noticed two grenade launchers sitting on a flat box near the door.

The heavy beat of the approaching helicopters filled the air.

"Helicopters are sixty seconds away," said Rockman. "We're sending everybody into the village."

"We'll be waiting," said Dean.

88

Jackson didn't realize anyone was in the room with him until he heard Rubens clearing his throat.

"Dr. Rubens," he said, starting to rise.

"Ambassador. Anything useful?"

"Just old reports on the Brazilian effort to develop a nuclear weapon," Jackson said, sitting as Rubens pulled over a chair.

"You're here late. It's going on seven."

"Really? Being underground means becoming something of a mole." He smiled to himself at the unintentional pun.

"I wonder if you'd be interested in going to Peru."

"When?"

"As soon as possible."

Jackson began thinking of what arrangements he would have to make. His cat needed to be fed—he hated the cat, but it did need to be fed. The plants.

"I'm afraid I can't go into detail unless you agree to go. You understand."

"Well, yes. I will go. If you need me."

"I have to arrange an aircraft first. And other details, such as a cover."

"What is it you want me to do?"

"The president wants to make sure that the candidate who is benefiting from General Túcume's money and his apparent maneuverings is aware of that. He wants us to send an unofficial emissary to deliver the information in person."

"To Hernando Aznar?"

"That's right. You would present just enough to show the link. And then you would return. We'll have a bodyguard with you, of course. There should be no personal danger to you, but one never knows in these situations."

"I would think the candidate would already know that he's receiving funding from the general," said Jackson.

"The president is not convinced. And in any event, Aznar would not know that *we* know. And that it's going to be made public."

"So we break the alliance when it's still vulnerable," said Jackson, "by putting Aznar on the spot. And best case, he ends up grateful to us, since we warned him."

He had seen this sort of play before. It could be very effective—or it could fall flat on its face. A lot depended on the person delivering the message.

"Please have some dinner," added Rubens. "We will get a driver for you, who'll take you to your home for a light bag, then deliver you to the airplane."

Rubens turned to go.

"There is one thing," added Jackson.

"Ambassador?"

"My Meals on Wheels assignment Tuesday."

"You'll be back in plenty of time. But just in case, I will arrange for a driver to substitute for you. Please give the contact information to Mr. Montblanc."

89

The helicopter dropped Dean, Lia, and their prisoner off at a mining complex to the east, dust swirling in the darkness. Two of the paramilitaries stayed behind as well. A team medic had seen to the guerrilla's knee, cleaning and bandaging the wound after knocking him out with synthetic morphine. It was likely that he would never walk properly again; Dean thought he was getting off easy. Servico was to be delivered to a U.S. Navy cruiser off the coast, part of the advance squadron of the carrier task force headed by the *Reagan*. His chariot, a Navy Seahawk helicopter that had run a transport sortie to northern Peru as a cover, was due in ten minutes.

The two PMs, or paramilitaries, helping them with the prisoner were former "blanket huggers"—Army Special Forces soldiers. They had gone to work with the CIA after their Army careers; Dean guessed both men were in their forties, not quite as old as he was, but definitely on the "mature" side. Both were taciturn, even for PMs. They stood quietly, each man holding his Colt submachine gun ready as he scanned the desolate landscape of the strip mine with his night glasses.

Servico, propped up against a huge rock nearby, shook off his drug-induced stupor.

"Where are you taking me?" he demanded.

"A helicopter's coming. It'll take you to a ship."

"Then where?"

"That hasn't been decided," said Dean. "You seem to be very popular with both the British and the Peruvians."

Servico's whole body shook. His voice cracked as he spoke. "I'd prefer to go to the British."

"You would, huh?" said Dean.

"Send me to Dartmoor," pleaded Servico, referring to the British prison. While not known as an "easy" jail, it was undoubtedly miles ahead of any place the Peruvians would put him.

"Not up to me," said Dean.

The guerrilla's lower lip quivered. Dean studied Servico, aware that he was at the very edge of breaking. His eyes swelled and his mouth hung open, his jaw not entirely under his control. But he managed to pull himself back from the edge, pressing his teeth together and raising his head.

Whatever he was holding on to inside wouldn't last, Dean knew. It would crumble soon, as the pain and pressure continued to build.

"You want more morphine?" said Dean.

A tear slipped from Servico's eye, but he shook his head. "No," he said.

His stubbornness impressed Dean. He didn't admire Servico, much less pity him, but recognized the man's struggle to remain true to what he believed, as misguided as that might be.

"If you cooperate with the Americans," Dean told him, "they'll be more likely to give you to Britain than Peru. You understand?"

Servico frowned but then bobbed his head up and down twice.

"You oughta take the morphine now."

"No."

"Fair enough."

Dean walked away, thinking sometimes you had to hold on to whatever you thought would make you whole, even if it was just pain. He walked up the ridge, surveying the area with his glasses. Satisfied they were alone, he found a large rock to sit on. He got a sports bar out of his backpack and nibbled at it, vainly hoping it might restore some of his energy. The adrenaline of the day had washed out of his body. He was beyond tired. His legs felt like they'd been worked over by someone with a baseball bat, and his fingers were cold and stiff.

Lia seemed like a bundle of energy, stalking around the area, taking it upon herself to make sure no one was lurking in the shadows somewhere.

Dean wanted to talk to her, but not about the mission—he wanted to talk to her about a lot of things, but this wasn't the time or place.

"Mr. Dean, this is Rubens. Lia, are you there?"

"Yes," she said, coming closer to Dean. He took out his phone, pretending to use it as Rubens continued.

In his usual bureaucratic cadence, Rubens began telling them the PMs would take the prisoner to the Navy ship. Their helicopter was ninety seconds away. The two Deep Black ops would not be joining them. Lia was to continue her mission at Nevas; Tommy Karr was already en route there. And Dean was to go to Lima, where he would meet a special envoy who was to talk with one of the presidential candidates. Civilian helicopters were on their way to pick them up.

Dean watched Lia. She'd been mad at him for helping her at the guerrilla compound, he knew; for coming to rescue her.

Well, tough.

"We'll be ready," Dean heard Lia tell Rubens. "And it would be nice if you could get me some new shoes."

"I'm sure Ms. Telach will see to that."

"She thinks of everything," snapped Lia. "Like my mom."

"You shouldn't be angry with the Art Room," Dean told her while they waited for Telach to come back on the line.

"What do you mean?"

"I came for you on my own. I heard you were in trouble, and I came."

"You left the mission?"

"Tommy didn't need me. You were in trouble."

"Bull."

Telach's voice boomed in, updating them on Karr. When she told them that the other op had found the place where the nuclear weapon had been, Dean felt a stab of guilt.

What if the weapon had still been in the barn?

He hadn't really considered that, not really, not thoroughly, not the way he should have. Not the way his duty demanded him to.

His duty. Who had a greater call on him? His country or his lover?

The Navy helo appeared above; Dean took up a post in the direction of the road, more for form's sake than out of any sense of danger.

"Wait," Dean said, grabbing Lia by the shoulders as she started for the chopper. "We have to straighten this out. You've been messed up since Korea."

"Me?"

"Yeah. Listen, I know that because of what happened you've been edgy. And I know I can't make it better. But I still love you. And—"

"I'm not edgy. And I'm past Korea." She stopped talking. "Why are you being so hard?"

"I just am. And you—I can't believe you did that. I can't believe you left your mission."

"What?" he shouted over the whine of the helicopter blades.

"You have to do your job. People are depending on you— an entire damn country. We don't matter, you and I—we don't matter."

"That's baloney."

"No, Charlie Dean, that isn't baloney. That's what Desk Three is about." Lia pulled away from his grip so fiercely he couldn't stop her. "I can take care of myself. Thank you very much."

Dean put his hand around the barrel of his MP5, tightening it in frustration as if to crush the metal. "I didn't jeopardize the mission. Tommy had it under control. You were in trouble."

Lia didn't answer. Instead, she turned and ran to the helicopter.

90

Certain things become ingrained in a man's being. Moving through a city, finding the alleys where people would do anything for the right amount of money—these had been an intimate part of Babin's life for nearly two decades before the accident, and even in his crippled state they were instinctual. The most difficult task was slipping from the hotel suite. But this proved easier than he had expected—the general himself had gone out, and the men guarding the rooms did not think Babin a prisoner.

As indeed he wasn't. Babin simply rode the elevator to the main floor and went to the concierge, who easily found him a car and driver whose fee could be tacked onto his hotel bill. Once in the car, he was tempted to keep going—to have the driver simply take him to the airport. But Babin had little money, barely enough to accomplish what he wanted to do tonight. A sizable amount of cash waited in Ecuador and more might be gotten from bank accounts, but it all might just as well be back in Russia at the moment.

He had the driver take him to the business area of old Lima—not a good section at night.

"Are you sure, *señor*?"

"Yes," Babin told him.

Babin leaned next to the window, watching the people and shops as he passed. Finally he saw what he wanted—a prostitute standing near a shuttered storefront.

"Stop here," said Babin.

"*Señor*—"

"I'm not going to do anything I'll regret," Babin told him. He pressed the button to lower the window, then held out a U.S. twenty-dollar bill. It was the only twenty he had—his two other bills were hundreds.

The twenty got the woman's attention, and she sashayed toward the car.

"Come with me," he told her, pulling the bill away.

The woman glanced at the driver. "I'll meet you at my hotel."

Babin rolled up the window. "Drive on," he said.

It took a half hour before they found a woman desperate or perhaps stoned enough to get into the car.

"I need to purchase a pistol," Babin told her.

The woman looked at him as if he were crazy.

"Your *pimp*—" he struggled over the word in Spanish, saying it in Russian and then finally settling for *hombre*, or man, not exactly a good translation, though it got the job done. "Maybe he can help us."

The woman started shaking her head and saying no. Babin calmed her and finally got the name of a club named Hopo, where he could look for a man named Jimenez. He gave her the twenty dollars and dropped her off.

Hopo in Spanish meant the wooly tail of a fox or a sheep; it was also an expression in some dialects for working hard—and an interjection along the lines of "get out." The place looked quiet on the outside, but the street was dark and narrow. Babin had frequented such places in Russia only to recruit toughs and laborers. He hesitated for a moment, then pushed open the car door.

"*Señor*, perhaps there is another way to get what you want," said the driver.

"What way is that?" said Babin, pulling himself out.

"Guns are illegal, but—"

"I'm interested in more than a gun," Babin told the driver. "I need some phones and other items. And I need them from someone who does not ask questions."

"Perhaps that could be arranged."

"Then come inside with me for a drink," said Babin, pushing the car door closed. He turned and began crutching toward the club. He heard the car move down the street but didn't look after it; either the driver would park and come behind him or he would be stranded here. To look back, he decided, would be an act of cowardice, as would deciding not to go in.

There was a bouncer at the door. Babin returned his snarling look. "Search me, if you want," he said in Spanish. The man waved him inside dismissively.

There were no more than a dozen people inside, scattered at tables and a long bar of dark wood. The interior was classier than Babin expected, its glory not quite faded.

Babin stopped near the middle of the bar. He saw from the bartender's look that his crutches were a curiosity; more than that, they made most people see him as someone who was not capable of threatening them.

A bad thing here.

"Vodka," he said. He pulled out some of the Peruvian bills he'd been given. "A shot."

The bartender put down a glass.

"I need to see a man named Jimenez about a business proposition," Babin said. "One of his girls said I would find him here."

The bartender glanced across the room but said nothing. Babin took his vodka and brought it to his lips, swallowing it in a gulp.

As he did, one of the men at the table the bartender had looked toward got up and came over behind him.

"What do you want?" said the man.

Before the accident that had left his back crippled, Babin would have dealt with the man simply—he would have stomped down on the man's foot and sent his elbow into his stomach, bending him in half. Now such a maneuver was impossible. So Babin chose another tactic.

"A drink for my friend," he told the bartender, pushing more of the money forward. "Whatever he wishes."

The bartender glanced at the man, then quickly got a glass of American whiskey for him.

"I would like you to tell Jimenez that I need to buy a pair of handguns. I can pick them up tomorrow."

"What makes you think he sells guns?"

Babin turned to smile in the man's face, then turned around and faced the two men at the table. "I hope you don't have the impression that I'm with the police. I wouldn't think they'd stoop to sending cripples to trick you."

One of the men frowned. By now, everyone in the room was either looking at Babin or pretending not to.

"Come here," said the thinner of the two men. He had a goatee, and a scar on his cheekbone.

Babin crutched his way over and sat. The pain had ratcheted up, but he was not going to admit it now. He was intoxicated, not by the small amount of vodka he'd drunk but by the *game*—being at the edge, negotiating what he wanted. The fact that he was at such a disadvantage added to the thrill and, somehow, to his confidence.

"What is it you need?" said Jimenez.

"Two Walthers would be perfect. Failing that, Glocks. Or Berettas."

"When?"

Babin reached into his pocket and pulled out the hundred-dollar bill. He dropped it on the table.

"Tomorrow. Here. At two p.m."

"The guns cost more than this."

"I understand."

"Ten times as much."

"That's not a very fair price," said Babin.

"I don't give handicapped discounts."

The man and everyone else in the bar began laughing. Babin felt his rage flicker, but he mastered himself.

"Perhaps in the future you will," he said, getting up. "I will be here at two, and pay your price."

"Wait," said Jimenez. "Tomorrow is too soon."

"For a thousand dollars, I would think tomorrow is not soon enough."

When Babin turned, he saw that his driver had come in and was standing near the bar, arms folded. He was a good-sized man, bigger than the bouncer, and looked suitably intimidating, though in a fight he would have been quickly overwhelmed by superior numbers and the bat the bartender had on the shelf above the back of the bar.

"You took a hell of a risk," said the driver, following Babin outside.

"I used to deal with trash like that every day. At heart he's a coward."

"He'll try to rob you tomorrow. How will you deal with that?"

"He won't rob me," said Babin. "You learn to judge these things. There are some other items I want. A satellite phone. Some tickets."

"I could help you."

"Yes, I thought you could. Come, let's go back to the hotel. I've spent all my money, but I believe the bar there will allow me to run a tab and charge it to my room."

"Are you sure, *señor*? It is getting late. There's always tomorrow."

"A crueler lie has never been told," said Babin. "Come."

General Túcume's late-night meeting with the chief of staff did not go smoothly. Major General Hector Maduro had never fired a gun in battle, but he had cut down countless rivals, and he clearly saw Túcume as one. Maduro started by asking pointed questions and within ten minutes was accusing Túcume of manufacturing a crisis to hurt the government and the army. The United States had shown far more interest in the weapon than Túcume had predicted, and this was causing considerable problems for Maduro. Peru's president and other members of the government were blaming the army for every imaginable problem in the country, saying its war against the rebels had been corrupt and ineffective. The criticism was nearly as bad as if the revolutionaries had exploded a nuclear device in Lima.

"The government may lose this election," said Maduro. "The polls are against Ortez. You've hurt him, and the army."

"The government I do not care about," said Túcume, waving his hand. "But I have spent my life in the army, and I have shed my blood for the army. How have I hurt it? By stopping the rebels? By doing my job?"

"You should not have allowed the newsperson to come. This should not have been announced to the world."

Túcume pressed his lips together. It was necessary for his plan that it *was* announced to the world, though obviously he wasn't about to tell the general that.

"The northerners are insisting on looking over our shoulder," said Maduro, referring to the U.S. "They want a team of their Delta Force to 'help' guard the warhead. They've already landed in Lima."

"We don't need any help," said Túcume. "It's in my custody."

"That is going to change. It must be under my direct control by noon tomorrow."

"There is no need to make new arrangements," said Túcume, taking a more diplomatic tack. "As the entire army is under your command, the warhead is already in your control. Perhaps you will accompany me to inspect it tomorrow. You might wish to bring guests, diplomats; naturally that would be your prerogative, as military commander."

Maduro's grimace did not melt entirely, but Túcume knew he was on the right track.

"You might bring this U.S. general, if you wished. But you, as the head of our military, would be the one to invite him. These Yankees—they assume sometimes we are children. We have control of our destiny."

"That is what is important."

"Their ambassador himself might also come with you," said Túcume. "That would be fitting. Not someone of a low level. The lower levels would work with me. You are head of the army, and deserve respect."

By the time the interview was ended, Túcume felt that he had mollified the general somewhat. Maduro was taking his suggestion of an inspection trip "under advisement," a phrase Túcume interpreted to mean he simply didn't want to admit right away that it was a good idea.

The meeting with the defense minister was far worse, though he began by congratulating Túcume on effectively dealing with the rebels. Within a few minutes, however, the minister was questioning how the revolutionaries could have built such a bomb under Túcume's nose. He pointed out that the weapon was not built by the revolutionaries but purchased. He hinted that perhaps one of their enemies such as Ecuador or Brazil had helped the New Path, but the minister dismissed this, saying that either country would have far preferred keeping such a weapon to itself.

By the time the session ended, Túcume realized he had miscalculated the reaction to the weapon by the U.S. It was the North's pressure that was making these people cross with him, turning him from a hero into a villain.

His confidence that he could control events had slipped, so much so that when the two guards at the door did not snap immediately to attention as he approached, Túcume took their momentary inattention as a personal insult and perhaps the result of orders from above. They finally stiffened, but still, he fought against a rising sense of unease and apprehension. Ordinarily he would have made a point of stopping and speaking with the men about their experiences; tonight he simply hurried out to his waiting car.

91

As most Deep Black missions progressed, Rubens began to lose track of the time. The rhythm of his days—meetings, conferences, meals—gradually fell by the wayside as he spent more and more time in the Art Room. There always came a point when he had no idea what time of day it was. Often, he lost track of the day as well. So he wasn't terribly surprised when Kevin Montblanc stuck his head in his office and said good morning.

"Would you like some coffee?"

"I suppose I would," Rubens told the Desk Three operations personnel director.

"Good, because I brought you some."

The coffee was freshly made and very strong. Rubens felt his sinuses tingle as he took a sip.

"You really should be getting more rest," suggested Montblanc.

"I suppose I will in a few days. What's on your mind?"

Montblanc's mustache drooped slightly. "Ambassador Jackson. He was holding something back during the interviews."

Rubens put his coffee down. Jackson was about two hours from touching down in Lima.

"What did he lie about?" asked Rubens.

"I don't know that he lied. But there certainly was anxiety around his son's death."

"You're a psychologist, Kevin—wouldn't you expect that?"

"Yes, but—"

"But what?"

"He's living in a bare-bones apartment. He doesn't even own the condominium. He's renting it."

"I hardly think that's a crime. He and his wife were never very well off. And he's paying his son's medical debts."

"Yes, and that's admirable. But why is he doing that?"

"Out of a sense of responsibility, I would imagine."

"Or guilt. His son died under suspicious circumstances. Apparently the young man was in the hospital receiving treatment when he died of an overdose of drugs."

"Suicide?"

"He was in a coma. The death was highly suspicious. At best, it's euthanasia."

"Were there charges?"

"No. Not even a grand jury. No publicity, either."

Montblanc didn't say anything else, but the implication seemed clear to Rubens—he thought there might have been some sort of local cover-up, possibly because Jackson had been an ambassador. In the scandal-averse culture of the NSA, a situation like this was almost always grounds for disqualifying a candidate for a sensitive job.

It was too late for that, wasn't it? And it was Rubens' fault and his alone.

"Investigate everything that needs to be investigated," said Rubens. "Put it on the highest priority. Do it yourself if you have to. And let me know what you find out as quickly as you can."

92

"Hey, Princess, how's it going?" yelled Tommy Karr as Lia climbed out of the boat at the Nevas dock.

"I thought you were over your juvenile phase."

"Nah, I'm just starting it. I was accelerated through school, remember?"

"This isn't Russia, Karr. You better watch what you're doing. You can't even speak Spanish."

"Por las buenas o por las malais," he said, starting to say that, whether she liked it or not, they were working together.

"Just peachy. You have the gender wrong, and the tense, and you sound like an American hick. Why didn't they send you to language school?"

"Wasn't time. But better a hick than a stuck-up princess."

Karr smiled at her and, knowing how much this annoyed her, started to laugh.

"I'm glad you're so amused."

"What's the sense of living if you can't have a few laughs? Come on, let's go grab some grub. Election center opens in an hour. I have the place scoped out. Oughta be as easy as falling off a log."

The voter cards were kept in a small room on the second floor of a local school building. As the Art Room had predicted, security here was considerably looser than it had been at Lima or even La Oroya. There was a metal detector at the main entrance, with two guards and a local election official, along with the deputy mayor. There was one guard on the top floor, stationed in the hallway in front of the room. There were no electronic security devices, and Karr had already concluded that most of the doors to the building were not locked.

"I put the video bugs in right before you got here. We're all ready to go," Karr told Lia as they finished eating. He pulled a small briefcase onto the table. "Even got you a new case and laptop."

"I have my own, thank you," Lia said.

"Yeah, but does yours have Zoo Tycoon on it?"

Lia rolled her eyes. "Be serious for once, OK?"

"I'm always serious."

The deputy mayor and another man were sitting at a table near the front door when Lia went in. The UN committee had contacted the local election people the night before and again in the morning, but if the deputy mayor was impressed by Lia's hardships, he didn't act like it. She greeted him in Spanish, but he made a face as if her pronunciation was bad. He addressed her in English—it was as good as her Spanish, which was excellent—and asked to see her credentials. After she showed them he claimed he had to call Lima for instructions.

Lia shrugged. "Go ahead and call them," she said.

"I will do that." He got up and began ambling down the hallway.

"We'll intercept the call; don't worry," said Rockman.

Lia wasn't worried. Annoyed but not worried. One more hurdle, she told herself, and the job was done.

"Back already," she muttered when she spotted him coming back down the hall.

"He didn't call anyone," said Rockman.

Gee, no kidding, she thought.

"Your belongings must be searched, going and coming," said the man.

"Of course," said Lia. She handed him the battered briefcase, even though it had already been checked at the door a few feet away. The deputy mayor eyed the laptop and its accessories suspiciously before handing everything back.

"The tests will only take a few minutes," she said as he led her up the stairs. "You can help if you want."

"I have better things to do. The guard will watch you."

He told the man in Spanish that she was a foreigner and bore very close watching. The guard nodded and followed her inside the room, which was an airless storeroom the size of a closet. The only furniture was a long table where the two boxes of cards were kept, and a simple folding chair against the wall.

Lia unpacked slowly, remembering how claustrophobic she had become in the Lima vault. She needed a ruse to get the guard away; she certainly didn't want him hanging over her shoulder—he smelled like a rat fresh from the nearby jungle.

There was an electrical outlet right next to the table, so she couldn't use her old standby of needing an extension cord.

"Are you in the army?" Lia asked the guard, in Spanish, trying to make conversation.

He shook his head.

"The army—and the police—helped me yesterday. They saved me from the rebels," she said.

There was no reaction from the guard. Lia booted up her computer and fussed with the equipment.

"It's kind of stuffy in here," she said. "Could you get me a drink of water?"

"I cannot leave my post," said the guard.

Heaven forbid, Lia thought.

She had the replacement envelope with its voter cards in the lining of the briefcase. She thought of just going ahead and pulling it out; the guard wouldn't know what she was doing anyway. But she worried that he might have some reason to tell the deputy mayor.

And the stench was really starting to get to her. She fingered the top of her computer, trying to think.

"Do you want water or not?" said the guard.

"Yes, I do."

"You can get it down the steps at the back of the hall. There is a machine there."

"I can't leave my laptop," she told him. "It's against the rules."

"So take it."

Lia was about to tell him that she had changed her mind, but then realized that if she had the card in her hand when she did the check, it would be easy to make the switch while she worked, even with him nearby. She could go downstairs and take the cards from the envelope, returning with them in her hand or even her briefcase. The only problem was that she wouldn't know in advance which card was which; she'd have to test them all.

"Hallway at the back?" she asked, packing up. "Are you going to show me?"

"I have to guard this room."

"That's what you should do," said Lia. "Don't be offended, but I have to take my laptop with me. Those are the rules that I have."

"Of course."

"Tommy's moving to the back of the room to cover you," Rockman told her. "Are you really that thirsty?"

"Oh, parched," she whispered as she walked down the hall.

93

The Art Room arranged a hotel room in Lima where Dean could take a shower and shave. He even managed a nap. The nap might have been a mistake, however: it left him feeling as if he had a hangover.

His new clothes were stiff, and while they fitted perfectly, they weren't exactly his style—a dark black suit with a crisp red shirt, fancy brownish shoes, and socks so thin they felt as if they weren't there. At least there was no tie.

Two Heckler & Koch P7 pistols had come with the clothes. They were easier to hide than the bulky Glock pistols he'd been carrying, but as he stepped into the terminal at Lima's Jorge Chavez Airport, Dean suddenly felt as if everyone were staring at the barely perceptible bulges at his ribs. He took careful note of the security people scattered around as he walked briskly toward the new arrivals board. And he made sure confusion registered on his face as he looked at it.

Ambassador Jackson had flown into Bolivia a few hours before. There he'd caught a flight bound for Lima on a commercial regional carrier for a modicum of cover. Peru's state-owned airline was not renowned for being on time, and the plane was reported fifteen minutes late. Dean folded his arms, made a show of looking put out—this wasn't hard—then went in search of coffee. He downed his first cup in a quick gulp, then ordered a second and found a small table to sit at. He took out his satellite phone, pretending to use it as he checked in with Rockman.

"The plane's about five minutes out," the runner told him.

"That's good."

"How you doing? You sound like you have a cold."

"Just tired. I'm all right." Dean took a nonchalant glance around him. Two men in brown suits were watching him from across the terminal. They'd be Peruvian intelligence agents. "How's Lia?"

"Sandy's running her," said Rockman, referring to Sandy Chafetz. "She's fine."

"I thought you always got the hot jobs."

"I do."

Dean glanced at his watch, a bit of stage action for the spies. "I thought this was a piece of cake."

"Doesn't mean it's not important."

"Yeah." He drained the last of his coffee. It hadn't made a dent in his fatigue. He decided he'd get another cup and rose. "Listen, I'm going to get some more joe. Anything is up, give me a shout."

"I don't think mineral salesmen use the word 'shout.'"

Jackson's plane had landed and the passengers were just starting to clear customs by the time Dean ambled over to the gate area. Even though he'd only been given a verbal description, he had no trouble picking out the ambassador. Besides being a good ten or twenty years older than the other passengers getting off the plane, he wore the casually dressy clothes Dean associated with prep schools and the foreign service—a two-buttoned blue blazer, slightly rumpled khaki pants, and well-worn loafers.

"Ambassador?" said Dean, approaching him as he walked onto the concourse.

"That was a long time ago," said Jackson.

"I have an uncle who's a painter."

"One of the great masters?"

"Yes," said Dean, completing the authentication process.

"Mr. Dean?"

"Charlie," said Dean, taking the ambassador's hand. The

spotted fingers clasped his in a firm grip. "Have a good flight?"

"Yes, I did. It's been so long since I was in an aircraft, I'd forgotten the pleasure of flying."

"We have a car this way," said Dean, taking his bag. He noticed the brown-suit pair watching across the way. "A lot of eyes are watching us."

"I would imagine there would be. Peru has always been known for its secret service. Very obtrusive. But I guess you get used to that sort of thing if you live here."

94

Karr walked around the outside of the building, toward a window he thought would give him a good view of the hallway that led to where Lia was going. He guessed—as Rockman clearly hadn't—that she was going to take the cards out of the envelope before swapping them. The guard was obviously standing over her shoulder making the swap difficult.

School was out today, but there were plenty of people inside. A nurse was holding some sort of clinic at the back of the first floor. As Karr watched through the vertical blinds, three people entered the room—a young girl, seventeen or eighteen at most; a nurse; and a well-dressed man whom Karr took to be a doctor. They closed the door, blocking off his view of the hall.

As Karr pulled back from the window, he saw the doctor take what looked like a pair of small balloons from a drawer at the side. His imagination stuttered; he couldn't quite piece together what was going on.

When he saw the girl take one of the balloons and hold it to her mouth, Karr finally got it—the kid was being prepped to take drugs to smuggle north to the U.S. The actual drugs weren't handed over here; it was more on the order of a job interview, with the applicants being screened.

Beautiful world, he thought to himself, moving on.

95

General Túcume did not like the news. Members of the general staff had spent the night calling every officer in his command, some four or five times, reminding them where their ultimate duty lay. As far as he knew—and Túcume had spoken to as many men as he could—no one had actually accused him of plotting a coup, but these sorts of calls were the first step; no one who had lived through the confusion and madness of the nineties could see it otherwise.

In today's Peru, to be accused of plotting a coup was a great slander. The new generation of military men—Túcume's generation and the colonels and majors they led—had grown up on the model of the U.S. military. They'd also learned from the failures of the past. His opponents were clever; he had anticipated jealousy but perhaps not with this vehemence.

Túcume had assigned one of his colonels to liaise with the U.S. Delta Force people, who were ostensibly here to help look for rebels. This was a major problem for the officer, since he had to check and double-check everything with the general staff. Túcume had no doubt that the U.S. soldiers' real aim was to be close to the bomb, though so far they had not made a request to see it—or rather, if they had, he had not been informed of it.

The U.S. had aircraft flying over the units guarding the weapon, and other airplanes were steadily crisscrossing the region, ostensibly searching for other rebel hideouts. The Peruvian air force was flying its own missions as well. It seemed ironic—for years he had begged for more helicopters and attack planes to support his fights against the rebel slimes; now practically the entire air force was in his region.

By 10:00 a.m. Saturday, Túcume had put two calls in to General Maduro, asking whether the general would accompany him when he returned to the unit that afternoon. The general's chief of staff was polite but could not say when the general would get back to Túcume.

When he hung up the phone after the second call, Túcume sat motionless for a few moments, contemplating the situation. Would the revelation that the bomb was not a real warhead diffuse some of the American pressure? If so, would that be enough to mollify Maduro?

It didn't matter. Aznar would win the election tomorrow, and after that, he would be fine. He had only to wait out his enemies to declare victory.

There was a sharp rap on Túcume's suite door.

"Come," said the general.

"There are more newspeople downstairs," said his aide, Chimor. "What should I do with them?"

"Tell them I don't have a statement."

"You ought to talk to them," said Babin, entering the suite behind the servant pushing in breakfast. "Public relations are important."

"Stephan. Good morning."

Chimor, who had not yet met Babin, looked at him crossly. He took him as a rival, Túcume realized.

"Señor Babin is a consultant who knows about nuclear weapons," the general told his aide. "He understands how they work. This is Captain Chimor, my most valuable officer."

Chimor preened for a moment, then lowered his head slightly.

"Your voice is very gravelly today, Stephan," Túcume said. "Did you stay up late last night?"

"I checked out the bar."

"And you used a car."

"I wanted to see the sights."

Túcume interpreted this to mean that Babin had spent time with a prostitute. He'd been shut up in exile for nearly three years. A man needed to be a man.

"Have breakfast with us," the general told him. "Captain, you, too. Please. Sit."

"If I may be excused, General. The press is waiting," Chimor explained. "What should I tell them?"

"Tell them that I do not have a statement now. I've told the story already, and there's really nothing to add. The army will defend the people of Peru until the death. I will defend the people of Peru until the death. I'm leaving for the base at three," Túcume added. "The defense ministry was to have arranged for experts from the International Atomic Energy Agency—perhaps they can join us. Contact the ministry."

"Directly? Or through the general staff?"

Túcume hesitated. "Directly."

"The American general, Spielmorph, is in Lima at the embassy," said Chimor. "He landed last night."

"If he calls, then we must share the request with General Maduro," said Túcume. "Personally, I would have no objection, but that is the major general's decision to make."

Chimor nodded, then left.

"Very politic," said Babin.

"Yes. Maduro is not pleased with me. He's jealous."

"The Yankees?"

"They are a problem. Nervous old aunts in the next room." Túcume smiled.

"Those experts will know as soon as they're close to the bomb that it's not real."

"That may be just as well now."

Babin scowled at him, obviously not understanding his point, Túcume thought.

"You should have spoken to the press," said Babin. "You need the people on your side, and the press will help you do that."

"I don't need a middleman. The newspeople are liars. Most are owned by the government anyway."

Babin seemed as if he were going to say something more but instead changed the subject. "I'd like to use a car today. I'd like to get some new clothes."

"I can send someone."

"I'd really like to move around, if you know what I mean."

"I have no objection," said Túcume. "Be careful where you spend your energy."

"I'm careful."

"The CIA has been sending many people into the city. I fear for your safety."

"I'll be all right."

"I can protect you after the election," said Túcume. "But until Aznar takes office, things will be difficult. You must be careful."

"Let me worry about that." Babin struggled to his feet.

"You must have a hangover. You're very disagreeable." Túcume watched the Russian crutch his way to the door. "Be careful."

"Good advice," said Babin, opening the door. "You should take it, too."

96

Lia leaned against the wall next to the water cooler and took a piece of elastic from her pocket, pushing it over her fist and up her wrist. Then she opened her briefcase and reached her nail beneath the top of the lining. She pulled, gently at first, and finally with a tug so hard she worried her nail would come off. The lining gave way and she pulled the envelope out, opening it just as she heard footsteps approaching. She pushed the cards up her sleeve, hooking them beneath the elastic. Closing the briefcase, she went to the water cooler and began pouring herself a drink.

A young girl approached her, a worried look on her face. The girl's hands trembled as she reached for the water.

"Are you all right?" Lia asked her in Spanish.

The girl turned suddenly, as if she hadn't even noticed that Lia was there.

"Are you OK?" Lia asked again.

The girl said nothing.

"Do you need something? Can I help you?"

The girl stared at her, still surprised.

"Quechua," said Lia, talking to Rockman.

She heard him sigh beneath his breath before the language expert came on the line.

"Are you OK?" Lià asked again in Spanish. And then she repeated the words the translator gave her.

"I am OK," said the girl, speaking in Spanish. "Thank you."

"Who are you?"

"Calvina."

"You should sit down, Calvina," said Lia. "Come on." She took the girl by the arm and led her into the hallway, but there were no chairs there. She turned back and led her to the stairway. As she sat the girl down, the deputy mayor's voice bellowed from the second-floor landing.

"What are you doing?" he asked in Spanish.

"This young lady seems sick," answered Lia.

"That's none of your concern."

Lia ignored him. "Are you all right?" she asked the girl.

Calvina nodded. Lia left her and climbed back up the stairs, where the deputy mayor was waiting, as if he were the principal and she an errant schoolgirl.

"Your guard wouldn't get me a drink of water. So I helped myself."

Lia ignored his glower and walked back down the hall to the room where the voter cards were. The guard stared stoically down the hallway. This time, he didn't follow her in. Lia made the switch quickly, expecting that either the guard or the mayor would come in at any moment. She sealed the old cards in her briefcase, then went through the testing procedure, relaxed now, confident that she had succeeded at her mission, happy to be done.

Calvina's hands trembled so badly she spilled some of the water on her dress. She finally managed to get up and went looking for the women's room to wipe it.

As she entered, she caught sight of her face. She seemed pale, another person. Until now it had seemed that she had stepped into another body, that the whole trip here had been a dream—a surrealistic nightmare, with leering strangers at every turn. But now she saw that it really was her, that she was neither dreaming nor inhabiting another body—it was her face in the mirror.

A pale, ghostly face. Fearful and worried. And sad.

What had she expected? Of course the people she was dealing with were cruel. That was their nature. Hadn't she expected that?

She would be taken to a border town near Ecuador, where she would take a bus to the capital. There she would go to the airport, where a man would meet her with balloons like the one she had been shown and she would be given a plane ticket.

If she tried to run away or made a mistake from that point on, she would be killed and her family would be killed.

Just looking at the balloons had made her sick.

The Chinawoman had appeared as if from a dream. Calvina wondered where she had come from—clearly she did not belong here.

She spoke many languages, including the Quechua, the tongue of Calvina's grandparents. She seemed . . . an apparition. Or an angel, trying to help? Calvina's guardian angel?

Just a kind woman, Calvina decided. She had only asked what was wrong, as anyone would.

Much was wrong. But these were the choices she had to make. She would be successful, like Señor DeCura. And when she returned to Lima and told the story of her younger days, she would not mention today.

Or the balloon.

Calvina fixed her dress, then crossed herself. She was to walk two blocks, where a woman in a red shawl would meet her. Then her journey would begin in earnest.

"Hey, stranger, fancy meeting you here," said Karr when Lia walked into the café two blocks from the school.

"Real coincidence," said Lia.

A waiter approached with a drink. "Same for her," Karr told the man in English.

The waiter swirled away before she could stop him.

"A lot of tourists come here," Karr told her. "They go into the jungle from here. That your idea of a vacation?"

"What are you drinking?"

"Bourbon."

"Oh jeez."

"Hey, we're done. Time to celebrate." He laughed and gave her one of his goofy smiles. "Who were you talking to inside?"

"Deputy mayor had a serious attitude."

"No, who were you asking if they were OK?"

"Just a girl in the hall."

"Drug smuggler."

"What do you mean?"

"That place is being used as a clinic by one of the local drug lords. The government officials are probably in on it. They get these young girls to swallow dope for them right before they get on the airplane to the U.S. or Canada. When they get there . . ." He made a face.

"What?"

"You know." He made the same face. "Terrible world out there, Princess."

"She's just a kid."

"Yeah," said Karr, looking up as the drinks came. "Life stinks."

97

Peruvian presidential candidates were as hard to schedule time with as American ones at the climax of a campaign but, like them, had an overwhelming need for campaign money. And so when Hernes Jackson was presented to Hernando Aznar, it was as something more than "just" a former ambassador to South America. His current connection as the international representative of Clyve Mining, a large conglomerate that owned several mines in Peru, was emphasized as well.

A connection that the Art Room had arranged, with considerable help from the State Department.

Jackson had mixed feelings about the charade. He had learned as a diplomat that lying could be an unpardonable sin. On the other hand, it was he who had suggested the specific cover story. It allowed him to mention his past while remaining distant from it.

Aznar was in Lima to give a speech at a local college. The talk had been planned more than a month ago; at the time, Aznar was running a very distant third and the organizers probably worried that he would have trouble filling the twelve hundred–seat auditorium. But by now Aznar was the most popular candidate in the race. The street outside the building was lined with media vans, and the crowd overflowed onto the front steps.

Dean and Jackson were led around to a basement door,

then up a back flight of stairs and into a small room near the stage. When they got there, Aznar had already begun his speech.

Jackson stood by the doorway, listening to the candidate speak. Dean disappeared for a moment, then reappeared with a chair.

"Thank you," said Jackson, sitting down. "I see what they're responding to."

"What's that?"

"He gives them hope. He talks of the future. Lifting them toward the future. That's a powerful message," said Jackson.

As Aznar wrapped up his speech, the auditorium exploded with applause. Jackson watched him soak it up for a moment—the candidate wasn't entirely comfortable with the adoration, he realized.

That could be a good thing.

Something in Aznar's expression reminded Jackson of his son. It unnerved him, made him lose track of where he was. Dean touched Jackson's shoulder and he got up just as Aznar was walking past.

"Señor Aznar, I—I have something critical to tell you," said Jackson, stammering, his throat suddenly dry.

He was Bobby's age, wasn't he?

"Who are you?" asked an aide who had been onstage behind him.

"I am Hernes Jackson," he said. Jackson pressed his hands together, pushed everything but the present away. "I have something critical to say. I was a U.S. ambassador."

They were the wrong words—his approach was far too tentative, completely off-balance. He came off like a flake, not the confident messenger he needed to be.

Aznar squinted, as if he was not sure whether to take the meeting or not.

"It's about General Túcume," added Jackson.

"What?"

Jackson looked into his face. He had Bobby's forceful gaze, but this wasn't his son.

"We should speak in a private place," Jackson told him, his voice firming as his confidence returned. "You would find it extremely valuable. And it will only take a moment."

"This is about the bomb?"

"No," said Jackson.

Dean walked up the steps, his eyes practically revolving around his head. They were surrounded by men armed with rifles and submachine guns. He could feel sweat running down his neck.

They reached the landing and walked into a hall of small classrooms. The vanguard of the candidate's group turned into one of the rooms. Dean closed the short gap between himself and Jackson, but as he stepped into the room behind him, two of Aznar's goons barred his way.

"No. You stay in the hall," one said.

"I'm with Jackson," said Dean.

"No." Another man stepped out, his hand close to his suit—obviously reaching for a pistol.

"What's the problem?" said Jackson.

"You don't need a bodyguard inside," said one of the aides.

"My friend is more than a bodyguard," said Jackson. "But if he makes you nervous, he can wait in the hall. All right, Charlie?"

"Yeah, all right," he said, stepping back.

Jackson watched Aznar's frown grow as he examined the copy of the bank transcripts. The sheets were not, as the analysts would say, "transparent"—in order to decipher what the sheets said, you had to know not only the bank codes but also which accounts the numbers referred to. And the page was half-filled with them. But they were definitive.

"This proves nothing," said Aznar finally.

"Oh, you and I know that's not true," said Jackson. Until now he had been speaking in Spanish; now he changed to English to make it difficult for the others to decipher. "I could go through it line by line with you if you wish. But perhaps it would be easier to talk in confidence."

"I trust these men with my life," responded Aznar.

In English. A good sign.

"Naturally," said Jackson. "But candor—that's a thing for privacy."

Aznar looked at one of the aides and nodded. Jackson noted that two of the men did not move quite as quickly as the others, but finally he and the candidate were alone in the room.

"What is the meaning of this?" Aznar demanded in Spanish when they were alone. He waved the paper in his hand. "Where did this come from? Are you with the CIA?"

"Señor Aznar, where the information came from is not very important. You surely can check it yourself, if you need to. Consider this: you've reached the point where you don't need anyone's help. You can free yourself."

There was a flash in Aznar's eyes. A recognition of the truth, or simply anger?

"These transfers are against Peruvian law. That alone is a serious matter." Jackson took out another paper. "This sheet shows that some of your people have been paid by these companies as well. Without your knowledge?"

Aznar studied the list. It seemed to Jackson that some surprise registered on his face, though the candidate fought to hide it.

"If you believe that speech you just gave," said Jackson, "now is the time to take the opportunity. There are newspeople downstairs. They'll broadcast anything you say. If you believe in a free future, as you told your supporters, you must take the decisive step."

98

Three years ago, it would have taken close to a half bottle of vodka to make Stephan Babin feel drunk and more than that to give him a hangover. Now his head pounded despite his having had only two drinks the night before. The pain seeped into unlikely places: his jaw ached, and his eyes felt as if they had been poked. And then there were the usual places, the spots where it always hurt: His back felt as if it had been trampled and then welded into a twisted knot. His right leg was immobile and his left throbbed with each breath he took.

Babin had already tried three of the four hangover cures he knew—strong coffee, aspirin, and a small dose of vodka. The first two had little effect; the third made him nauseated.

The final remedy—sleep—he could not afford. Instead, he made his way downstairs to the lobby. The driver was not due for another two hours; Babin decided that he could arrange a bank transfer in the meantime, using a local bank. But the pain overwhelmed him only a few crutched steps from the elevator. He struggled to the lobby and dropped onto the couch like a felled tree.

The scene before him blurred, and so did his sense of time. He stared across the large open room, watching shadows swarm and flit away.

Anger restored him, finally—bitterness at what he had lost, the rage at betrayal. He had given the Americans everything, and how had they repaid him? By shooting a missile at his airplane, trying to assassinate him. Their attempt had proven that he was right to hold on to the third warhead.

His mistake was not being paranoid enough. He'd trusted his so-called case officer and the officer who had approached him on the warhead matter, the lying prince of Satan, Jorge Evans.

Evans would pay—not with his life or even merely with his family's lives, but with his city's.

Four soldiers emerged from the blurred shadow entering the lobby as Babin's vision sharpened. One mentioned Captain Chimor—Túcume's aide. The clerk at the desk offered to phone.

Babin took hold of his crutches and pushed himself to his feet. The pain in his head had subsided slightly, but his back felt even worse. His legs—his right leg today seemed almost strong, and he crutched to the door steadily, surprising himself.

The door flew back. There were more soldiers outside, soldiers everywhere.

"Taxi," he said, stopping and holding up his hand, though there were none nearby.

One of the soldiers nearby mentioned Túcume. His tone sounded bitter. Babin understood Spanish, but their accents and the speed of their words made it difficult to decipher what they were saying until he heard the word *traición*—treason.

He turned his head. The two men looked at him. A taxi pulled around the corner and Babin yelled at it, crutching into the roadway. Right until the moment the cab turned the block, he thought the soldiers would stop him.

"A bank," Babin told the driver. "The nearest HSBC branch."

The driver nodded.

"What was that business with the soldiers?" Babin asked him.

The driver glanced back in Babin's direction, then shrugged, as if to say, *You were there; you tell me.*

When they reached the bank, Babin leaned over the front seat. "I need you to wait. This should only take a minute."

"The meter will run."

"I understand," said Babin, crutching out.

There were four policemen in front of the bank, and inside, Babin noticed several more. The receptionist's desk was empty, and he didn't see anyone in the open bullpen area behind her. Rather than simply waiting, he decided to try to make a withdrawal from one of his old accounts.

The number came too slowly. He had always been good with numbers, but this was one of the accounts he never used, relying on its secrecy for an emergency. He had arranged years ago to keep it active, but after so much time thought his odds of getting any money at best one out of ten. But a problem would bring a bank executive immediately, and he would be able to complete the wire transaction.

To Babin's surprise, the teller quickly counted out the equivalent of five hundred euros without even asking a question.

"Who would I speak to about a wire transfer?" Babin asked, taking the money.

"It's not possible today," said the teller.

"Why not?" said Babin.

"On Saturday, the officers are gone. You must come back on Monday."

"Is there another branch?"

"Not in Lima. Monday."

Babin smiled, then crutched away, angry with himself for not realizing that might be a problem. He reassured himself that not every bank would have such limited staff; it was just a question of finding a larger bank. As he approached the door, a security guard nearby stepped toward him, keys in his hand.

"Closing early, sir," said the guard. "Because of the political rally."

"Expecting trouble?"

The guard simply shrugged and held the door for him.

Outside, Babin heard sirens. As he approached the car, two army vehicles turned around the corner and sped past.

"What's going on?" he asked the driver.

"The radio says there was an attempted coup. They're calling for calm."

"A coup?" Babin felt his heart grab. "I want to find a large bank that would be open. Where would be the closest?"

The driver shook his head. "I'm not sure. The state bank in Miraflores, I would guess."

"How far is it?"

"In distance, not much. But with the traffic, because of the rally and with this now on the radio, it could be hours."

99

Túcume's first hint that the army had moved against him came when Captain Chimor failed to answer either the phone at the hotel or his secure satellite phone. Still, the general remained so focused on his morning tasks that he did not truly sense the danger until his three-car motorcade turned onto the road near the restaurant where he was to meet Aznar's Argentinean speechwriter, Geraldo Stein. Túcume caught sight of two large olive-drab buses, typically used to cart soldiers around. He rapped his knuckles on the glass divider to the front of the car and told his driver not to stop. Then he called Stein on his civilian cell phone.

"Aznar's denouncing you," said Stein, who answered on the first ring. "The bodyguards you hired have been dismissed. Don't call me."

The line went dead.

Stein was on *his* payroll, and hanging up on him was an incredible insult. It was also completely out of character for the Argentinean, whose prose was florid but whose actions were normally timid. The only explanation was that things were much worse than Túcume could have supposed.

Aznar denounce him?

That seemed impossible. It *was* impossible. He told the driver to take him to Plaza San Martin, a large downtown park where Aznar was scheduled to hold a rally. As they approached the area, Túcume was amazed—the streets were packed with people rushing to hear the presidential candidate. Supporters with signs clogged the streets, and the daily gridlock was several times worse than normal. Finally there was no question of forging ahead and Túcume decided to get out of the car. With his six bodyguards—he'd decided on the precaution before he knew there was real trouble—he began threading his way forward on Jirón Belén, wading through the flood of Peruvians.

Ordinarily his uniform would have engendered a certain respect and distance, but today he might have been wearing a peddler's rags for all the deference he received. They were still two blocks from the park and quite a way from the actual rally when the candidate's high-pitched voice reached Túcume's ears through a set of outdoor speakers set up on the streets nearby. The opening was pure Stein—thanking the people for their faith, invoking the past, and then looking toward the future, all in the space of two sentences. Even Túcume, who had heard the basic formula many times, was stirred.

But with the third sentence, the tone changed abruptly. For the first time, Túcume heard his own name mentioned.

Not as a hero but as a blackmailer and villain.

"He came to me not a week ago, threatening to ruin me unless I went along with him, which I would not do. And when I told him this, he hinted that all Peru would bow to him soon. He did not spell it out, but I realize now that he was speaking of this bomb he claims to have wrested from the guerrillas' hands. I suspect he has made demands to all of the other candidates—let them come forward and admit it. . . .

"I tell you what I believe, though as yet there is no proof: General Túcume has been working with these guerrillas all along. Tell me, friends: Why has a puny guerrilla group not been defeated despite two years of pursuit? How could a man who vanquished Ecuador not defeat a dozen lawless guerrillas? He must be stopped, and stopped now. I call on the other candidates to join me—I call on the government to join me. We stand as one against this general. If this is not a coup by one general, let the army prove its goodwill by arresting him and seizing his weapon. It belongs to the people of Peru, not a blackmailing general who clearly is planning a coup. . . ."

Each word felt like a hot poker jabbed against Túcume's temple. They were lies, incredible lies!

But the crowd sopped them up, roaring approval.

Túcume raged, but there was no place to vent his anger. Even the speakers were out of sight, a block or more away.

"We must seize this weapon as we seize the future," continued Aznar. "We will not be blackmailed by the past. The people of Peru move onward!"

Túcume changed direction as the crowd continued to erupt with cheers. Fear mixed with anger, true fear—he had miscalculated badly; utterly surprised by Aznar's betrayal, Túcume had no plan to deal with it. The only thing he could do was retreat.

As he reached the block where he had left his car, he saw a phalanx of green uniforms surrounding it.

Was he to be arrested? On what charges?

Maduro wouldn't need charges. Any lie would be believed, as Aznar was now showing.

Cursing, Túcume quickened his pace and reached into his jacket for the small pistol he carried for protection; for the first time in his life he thought of using the gun on himself.

He dismissed the idea and continued moving. A half block later, his satellite phone rang. He took it from his belt, but then hesitated, wondering if it was a trap: the phone might be used to locate him.

I am not a coward, he told himself, and he pressed the receive button and held the phone to his ear.

"They've betrayed you. The Americans have pressured them, and they have betrayed you."

"Stephan?"

"Try to get to Avenida Roosevelt where it meets Cotabamas. Don't go to your hotel."

"Stephan?"

The line went dead.

• • •

Babin hung up the pay phone, then crutched back to the cab. Soldiers and policemen were flooding all over the city. The radio in the cab reported that presidential candidate Aznar—now declared the "favorite" for president—had denounced Túcume, charging that he had tried to blackmail him by making illegal contributions without his knowledge. It was believed that this had happened to other candidates as well, the commentator added, but that Aznar was the only one with the courage to admit it.

This was only the tip of the iceberg for this general, continued the commentator, mixing speculation with malicious lies.

People would believe what they wanted to believe, Babin thought to himself. Once they had chosen a villain, they would weave whatever facts supported their view. Intellect followed emotion, not the other way around.

In his case as well, perhaps. Babin told himself that he was trying to help the general because he needed him to get out of Peru. Even if the situation had not been so chaotic in the city, Babin's plan to get the gun and phone and leave the country was fraught with peril. Túcume would be grateful at worst, willing perhaps to give Babin money or the names of others who could help. And at best, Túcume would be a useful ally, certainly better than a driver selected largely by chance.

But Babin's decision went beyond the logic. Not only did he feel that he owed the general a debt; Babin was sorry for him as well. Túcume had succumbed to the same flaw Babin had: he had trusted people he should not. He had failed to be paranoid enough.

"We'll wait here only a half hour," Babin told the cab-driver. But it was forty-five minutes before Babin spotted the general, and in truth he might have waited until nightfall.

"My men?" Túcume said as he approached the taxi, gesturing to his bodyguards.

"If you think they're loyal to you, release them," said Babin. "Otherwise, shoot them. Better yet, shoot them no matter what you think."

Túcume frowned. He turned back and waved the men away before he got into the cab.

100

By the time Dean and Ambassador Jackson returned to Dean's hotel room, the army had decided to arrest Túcume on charges that he was fomenting a coup. Knots of businessmen stood around the hotel lobby, trading rumors of coups, countercoups, and rebel uprisings.

Dean and the ambassador went up to their room. Tired from the long flight, Jackson took a nap while Dean checked for bugs—only one, in the TV—and then checked in with the Art Room.

"Mission accomplished," he told Telach.

"In spades," she replied. "The army has decided to arrest Túcume."

"Are they shutting down the city?" said Dean. "Should we go to the embassy?"

"That shouldn't be necessary. We'll keep an eye on it here. There are two army helicopters at the Lima airport that can grab you if it comes to that. The Peruvian army has moved a battalion's worth of men into the city area, but everything's calm. The units Túcume commanded in the north have already made it clear that they're not rebelling and are following orders from the general staff. Air traffic has been temporarily shut down, but we expect it to resume in a few hours. We'll update you on that."

Dean flipped on the TV when they were done. The reports varied wildly. Some claimed a coup had been under way since the night before. Others said that the New Path guerrillas were rising all across the country. Several stations carried a taped message from the country's commanding general announcing that "certain rebel forces within the armed forces' ranks" had tried to force their way into the election. The "people of Peru must not worry. The army will preserve our institutions."

Dean, who'd never put much trust in either politicians or the media, smirked as the reports continued. There were rumors that Túcume had been arrested in the city, others that he had threatened to detonate the nuclear bomb if captured. Politicians appeared one after another, assuring the public in almost hysterical tones that there was no need to panic.

As far as Dean could see, no one had. Every image of crowds on TV showed peaceful, smiling faces. The highway beyond the hotel remained about as busy as it had been when they arrived.

Dean checked in with the Art Room every half hour. By nightfall, it was clear that the immediate crisis had passed. The election was going forward. Túcume had been discredited, though he remained at large.

An international inspection team had gone north to inspect the nuclear weapon. Once that was done and the bomb announced to be a phony, the crisis would be diffused completely—on the surface. Meanwhile, the U.S. would continue scouring the country for a second warhead, this one believed to be real. The search was being coordinated by the U.S. military and State Department; the NSA would play a supporting role.

"The ban on air travel is going to be lifted at nine p.m.," Telach told Dean at six. "We've arranged a ticket for Ambassador Jackson on the first flight out. It's first class and it's direct to Miami."

"All right."

"We'd like you to stay in country for the next twenty-four hours or so, just in case you're needed. This isn't our show anymore, Charlie, but if you're needed . . ."

"Yeah, that's not a problem. How are Lia and Tommy?"

"They're fine. They're going to stay in the north for now. Things are in flux."

Dean thought of asking Telach to put him in touch with Lia but decided not to.

He woke the ambassador a few hours before the flight. Traffic was light on the way to the airport. There were army vehicles parked on the roads, and soldiers in twos and threes patrolled the entrances to the parking lots and terminal. Dean took off his holsters but kept one of his pistols in his belt before leaving the car.

"I'll wait with you at the gate," he told Jackson. "We're a little early."

"Can you get your gun past?"

"Probably. But I'm not going to try."

"Have you been doing this long?" asked Jackson as they walked through the lot.

"Awhile."

"You were in the Marines."

"Yes."

"Someone mentioned it. But I think I would have known. You hold yourself like a Marine."

"I didn't realize there was a Marine way of walking," said Dean, amused.

"Oh, absolutely. And standing. I remember the young men who guarded our embassies. You remind me of them."

"Thanks."

"It's quite all right, son. You're in good company."

Amused at being called "son," Dean led Jackson through the building, walking by the empty airline desk, then over to a café area, where they were the only customers. Dean ordered coffee; the ambassador had water. Two of the workers were talking about the election and the tumult in the city. After listening for a moment Jackson got up and went over to talk to them. Dean watched, not sure whether to be impressed or alarmed by the older man's calm matter-of-factness. By the time Jackson came back, Dean had finished his coffee.

"They think Aznar is going to win," said the ambassador. "They're voting for him."

"Is that good or bad?"

"That depends entirely on your perspective," said Jackson.

"From *our* perspective."

"From our perspective, it's not as good as we would like. Imberbe's a better candidate. Not just because he's pro-U.S., either. I think it highly likely Aznar knew that Túcume was helping him. Maybe he didn't want to be beholden to him, and saw this as the perfect opportunity to get rid of him. Or maybe he just saw that his hand was being forced, both by us and the Peruvian military."

Dean nodded.

"On the other hand, with Túcume neutered and the vice president on the way out, it's not as bad as it could have been," said Jackson. "We're dealing with a difficult situation, so complicated that the implications of what we do are sometimes not knowable until long after we've acted."

"Yeah." Dean leaned back in the chair.

"But there are times you can feel what you have to do in your stomach," said Jackson. "To do anything else would make you feel sick."

"Yes," said Dean, surprised. "I feel that way sometimes."

"But then you worry afterward whether you were right or not," said Jackson. "It's not easy."

The ambassador stared at the table. He seemed to have aged another decade; the energy that had followed his nap had dissipated.

"Come on, let's go find a place to park my metal," Dean told him. "Then swing by the airline counter and get your ticket. They should have gotten the all clear to open up by now."

Jackson waited while Dean cleared the metal detector at the gate entrance. He'd stashed his gun at the bottom of a waste can in one of the men's rooms while Jackson played lookout; it seemed like an apt coda to the caper. The cloak-and-dagger mission surpassed anything he had ever done at the State Department, and Jackson knew he'd be on a high for days, if not weeks.

Dean pulled on his shoes and joined him, and together they walked toward the gate where the plane would board. Dean had a ticket but was not going to join Jackson on the plane. Though curious, he knew better than to ask Dean what he was doing next.

The attendants were calling for first-class passengers when they arrived.

"You better get going," Dean told him.

Jackson gave Dean his hand. "Thank you very much, Mr. Dean."

"You're welcome."

Jackson started away but then stopped. He turned back to Dean. "It bothers you a great deal, doesn't it?"

"What's that?"

"Your problem earlier. You're worried about something specific."

"I guess I am."

"I think the fact that it bothers you is a good thing," said Jackson. "But I wouldn't let it paralyze you. You have to move on. Don't let it consume you."

"Thanks." Dean's face remained a stoic mask—the Marine way, thought Jackson. Emotion swirled behind it, but the face revealed nothing.

"I hope to see you again," said Jackson, waving and heading toward the door to the boarding tunnel.

101

The twenty-four hours that followed Túcume's decision to get into the taxi with Babin passed like the landscape viewed from a jet dashing over mountainous terrain. It was pockmarked with humiliations, large and small.

The first came at a bus station in a small town a few miles west of Lima. Mindful of the inherent risks in Peruvian military politics, Túcume had stashed money, clean credit cards, a small pistol, and—most important—passports in several places around the country, including the ancient lockers in this small building. When they arrived, Babin told Túcume he must stay in the car with the driver; he was still wearing his uniform and might be recognized. Reluctantly, Túcume gave Babin the locker number and the combination, then gritted his teeth and waited in the car like a common criminal escaped from jail.

The second humiliation came a few hours later, on the road west in the mountains. Babin had promised the taxi driver a good sum to keep his mouth shut, and, though wary, the driver initially believed him. He grew more nervous as night fell, however. Finally the man's hands began to shake when Babin told him he must pull off the road so that he could relieve himself. Tears fell from the man's eyes as he stopped. Babin took out the small pistol he had removed from Túcume's box and ordered the man out to the nearby brush.

Túcume didn't say a word, remaining silently in the car. Two shots resounded against the nearby mountainside, long, thin echoes that stung Túcume's conscience. But louder and more painful still was the knock on his window—Túcume turned to see Babin's face leering at him.

"Take his clothes. They will do for a short while. We must find another car."

Túcume did as he was told.

They used no fewer than six cars, beginning with the stolen taxi and ending with one bought with cash in a mountain town in the Andes. For Túcume, the journey was a succession of revelations showing how deeply he had miscalculated. The worst came Sunday morning, when a radio station aired an interview with Captain Chimor claiming Túcume had prepared a coup.

Túcume insisted on listening to it as they drove, wincing at every lie and falsehood. Clearly, Chimor had made some sort of deal with the general staff, either to save himself from whatever charges they were inventing or to salvage his career.

Chimor did not know of the bomb plot, but he knew of much else. And sooner or later the handful of men who did know what had happened would be pressured to tell more. Túcume clung to the hope that he might reach the barn before the warhead was discovered. What he would do then he did not contemplate.

He and Babin made their way westward and then north through the Andes. They changed their clothes and dyed their hair, dressing in simple garb to fit in. Only Túcume's shoes suggested that he was not a simple peasant; he scuffed them to make them appear older than they were, tokens of a prosperous past now distant.

Túcume's fluency with Quechua and his native accent were advantages, but they did not guarantee safety. They had plenty of money: besides ten thousand euros from the box, Túcume maxed out cash advances on his legitimate credit cards in Lima, then left them in the machines at Babin's advice, hoping some thief would take them and confuse the authorities with a false trail. Babin spoke of other sums that he might get, arranged through wire transfers with foreign accounts. In the areas where they were, however, such arrangements would be difficult at best, and for the moment they had no need of them. At the border, they would have the choice of using either Peruvian or Spanish passports; they would only have to get photos made at one of the many cheap shops nearby to establish their new identities.

Túcume, naturally, did the driving. Babin spent much of the time sleeping, worn out by exhaustion and pain.

Sometime after three on Sunday, General Túcume decided to stop for lunch. He found a small town several miles from the highway and parked the car. He left Babin sleeping and went to negotiate some food. The local restaurant sold french fries and chicken, and Túcume managed to persuade the owner to make some plates "for a picnic." He found Babin awake in the car when he returned.

"I thought you abandoned me," said Babin as he got in.

"I would not leave you, Stephan."

The Russian shook his head when Túcume offered him some food.

"You need to keep up your strength," the general told him. He started to eat himself and soon was glad Babin wanted nothing; his hunger was much greater than he'd reckoned.

"Put on the radio," said Babin.

"It's only bad news."

"We need to know what's going on."

Reluctantly, Túcume agreed.

"They turn against you quickly," said Babin as the radio finished replaying a bit about Aznar.

"Very."

"The CIA helped them. The Yankees were behind everything. They decided they had to stop you at all costs."

"Do you think they'll find the real bomb?" the general asked, changing the subject.

"It's only a matter of time before they go to the barn," said Babin.

Túcume knew this was true and didn't argue. "If we beat them, we can sell it."

"The Americans will never let it be sold," continued Babin. "The only thing to do with it is to use it to get revenge. There's no other choice."

"I can't kill my countrymen," said the general softly. "If the traitors alone were gathered—Aznar, Chimor, the general staff, the president, the defense minister. If they were put together, those people I would gladly kill. But not the innocent."

He shook his head. His stomach had begun to revolt at the very idea.

"I wasn't talking about Peru," said Babin. "The CIA. The Yankees, General. They are who did you in. Your countrymen were only pawns. The Americans are your enemy."

Túcume pushed his unfinished lunch back into the bag.

"I only wish that were true," he said, starting the car.

While Babin knew it was only a matter of time before Túcume agreed with him about what must be done, time was an extremely limited quantity. From what he could determine by looking at the map, within four or five hours they would reach a juncture in the highway where they would have to either proceed northward toward Ecuador or turn right toward the region of Túcume's military district and the barn where the warhead had been kept. Proceeding eastward toward the barn was suicidal, and in no way would Babin do so. In the worst case, he would insist that the general help him find a driver to take him to Ecuador, and he had the general's small pistol to use if absolutely necessary.

It would be considerably more convenient to convince Túcume that he should join in Babin's own plan to take revenge on the U.S. To do this, Babin had to tell him that he had the warhead. But he needed the right moment.

Babin watched the general as they drove, staring surreptitiously at his drooping cheeks and heavy frown. Túcume looked different, not just because of his dyed hair and clothes, but also because something inside him had dramatically changed. He had lost the thing that had driven him. More than that, he had seen that his own instincts to trust people close to him had led to his downfall. In a sense, he had betrayed himself. If he couldn't trust his judgment, he couldn't trust anything. He had lost his dream, and he had lost his own sense of who he was.

Babin knew the feeling intimately. He had not begun to climb from the deep hole the crash had ejected him into until his plan for revenge took shape.

The general had cared for Babin then, arranging his hiding place and home, bringing Rosalina to watch him. It was partly in the general's interests, surely; he did not know much about the warhead, and Babin wasn't even sure at what point the general realized it was a nuke. But killing Babin would have been easy to do at any point; instead, Túcume's instincts led him to a role more like that of a father or uncle.

Or Inca, to hear Túcume describe his ancestors.

Now their roles were reversed. Though his body was racked with pain, Babin was the strong one. Túcume was now a shell, crippled within.

They stopped around five to get gas in a village that looked like something that came out of the eighteenth century. The station was modern enough, but there were two burros tied to a pole near the building, and just beyond the gas pumps sat a row of huts that from a distance seemed to be made of straw and dried mud.

"Are you hungry?" Túcume asked.

"No, but I could use something to drink," said Babin.

"There will be food and drink over there," Túcume said, gesturing across the street. To Babin, the building looked the same as the other hovels, but it proved to be a restaurant, and they were soon eating a kind of casserole of potatoes mixed with tiny bits of chicken. The dining room was open to the kitchen; a TV played in a corner above the stove. Babin winced as the general's face was flashed on the screen.

Túcume ignored the program, devouring his food.

"They'll be looking for you in your military district," said Babin, his voice almost a whisper.

"Sshh," said Túcume.

He'd found a woven hat to wear, and it made him look like one of the locals. Still, it was not a complete disguise.

The picture changed—there was a shot of Inca ruins from the distance, then the house where Babin had stayed for more than two years.

"This is where the weapon was stored, intelligence agents believe," said a voice off-camera.

"Rosalina," said Túcume, but she didn't appear and there was no mention of her as the program continued. The original footage that had been shot when the bomb was discovered followed, with the commentator describing some of the authentic combat with the rebels that had taken place in the region over the past several months. The scene then changed to a military base in the region, and Babin realized that he'd been watching a lead-in for what the newspeople thought was the main event: a live press conference with the head of the military and several experts who had examined the bomb. Immediately behind the podium were two American military people in freshly starched fatigues.

"The snake," said Túcume as Major General Maduro stepped to the podium.

Words flashed on the bottom of the screen; *Channel 37 exclusive—the bomb is a fake.*

"We must leave," Babin told Túcume.

Túcume stayed motionless as Maduro announced that experts from the International Atomic Energy Agency had discovered that there was no uranium or plutonium warhead in the weapon.

"The Yankees have the warhead," whispered Túcume.

"No, they don't," said Babin. "Let's pay and go, before someone recognizes you."

102

After Jackson got on the airplane, Dean went to a new hotel a mile away, got a room, and went to sleep. He slept so soundly that the Art Room became worried about him and finally had someone from the embassy go over and check on him. The woman they sent knocked on the door for so long that someone from hotel security was sent to investigate; the detective was just getting off the elevator when Dean finally opened the door.

"Charles Dean?" asked the woman.

"Yeah?"

"The embassy sent me. Are you OK?"

Dean saw the detective eyeing them suspiciously. "Come in," he told her, pushing the door closed so he could undo the chain. He kept his gun behind his back as she came in, not sure who she was.

"What's up?" he said to her, letting the door close.

"Someone back home wanted to make sure you were all right."

"Who are you?"

"Lisa Tomari. I'm with the embassy."

"Which means what?"

The woman glanced around the room, obviously trying to indicate to him that she was afraid it might be bugged.

"I got it already," said Dean.

She was in her midtwenties, very pretty. Looking at her made him ache for Lia.

"I guess you should call home," Tomari said. Her face blanched white; she'd finally realized he had a gun behind his hip.

"All right. Sit in the chair," he told her.

He went and got the sat phone, using it rather than pulling on his shirt with the wiring for the com system. Sandy Chafetz answered immediately.

"You wanted me?" Dean asked.

"We hadn't heard from you."

"I was sleeping."

"Can you talk now?"

"Somebody from the embassy is with me."

"Tell you what—why don't you go over to the embassy and we'll update you there?" Chafetz said. "There's a fresh ID and a credit card waiting for you. Don't use the rental car; the Peruvian intelligence service has it staked out."

"All right."

Dean slapped off the phone.

"Can you give me a ride to the embassy?" Dean asked Tomari.

She nodded, her eyes still fixed on the pistol.

"Just a precaution," he told her, putting it in his belt. "Let me take a shower first. All right?"

Dean was done in under five minutes. Tomari had flipped on the TV and was watching a news report. Dean went over and looked at the screen. Hernando Aznar was holding his hands over his head in victory.

"He won, huh?" said Dean.

"Yes, quite a surprise. This is from one of the celebrations last night," Tomari said. "They had quite a celebration in Lima. People were partying in the streets. They really seem to like him."

"Feel like some breakfast?"

"It's six in the evening."

"How about dinner then?"

"OK."

"I'm not going to shoot you. Don't worry."

He could tell by the way she laughed that she was attracted or at least intrigued by him. If he was the kind of man who indulged in casual affairs, finding a way to bed her would not have been difficult. But he wasn't that kind of man.

When they arrived at the embassy, the newly elected president was finishing a courtesy call to the U.S. ambassador. Aznar and the ambassador had just concluded a press conference, but the media continued to press him as he walked toward the door. Dean stood to the side, watching the politician make his way forward. He seemed even more tired than he had been the other day, fatigued, already weighed down by the office he had won. Yet when he stopped to give a statement and the television lights were flipped on, he straightened and seemed invigorated. His words were just as assured as they had been the other day when Dean saw him from the side of the stage.

"Peru's election stands as an example to the rest of South America," said Aznar in Spanish. "The people have been heard. My administration will work closely with the United States on economic issues, and to combat the spread of drugs. We will be more aggressive than our predecessors; I guarantee you that."

Dean watched with a jaundiced eye, wondering how long it would be before Aznar fell back on the much easier line of America-bashing. The new president answered a few more questions, then pushed on.

He saw Dean as he came down the steps. After a moment's hesitation, he came over to Dean.

"Tell your friend I won't forget the service he's done for me," whispered Aznar.

Dean nodded, and Peru's newly elected president moved on.

The embassy was packed with CIA officers, military people, and State Department experts. Dean collected his new ID and credit card, then called the Art Room using one of the secure lines in the communications center.

Telach filled him in, saying Jackson had gotten back safely and congratulating Dean on a good mission.

"What do I do next?" Dean asked.

"General Spielmorph is in charge of the task force that's conducting the search. He'd like you to brief some Delta people at the embassy tonight; they're heading north as soon as you're done. They want to know about the area where the bomb was found."

"I can go with them if they want."

"At this point, they're spearheading the search down there."

"What about a recovery operation if there's another bomb?"

"Again, that's going to be a Delta mission most likely. Tommy and Lia are in country to help out. Mr. Rubens would like you back in the States."

"Time to face the piper?"

"I'm sorry?"

"That's all right, Marie. Tell me what flight you want me on, and then I'll go find the Delta people."

103

Calvina Agnese pulled the thin sweater tighter around her shoulders, more to move her stiff limbs than to ward off the early-morning cold. The Ecuador-bound bus wasn't due for another three hours, but the line for spots already stretched well past the stones that marked the spot where people were usually turned away. Calvina was two people beyond the stones, but the veterans in the line around her said it was likely she would get in anyway. A small bribe to the driver might help, they'd added, and Calvina had allocated a few soles from her meager supply for that.

Calvina had had to pay for the boat and bus from Nevas and would have to spend her own money to get to Quito, the capital of Ecuador, and the airport, where the man with the balloons would meet her. She did not know which city she was going to and would not until she was at the airport. Nor had the details on what would happen when she arrived been explained.

The passport she'd been given had spelled her name wrong and gave as her address the school in Nevas where she had gone. They had not even bothered to ask her real address, and she thought it better not to question them about the name.

"What are you doing in Ecuador?" asked an older gentleman near her as she waited.

"I have a job," she lied.

"A young girl like you should go to the North," he said, meaning the U.S. "There are many rich people there, if you work hard."

She smiled at him.

"You're not so pretty," the man added. "But a hard worker would make a good bride."

Calvina felt her face flush red as she turned away.

"All the others I could accept, but to lose Rosalina as well— that is the final blow," Túcume told Babin as they waited for petrol.

"I don't think she would betray you," Babin replied. "Not Rosalina. Why do you say that?"

"She did."

Túcume threw his head back on the seat. Babin thought he wore the look of a man crushed by the world.

"She was a descendant of the people who had sheltered my ancestors," said the general, his voice almost a moan. "Now even they turn against the Inca."

Depression made Túcume compliant, but Babin worried that the general was sinking too deep. He had hardly said anything as Babin explained his plan to take the weapon to the North and extract revenge; the Russian had had to ask point-blank whether he would do it before getting a "yes."

"Why would Rosalina give me up?" Túcume asked.

"I don't think she did."

"This is just like the natives—like all of our people. You see from the vote—no one came to the polls. Did you even hear talk of an election in any town we stopped in?"

"No," said Babin. The news reports had said that turnout in the native regions had been low, running at about 10 percent—far under Túcume's expectations, though actually in keeping with most elections in the past.

"This is how the conquistadors won," said Túcume. "They used our people against us."

"Perhaps you should sleep," suggested Babin. "We don't want to cross until nightfall anyway."

"Sleep. I cannot sleep."

"What do you think about getting another driver?"

"Who would we trust?"

Babin nodded. It would be risky to take someone with them, too tempting—even if the man could not see beyond the general's ill-fitting clothes and realize who he was, he would know they had money, and they would have to be on their guard constantly.

But another helper, someone to get them food even, to buy tickets when they went to Ecuador and Mexico—above all, someone to distract the general even slightly—that would be *most* useful.

"I think I will stretch my back and legs," said Babin, getting out of the car. Túcume said nothing.

Though tiny, the town was something of a way station for travelers. A long line snaked in front of the local café: a mixture of workers, northern tourists, would-be emigrants, and adventurers waited for the daily bus to Ecuador.

A helper might be found here. Not a driver—it occurred to Babin that most of these peasants probably had never driven in their lives.

They'd lie, of course, if asked.

He couldn't trust a man, not even an old one.

A woman?

Babin crutched forward, pondering the idea, its risks and rewards, even as he eyed the crowd. A woman *might* be trusted. Certainly a pretty one would take Túcume's mind off his problems.

Or not. That would be too obvious.

An older woman was out of the question. Anyone who reminded him of Rosalina would be a terrible choice.

A girl, barely out of her teens, not quite experienced enough to cause too many problems but smart enough to do as she was told.

A good idea? Or more complications?

Babin saw two, maybe three girls who would do in line. It

was hard to judge ages without staring, and staring would make them suspicious. He turned and crutched back toward the car.

He would send Túcume to choose.

The gray-haired gentleman who approached the line at the bus stop reminded Calvina of Señor DeCura even before he began to speak. He was taller than Señor DeCura, bigger, more clearly native by birth. But his accent was the same. The first words from his mouth were Spanish, asking if everyone here was going north across the border, when the bus was expected, and when the ride was due. Then he began speaking in Quechua, repeating the questions.

No one answered. Calvina saw a look of hurt cross his face and felt sad for him; she glanced to her left and right and, when she was sure that no one else would speak, told him in the language of her grandparents that yes, it was a long wait until the bus came.

"You live nearby?" asked the man.

She shook her head, then added, "Lima."

"Why are you going to Ecuador?"

She felt her face flush. "Work."

"Where?"

"The capital."

"When do you need to be there?"

"The work begins when I arrive."

The man paused, considering something. Then he said, "I need someone to help me with my friend, who is a cripple. The work is not hard, and I will pay with a ride to Ecuador as well as a modest sum."

At the mention of a job—even though the words were in Quechua—Calvina felt several of the people around her stir.

Should she go with him? Perhaps it was a trap. But he seemed so reassuring, so much like Señor DeCura.

Hadn't Señor DeCura proved to be less than he seemed?

No. Whatever trouble he had gotten into was not his fault. Señor DeCura was too kind, too wise. Others had been jealous and brought him down.

"What sort of job, *señor*?" said an older woman in Quechua.

As the gentleman turned to her, Calvina stepped forward and touched his arm. "What is it I should do?" she said.

104

The Art Room told Dean he didn't have to report back until Wednesday, and he took them at their word, going straight home Monday night and planning to sleep in Tuesday. But he woke up around two in the morning, restless. He kept thinking about Lia and leaving Karr.

Leaving Karr was the wrong thing to do. It had been a mistake—he should have let the Art Room handle it. It had been a dumb *kid* mistake, something he should have grown out of years ago, around the time he was hunting Fu Manchu with Turk.

Worse than that was the fact that it had felt like the right thing to do. It still did.

Could he trust his judgment anymore?

Dean got up and turned on the TV. The news channels had nothing about Peru.

Around five he decided to go for a run. He pulled on his baggy sweats, laced his sneakers up, stretched out front, and began jogging lazily through the still-slumbering neighborhood.

Maybe it was Lia he couldn't trust. Not her—his feelings for her.

If it was a struggle between doing his job and protecting her—not even protecting, simply loving—she won.

She won.

How did that jibe with his duty to his country? When you

were a member of Deep Black, a Marine, a soldier, you had a responsibility to your country first. Or you should.

You had to. And you had to feel it in your gut.

He did feel it in his gut. That was the problem. What he felt for her was stronger.

He pushed himself through the streets, hoping the sweat would help provide an answer.

105

Tuesday's morning brief included a long list of the searches that had been conducted in Peru, but the bullet summary at the top said it all: no second weapon found.

Rubens killed the e-mailed newsletter. It was barely four and a half days since the weapon had first been sighted, and by any realistic measure, the search had a long way to go. But by nature, these sorts of missions tended to play out in one of two ways: very quick results, based on hard work and perhaps a break or two; and long-drawn-out, often inconclusive operations where energy flagged over time.

While the search was only a few days old, already the most likely places to find the bomb had been carefully inspected. The Peruvians were already chafing at the continued U.S. presence, especially as the search agenda deviated from the war against the New Path rebels.

The CIA analysis—and for once Rubens actually agreed—was that the general would follow the lead of his ancestors and hide in the jungle. Vast stretches of Amazonian jungle in the far northeast were essentially outside of the central government's control; he might stay there forever and not be found.

A bomb might as well. The NSA had tried various data searches to try to re-create movement in and out of the region, but the primitive nature of the transportation and communications system there meant there were few records to look at.

As for Babin, he, too, had disappeared. Or more accurately, had never appeared in the first place. They had put together a reasonably decent description of him, and several Army Special Forces soldiers fluent in Spanish had been detailed to search the slums of Lima for him. The Peruvian intelligence service and military had been given his description and told that he was a technical expert who'd helped Túcume fake the warhead. They, too, were looking for Babin, though with somewhat less urgency than Rubens would have liked.

There was a knock on his door.

"Come in," said Rubens, pushing the blanket over the top of his desk.

"I was to report to you this morning," said Ambassador Jackson, shuffling tentatively into the office.

"Yes. Take a seat, Mr. Ambassador."

Jackson pulled over a chair. He had an inquisitive expression on his face.

"You're rested from your trip to Peru?" asked Rubens.

"Quite."

"And it went well."

"My small part went as required, I think. Beyond that, I'm not in a position to say."

A measured, thoughtful answer. It did not make things easier.

"Ambassador, I find that I have to talk to you about a matter of grave concern," Rubens said. "I find that you were not completely candid with our interviewers during your intake sessions."

"Intake?"

"During some of our routine screening," said Rubens. "Specifically, you omitted the controversy regarding your son. The district attorney's office kindly filled us in yesterday afternoon."

"Kindly?" Jackson's voice was almost inaudible.

"They claim that they haven't decided whether to press charges or not. Though they gave me to understand that, given the time that has now passed, it's unlikely."

• • •

Jackson stared at the carpet in front of Rubens' feet. He was under no obligation to explain what happened; nor did he think that Rubens—that anyone, really—would understand if he did. And yet the impulse to speak was very strong.

"It's a wonderful thing to see a young man grow from an infant to an adult," he said. "He was a very fine young man. Due to my wife, I'd say. More than me. After college, we became much closer. A few years ago, he introduced me to instant messaging on computers and cell phones. We would talk several times a day while he was in law school. I like to think I may have helped him with his studies. He was a wonderful young man." He raised his eyes to meet Rubens'. "If you have specific questions, I'll answer them."

"Did you use any influence at all with the district attorney?" Rubens asked.

"Not at all."

"He knew you had been an ambassador?"

"I don't think it was a secret," said Jackson. "I never asked for any special consideration. And I told the truth."

"You spoke to the DA without an attorney present?" asked Rubens.

"I didn't see the need for one."

Jackson waited to be asked if he had killed his son. He hadn't, not in a moral sense; his boy had gone on long before that long night Jackson cried over him as the heart monitor began to sound. But if he was asked, he would describe exactly what he did, step-by-step. It was a simple matter of changing a setting on the machine. He knew the night well; it replayed regularly in his head.

But Rubens didn't say anything.

"Should I get to work?" Jackson asked finally. "I have to leave at eleven for my Meals on Wheels route. But I will be back."

"We'll speak again," said Rubens, dismissing him.

• • •

What struck Rubens was the fact that Jackson had not tried to justify himself or excuse his actions.

Rubens had spoken personally to the district attorney. Jackson's son had been on life support for more than two years before he died of an apparent overdose of his painkilling medication. The circumstances strongly suggested that Jackson had administered it, though as the district attorney admitted, the evidence might not rise to the level of "beyond reasonable doubt" in the eyes of a jury which could gauge in person the suffering of a distinguished and anguished father.

Montblanc's investigators said there was no evidence of Jackson's having used any sort of political influence with the DA. For one thing, the district attorney was a Democrat and Jackson a registered Republican. Nor did Jackson have any roots in the community where his son had been taken for treatment.

Montblanc told Rubens that if the young man had been at a different hospital in another state or even county, very likely he would have been removed from the respirator long before. And the astronomical cost of the care did not seem to have been a factor—the hospital hadn't even considered that Jackson might pay the bills until after the young man died. Jackson himself insisted on it.

And yet the agency had always avoided even the potential for scandal.

Had Rubens not intervened, Jackson would not have been brought on until the investigation was completed. In that case, he wouldn't have helped Desk Three reach the conclusions it had—no one might have undertaken the mission in Peru that discredited General Túcume.

Would he have taken Jackson on, knowing this?

If there were no charges, then it wasn't a crime. But . . .

But . . .

And what would Rubens say if Collins or someone else brought it up with the president to embarrass him?

Did you know, Mr. President, that you sent a murderer to Peru to speak to a candidate on your behalf?

Or worse—*pulled strings to have a grand jury convened and charges filed?*

What would he do then? What would it change?

Nothing—and yet everything, as far as politics were concerned. The battle lines would be drawn instantly. The controversy would have nothing to do with national policy and yet *everything* to do with it. Could he afford that risk? Not if he wanted higher office.

Rubens hated this. He hated parsing decisions into political pluses and minuses. If this was the price of being national security adviser . . . then he didn't want it.

He didn't want it.

Rubens rose from his desk. Jackson had proved his worth. If the matter came up, Rubens would do the thing that *should* be done—he would admit that he had installed Jackson before the vetting procedure had been complete and had made the judgment that he should be kept on. It was the right decision given the larger circumstances, and he would stand by it.

Rubens also made another decision. He didn't want to be national security adviser. He didn't want to deal with the politics. They would corrupt him. He would do things not because they were right or wrong, but because of how they would look and whom they would influence.

"I'm not going to take the job," he told himself out loud. "I'll send a message to the president that I'm not interested."

People said that when you made the right decision, you felt like a great weight had been removed from your back. But Rubens didn't feel any freer now. If anything, he felt a little depressed.

106

Babin put his hand on the back of the plastic chair in the waiting area at the Manta airport, waiting for their flight to begin boarding. They had driven much of the night and nearly all the day to get to Manta, in the northeastern corner of Ecuador, but Babin thought it far safer than Quito or any of the smaller airports in the south. The police here seemed to take little notice of them. He was not so sure it would have been the same near the capital.

Túcume sat in the next row, stony eyed and tired. But at least he had not deteriorated any further.

The girl was to thank for that. She had proven useful, not only in buying food and then tickets, but also at the bank a few hours before, where with the help of a new dress she had posed as Babin's secretary as he arranged the final money transfers and a sizable withdrawal.

He had decided not to kill her for several reasons, all practical. She was what some people called simple and lacked the mental capability to betray them. More important, he did not think the general could withstand the shock. Here was a man who had probably killed hundreds during his military career, and yet he had been trembling after the taxi driver was executed.

As the attendant moved to the desk to announce the flight, Babin took up his crutches and went over to the girl.

"Calvina, here," he said, taking the ticket for Quito from his pocket. "Your flight leaves in two hours. Go back into the terminal, past the shop with the shawls. Match the number of the gate to this number here. That is where you should go."

She nodded as she took it.

"Why don't you come with us?" said Túcume, looking up from his seat.

"I—"

"You want to go to the North, don't you?"

"I'm not sure that would be the best for all of us," said Babin.

"I think she should come. You had to buy a ticket for her to get to the gate area," added the general. "It's no more of an expense."

"Money has nothing to do with it," said Babin.

"I don't know if I can," said Calvina.

"You're scared of the men who gave you the passport?" asked Túcume.

"Might I suggest we discuss this nearer to the aisle, where there are no ears to listen in?" said Babin.

Túcume got up and walked to the opposite end of the waiting area. By the time Babin reached them, tears were slipping from the girl's eyes.

"Now what?" he asked Túcume.

"She was supposed to bring drugs to the United States. I told her what would happen in the North, when she arrived."

Though she hadn't said, Babin had easily guessed why she wanted to go to Quito. The general must have as well.

"Of course," said Babin.

"She didn't understand everything."

There was little time to argue.

"Won't they kill her family if she doesn't go?" said Babin.

"Not if she hasn't taken money from them. They are cowards."

Túcume's voice was forceful—not its old self but a shadow of it at least.

"Why not?" said Babin, hearing their aisle called behind him. "We'll keep her with us, and perhaps she'll be of some use."

Calvina looked out the window of the airplane. Señor Oroya said they were nearing Mexico, but all she could see were the tufted gray tops of clouds—a wondrous, incredible sight, the sight angels would see when they looked down at earth.

Señor Oroya—she believed that was not his real name, though it fit him—had proven very kind. He and the other man, the one with the crutches called Stephan, had asked her to do almost nothing, and in return had fed her and bought her clothes, been so very kind. She felt she could trust Señor with her life. He seemed like a protector, a true godfather.

He told her the men who had given her the passport were evil. Not because of the drugs but because of what they did to souls.

Calvina believed him. He was the sort of man who knew many things and could make much happen. He was rich and wise, and if they came for her now, he would protect her.

Calvina's thoughts went back to the school and the man with the balloons. And then she thought of the Chinawoman, the apparition that had appeared, talking in many tongues so Calvina could understand.

Like an angel would.

Just a woman. A kind woman.

Sent by the Blessed Virgin, perhaps. To find out how to help. Nothing occurred by accident.

Calvina continued to gaze at the clouds, wondering what the future would bring.

107

Lia gripped the side of the MH60G Blackhawk as it sped along the river west of Iquitos. The drumming rotor overhead numbed her head, mixing with the heavy fatigue of the last week. She knew today was Wednesday only because WE was underlined on her watch face.

She thought about Charlie, missing him. Every cross word she'd ever said to him came back to her, rumbling in the roar of the blades.

The helicopter banked sharply. It was at the end of a six-helicopter procession speeding toward a former Baptist missionary compound deep in the Amazonian jungle. The compound was occupied by a dozen natives the Peruvian intelligence service believed were part of a group called Sacred Right, dedicated to returning native land to native tribes. Though obscure, the group had issued a communiqué praising General Túcume eight or nine months before, calling him a "pure hero for the people." The proximity of the river would have made it relatively easy to transport a warhead here. Beyond that, though, there was no evidence that this raid was anything but a long shot, one of several the Army had been on in the past thirty-six hours. Karr had been asked to come because of his expertise in nuclear weapons. Lia was simply backing him up; she herself knew very little about the weapon's hardware.

"Up and at 'em!" yelled Karr as the helicopter shifted for

its final approach. The big blond giant rising from the nearby jump seat, standing with Lia as the helo pirouetted toward the landing zone. The Air Force crewman manned a machine gun at the door, grim-faced and determined as he scanned the jungle. An AC-130U gunship was circling overhead, covering the landing area.

The special operations radio channel began buzzing with chatter. There were flares on the ground. The first team was down. No opposition had been encountered. The three Special Forces pathfinders who'd infiltrated into the area earlier that morning were reporting in—everything is good; everything is good; everything is good.

Lia flashed back to an incident when she'd been on a Delta mission before coming over to Deep Black. As a woman, she'd been part of the officially nonexistent "Funny Squadron"—an all-female Delta unit that mostly undertook undercover missions in foreign urban areas. On this occasion, however, she happened to have been part of a team assisting locals trying to apprehend terrorists who'd taken refuge at an African elementary school. One of the people at the school used that very same phrase, "everything is good," to say they hadn't meant any resistance and the hostages were free.

A second later, the school blew up.

"Let's go, Princess," shouted Karr, leaping from the helo as it touched down.

Lia jumped out after him, pistol ready, trotting behind him as he strode toward the buildings, laid out in a horseshoe. The captain commanding the unit met them near the opening of the horseshoe, signaling for them to wait while the Army Rangers and Special Forces troops secured the buildings.

There was a certain rhythm to entering a dangerous and unknown space. The soldiers didn't take any chances, dropping flash-bang grenades through windows, blowing off the door hinges, moving inside quickly. Two Peruvian army officers were with them, acting as translators. Lia and Karr kept their distance from them, not wanting to have to answer any questions.

"Looks good," said Rockman over the communications system. He was watching a feed from a Predator unmanned aerial vehicle that had been launched to provide reconnaissance earlier.

"It's too easy," said Lia.

Gunfire erupted from one of the buildings near the head of the horseshoe. Two, three men with automatic weapons began firing from one of the windows. One of the American soldiers launched a grenade into the window; it burst with a cut-off boom and smoke curled out.

Lia glanced at Karr nervously. The experts said the warhead couldn't explode if it was jostled by another explosion. She wasn't so sure.

"Clear!" yelled someone in the building.

There were some more pops and rattles, but the main resistance was over. Six of the native guerrillas were dead; five others had surrendered or been captured after being wounded. They denied any knowledge of Túcume.

It took an hour for the troops to search the buildings. Karr was his usual good-natured self, waiting with his arms folded and his rucksack hanging off his shoulder. The ruck had the nuclear testing equipment—and tools he could use to de-arm the bomb if necessary.

Finally cleared, they walked to join the soldiers searching the buildings.

Karr kicked at the metal door covering the cellar entrance in the old tool building.

"What do you think?" asked the sergeant in charge of the detail searching the place.

"It ain't nowhere else," said Karr. "Hang on."

He bent down and ran his PDA around the side, looking for electrical or magnetic currents.

"What's that thing?" said the sergeant.

Karr smiled but didn't answer.

"There's no electrical booby traps," he said when he finished. "But I have a bad feeling about this. You got a rope? We'll rig it so we can yank it open from outside."

The soldiers quickly rigged the rope. Karr pulled; the door opened; nothing blew up.

"So much for feelings, huh?" said Karr, easing in.

"Look at this!" shouted the first man down in the hole. "It's a wine cellar!"

"Bust, huh?" said Rockman as Lia and Karr waited for the soldiers to saddle up.

"Except for the wine," said Karr.

"Catch a ride back to Iquitos and head down to Lima," said Rockman. "There are enough Atomic Energy people in Peru now. We're going to get you home."

"Who says we want to go home?" protested Karr.

"I wouldn't mind going home," said Lia.

Karr laughed, as if she were joking.

Later, as they walked toward the helicopter, Lia glanced across the clearing toward the other riverbank. An eagle had just come out of one of the treetops. He seemed to stumble in the air, but after two strong strokes, began to soar, gliding upward.

She didn't know why, but the sight cheered her up.

108

Deep Black missions were debriefed in a special area of the underground complex devoted to supporting Desk Three missions. Called the squad room by the ops, the facility looked like an oversize living room, and the process itself was designed to be as painless as possible for the ops. When the mission was complete, the agent took a small digital video camera and recorded the details in one of the two cubicles down the hall. They were outfitted like studies and reminded Charlie Dean of what a doctor's or lawyer's private office might look like; the books in the bookcases were English translations of classics, such as Plutarch's *Lives*.

In the past, Dean handled the reports with the briefest possible accounts. He thought the famous "We came, we saw, we conquered" report delivered by Julius Caesar to the Senate after he defeated Pharnaces too long by a third. But this time Dean gave an especially detailed account, including the part where he left Karr and went to find and help Lia.

He'd spent the flight from Lima thinking about what he was going to say. What truly bothered him wasn't the fact that he had made a mistake, but that even now he didn't feel as if it were a mistake. His head said it was, but his gut didn't agree.

And that, he decided, was a major problem.

"Mr. Rubens wants to see you," said Montblanc when Dean handed the recorder to him.

"I want to see him, too."

Montblanc's mustache bobbed. "He's up in his office. I'll let him know you're on your way."

Rubens was still struggling to get through the mountain of paperwork that had piled up over the last few days when Dean knocked on his door. He had Dean wait while he folded the gray blanket over the papers on his desk. Then he called the op in.

"I was really surprised at you, Mr. Dean," Rubens started as soon as Dean had sat down. "We do have a certain procedure and chain of command, and when we're in—"

"That's all right," said Dean, putting up his hand. "I was wrong. I know it. I've written up my resignation."

"What?"

"I don't know if this is the right language to use," he added, taking a folded letter from his shirt pocket. "I can adjust it if you want."

"You're quitting?"

"I can't trust my judgment."

"Charlie. Wait. Let's not get ahead of ourselves here."

Dean stared at him dispassionately.

"You just need a rest," Rubens told him. "A few days. You've been under considerable strain. A great deal of stress. On this mission and the others. You should take this under advisement."

"What's that mean?"

"Think about it."

"I have."

"You're tired, Charlie. You've just come back from an exhausting mission. We push you all too hard; I realize that. But you shouldn't—"

Rubens stopped, unsure of what words to use. "My family has a small cottage on Martinique. Why don't you take two weeks off and have some fun there? Just yourself. The servants will see to your needs. You need a *real* vacation."

"Trying to bribe me?"

"Bribe you?"

"I'm only kidding." Dean got up. "Thanks anyway."

"Charlie—take a few days off," said Rubens. But Dean was already out of his office.

"How are you, Charlie?" said Montblanc when Dean went in to see him. "I hope Mr. Rubens didn't come off too harsh. He thinks the world of you. That little confusion about your assignment isn't going to affect you long-term. I've seen these things blow over time and again. Operatives are expected to use their own judgment—that's why you're here. Conflicts are inevitable."

"Yeah, I guess." Dean wasn't sure how much of Montblanc's manner was genuine and how much was intended to be therapeutic. He was a psychologist, and his job was basically to seem as reassuring as possible to the Deep Black ops. In a way, thought Dean, he was a bit of a rat, pretending to be your friend and then probably filing reports behind your back.

"You know, you're due a lot of time off," said Montblanc. "And it happens that I have some tickets to Disney World."

"You, too?"

"I don't understand."

"Thanks. I'm a little old for Mickey Mouse."

"Oh, you'd be surprised at how much fun it can be. It's very relaxing."

"Thanks. I am taking some time off," Dean told him. "Friend of mine has a hunting lodge up near the Delaware, couple of hours north of Philadelphia. I'm heading there."

"Excellent," said Montblanc. "Very good. Of course, you do have to check in with me every twenty-four hours. There's a number to call, and we need to be able—"

"Yeah, I know the drill. Don't worry. I have a cell phone. Listen, there's something you ought to know. I'm quitting."

"Quitting?"

"Desk Three was supposed to be a temporary assignment. I have other things I have to do."

"Wait a second, Charlie. Charles—you can't just quit. That's *not* the way it works."

"I'm not walking right out. I know I have to go through discharge or whatever the procedure is. I just want you to know, I'm giving notice."

"No, you don't want to do that."

"I don't?"

"Charlie—"

"I'll be back in a week. We can talk about it then, but my mind's made up."

Dean started to leave.

"Is it hunting season?" said Montblanc, his voice wrought with frustration and confusion.

"Depends on what you're hunting."

109

The container was one of two dozen carried on the ship. They all looked exactly alike, and at first Babin was worried that the paperwork had been filled out incorrectly and that he had been led to the wrong truck. But his fear vanished when he opened the back and peered in. The crate, its freight labeled as cast-iron bathtubs, sat near the front, secured to its tie-downs.

He nodded to the yardman, who closed the rear of the container up. Babin crutched over to the waiting tractor.

"It's all right," he told the driver. "We'll meet at the park as I told you."

"My pay."

"I'll pay you the money I promised then," said Babin.

The Mexican was a scoundrel; he'd been promised twice the going daily rate to take the truck north to the U.S. and then had the gall to ask for a "tip" because the cargo container had to be picked up. Babin worried that the idiot would take off with the bomb, but there was no way he could climb into the cab.

Túcume had said very little since Ecuador. Even the girl was more talkative, telling them about her dream to make money in America and then return to buy a restaurant. Babin had considered telling her how things *really* worked but decided it was better to leave her naïveté unchallenged.

"Don't let him get too far ahead," Babin told the general

when he got back to the car they'd bought for cash at a small gas station not far from the airport. The truck was just turning around and heading for the exit.

"I don't trust him," said Túcume. He used English so the girl couldn't understand. "We should get rid of him."

Surprised, Babin asked the general if he was prepared for such a thing.

"We can't trust him," replied Túcume. "So we had best deal with him sooner instead of later."

"Good. Yes."

"The road would be the best place to dispose of him," said Túcume. "A stop."

"Yes. After we make the switch."

110

Though Rubens had spoken to George Hadash several times since the national security adviser had returned to Washington late Monday, the circumstances were never right for the kind of personal discussion he wanted to have with him. Nor did he think speaking to Hadash by telephone was the right way to handle what he wanted to say.

A full briefing for the National Security Council was arranged for Wednesday evening at seven; Rubens knew from past experience that Hadash's ever efficient secretary would block off the last hour before the meeting to make sure he would get there on time. He also knew that Hadash typically skipped dinner when an evening session was planned—not out of design, but because he inevitably got caught up in last-minute details for the meeting. So Rubens decided to stop by Hadash's office a little past six, gambling that he would manage to get a few minutes alone with his one-time college mentor.

"Have you had dinner, George?" asked Rubens, walking in on him.

"I was going to have something sent up."

"Mind if I join you?"

"No. Please. I'm just looking over some of the most recent updates."

Rubens went to use the secretary's phone to order Hadash's

normal dinner: a roast beef on rye, heavy on the mustard. He got a club sandwich for himself.

"Anything new in the past two hours?" asked Hadash.

"No," said Rubens. Even so, he began cataloging some of the rumors that had fizzled and a few relatively insignificant details gleaned from intercepts of Peruvian army units. He realized he was going on a bit too long, but had trouble stopping himself.

"How smooth do you think the transition will be between the present government and Aznar?" asked Hadash when Rubens finished.

"Aznar has appointed a former air force general as his top military adviser. That's being taken as a sign that he wants status quo with the military."

"Do *you* take it that way?"

"I have no evidence one way or the other. It's too soon after the election. He did make a point of going to our embassy and talking to the ambassador. That I suppose is a good sign. He thanked us."

"We'll see what that translates into in a few months," said Hadash. "The CIA is starting to believe that the general staff may be hiding Túcume, or at least dragging their feet on finding him. The feeling might be that there's no reason to disgrace him further."

"Just speculation," said Rubens. "Everything we've seen indicates the generals are serious about finding him. They haven't been looking for Babin—Sholk—the Russian arms dealer. They issued a bulletin, but they've left his search to the police and intelligence people, and they really haven't done much."

Hadash grimaced. At first, Rubens thought it was in reaction to what he had said, but then he realized it was something else.

"Are you all right, George?"

"Yes," said the national security adviser, though he obviously wasn't.

Rubens watched as Hadash put his hands over his eyes, squeezing his head.

"I've been getting migraines," Hadash said. "Terrible."

"Is that why you're resigning?" The words came out in a blurt, but at least they were out.

"I have a tumor, George."

"A tumor?"

"It's operable. That's a start. Not a death sentence."

"But—"

"I found out the day before I left for China. It seemed proper to deal with it immediately. I told the president, and no one else. I'll be leaving as soon as it can be arranged. The end of the month, I hope."

"You shouldn't resign. You're too valuable to us. To the country."

"Thank you for that. But I don't see how I can do my job." Hadash rubbed his head again. When he continued, his voice was awkward, his words tripping over each other. "I'm sorry. I hadn't planned on telling you quite like this. I thought it would be better to have a different setting. More relaxed. But circumstances haven't allowed."

"The president didn't say anything about this."

"I asked that he not."

"He told both myself and Debra Collins that you were resigning, but he did not offer an explanation. He made it sound as if we were both being considered for your position," said Rubens.

"Do you want it?"

Did he? Yes, *yes*—he definitely wanted it.

But he didn't want to be the person it would make him.

"I don't think I want to play the political games that you have to play if you're in the White House."

Hadash glanced at him from beneath his clasped hands. Rubens realized, belatedly, that what he had said could be interpreted as an insult. But all Hadash said was, "I know what you mean."

Rubens thought his old friend might talk him out of it, but instead, Hadash began speaking about China and continued to do so right up until the time came for them to leave for the session.

111

Robert Gallo ran another of the "Dredge" searches across the database of NSA electronic intercepts, this time using the tool to cross-reference those intercepts against financial data from banks that had had any association with Stephan Babin during the time he was working as an arms dealer. While Gallo considered it relatively easy to break into the computers that contained the data without being detected, the sheer size of their data files was overwhelming. The project had started five days before, and it had taken over one hundred hours to clandestinely "squeeze" all of the transaction information from the targeted computers.

Unlike targeted attacks such as those on General Túcume's family holdings, this was a brute-force "tell me all" data dump, made possible only by the massive power of the NSA's computers. The information retrieved was so vast that Gallo and the others working on it literally didn't know what they had. And so after a few "simple" and straightforward searches to see if there were any links with Babin's known accounts, Gallo had turned to Dredge, hoping it would turn something, anything, up.

That was the value of Dredge: you didn't know what the search engine would find before it went to work.

The tool's nickname referred to the program's ability to dredge up important facts from a vast pile of information without being told what it was looking for. It worked by finding patterns in the data similar to things that had been found in other searches. If, for example, five keyword searches had picked out bank accounts connected with a keyword, Dredge would look at the data discovered, decide what else was unique about it, and then hunt down similar patterns in the database. Maybe the accounts always had deposits made on Mondays; Dredge would find others that fit the same pattern. It could also find missing items in patterns—say the accounts had withdrawals every day but Thursday; it would find accounts that had only Thursday withdrawals, looking to fill in the missing gap.

The reason the search engine was valuable was that the operator didn't have to know what to ask for. You couldn't search the Web with Google unless you knew what you were looking for. Dredge was all about guessing. The more complex the data it started with, the "richer" the results were.

"Richer," in Gallo's experience, was a synonym for "bizarre." But even the bizarre had failed to turn up Babin.

The computer compiled a list of 145,375 accounts in the six banks Babin had used while in business that had been accessed in both Russia and South America in the year Babin disappeared. That sounded to Gallo as if it was a lot of accounts, and apparently the computer thought so, too, because it delivered twenty-eight pages of possible patterns analyzing those accounts.

"So what's unique about these accounts?" he asked himself and then the computer. Dredge brought up page after page of differences, finding patterns in odd balances and withdrawals, listed owners, even tax rates.

On the third page, at the very bottom, it red-flagged a category he'd never thought of—accounts that had had no activity except for interest accruals and deposits for three years until the past seven days.

There were fifty-three accounts, none of which were connected to Babin in any way.

Except for the one that was set up in Austria just over the

border from the Czech Republic on a day Babin was known to be in Prague.

It had sat dormant until this past Saturday in Lima, when it received a wire transfer from a bank that, until now, had no connection with Babin at all.

Rubens was just about to go and get some lunch when Johnny Bib ran into his office, waving his arms. He was hopping up and down, more excited than usual.

"Container ships!" he sputtered. "Containers!"

Rubens folded his arms, waiting for Johnny to explain. Experience showed that asking any questions when he was in this condition tended to delay his pronouncement.

"Moscow Fabric Importers—that's the name in Russian. Sholk was the code name, wasn't it? Silk?"

"You found his account?"

"Ha!"

Johnny Bib explained that the Desk Three computer people—Gallo mostly—had found three accounts until now not known to be Babin's. One of the three was with a South American bank, El Prio, a relatively small institution based in Argentina. The account had made a wire transfer to an account in Austria that hadn't been used for more than three years on the Saturday afternoon that Túcume had been denounced.

More critically, it had been accessed several times over the last few days.

Rubens started to get lost in some of the details of the bank accounts and the network of transfers.

"The bottom line, Johnny," he said.

"There was a cash withdrawal in Lima on Saturday from an HSBC bank account set up in Singapore while Babin was there five years ago. A few hours later, that account was used to transfer money to another bank account, which had made a payment to a container shipping company in Peru the week before. That payment was the third in a series, and coincided with the sailing of a ship to Mexico. Last week—the day before the warhead was found. It docked yesterday. We're working on tracking all of the cargo containers."

Rubens picked up the phone to talk to the Art Room. "Give me the location, Johnny."

112

Driving the 18-wheeler took Túcume back to his earliest days in the army, when he worked with a supply company in the southern Andes and made sure to familiarize himself with the equipment his men used. Their trucks had been geared differently but were very similar to drive. He knew he would not do well in a city or parking the rig, but on the highway he was mostly all right, lurching a bit when in traffic and probably driving a bit too slow overall, but certainly all right.

The girl slept between him and Babin. Her weight felt pleasant on Túcume's shoulder, even reassuring. In their short time together, he'd come to like her very much. It wasn't a sexual attraction; it was more as if she were the child he would have had if he'd married. It was clear from what she had said that she had intended to sell herself as a drug mule; he was glad to have saved her from that.

She would be a ripe target in America. She was too naive, too young, to survive on her own. The predators would snatch her up in a moment. Túcume didn't think she was pretty enough to be a whore, but that wouldn't save her; she would end up being used in some other way.

As he drove, he fantasized about how he might protect her. He could let Babin take the weapon and go on without him. But that made no sense; his course was set. Sooner or later, the Peruvians and their CIA collaborators would hunt him down. Most likely, they were already on his trail. The CIA had its tentacles everywhere.

Túcume glanced in his mirror, looking at the sparse head-lights behind him. Maybe they were behind him already.

Babin stirred. "Where are we?" he asked.

"The border is a few miles ahead. What do you want to do?"

The Russian glanced at his watch. "Near midnight. We will cross now."

"Do you think the passports look good?" asked Túcume.

"They're fine. I've used much worse."

Túcume was not so sure. They had bypassed the border controls to get into Ecuador—not very difficult in the moun-tainous jungle—and getting into Mexico had been easy. The Spanish passports they had used were of the highest quality; even the holographic laminate they pasted over the photos looked perfect. The only comment the passport official had made was one of condolence to the alleged Señor Oroya on the graying of his hair.

But the United States would be another matter entirely. Babin had obtained his own documents for their use and in-sisted they use them. They would appear to be two long-distance drivers who had picked up a paying passenger.

"What about the girl?" Túcume asked.

"We can leave her if you wish," said Babin. "But here is what is likely to happen if she is with us. If we are stopped, the agents will spend their time questioning her story, not ours. Her documents are excellent, and they will have to let her go. They won't even bother us."

"The truck—"

"You worry too much."

"Maybe a little rest before we continue."

"No, we go now. If you're worried, waiting will only make you more nervous. Once we're past the border, you will feel much better."

113

Even in the CIA's custom-built Gulfstream V, it took roughly six hours to fly from Lima to Manzanillo, on the western coast of Mexico. Karr spent the whole time sleeping. Lia, sitting next to Adam Winkle, the head of the CIA working group on the warhead, spent the whole time thinking about Dean. The Art Room told her that he'd decided to take a week off. Telach made it sound like he had gone at Rubens' urging, but it all seemed too out of character for Dean.

Less than eight hours before, NSA analysts had located a cargo container apparently connected with Stephan Babin in a transport yard in Manzanillo's port. The container and the yard were under surveillance, with two CIA teams hidden nearby and ready to pounce if the truck was moved. A third team, which included U.S. drug enforcement agents and Mexican police, as well two CIA liaisons, was stationed at the entrance to the lot, inspecting every cargo truck that left.

In the meantime, the NSA had been using the shippers' records to check on the trailers that had left the yard. On paper at least, all of the container trucks checked out. Most belonged to a company that made mining equipment about thirty miles to the north; the company was being inspected by another strike team, this one organized by the FBI.

Winkle checked in with the ground teams as they approached the airport. The cargo container had not been moved or approached overnight. Lia heard the disappointment in his voice—while the teams had been ordered not to move in until bomb experts were nearby, there had also been some hope that Babin or even Túcume would come by to pick up the container.

"It'll be dawn soon. We've got to move in," said Winkle. "I have two Department of Energy people with me, along with another bomb expert. We're five minutes from the airport. Helicopters are waiting for us. Go ahead and move in."

He snapped off the phone and turned to Lia. "We have to find out if it's real, or if we should look somewhere else."

"Absolutely," she told him.

114

Babin's prediction about the border agents had proven correct, and Túcume felt himself relaxing as they continued north toward Houston. The girl had fallen asleep and lay slumped against his shoulder.

"We should change vehicles again," said Babin. "Sooner or later they will look for this one."

"We can't unload all the boxes," said Túcume.

"We only have to unload one."

"Two hundred kilos—"

"Two hundred and fifteen."

"Too much weight, and no one to help this time."

"That we can change easily. What we will need is a suitable vehicle." Babin stared out the window. "Take the next exit. I know what we can do."

Babin surveyed the vehicles parked in front of the bar two stores down from a large all-night supermarket. There were pickup trucks, but they were too obvious a choice, as bad, he thought, as another tractor trailer. A large station wagon on the other hand—that would be perfect, as long as he could find one with a rear hatch large enough to accommodate the crate.

He had listened to the radio religiously on the way north. There was no news about Peru, let alone his warhead. Still, he thought it possible that the Americans would be looking for him. He had the advantage of knowing where he was going—the conceited Yankees would no doubt think he would strike at Washington, D.C., a symbolic gesture against the world's tyrant. But he was not so simple; he had never believed in symbols.

Still, if they were on his trail, they would be looking for a large truck. It was best to find something completely different.

There were no station wagons near the bar. He was just about to tell Túcume to start up the truck and move on when a small SUV pulled up in front of the bar. Two men got out—young men, Babin thought, though he couldn't get more than a glimpse.

"Let's try with those two," said Babin, pulling open the cab. "Wait for me at the old building we saw. If I am not there in an hour and a half, come back. I will be in the supermarket."

Getting down from the truck was a struggle, but the pain made him more determined. He crutched across the parking lot, avoiding the puddles left by a recent rain. He examined the rear of the car, noted the license plate number, and went inside.

The room was almost empty. The two men who had just come in from the lot were sitting at the bar.

"Bartender, there was a car outside with its lights on," he said out loud. "A red vehicle." He gave the license plate.

"Yo, I left my lights on?" said one of the men, starting to get up.

"I turned them off for you," said Babin.

"Good thing I don't lock it, huh?"

"Nice car," said Babin. He found English awkward after having gone so long without using it very much, and his unease dampened his courage.

"Have a drink, y'all," said the man. "What are you havin'?"

Remembering his last experience with vodka, Babin ordered a beer.

"Messed up your leg, huh?" said the man's friend. They were in their early twenties, relatively big.

Could they lift five hundred pounds between them?

Probably not. Babin had a ramp in the truck, though. They

could angle it down into the back of their car and manhandle the crate inside.

The trick was to get them to want to do it.

"My back is the problem," said Babin. "It's a big problem. My partner and I were supposed to make a delivery to one of the construction sites up the road. A bathtub. Special order. But the trailer can't make it past the mud and, with my back, I couldn't help him unload it anyway."

"Bummer," said the man who owned the car.

"Maybe I could hire some help," said Babin, taking the beer.

The man closest to him turned and winked at his friend. "Five hundred bucks cash, no questions asked," he told Babin.

"Five hundred?"

The man leaned toward him. "What you're delivering's hot, right?"

"Hot?"

"You're going to remember you need to deliver the whole load, right? Five hundred bucks. Each of us."

"It's just one."

"Oh, OK," said the man, smiling and returning to his beer.

The liquid stung Babin's mouth. He took another sip, realizing this would be much easier than he thought.

"Careful, man, this car has to last me another year," said the American as he and his friend began easing the crate into the back of the Subaru Forester.

Though they were using the ramp, the job was made more difficult by the fact that the car's rear hatch opened upward. The front of the wooden crate cleared easily, but then it hung up about three-quarters of the way in. Túcume came and helped, pushing on the crate with one of the Americans while the other held up the hatch. Finally, the crate made it all the way in.

"Take the girl for something to eat," Babin told Túcume. "Then come back for me."

"She's still sleeping."

"There was a McDonald's restaurant down the street. Have her wait for us there."

Túcume nodded. Babin walked back to the two men, who were trying to close the rear door on the crate. It was about an inch too long.

"We'll just get some rope and tie it down," said one of the men.

Babin looked at it. Clearly, this would not do; he worried that there might be some highway regulation about driving with an open hatch and they would be stopped. The rear portion of the crate could be pried away. Then it might fit.

They'd have to get different license plates, preferably from out of state. From as far from Texas as they could find.

"So what's really in there, dude? You moving dope?"

Babin swung around, filled with fear. He expected the man would be holding a gun in his hand, but he was not.

Too bad for him, for Babin had pulled the general's .22 from his pocket.

Without answering the man's question, Babin fired quickly. As the man crumbled, his friend began to run. He got only a few feet away before Babin put a slug in the back of his head.

Túcume dragged the second body to the Dumpster, holding his nose as he picked the dead man up and dropped him over the side. He felt like a grave robber.

"How low I have fallen," he mumbled to himself, going back to the car.

Babin had pulled part of the crate off to get the weapon to fit inside.

"We'll need to find a blanket to throw on top of the crate," said the Russian. "But let's get rid of the truck first."

"Why not leave it here? The building's old. It looks as if it's abandoned."

"It will blend in better in the salvage yard up by the highway," said Babin. "No one will look for it."

"It's a mile away."

"I'll wait."

"The girl."

"We should leave her."

"No."

"Then hurry or she'll run off on her own."

Túcume gritted his teeth, then climbed into the cab.

115

The Mexican port of Manzanillo had admirably modern facilities—which made it easy for the Art Room to obtain information about the location of the container. According to the computer, it was still parked in Lot 5A—and in fact, Rubens and the rest of the people in the Art Room could see it on the infrared feed from a U-2S that had been specially detailed to the strike team.

"Lia and Tommy are landing now," said Rockman. "The CIA team is moving in."

Of course, thought Rubens. They want to get the credit.

Three large black SUVs appeared in the frame at the right. Rockman toggled the controls for the viewer, zeroing in on the target. A dozen men jumped from the SUVs and surrounded the container, their M4 carbines and grenade launchers clearly visible.

Then the image blurred. The screen dissolved in whiteness.

"Technical glitch," said Rockman. "Something in the air force system. Theirs, not ours."

Rubens stared at the screen, waiting for information. They were just a resource here—helpers, rather than the lead agents. He'd have much preferred it if his people were the ones going into the truck.

Desk Three wasn't set up to conduct an operation on such a massive scale as the search for the weapon in Peru; even when it took the lead on a mission, it had to draw on many other agencies for support.

Its capabilities should be expanded and extended to include others. The CIA and the military special operations should have Desk Three's capabilities as well—in fact, they should work together seamlessly, as the original plan had called for.

His original plan.

If he had taken the job as national security adviser, he would have made doing so a priority.

Telach cursed as the image came back on the screen.

"It's the wrong container," she said. "The boxes are too small. Listen."

An audio report came over the speakers, an account from one of the CIA people back to Langley. The boxes he was describing were about three feet by two feet by two feet.

"The radioactive kernel could be inside one," said Rockman. "The bomb pit itself weighs only a few pounds."

Rubens watched the screen, trying to remain optimistic though he agreed with Telach. The image from the scene showed the team beginning to remove the contents. The chatter began taking on a pessimistic tone.

"Maybe it's further back," said Rockman.

"No, I believe we've missed something," said Rubens. "They'll be going to Plan B next." He turned toward the back of the room, where Johnny Bib was waving his hands furiously behind a bench of analysts.

"Working, working, working!" Johnny yelled before Rubens could say anything.

116

Plan B for Manzanillo was to check *all* of the other containers in the lot and then to look around the industrialized area for other possible hiding places. A second wave of DEA and FBI agents, along with a contingent of U.S. Army rangers, began fanning out across the area. Lia and Karr joined in the hunt. They were tasked to work with a CIA agent named Jason Milano and check a string of industrial parks several miles from the port.

This was detective work at its shoe-leather worst. Or, as Tommy Karr put it, driving from the airport to begin their search, "Needle in the haystack time."

"Yeah, but don't you want to be where the action is?" asked Milano from the backseat.

"Action," said Lia sarcastically.

This made Karr laugh so uncontrollably that he nearly missed the traffic light. He jammed on the brakes.

"Being where the action is is no big deal," said Karr. "What we want to be near are the babes."

"Real funny, Mr. Comedian," said Lia. "I'm just rolling on the floor here."

"I thought so." Karr glanced back at the bewildered CIA officer—he was a paramilitary with about three months in the agency. "You OK, Spook Dude?"

"You can call me Jason."

"Once he gives you a nickname, you're stuck with it," Lia said.

"You tell him, Princess."

"One of these days, Tommy, I'm going to strangle you."

"If your hands fit around my neck I'd be scared."

"Mr. Karr, this is Bill Rubens. We have a truck you should make your top priority. It's in a lot not far from where you are. The U-2 took a picture of it a short while ago. It's not attached to a tractor, or I should say it wasn't when we last looked at it. It's isolated. It should be eminently approachable."

"Great. Give me some direction," said Karr.

"Who are you talking to?" asked Milano.

The Deep Black communications system was classified; while technically it was considered all right to tell him about it since he was working with them, as a general rule Karr wouldn't unless it was absolutely necessary.

Besides, he *loved* goofing on CIA people.

"I hear voices," Karr told him, turning left as Rockman began directing him. "Some people think I'm the reincarnation of Joan of Arc. Get that submachine gun out and make sure you have it loaded."

The container truck was at the rear of a warehouse lot, parked near a fence that ran along a road. Lia got out of the car two blocks away and began trotting toward a cluster of small industrial buildings that lay between her and the target.

"We're about three minutes away from getting the overhead view online," Rockman said in her ear. "The U-2 is still covering the cargo container park."

"It's all right," Lia told him.

Lia slowed her pace as she reached the buildings. A group of women waiting to start work were standing nearby, gossiping; they glanced at her as she walked toward the back of the building. Lia had a pistol under her jacket, but if challenged she would just back off; the container wasn't going anywhere and there was no sense upsetting the locals, at least not yet.

A chain-link fence separated the warehouse lot from the yard behind the buildings. Cars were parked close to the fence, blocking her view.

"I'm going over the fence," she told Rockman.

"Wait until Tommy makes his pass."

"You sure this is the right truck?"

"No," said Rockman. "We're guessing, but it's a good guess. We think someone was bribed to change the registration numbers around when the container was loaded. The shipment in this truck matches the cargo that was found in the trailer back in the lot. Paper. Here comes Tommy," added Rockman.

Lia heard Karr "yee-hah" over the communications system. Karr was always a pill, but he was insufferable when working with anyone from the CIA.

Not that he was actually taking things lightly—he had placed a sawed-off shotgun on his lap as he dropped Lia off and had a flash-bang grenade in the armrest in case he had to divert attention and make a quick getaway. But she was sure the poor liaison in the backseat thought he'd hooked up with the teenage son of Genghis Khan.

"Clear," said Rockman. "Go."

Lia took a quick glance behind her, then jumped up on the fence. As she reached the top, she saw that the container sat all alone—and that its rear door was ajar.

Not a good sign.

"Señorita?" called someone behind her.

The voice sounded more inquisitive than hostile, so Lia didn't bother to turn around. Instead, she continued over the top and dropped to the ground on the other side. An older man stood near the side of the building watching her, literally scratching his head.

By the time Lia reached the truck, Karr and their CIA sidekick had circled around and parked their car on the side of the road twenty yards from the container.

"Door's not locked," Lia told Karr, who was standing near the fence, shotgun pressed against his jacket.

"Watch out for booby traps."

"Yeah. Rad detector's quiet."

"It would be if it were a bomb, unless you're right in its face," said Karr. "You have to get real close. Check the door first."

"Yeah."

"Watch for booby traps."

"You're getting as bad as Rockman."

By the time she was sure it was clean, Karr and their CIA sidekick were standing on the ground behind her.

"Nothing," she said.

"Get back," Karr told her, taking hold of the long pipe that worked the external door latches.

"I'll do it."

"No, no. You stand back," he said. He waited a second—probably just long enough to see that she wouldn't move—then threw the door open, ducking around as he did, as if he expected an explosion.

"Empty," said Jason, standing with his hands on his hips.

Lia climbed into the interior. A few pieces of wood lay scattered on the floor. One was stamped with black letters; half of the word was cut off, but she thought it read *baño*—bath.

"That would make sense," said Karr. "Because that factory over there makes bathtubs."

117

If it had been November rather than early June, Dean would have bagged the biggest buck of his life, a magnificent animal with a rack wider than a limo. Even now, with some months' worth of growth left, his horns made a magnificent crown at the top of his head.

Dean stared at the animal through his binoculars, no more than fifty yards away, mesmerized by the deer's haughty stare through the morning mist. Clearly, the buck knew he was here, and yet the beast didn't seem to care, so assured it was in the wild of the upper Delaware River Valley. It lowered its head slightly, then raised it back upright—a challenge, Dean thought, or perhaps an acknowledgment, before it turned and slowly trotted away.

"Even if it had been hunting season," Dean told the deer as it left, "I might have let you go."

He let the binoculars fall to his chest and walked back to the streambed, swollen with the recent rains. He'd come here to clear his head, and he had. What he hadn't done was replace the clutter with a specific plan on what to do.

He longed for Lia—he could feel the familiar ache in his chest—but where exactly she would fit in his future, he didn't know. As for everything else, including what he would do for work, all of that would have to wait. For now, he was simply experiencing what was around him.

Something rustled in the bushes ahead. Dean stopped.

Before he could raise the binoculars to examine the area, a chipmunk darted out and ran across the gnarled roots of a nearby tree and disappeared. From the noise it had made, he expected something closer to a mountain lion, and he laughed when he realized the tiny rodent was all that was there.

A humbling experience, the woods.

118

The CIA, the NSA, and the Department of Homeland Security had all prepared computer projections on how far a truck could have traveled from Manzanillo in the roughly thirty-six hours since the ship had docked. While the projections differed around the margins, they all agreed on one thing: it was possible that the truck had already crossed the border into the U.S.

"But that doesn't mean we shouldn't close the border right now," said Griffin Bolso, the FBI director, as representatives of the agencies involved in the crisis met via video-conference Thursday to update one another and the national security adviser. "We should close it immediately."

"Closing the border is not going to accomplish much more than we're doing now," said Cynthia Marshall, representing Homeland Security. "We're searching every truck that comes across the border, and traffic is already snarled beyond belief. If we close everything completely, we have to say why."

"We've already said we're looking for a bomb," suggested Bolso. "I don't see why we need to say anything else."

"The president has reserved to himself the decision on what information to release," said Hadash, who was chairing the meeting. "Bill, do you have better information on the possible truck?"

"I'm afraid we don't. At least a dozen vehicles were rented and picked up that day, and two were stolen as well. They're all tractor-trailer types," said Rubens. "We think there's a possibility that someone was hired to help, and the CIA is talking to day laborers in the area."

"Yes, we are," said Debra Collins smugly, as if no one else had the right to mention what her people were doing.

Besides the descriptions of the size of the crate and the type of vehicle, the border patrol and police agencies in the area had been given computer-generated images and artist renditions of Babin. It was not known, however, if Babin was with the truck—he had been in Lima while it was in transit and then in Ecuador before it docked. But there was no proof that he had hooked up with whatever accomplices or helpers were transporting it.

"The thing we have to remember," said Collins, "is that there's no evidence the bomb is actually coming to the U.S."

"Where else would Sholk go?" said Rubens. "He wants to pay us back for betraying him. Or rather, pay the CIA back."

Ordinarily, Rubens hated using the videoconferencing system, but in this case he thought the camera caught her perfectly—her face drawn, her eyes shifting back and forth.

"He's a businessman, not a psycho," she said. "He'd try to sell the weapon."

Resistant to the bitter end, thought Rubens. But at least she was no longer trying to discount the possibility that Babin was alive.

"I'm not saying we shouldn't be searching," insisted Collins, softening her tone as she continued. "We have to conduct the largest possible search. I don't want to be blindsided elsewhere, that's all."

"The question I have is how soon to extend the warning beyond the border states," said Bolso. "And in what degree of detail. Telling these people we're looking for something the size of a bathtub is just not enough."

The discussion focused on the allocation of resources to check the highway system in the Southwest U.S. Searching

Peru had proved a daunting task. Now the task was even greater. There were hundreds of thousands of trucks in the targeted zone, and every hour the zone's radius increased by fifty miles. Army troops had been moved in to help patrol the Texas and New Mexico border areas, with aerial reconnaissance being conducted by Air Force, Army, and Coast Guard units. Homeland Security had taken charge of a new task group coordinating the search in the U.S.; the military's Southern Command was coordinating search efforts in Mexico. General Spielmorph's group was still in Peru, but some of his resources were being shifted north.

Rubens tapped the key controlling the different available feeds on the conference system, putting Collins on the small screen to his left.

She seemed to be staring directly at him, with all the venom of a cobra disturbed in its den.

If she takes Hadash's job, I'll resign, he thought.

Wouldn't it be better, then, to take it himself?

"All right, thank you, everyone," said Hadash. "The president wants updates on the hour. We'll reconvene at ten o'clock, sooner if necessary."

119

"What do you think the possibility is this has all been a bad dream?"

Lia looked across the aisle of the Air Force 737 that was ferrying her and Karr back to the Washington, D.C., area. He had contorted his huge frame between the seats in an effort to get comfortable.

"I don't think it was a dream," she told him.

"A nightmare?"

"No."

"But it could all be a wild-goose chase," said Karr. "We've been on them before."

"You mean, what do I think the odds are that there's no nuclear warhead?"

"Yeah. Look at it this way. Babin or whoever he hired to get the bomb could have been at the border twenty-four hours ago."

"If he drove like you. And flew over the mountains and desert."

"If he drove like me. Right. Now, twenty-four hours from the border—he could be just out to D.C."

"Or he could still be in Mexico, which is the CIA theory," said Lia.

"Yeah, but they're always wrong. Good job, by the way."

"What?"

"With the election cards. And the neo-Marxist wackos in

the jungle. That's all gonna get lost, you know. We're not going to get any attaboys for it."

"We don't need any attaboys."

"Speak for yourself, Princess," said Karr, shifting his legs against the seat backs. "I need all the attaboys I can get. And steaks."

120

Rubens bent over the console at one of the stations at the rear of the Art Room, watching the screen of an analyst who was monitoring and assisting police activity in Texas. He had a feed from a Customs Service aircraft, supplying an overhead view as an emergency response team of FBI and border patrol agents surrounded a tractor trailer south of Houston.

A series of links with Homeland Security gave the Art Room access to police networks as well as the FBI. The Texas Highway Patrol had found a truck with Mexican plates apparently abandoned at the edge of an auto wrecking yard. The plates were not on the watch list the Art Room had developed, but otherwise the truck looked very much like what they were looking for.

"No audio?" said Rubens.

"They're using standard radios," said the analyst. "We can get to the commander through the Homeland Security line and vice versa, but we don't have real-time communications with the people on the scene."

Rubens watched as the emergency response team—essentially a SWAT squad—cautiously approached the truck. Rather than risking a booby-trapped door, they climbed to the top, where they began cutting a hole to get in.

What if he was wrong? What if the warhead didn't exist or was back in Peru? Babin certainly could be there, hiding somewhere in the Amazon with Túcume.

That mistake Rubens could live with. Far worse was a mistake that led to the destruction of an American city.

"Won't be long now," said the analyst.

"You have a list of stolen vehicles from this area?"

"As soon as the alert came in, I got it. I went all the way back to the border, tracing the route. There are only a dozen."

"Only a dozen?"

"Not many people steal trucks, I guess."

"Expand the search to include any sort of vehicle, anything large enough to hold a crated weapon. Sixty-six inches," added Rubens. "Approximately."

"Are you praying?" asked Johnny Bib.

"Uh, just stretching my back," said Robert Gallo, twisting up from the floor. Though perhaps prayer would not have been inappropriate—he was having a very hard time nailing down any sort of indication that the container truck had made it into the U.S., let alone where it was going.

"Nothing in the state databases that you can use to find what sort of truck it is?" asked Johnny Bib, coming over to look.

"The states don't keep very close tabs of trucks," said Gallo. "I've, like, checked through the lists of, you know, road stops and stuff, those weigh-in things. Looked for mismatches and stuff. But nothing jumps out. This kind of isn't my thing, you know? Searches? And like, what would I check? Vehicles most unlikely to be stopped?"

"I hope that's not going to become your slogan," said Johnny Bib. "Defeat."

"It's not defeat."

Johnny began to shake his head back and forth without saying anything. He looked like a kid's wind-up toy gone berserk.

"What if I looked for the target rather than the truck?" said Gallo. "What I was thinking was, check everything we have related to Babin, right? And then see if there are any links. Jeez, Johnny, could you stop? You're giving me vertigo."

"Exactly," said his supervisor, without explanation. And he turned and walked from the room.

Puzzled, Gallo returned to his computer. He began another set of searches, this time a keyword search of NSA South American intercepts over the past week using "Stephan" rather than "Babin" as a keyword. Not surprisingly, he got about ten thousand hits.

He was about to run a Dredge search on the hits when he noticed that one of the entries on the last page had a name very similar to Babin—Baben. He looked and confirmed that it was simply a misspelling by the computerized transcription programs, which often relied on phonetic spellings and best choices if the intercept data was unclear.

The search system was programmed to find near misses in spelling. But did that tool apply when you were searching in foreign character sets?

Or rather, had the tool been in place three years before when the Babin intercepts were being compiled in Russian and the Cyrillic alphabet was being used?

As a matter of fact, it had. But to keep the tool from matching every possible word, Gallo realized as he played with it, it assumed that the first two letters were *phonetically* correct. So if "Ба" (the sound that began "baby") was entered incorrectly as "Ba" (the sound, in Russian, that began "vacation"), the tool rejected the string as a match. That made sense in most cases, but in this particular instance, a human operator who was a native English speaker could easily choose "B" by mistake rather than "Б" and the error would not be picked up.

"This isn't my thing," mumbled Gallo as he retrieved a list of old databases to apply the new search term to.

121

Rubens stared at the map on his computer screen, showing the area Babin could have reached by now. The purple swatch covered almost three-fourths of the country, with the tip just reaching toward the Beltway below Washington, D.C.

The truck in Texas appeared to have been the one Babin had taken from Mexico. The rear compartment had contained bathtubs—and the bumper had traces of blood. But that was all that had been found. How long the truck had been in the lot, where the blood had come from, what had happened to the bomb, assuming it had been there . . . no one knew.

All sorts of other leads were being investigated in Mexico as well as the U.S., including the murder of a truck driver near Mexico City and another closer to the border. But real information—the sort that would help them find Babin and the bomb—remained elusive.

At Montblanc's suggestion, several psychologists had been consulted about the situation; all thought it likely that Babin would try to seek revenge against the people who had wronged him. This seemed rather obvious to Rubens as well.

The warhead's arming mechanism had to be altered for it to explode. Babin had an engineering background and knew explosives; he was probably capable of doing the work.

But where? And when?

On this the psychologists divided. Washington, D.C., was

an obvious target. So was Langley, Virginia, the home of the CIA. Beyond that, it was very possible that any city might do.

And when? Right away, said a narrow majority of the psychologists. He'd been waiting for years and now had his chance. At his own leisure, said the others. He'd been waiting for years and could afford to wait for weeks or months or even far longer.

Rubens thought sooner. But he had no *evidence*. And evidence was what he needed.

Large parts of the picture were still unseen. What was the connection between Babin and General Túcume? The housekeeper Karr had talked to had been taken into Peruvian custody, but she had apparently supplied very little information. Others in Túcume's circle were still being debriefed, but the CIA summaries of the interrogations had no references to Babin, with the exception of a very brief appearance in Lima the night before the dam broke on the general. Investigators were trying to track down the men who had been under his command at the time the weapon was found; so far, they had little luck.

Eventually, they would have more information. But eventually might be too late.

If a bomb exploded—if hundreds of thousands, maybe a million, Americans died—Rubens felt it would be his responsibility. A classic intelligence failure, by definition.

And yet they were looking at every possibility.

Rubens killed the computer program and secured his desk, throwing the security blanket over it. He walked to the small space between the desk and door, stopped, and put his hands together in a simple yoga pose, steadying his breathing. He took two very long, slow breaths, then arched his back, rising on his toes as he brought his arms up and around.

As always, the stretch calmed his restlessness somewhat. And as always, the calm had dissipated by the time he reached the Art Room level in the subbasement below.

"Still status quo," said Chris Farlekas, the on-shift Art Room supervisor. "Lia DeFrancesca and Tommy Karr are with the task force around Washington, D.C. We have a helicopter which can take them to the scene if a truck is apprehended. I tried to tell Lia, gently, that it was all right for her to take a break if she wanted."

"I don't imagine she took that very well."

"No," said Farlekas.

Since he'd been trained to disarm Russian warheads, Karr was an important asset; there were only a few dozen such experts in the country, and Karr had the advantage not only of having actually worked on a live warhead but of being able to tap the Art Room's experts as well. Lia, on the other hand, was Lia. And no one was going to force her to take a rest until she felt like it.

"Even Mr. Karr will have to take a breather at some point," Rubens told Farlekas. "Don't push him too far."

"I'm not pushing him. He's alternating with two other people from the Energy Commission."

"Very well. I am going to speak to Johnny Bib's people. Buzz me if you need me."

Rubens walked up the corridor and up the stairs to the computer labs where many of Johnny Bib's people were working. If he were national security adviser, he would make sure there were more Tommy Karrs on the front lines of the nation's intelligence services. He'd do more to get the CIA and the military working together. He would use intelligence to help the president make more timely decisions . . .

Why was he torturing himself with so many "ifs"? Did he want the job? The opportunity was lost; he'd said he didn't want it. To change his mind now would make him look weak. Indecisive.

Would it, though? Was he not entitled to a mistake?

Not a mistake—a reconsideration.

Rubens went through the suite of rooms, looking in on a few of the analysts and cryptographers, making his presence known but not interrupting them. When he saw Ambassador Jackson leaning over Robert Gallo's shoulder in one of the rooms, however, Rubens couldn't help but ask what they were doing.

"A theory," said Jackson. "On a target."

"How about Philadelphia?" said Gallo.

"Why do you say that?"

Gallo began telling Rubens about a Russian intelligence file listing phone calls that had been made to Babin in the months before Iron Heart. The file included three calls from Philadelphia pay phones.

"Philadelphia is where Evans comes from," explained Jackson.

"He was probably trying to recruit him," said Rubens—though there were other possibilities.

"Yes, but that's not actually the point," said the ambassador. "Babin knows where Evans lives, where his family is."

"And he would blame Evans for betraying him," said Rubens, finally understanding.

122

Dean had gone over to a nearby diner for dinner and was just getting back to the cottage when his cell phone began to ring. He knew that it had to be the NSA; they were the only ones he had given the number to.

"Dean," he said, flipping it open.

"Charlie, we need you to go to Harrisburg, Pennsylvania," said Chris Farlekas. "To the state police headquarters there."

"How are you, Chris?"

"Very busy at the moment. How long will it take you?"

"I don't know. It's pretty far away. If I left now . . . six or seven hours by car maybe." He glanced up and saw a bat dart overhead, grabbing flies in mid-air.

"You won't go by car." Farlekas was silent for moment, apparently consulting with someone. "Can you get to a city called New Milford, Pennsylvania?"

"It's more like a village. Yeah, it would take about a half hour."

"Leave now, please. A helicopter will meet you outside the city, at the police barracks. We're making the arrangements right now."

"What's going on?"

"The item you were looking for in Peru may be on its way to Philadelphia. I'd prefer not to discuss it on this line. If you would kindly change, we'll be able to use our usual method while you're on your way."

123

One of the things that had made the SA-10 warheads easy to get out of Russia was their compact size and weight. But these were relative qualities: the crated warhead was so heavy that it snapped the makeshift wooden ramp Babin had Túcume place between the back of the car and the cargo van he wanted to transfer it to. He saw the disaster happening in slow motion—the wood splintered, the front of the crate tipped, and the crate fell between the two vehicles.

Babin closed his eyes as it slipped. When he opened them, he realized it wasn't quite as bad as he had feared: the bomb had enough downward momentum to slide halfway into the van, where it got stuck, wedged more in than out. The front of the crate, which he'd taken off to get the bomb in, had come apart, but the weapon itself was still firmly in its skeleton cradle.

Túcume cursed. It was the first time Babin could remember him using any profanity since they had met.

Babin peered into the van, then moved to the crate, pushing against the side in the vain hope that it might slide in. It was a useless gesture; it didn't even help him vent his frustration.

"Let me see one of your crutches," said Túcume.

Babin gave it to him, and the general climbed into the van. He tried using the crutch as a lever, but the crate didn't move.

When Túcume came out, he was holding the top of the crutch in his hand. The bottom had broken and was still lodged between the box and the side of the truck.

"I'm sorry," said Túcume.

"I have another idea," Babin said, ignoring the now-useless stick. "Get in the car."

Calvina watched the two men as they maneuvered the vehicles and the large crate, trying to push the box into the van.

The van did not belong to them. She knew this because of the way they had had to start it, jiggling with something under the hood and dashboard. She realized now that the trucks and the red car probably had not belonged to them as well and wondered if the papers were stolen, too.

Until that moment, she had trusted the *señor*. Not the foreigner—she could tell just by looking at him that his soul was twisted. It wasn't a matter of his legs; something in his face and eyes spoke of hatred and worse, and though he had never threatened her, she knew he would be capable of strangling her in a moment.

Calvina thought of the woman she had seen in Peru, the Chinawoman who had been able to speak in Quechua as well as Spanish.

The woman had asked if she wanted help, and Calvina had refused. Truly she must have been an angel sent by the Virgin to warn her. She'd been a fool not to understand.

She remembered the woman so vividly that it almost seemed that she was here with her.

"What should I do?" Calvina whispered.

There was no one to answer, but as the words left her mouth, Calvina knew: *run!*

She turned and bolted toward the highway.

"Good! Good!" yelled Babin. "Stop."

Túcume set the parking brake and got out of the car. He'd managed to push the crate another foot into the van, and it now hung about a fifth of the way out. They could turn the car around and use it to push it the rest of the way.

"The girl!" yelled Babin. "She's running!"

Túcume looked up and saw her going up the ramp toward the highway. He started after her, running up the grass infield to the ramp and cutting the distance between them in half. He had to stop momentarily at the highway, unsure of which way she had gone. Finally the lights of a passing car silhouetted her moving along the shoulder. Túcume threw himself forward, running steadily. The mountains he had grown up in had inadvertently trained him to be a good long-distance runner; his lungs and heart were naturally big, and he got a natural boost from the richer oxygen of the lower altitude where he found himself. His legs began to tire, but he pushed on, continuing to gain. Before he had gone twenty yards he had cut the distance between them once more in half; another twenty and she was only ten from him. A car passed and he saw her look back, glancing over her shoulder toward him.

He'd never seen such fear before. It stopped him cold.

Go, he thought. I won't harm you. Go.

Túcume waited until he no longer could see her in the shadows; then he turned around and went back.

Babin struggled to get the crate the rest of the way in, clawing and pushing at it but not budging it. All that was needed was another push from the car, but he didn't trust his legs enough to try it. He'd have to wait for the general to return.

The effort exhausted Babin; finally he gave up, leaning against the crate, chest heaving.

After a few moments, he forced himself to move. He took out his knife and pried open the top of the crate, carefully removing one part of the top layer of lead foil and sliding it aside so he could reach to the trigger panel at the top of the bomb.

The timer mechanism was easily set. Once it was started, the fail-safe system could not be unlocked and the weapon defused without entering a release code. Babin didn't even know what it was, since it was keyed to the weapon, not the timer.

How much time should he set it for?

He wanted it to explode in Philadelphia, where the CIA officer who had betrayed him lived. From the map, Babin thought it might take two hours to get there, perhaps more, since they would not use the highways.

Explode it now—be done with it.

Babin resisted the temptation. With the phone he could always set the bomb off. The timer was just a fail-safe.

Should he give Túcume a chance to run if he wanted?

That seemed absurd. Why would the general choose to save himself? He was not a coward.

How long would he need to escape?

Days really. It was impossible.

Babin tapped the small button on the timer. The digits moved forward, filling the dial, but not smoothly—1 appeared, and then a 0.

Ten minutes?

Ten minutes was not what he wanted. He pushed his finger against the small button, but nothing happened. He felt himself starting to sweat.

If it must be ten, he said to himself, then ten will be all right. Let it be whatever it is.

The numbers began draining on the timer.

They were seconds.

He pushed the button quickly.

The timer was set to work in increments. From ten seconds it went to sixty seconds, then three minutes, then a hundred.

Too soon. He pressed again. Three hundred.

Five hours. Good enough.

Even if he did nothing, the bomb would explode at 4:03 a.m.

He put the top back on the crate and lowered himself to the ground. He was so exhausted that he simply collapsed, lying flat on his back until the general returned.

"What happened?" Túcume asked, standing over him.

"I couldn't push the crate in by myself. We need another push from the car."

The general extended his hand.

"The girl?" said Babin.

Instead of answering, the general stared at him for a moment, then went to get in the cab.

"We don't need her. It's OK," said Babin. He picked up his crutch and went toward the van, steadying himself against the fender. "Take the road atlas. And maybe we can find a place open to get gas and something to eat."

He stood back as Túcume started the Subaru. Hobbling with one crutch was very difficult, but he wouldn't have to do it for very much longer.

124

The captain in charge of Homeland Security matters for the Pennsylvania State Police was about Dean's age and like him had close-cropped hair. That was as far as the similarities went—the captain stood several inches shorter than Dean but outweighed him by a good bit, even if one ignored the bulletproof vest under his uniform shirt.

His agency had already been alerted that Philadelphia might be a target of a terror attack before Dean got there, but Dean's impression when he walked into the tactical center shortly after eleven was that the troopers were more annoyed than alarmed. Most of them looked as if they'd been working the day shift and stayed on through the night.

"You're from Washington, right?" said the captain, whose name tag read: DANIELS. He didn't offer a first name to go with it.

"That's right."

"Homeland Defense?"

"I'm helping them out."

Daniels gave him a puzzled look but didn't press. He gave Dean a brief rundown of the extra units they'd called on duty, the patrols they had initiated, and the alerts they had sent out.

"I have to tell you, we get these advisories all the time," said the captain. "We've been tracking this since it broke a day and a half ago. We've watched the highways at the border.

We shut down I-Ninety-five for a while. We're still taking all the trucks off the road there. No truck passes without being searched."

"That's a start," said Dean.

"The reports we've seen were related to Washington and Virginia," said the captain.

"My information is more up-to-date," said Dean. "There's a good chance the truck is on its way to Philadelphia."

Daniels unhooked his tie—it was a clip model, a precaution all police took against it being used for a choke hold—and set it on the desk. "Mr. Dean—"

"Charlie."

"No offense, but looking for a truck packed with explosives is only a little easier than looking for a needle in a haystack. We can cover the major highways, but once you start including country roads, local roads—"

"If I were you, I'd stop every truck in the state," said Dean. "Every vehicle. The bomb is that big."

125

Túcume pulled the van to the side of the street. They were near or inside the city borders, but he had no idea where precisely they were. Babin's directions were confused and confusing.

"I need to rest," Túcume told Babin. "Let's stop here awhile."

"No."

"I need to rest," he said. The voice seemed loud even to him. And stronger.

It was his voice. He'd lost it but now had it back.

A deep anger welled up within him. When he looked down at his fingers on the wheel, he saw that his knuckles were white.

"Relax," said Babin. "We can rest. Let's find a place for coffee."

He should have gone with the girl, Túcume thought. She'd been his chance to escape.

Hadn't he made that same decision years before, when he chose to pursue his dream of leading the people? He had given up everything for it.

What did he have to show for his decision now? Bitterness. The sum of who he was.

No. He was the leader he had hoped to become. He had made mistakes—fatal mistakes, errors that came from his own character. He had trusted people who should not have been trusted. But in every other way, he had made himself the leader he had wanted to be. *He was an Inca.*

Would an Inca have sought blind revenge, even in defeat? In triumph they were generous. In defeat . . .

Would his namesake have called on the sun god to obliterate the earth so that his wrath might be appeased?

"General, coffee and something to eat," suggested Babin. "We passed a small restaurant not too long ago. A diner, the Yankees call it."

"Coffee would be a good idea," Túcume said. "Direct me."

126

Among the assets that had been allocated to the Pennsylvania task force was an Air Force Special Operations Pave Low MH-53J. The large two-engined helicopter was specially equipped with infrared radar to see in the dark, and extra-large fuel tanks that would allow it to stay in the air for several hours. Captain Daniels had decided to use the helicopter to go up to Philadelphia to inspect preparations there, and Dean went along.

The crew chief gave Dean and Daniels radios and headsets to allow them to connect with both the helicopter's interphone system and the emergency network being used to coordinate the search.

"You with me, Rockman?" Dean asked as he pulled on the headset, pretending to fiddle with the controls.

"I'm always with you, Charlie. You never told me how your hunting trip was."

"Too short. How are we looking?"

"Situation is basically unchanged since Marie spoke to you a half hour ago. Truck with small bathtubs was found outside of Houston a few hours ago. Two dead males were found not too far away. Haven't been identified yet. They haven't established time of death precisely, but it's likely to be a little over twenty-four hours ago. We've been looking at stolen vehicles in the area, also rentals, and even purchases. We've got a couple of tractor trailers, U-Hauls—basically everything we've been looking at up until now. We've expanded the search to include vans, SUVs, and station wagons. I realize this isn't much use to you."

"Yeah."

"State police have barricade checkpoints around every major highway. Two Coast Guard aircraft are surveying the roads south of Philadelphia and local police departments are stopping every cargo carrier and large truck they see. You know all that?"

"Yeah."

"They're holding a marathon cabinet meeting about what to tell the public," added Rockman. "Mr. Rubens is down the hall, talking to them. They're debating whether to go to Red Sky even though they haven't definitely found a bomb. Some of the key personnel have already gone into shelters. Personally, I think it's overkill. I think this whole thing may just be a wild-goose chase."

Dean didn't particularly care to hear the runner's opinions.

"Red Sky" was a procedure to be invoked in the event of a nuclear terrorist attack. Among other things, it would shut down all air traffic in the country, close the borders, and send cabinet members and other important leaders to bomb shelters. The federal government would exercise direct control over the affected area, in effect declaring martial law.

"Is this radio going to work or what?" he said, changing the subject.

Rockman reminded Dean that they were supposed to maintain organizational secrecy "to the extent possible if the target is discovered."

Dean smiled to himself, thinking of the cracks Tommy Karr could have made about that.

127

A cacophony of confusion spread out in the darkness below
the MH-6 "Little Bird" helicopter Lia and Karr were flying
in north of Washington, D.C. The helicopter and its pilot
were members of the famed 160th Special Operations Avia-
tion Regiment. Besides carrying surveillance gear that included a forward-looking infrared radar capable of seeing in
the dark, the helicopter also had a .50-caliber machine gun,
which was loaded and ready for use.

The road network around the capital had been effectively
shut down, and while it was very late—or early, depending
on how you interpreted 12:30 a.m.—the traffic jams were
massive. Air traffic had been curtailed, and civilian flights
that were allowed had to fly very precise routes or risk being
shot down.

"What's your estimated time of arrival at Crypto City?"
Telach asked Lia over the Deep Black com system.

"Another ten minutes," she told Telach.

"Good. As soon as you refuel, head up to Pennsylvania.
They only have one AEC person covering the area up there."

"AEC" stood for the Atomic Energy Commission—other
bomb experts assigned to work with the local task force.
There were already two in the D.C. area and another three in
nearby Virginia.

"Where's Charlie?"

"He's in a helo en route to Philadelphia with the troopers there."

"Tell him I said hi."

"Will do."

Lia looked out the side of the small helicopter. If you ignored what was going on and just stared at the lights, they looked beautiful.

128

"Town police in Wellington, Pennsylvania, are asking for a license plate ID on a Forester. A Subaru Forester!"

The shout from one of the people at the back of the Art Room was like a bolt of lightning. Everyone stopped what they were doing.

"New York plate," added the young man, instantly depressed. An assistant computer scientist, he had been pressed into work as a monitor, using a computer tool that watched queries on the various state motor vehicle departments to see if any matched the Deep Black watch lists. He punched the keys to capture the plate number, then thumbed through a menu of state registrations for a search through a Department of Transportation connection arranged when the crisis began.

"Oh my God! This is something! The plate comes from a Nissan Maxima, not a Subaru. This is something."

Telach walked over to the young man and put her hand on his shoulder. The Forester was a small SUV, with an interior capacity that could just squeeze the weapon inside.

"Easy, Peter. Let's do this together." She knelt down next to him and hit one of the function keys, bringing up ID data on the local police agency. "Call the dispatcher on the Homeland Security line and ask for the vehicle ID. Then check it against the stolen vehicles."

"Yeah, yeah, yeah," said Peter, pounding on a numeric keypad.

Telach tapped a large red button that sent the data to a window on Rockman's console.

"They already have the number," said Peter. He punched it into the computer. A second after he hit the enter key, the screen blinked back with a long list; one line in the middle was highlighted.

The vehicle was registered to a man in Texas, who lived a few miles from where the abandoned truck had been found.

"Jeff, get Charlie down to look at this car right away," said Telach.

She glanced down at her belt and hit the key on her communications set to alert Rubens that she needed him.

129

"You ever hear of a place called Wellington?" Dean asked Daniels.

"Little town outside of Philadelphia. It was mostly farms ten years ago," said the state trooper.

"We have to get there. Local police found a car that was stolen in the same area that the truck from Mexico was found."

"How come they haven't reported it?"

"They're doing it right now," said Dean, reaching to the switch to connect with the pilot. "Trust me on this—like I say, my information is always a little ahead of the curve."

The big helicopter scattered dirt and papers before it as it fluttered down in the small lot near the road of the county highway. Dean hopped out, trotting toward the row of revolving police lights nearby. Two sheriff's deputies met him; Daniels and two of his aides trailed behind.

"Where's the vehicle?" said Dean.

They led him to a battered Subaru Forester, surrounded by local detectives and policemen.

"You FBI?" asked a white-haired man in a blue uniform.

"Dean. I work with Homeland Security."

"I'm Chief Dalton. We're waiting for some crime scene people from the state police."

"Yeah, they're on their way. That's Daniels, from the state

police," Dean said, thumbing behind him as the captain huffed across the macadam. "He's in charge of the task force."

Dean took his phone out as he walked over to the car so he could talk to Rockman without looking too peculiar. He bent down in front of the car, reading the New York license plate for verification and examining the front of the car. It looked as if it had been in a light fender bender. Bits of wood were stuck in the front grille. Dean stepped back, looking around.

"Part of a broken crutch," he told Rockman, walking toward it.

"Mr. Dean, this is Rubens. Describe the crutch as precisely as you can for Mr. Rockman. Then please do two things. Find out if there are any tire tracks or other indications of what sort of vehicle the weapon was loaded into—"

"It's asphalt pavement. No tracks."

"I see. Then please describe the pieces of wood you mention to Mr. Rockman, and any other items at the scene, inside and outside of the car. Any items at all."

Rubens walked to the front of the Art Room and stood over the communications console. He put his finger on the button of a voice-only scrambled phone, connecting himself to George Hadash in the situation room under the White House.

"We have evidence that Babin has reached the Philadelphia area."

"The warhead?"

"We have no direct evidence of the warhead. However, we have wood that might have been part of a crate. I urge a full Red Sky alert at this time."

130

"Tommy, this is Rubens."

"Hey, boss," said Karr. "Got something?"

"We've discovered a vehicle we believe Babin used about twenty miles southwest of Philadelphia. Mr. Dean is there now. The president is going to declare a Red Sky alert."

"OK."

"Instruct your pilot to proceed outside of the probable shock area. Mr. Rockman will give you precise directions."

"Boss—"

"Stay outside of the danger area until the weapon is located. You understand."

"Yeah, all right."

"I have something more. Stand by. Mr. Bibleria's people are just presenting me with information."

"Lia, check this out," said Karr, poking her in the back with his handheld computer.

She turned around and took the device. The screen was filled with text.

"What am I looking at?"

"They found a vehicle in Pennsylvania they think Babin used. We have to stay away from Philadelphia. This is some data about someone the police a couple of towns over picked up on the highway, nearby according to Johnny Bib. She's

from Peru. Gotta be a connection. Talk to Telach while I get
our flight plan worked out with the pilot."

Lia looked at the information. According to the bulletin,
which had been shared over one of the Homeland Security
information sites, the young woman—Calvina Adnese, according to her passport—was nineteen. Her address was in
Nevas—at the school Lia had gone to, one of the Art Room
analysts had noted.

He'd also pointed out that Calvina had taken a flight from
Ecuador to Mexico a few days before.

A picture from her passport was included on the next
screen. Lia stared at it. It looked to her like the girl she'd
seen in the hallway, the one who'd been sick. But of course
hundreds or even thousands of girls would go through that
school.

Had her name been Calvina?

"Marie?" Lia said to Telach over the Deep Black com
system.

"I'm here."

"This girl the police picked up in Pennsylvania," she said.
"Has she been interviewed?"

"No, the FBI is still en route. We're setting up our own
phone interview with one of our translators in the Art
Room."

"I'd like to talk to her myself," said Lia. "I'll put a video
bug on the dashboard here so she can see me."

"We'll have to see if they have a video hookup. Otherwise you can do it by your com system."

"I want to see her, and I want her to see me. Have someone go back in the mission tape for the school at Nevas.
I talked to a girl there. See if her name was Calvina."

131

Calvina Agnese—*Adnese* on her passport—stared as the door of the room in the small police station opened. The officer who had brought her here wheeled in a computer on a small stand, smiling apologetically. He said something to her in English, a long explanation probably, though she had no idea what he was trying to tell her. He'd been very nice since stopping for her on the road, nicer than she expected, even giving her food. One of the men at the station spoke a few words of Spanish, enough to ask who she was and what she was doing on the highway in the middle of the night.

"Running from someone?" he asked.

She'd cringed, then shaken her head. When he asked for identification, she handed over her passport. It seemed to satisfy him.

She thought they would either put her into jail or send her back home, or somehow arrange to do both. She'd been a foolish girl to dream of being like Señor DeCura; she was just a girl who washed floors and always would be.

The policeman left the room, then returned with a telephone. A long cord stretched out from behind it into the other room. He pulled a keyboard out from the shelf under the computer, then turned it on.

He fiddled with the keyboard. A picture appeared in the center of the screen. It had a whitish-brown tint, and the figure in it moved in jerks and starts. But as Calvina stared, she realized it was the woman she had seen in Ecuador—her angel.

"*Hola,*" said the woman.

"*¿Hola?*"

"Do you remember me?"

Calvina didn't answer.

"Should I speak Spanish or Quechua?"

"Spanish."

"You were in the hallway and I asked if you needed help. Am I right?"

"Yes, Your Highness."

"Calvina, how did you get to the U.S.?"

"Two men helped me. One was older and very kind."

"Did the other walk with a cane or crutches?"

"Yes."

"Can you describe them please?"

She did. When she was finished, the angel asked her about the truck she had been in. Calvina described it carefully.

"And the men used another car or truck, didn't they?" said the angel.

"Yes," said Calvina Agnese, nodding.

"Tell me about the last vehicle they got into," said the angel, leaning closer to the screen.

132

The city was a confusing tangle of one-way streets, and Tú-cume feared that he would make the wrong turn every time he came to an intersection. They could hear police sirens in the distance but had seen no police cars since they had left the main roads. Their maps were not very detailed, they had gotten lost several times, and even Babin wasn't sure exactly where they were.

But they were very close to the center of the city.

"That way, go that way," said Babin, pointing to the right. "You see the sign? Independence Mall."

Túcume did not see the sign but turned anyway. Babin leaned forward against the dashboard, looking past him.

"Turn!"

"Where?"

"Just turn."

He did and found himself on a narrow one-lane street.

"There were police and military trucks on that street. We have to stick to the side roads."

"Which way?"

"I don't know," said the Russian, studying his map.

Babin had trouble reading the map in the dark but feared do-ing anything that would attract any attention to them, includ-ing turning on an interior light as they drove. He'd mapped the route earlier, avoiding what looked like the larger streets.

He wanted to be on Chestnut, he thought, but he couldn't find it now.

Anywhere nearby would do. They were close to the famed Liberty Bell and the center of the city. His heart pounded crazily; he could feel the pulse throughout his body, throbbing in every bone and muscle.

"Take a right," he said.

Túcume turned left. They went about halfway down the block, then saw it was a dead end.

"I told you *right*," Babin said angrily.

"It was one-way."

Babin rolled down the window and looked out. "Back up. Back up quickly before someone comes."

"If you can do better, you drive." Túcume opened the door and jumped out of the truck.

Babin cursed and pounded on the dashboard. He pulled out his pistol, then realized there was no sense going after the general. What difference would it make a few seconds from now whether the bomb exploded here or a few blocks away?

Babin left his gun in his lap and bent to retrieve the cell phone from the well between the seats. He picked it up, his fingers jittering.

He'd never felt anxiety like this before, the anticipation of revenge, the final payoff to Evans and the CIA people who had betrayed and maimed him.

He pressed his thumb on the button to activate the phone.

"No!" yelled Túcume, suddenly at the open passenger window. In the same instant, Babin felt the general's fist hit him square in the side of the head.

133

"If the time they picked the girl up is even close to being right, they may be in Philadelphia already," the state police captain told Dean as the helicopter became airborne.

The girl had described a long light-colored cargo van, with no windows. An Army surveillance aircraft and a Coast Guard plane normally used for work against drug smugglers recalibrated their search grids and began hunting for the vehicle in and around the city. At the same time, police and National Guard units moved to shut down the roads completely. The alert going out over the police and Homeland Security networks added a description not only of Babin but of a man who was probably General Túcume. The Art Room was supplying several *.jpg files, digital photographs that could be shown on computer screens or printed out.

It was after 1:00 a.m. The city loomed in the distance, its well-lit skyline proclaiming that it would survive even this challenge. It had witnessed the birth of democracy more than two hundred years before and withstood the wrath of what was then the greatest army in the world. It would not cower tonight.

"If I were going to blow up Philadelphia," Dean said to Daniels, "I'd make Congress Hall ground zero. That or the Liberty Bell. We should start searching there."

"We will," said the trooper, pushing his headset lower on his head.

• • •

"They're in the city by now," Lia told the helicopter pilot. "We can help the search."

"Uh, I have orders to get out of the blast area," said the pilot. "Specifically, Red Sky—"

"Nah, that doesn't apply to you," said Karr, leaning forward. "Let's go."

"Sir—"

"We're looking for a light-colored van," Lia told the pilot, reaching for the controls to the forward-looking infrared radar.

134

Babin fell over to the driver's side of the truck, the phone bouncing from his hand to the floor. He raged against the whirlpool of pain that enveloped him, screaming and flailing and refusing to give up, refusing to be cheated of his revenge. He rolled and tried to grip his assailant, remembered his gun, then saw the cell phone a few inches from his head; unsure which to grab, he hesitated, and in that moment the pain increased exponentially. He felt himself falling, surrounded by flames—he was back in the aircraft, back in the ambush, screaming at the pilot and yelling at himself, tricked by the CIA liar, murdered, murdered, murdered.

Túcume lowered the pistol, then reached through the window and pulled Babin's body upright. He had killed a number of men in his life as an army commander but never one so close to him.

He went around to the other side of the van and opened the door. He reached on the floor and picked up the cell phone, then dashed it on the street. It broke in two. Not satisfied, he stood over each piece and shot it. It took two bullets to hit the second piece, his hand was shaking so badly.

He threw the pistol aside and went back to the truck. He thought from Babin's directions earlier that the waterfront was nearby somewhere; he'd drive the van into the water and be done with it all.

But which way was it? Left? Right?

Slowly, he backed down the road, struggling to see and control the van at the same time. As he reached the intersection, the ground began to shake with the heavy beat of helicopters overhead.

135

One of the crew members in the cockpit spotted the van backing down the dead-end street a few blocks from the historic district in downtown Philadelphia. Dean went to the side of the Pave Low, peering down through the open door.

"Yeah! Could be it," he yelled into the interphone. He grabbed hold of the rail near the door and punched the button to the shared police channel, starting to describe the vehicle.

"They're in the center of the city, not far from Congress Hall and the Liberty Bell," the pilot of the Little Bird shouted to Lia. "We're real close."

"Get us there!" she yelled.

Karr jerked behind her, the whole helicopter seeming to rock as he leaned out the side and looked down. They were maybe fifty feet over the street, so close to some of the rooftops that they could have stepped off onto them. The pilot barked into his microphone, talking to another nearby helicopter.

"That's got to be it," yelled Karr. "Watch him—he's going up Eighth."

The helicopter veered left, spinning around a building and then running in the direction the van was taking. It went in the direction of 676, the arterial that ran between 76 and 95 north of City Hall. It cut left, then right, veered suddenly, and bashed the end of a police cruiser parked across the entrance ramp to the highway. The van veered onto the side-walk, careened against the guardrail, and made it onto the roadway.

"Stop him!" Lia shouted to the pilot. "Use the machine-gun."

"We're going to."

The small helicopter bucked and pitched almost straight down, its tail whipping around. The truck veered across the divider as the pilot began to fire; bullets flashed along the roadway and right under the truck. The wheels blew out as the chopper veered off.

"All right, all right, he's stopping," yelled Karr in the back. "Get us down! Get us down!"

"We're in," said the pilot, gliding for a landing on the roadway ahead.

As they settled down, Dean's helicopter appeared right above. Lia closed her eyes, sure they were going to hit.

"Oh God, Charlie Dean," she whispered. "Oh God."

"Lia, come on!" yelled Karr, jumping from the rear as the Little Bird set down. "Let's go, let's go! I got the front; you got the rear. Go!"

Lia, in disbelief, pitched herself out of the cockpit, amazed that they hadn't collided.

"No offense, but we'll do better if I use that," said Dean, putting his hand on the M4 carbine the crew chief had in his hand. It wasn't a request; Dean took the gun firmly in hand and in the same motion leapt to the ground, running forward as the van slammed to a stop against the concrete road barrier and spun sideways.

Dean took two steps. The driver of the van turned his head toward him.

When you have the shot, fire. That's the only thing that ever matters, kid. When you have the shot, fire.

The voice Dean heard was Turk's, muttered in the jungle some thirty years before. It was the one piece of advice no experience had ever contradicted, the one thing anyone had ever told Dean that he knew to be true under any circumstance.

And by the time Dean heard it in his head, he had already pressed the trigger on the automatic rifle. Three bullets struck the driver of the van in the head, taking off a good part of the skull and killing him instantly.

"Charlie Dean!" yelled a voice close to him, and for a second Dean thought it was Turk, back from the dead, back from the war he would always be fighting, congratulating him. But it was Karr, yelling at him, telling him he was going to flank the van and to watch out for the rear.

"I got the back! I got the back!" screamed Lia, appearing to Dean's right.

Dean covered them, advancing slowly, gun trained on the van.

"Dead guy!" yelled Karr. "They're both down. We're OK! We're OK!"

"We have the bomb here!" said Lia in the back. "Jesus, Charlie!"

"I'm here," said Dean. He went around to the back of the van. "Are you all right?"

She bent over the large crate in the back. "I love you," she told him.

Dean stayed still for a moment, frozen. "I love you, too."

Karr had climbed into the back, pulling off the blanket and wood to expose the guts of the bomb.

"There's a timer here," Karr told them. "Moving."

"The bomb's set?" said Dean.

"Oh yeah." Karr got down on his knees next to the warhead. "We need the tool kit. Tool kit!"

Lia jumped from the van to get it. As she did, Dean grabbed her arm. They looked at each other, only for a moment; then he let go and she ran to the helicopter.

Leaving Karr to help her might not have been the right thing to do, Dean realized. But he'd do it again in a heartbeat.

Dean climbed into the back.

"You got a flashlight, Charlie?" said Karr, who already had one out.

Dean took out his penlight and shone its beam on the area where Karr was working. What looked like a large digital clock dial sat at the side of a metal cage with circuit boards in it.

"Tommy, Charlie, Lia, stand by for Mr. Rubens," said Telach over the communications system.

"We're here," said Karr.

"Very good, Tommy," said Rubens. "What's your situation?"

"Looks like they grafted a cell-phone type trigger in, along with a backup timer, wired into the trigger section on a bypass. Taking the place of the proximity stuff, that's gone. Cell phone setup looks like a Chechen IED."

"The bomb people are on the line," said Rubens. "What does the timer say?"

"Twenty-two minutes."

"We can put it in the Pave Low and take it out to sea," suggested Dean.

"Never make it, Charlie," said Karr, looking at the circuit boards and describing them to the people in the Art Room.

"Tommy, go directly for the lookout code," said Rubens.

"Yeah, that's what I'm thinking."

"You have much more time than you require," said Rubens. His voice was cold and distant, an accountant adding a long and boring sequence of numbers.

Karr looked up at Dean. "You sure you want to be this close?"

"Does it matter?"

"No, I guess not."

Lia slid the tool kit across the van floor. Dean took out a bigger flashlight and held it for Karr.

Emergency vehicles were arriving around them, and two more helicopters hovered overhead.

Karr took a tiny jeweler's screwdriver and hex wrench and eased one of the circuit boards up from the assembly, being careful to keep the wire harness attached. He did the same with the second board, revealing a small panel with what looked to Dean like a miniature bicycle tumbler embedded in a long plastic box.

"OK, what I need here is more light," said Karr. He

straightened, blew a big wad of air through his teeth, and then took another long and thin jeweler's screwdriver from the case. In the meantime, Dean took two of the flashlights from the tool kit and held them over the work space.

"A little closer," whispered Karr.

Dean lowered the lights. His arms were starting to get heavy and tired. He remembered holding a work lamp for his dad when he was thirteen or fourteen, trying to fix the family car in the driveway one night after dark.

"Ready for the code," said Karr. He blew another long wad of air from his chest, hunkering over the bomb with his tiny screwdriver.

"Six characters, all the same? That's their kill code?" said Karr after they were read. "You sure?"

The expert on the other end of the line assured him that he was.

"I'm not arguing with you," said Karr. "But I really want to be correct here."

The expert replied that there was no doubt.

"All right. But man, did these Russian guys go to MIT or what?"

Karr—an RPI graduate—moved the tumblers one by one to proper stops.

"Done?" asked Dean as he straightened again.

"Heh," said Karr, fishing a set of probes connected by a nest of wires from the bag. He placed the needlelike tips of the probes into the board one at a time, then took a small oscilloscope from the tool kit, along with a voltage / resistance meter. He scowled at the interior of the bomb as he found the right places to connect the wires, but otherwise he could have been working on a copy machine rather than a nuke.

"You want the one with the red wires," said the techie.

"Are you sure?" asked Karr. "I think it's the yellow."

"Yellow? Hold on, hold on," said the techie.

Dean glanced at Lia, then at Karr, who remained bent over the front of the warhead, his head so near the device he could have kissed it.

"Red or yellow?" said Karr.

"It's red here."

"Are you positive?"

"I—let me double-check."

"Don't bother," said Karr, straightening. He was grinning. He pointed to the oscilloscope. "Flatline, Charlie. See that? This baby is dead."

"What?" said the techie.

Karr pointed at the scope. "That's flat, right?" he asked Dean.

"Yeah," said Dean.

"It's disarmed."

"How did you know which wire?" asked Dean.

"Sometimes you just got to go with your gut," said Karr. He stretched his neck; Dean heard it crack.

Lia had her arms folded.

"They sent him to school last year to learn how to defuse Russian nukes for a mission we were on," she said. "He memorized all of the tech manuals. He probably knows more than the experts they have in the Art Room. I'll bet he didn't even need them to read their kill code."

"Still comes down to a guess, Princess," said Karr, laughing as he hopped out of the van.

Dean looked at the framework of the now-inert warhead. There were no yellow wires to be seen anywhere.

"Tommy can be a real jerk, you know that?" Lia told Dean.

"That wasn't exactly what I was thinking," he said, leaning over to kiss her.

136

The president had never been to the Art Room, and so his visit to the NSA two days after the bomb had been defused presented Rubens with a rather unique problem: should the President of the United States go through the rigorous search procedure that everyone else had to?

The president took the weight off him when he arrived, telling Rubens that he wanted to "experience everything like your people do." Still, Rubens worried—irrationally, he admitted to himself—that the security people would inadvertently find some reason to require the president to go through a strip search. Downstairs—two Secret Service people accompanying him—Rubens let Telach describe some of the capabilities and functions of the Art Room. Marcke was duly impressed and even asked Rockman if he played reruns on the monitors when he got bored.

"Just joking, son," said the president as the runner blanched.

A small awards ceremony had been arranged in one of the upstairs lounges. Tommy Karr beamed as the president strode over and shook his hand.

"We meet again, Mr. Karr," said Marcke, who had stopped by Karr's hospital room in Europe several months before. "Where's that girl of yours?"

"At school in France, sir."

"You better hook up with her soon, or whatever you

young people are calling it these days," said the president. "Don't let her get away."

Karr blushed.

"Ambassador Jackson, I was hoping I would see you," said Marcke, taking Jackson's hand. "You did a good job with Aznar. He told our ambassador he owes many favors in the future."

"Yes, sir."

"We'll see how much that means when we actually want something down the line," added Marcke wryly. "Mr. Rubens told me what a help you'd been. I hope you'll stay on."

"He asked me to, sir."

"Good. Please do."

"Yes, sir."

Marcke turned to some of the young people on Johnny Bib's staff, congratulating each one by name. His recall was incredible, thought Rubens; he'd given the president a list with faces the day before when the visit had been arranged, but how much time could he have had to memorize it?

Marcke worked his way through the small group, then said good-bye; he was on his way to Pennsylvania to thank the people of the Commonwealth for coming through the crisis.

"I understand the warhead has been taken to Nevada to be disassembled," said Marcke as they rode down in the elevator.

"Yes, sir."

"Would it have exploded?"

"No question."

"Some people think it would have been inert."

"No. It would have gone."

"Good work on this, Billy. It was a gutsy call on Philadelphia."

"It was—the product of a great deal of staff research," said Rubens. "I was only the messenger."

Marcke smiled at him. Rubens glanced at the two Secret Service people at the back of the elevator car. This was as alone as they were going to get.

"I wonder, sir—about the national security adviser's post. I—I would like to be considered."

"George told me you didn't want it."

"I believe I made a mistake. I was hasty, and did not give it the proper consideration."

"I'm sorry to hear that." The door opened behind them. The president's aides were standing in a knot nearby.

"Oh." Rubens felt as if the elevator had suddenly plunged a hundred feet. "Ms. Collins?"

"At the present time, I don't think anyone from the CIA would do well in the spotlight. I've gone ahead and chosen Donna Bing out at Stanford. She worked for George Bush as undersecretary of defense; I believe you know her."

"An excellent choice," said Rubens softly. He remained in the elevator, watching as the president and his aides strode away.

137

Dean climbed up the small rise from the stream and gazed in the direction of the narrow clearing where the huge buck had appeared a few days before. He brought his binoculars up, scanning the nearby woods carefully, hoping he would see the buck again.

"You're not really quitting, are you?" said Lia, trudging up behind him.

"Ssshhh."

"You can't leave."

"I thought we weren't going to talk about it."

"Mr. Rubens is going to get that girl from Peru a job. He thinks he can find something in the non-secure section of the agency. Or over at State."

"That's good."

"I know you're not leaving," she added.

"Maybe not," Dean admitted. "This is where I saw that buck I told you about."

Lia took out her own binoculars and examined the woods. They stood there for five, ten minutes, neither talking. Dean had suggested they come here after the mission was over. Rubens had called yesterday to tell them that the president wanted to honor them as heroes; Dean had told him, not with much diplomacy, that he'd prefer to stay in the woods.

And Lia said she wanted to be with Dean.

"I shouldn't have yelled at you when you came to help

me," Lia told him now, putting down her field glasses. "I—I thought that being helped meant I was weak. All my life, I guess, I've thought that."

"It doesn't."

"I don't like being scared, Charlie Dean."

He turned and looked down into her face. "It's not the worst thing."

"What is?"

"Being scared for somebody else when you can't do anything about it."

"Being alone is worse, I think. Not on a mission—really alone. I think that's really what I'm afraid of. That's the real fear. Everything else—it's a reaction to it."

"You're not alone."

As he bent to kiss her, he thought he heard something moving in the woods. How perfect it would be, he thought, if the big buck appeared now.

He straightened and picked up his glasses. Lia did the same. But they saw nothing, and though they stayed on the knoll for more than an hour, the big buck never came.